Who Brydles Heavens most Cleare

To Dave
Best Wishes
Steve R.

Also by Steve Ragnall

Fiction

A Sea of Contumely

Non-Fiction

"Better Conceiv'd than Describ'd" – The Life and Times of Captain James King

Pandora's Box and Other Stories

As Editor
Ollie's War

Who Brydles Heavens most Cleare

A Dr Webster Story

Steve Ragnall

Troubador Publishing Ltd
Unit E2 Airfield Business Park,
Harrison Road, Market Harborough,
Leicestershire LE16 7UL
Tel: 0116 279 2299
Email: books@troubador.co.uk
Web: www.troubador.co.uk

ISBN 978 1 83628 127 6

British Library Cataloguing in Publication Data.
A catalogue record for this book is available from the British Library.

Printed and bound by CPI Group (UK) Ltd, Croydon, CR0 4YY
Typeset in 12pt Jenson Pro by Troubador Publishing Ltd, Leicester, UK

Matador is an imprint of Troubador Publishing Ltd

MIX
Paper | Supporting responsible forestry
FSC www.fsc.org FSC® C013604

Dedicated to my dear friend Isabel Norton.

O ye that wolde your browes with Laurel bind,
What larger feild I pray you can you find,
Than is his praise, who brydles heavens most cleare
Makes mountaines tremble, and lowest hells to feare?

From L'Uranie by Guillaume Du Bartas, circa 1578,
as translated by King James VI of Scotland
(later James I of England).

Contents

List of Maps and Illustrations x
Cast of Characters xi
Prologue xvii
Part One xix
Part Two 165
Postscript 291
Author's Comments and Historical Notes 295
Notes to Chapters 298
John Webster Biography 302
Medical Practise in the Seventeenth Century 305
Acknowledgements 307

List of Maps and Illustrations

Dr John Webster xiii
Webster's Ribble Valley xiv
Webster's Clitheroe xv
Webster's Clitheroe from Castle xvi
Webster's journey to Colne and Heptonstall 42
Downham Hall and environs 123
To Hornby and back 166
The Chapter House of Cockersand Abbey 166
Hornby and the attack on the Castle 187
The raid on Read Hall 269

Cast of Characters

Dr John Webster: *Currently acting Surgeon to Parliamentary forces but still holding the title of Master of Clitheroe Royal Grammar School.*

The Widow Slater: *Webster's housekeeper.*

Nate Slater: *The housekeeper's son and assistant to Webster. Age: Almost 13.*

Pod: *Orphan taken in by Webster. Age: 9.*

Cas: *Black servant in Webster's household. Age:14 (probably)*

Sir Ralph Assheton of Downham: *MP and School Governor. Parliamentarian.*

Lady Katherine Assheton: *Wife of Sir Ralph.*

Will Cummins: *Master-at-Arms for Sir Ralph of Downham but seconded as bodyguard for Webster.*

Colonel Ralph Assheton of Whalley: *Son of Sir Ralph of Downham. Parliamentarian.*

Colonel Rigby: *Parliamentarian.*

John Aspinall: *School Governor and Magistrate. Political allegiance unknown.*

Sir Christopher Kendall: *Webster's nemesis, current whereabouts unknown, presumed dead. Royalist.*

Tench: *A creature of Kendall's, and thus another threat to Webster.*

An impression of Dr.John Webster. Painting by the Author.
No actual portrait of Webster is known to exist.

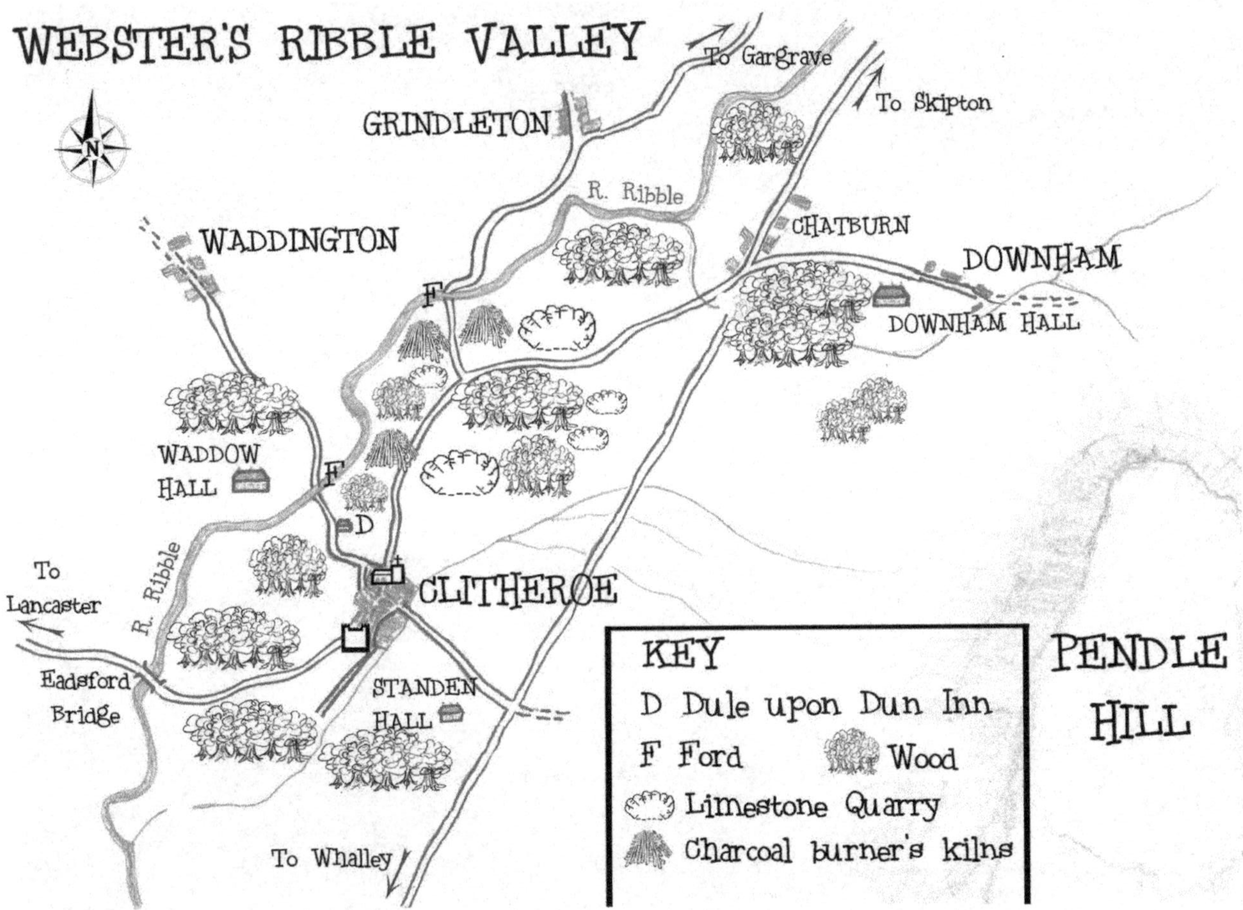
WEBSTER'S RIBBLE VALLEY
N
To Gargrave
To Skipton
GRINDLETON
R. Ribble
CHATBURN
WADDINGTON
DOWNHAM
F
DOWNHAM HALL
WADDOW
HALL
F
D
To
Lancaster
R. Ribble
CLITHEROE
Eadsford
Bridge
STANDEN
HALL
To Whalley
KEY
D Dule upon Dun Inn
F Ford
Wood
Limestone Quarry
Charcoal burner's kilns
PENDLE
HILL

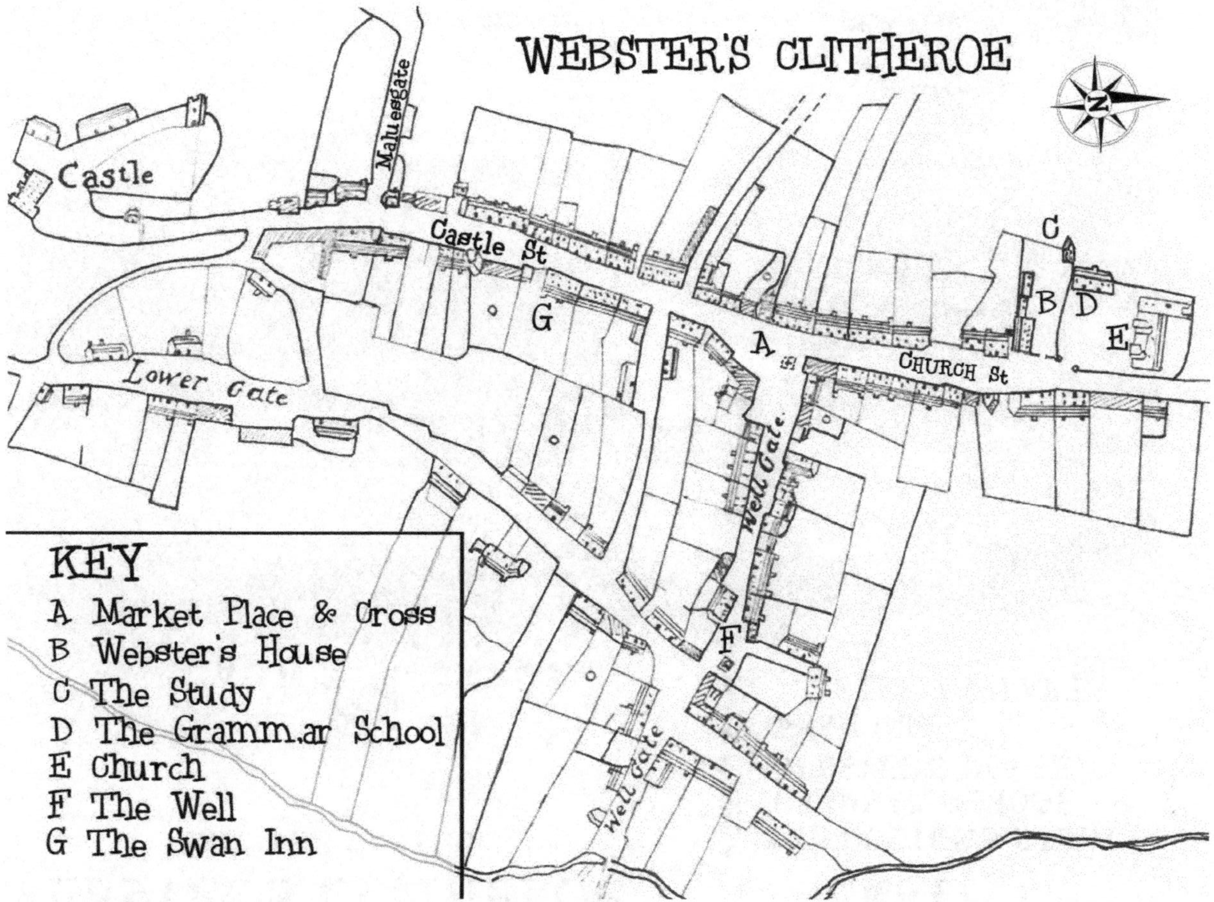
WEBSTER'S CLITHEROE
Castle
Malmesgate
Castle St
G
Lower Gate
C
B
D
E
A
CHURCH St
Well Gate
F
Well Gate
N
KEY
A Market Place & Cross
B Webster's House
C The Study
D The Gramm.ar School
E Church
F The Well
G The Swan Inn

WEBSTER'S CLITHEROE

FROM THE CASTLE

KEY

A THE DOCTOR'S STUDY
B GRAMMAR SCHOOL
C WEBSTER'S HOUSE
D SWAN INN
E CASTLE RAMPARTS

Prologue

It is 1643, the second year of Civil War, and Dr John Webster, Schoolmaster, Alchemist, Astrologer and Physician, is recovering from wounds received at the Battle of Read Bridge. The last eighteen months have been amongst the most traumatic of his life – so far!

After uncovering a fraud in the accounts of the Grammar School of which he was Master, he has been forced to leave his home in Clitheroe due to the vicious murder of one of his servants by his nemesis, Sir Christopher Kendall, along with his devilish henchman Tench, who have also painted Webster as being in league with the Devil. It is true that his Alchemical experiments have been equated to witchcraft by many.

The whereabouts of Kendall and Tench are unknown.

He feels that he has been living in 'A Sea of Contumely', people not showing him due respect for his skills and knowledge, though he doesn't recognise that he treats many in the same way.

Given sanctuary in the village of Downham, under Pendle Hill, by Sir Ralph Assheton, he has been pressed into service as surgeon to Parliamentary forces, when all he really wants to do is return to his beloved library and experiments.

But Webster believes that King Charles I is trying to turn the country back to Catholicism and, as a dissenter, is opposed to the King's personal rule and is thus a Parliamentarian by inclination. Neither does he believe in witchcraft, unlike most of the country's population.

Now read on as he continues his story...

PART ONE

One

A Captive of Capricorn

If I knew the exact date and time of my birth, I could make a perfect chart, a forecast, that might save me much worry. I had been reading a book by a Hungarian, Johannes Kepler, who had divined God's geometrical plan of the Universe. The book was already some fifty years old, but it made sense. He agreed with Copernicus that the Sun was at the centre of everything, all the planets and stars circling it, and I also agreed with that. The sun was the start of all. My bible says that on the first day God created light. That's the Sun. The beginning of everything. You've only to look at the seasons, where growth is determined by the Sun's light and how nothing grows when its light is missing to see the truth in that. Obviously, the Sun is the centre, not the earth, a view that some still consider heresy, the idiots.

The circumnavigation of the Earth by the Moon is another case in point. The movement of the seas are dependent on the orbit of that celestial body as any mariner will tell you. Even the Venerable Bede of antiquity knew that, for I have it in his book, *De Temporum Ratione*.

As I know from medicine, a full moon can intensify a patient's fever, whilst its waxing phases enhance the benefits of letting of blood. I have my discs, my *Volvelles*, to keep track of the Moon's position for this very purpose as do most physicians. And, of course, Apothecaries create their remedies using watery plants that are influenced by the Moon.

It then follows that these influences must also apply to every other body in the firmament. All must have an effect not just on the Earth but on each and every one of us.

If I construed Kepler's argument correctly, he had connected the physical shape of the universe to the spiritual, which I had long believed in. It seemed to me to fit with the work of my friend William Lilly, the Astrologer. Perhaps 'friend' is too strong, acquaintance would be more exact. I'd met him when at Oxford and he showed me how to cast a chart. Given the exalted figure he is now, calculating for both King and Parliament, I trust his art.

I would like to cast my own chart but, though I know I was baptised on the third of February in the year 1610, I know not if this was the usual month from the day of my birth. Neither do I know the hour that I appeared, which I also need. An hour or two one way or the other can make a complete difference to a life; death in old age or young; a happy life or one of sorrow; one dominated by Mars or Venus. You get the picture.

My life has certainly not been dominated by Venus.

My parents are now long dead so I cannot ask them. Edward, my elder brother, always said that I was born at midnight at the full moon, with wolves howling at the door and a wild tempest blowing, but then he would say such things.

No, I believe I was probably born in the house of Capricorn and thus am strong, wise, independent, resilient, serious, and even visionary. My charts tell me the moon was waxing and that would reinforce those qualities, all of which sounds accurate. I cannot be sure of which planet or planets were in the house at that time, which is why I cannot complete my chart. Saturn should rule all of this sign but instead Mars seems to have been present, which would have made me impulsive, to act first and think later, which doesn't seem to fit my character at all.

I'm not emotional like someone born in Virgo, otherwise I might find my surgical works distressing, but other virginal signs are practicality, loyalty and stability and I'm sure I have those qualities. I also have Libran qualities of rationality and intellect, but not its joy of the company of others. With a few exceptions, I find most people annoying and am happy to be on my own with my books. Now that is a Capricorn quality, so I'll go with that as the nearest to my composition because I, like all humanity, am designed by these two things: the sign under which I entered the world and the power of certain heavenly bodies. And the one thing that commands and governs all those elements: God.

Despite being thrown out of my curacy in Kildwick a few years ago for disagreeing with my Bishop (the ass), my faith in God is more or less undiminished. It's just the people who pretend to disseminate His word; those who try to tell us how to interpret the Bible; those like Archbishop Laud who would try to return us to the Roman way of things. Don't mistake me, I agree with Laud that predestination is wrong – everyone has the opportunity to redeem themselves. Well, almost everyone.

There you have it. A real conundrum. How can I fit my belief in Astrology with my disbelief in predestination? God works in mysterious ways is all I can say.

Two

'A Cuckoo in my Nest'

I was in a real quandary and it was the widow Slater's fault. She was my housekeeper and liked to think she ruled me. We'd been living under the protection of Sir Ralph Assheton within his lands surrounding Downham Hall ever since life in Clitheroe had proved untenable. Near eighteen months my household had been here, with a small cottage and barn, enough time for Slater to make her mark. She preferred Downham because she believed that she had improved her standing in life, consorting with Sir Ralph and his Lady. With their blessing she had improved their cook's offerings and brought better order to the Hall. Now, though, I thought it time to see how the land lay back in the town, or else we might never leave.

I was known to all as Doctor Webster. That title was an honorific as, though I call myself a physician, I'm not truly one, for I am not actually registered with the College of Physic, but I have amassed much medical knowledge that lets me mix and prescribe cures, salves, potions and the like with as much success as most. And I can whip off a leg or arm as well as the best surgeon, as some of my patients will affirm. My true title was Master of the Grammar School in Clitheroe, but my uncovering of the embezzlement of school funds by one of the Governors, Sir Christopher Kendall, and his subsequent persecution of me, had driven me from the town.

I believed Kendall to be dead. He had wounded me quite badly earlier in the year when we fought, and beat, Lord Derby's Royalists at Read Bridge, a great victory. Whilst I was treating the wounded he came out of nowhere but, as he struck me with his sword, one of our men fired a musket directly at him. Our soldier, God bless him, had undoubtedly saved my life. True, Kendall's body hadn't been found amongst the slain but, surely, he couldn't have survived that shot.

Over the months that we'd been at odds, Kendall had suborned people close to me, murdered my dear servant Sam in as awful a manner as you could imagine and fired the building that people called my study. He made the townsfolk of Clitheroe believe I was in league with the Devil, fools that they are. The School then lost its pupils, and we were obliged to move to Downham. So, a straightforward series of events that could happen to anyone, do you think?

In return for our sanctuary, I was happy to give my services to Sir Ralph and the Parliamentarians, my inclinations being to their side. I certainly couldn't support King Charles, that divisive Monarch, with his 'Divine Right' to rule. He had proved himself duplicitous, incompetent and Catholic in intention and, though I had no difficulty with the principle of being ruled by a King, it should not and must not be done without consent of a Parliament. Charles had denied that and, until he should return to reason and to the rights and freedoms gained since bad King John's times, I must oppose him.

'Morning, sir. I have brought your posset.' It was Nate with my morning cure-all, courtesy of his mother. She found it her duty to build me up since the wounds inflicted on me at the battle, and its following fever, had left me as weak as a kitten.

Two weeks had passed since the battle, for most of which time I'd been bed-ridden, but in the last few days I'd managed to rise and take short walks through the village with the assistance of my trusty stick. The sword slash to my back was now healing well, as was the wound to my right side and arm. I don't know whether my ribs had been broken or just chipped, but they had ceased to trouble me and, though I had lost a little movement in it, my right arm was almost back to normal. The scars still looked rather red but there was nothing in that. Nate had done an excellent job in keeping my cuts clear of infection and sewing me up so neatly. His improvement since virtually betraying me to Kendall's men, now more than two years past, had been astonishing. I was right in having pardoned him for that.

Nate was now almost thirteen years of age, moderately tall already, dark brown hair and eyes, voice beginning to break. He'd accompanied me to Preston when I followed Sir Richard Shuttleworth's men and I had used him mercilessly as an assistant when dealing with the wounded of that battle. Quickly he picked up the art of surgery and I began to rely on him despite his youth. His early wish had been to apprentice to a smith or farrier and follow in the steps of his long dead father, but I could see a better future for him should he wish it. As I had lain in bed, confined by wounds, I had decided that I would sponsor his apprenticeship to an Apothecary or, if we could improve his schooling, even to a Physician, subject to his own wishes. And, of course, to those of his mother.

I dutifully downed the posset, as good a way to start the day as any, and rose to my feet, feeling less weak and unsteady than previously. My arm was aching and, true to form, when I looked out of the window it was raining. Why my arm should act as a pointer to weather I do not know, but I've heard others remark on such phenomena, especially in the case of the cold working on those with rheumatism and the like. The sky looked to be clearing from the west so today, I thought, I will take a ride when this drizzle stops. Bay, my lovely horse, is a sensitive creature and will know to carry me with care. Having lost weight whist confined to my bed, I tightened my belt to the new holes now punched through the leather.

'No, Doctor. I won't allow it. You are not returned to full health.' Slater can be so shrill at times. My housekeeper could be perfectly cast as the termagant in a play and tries to rule my life with a rod of iron. My attempts to stand up to her are not always successful. I pretend that I have little time for her and that she annoys me but, in fact, she gives me excellent service and I admire her resilience and fortitude. I do care for her. Not that I would tell her that of course.

This time, though, she reminded me that Sir Ralph had asked that I call on him, so I was obliged to bow to her wishes. At least, that was what she thought, I expect. I resolved to ride later in the day and took the short walk to the Hall, leaning heavily on my stick.

Sir Ralph's Hall has a beautiful aspect. In many ways it is a modest building, though long and fronted by a pillared portico. Its dark, mellowed gritstone stands at the top of a rise whilst its rear looks down, past a venerable church, to a well-ordered village. Beyond stands Pendle Hill and its wild moor. In sunshine the hill can sport a benevolent face but most of the time there is a brooding quality to it, a darkness, a terrible grandeur. It is a landmark that many equate with witchcraft since the infamous trials that took place thirty years ago. Just the name of Pendle has some folk crossing themselves. Whilst I have no time for such foolishness I, like most, would never venture to climb its steep slopes, though Sir Ralph has and says that you can see clear across the country from its lofty summit, even to York Minster.

I turned past the barn that adjoins our cottage to cut across to the front of the Hall. The latest addition to my household was sitting slumped on a stone with his back to me. I didn't know what to make of him. During my weeks in Preston had come the news that 'another Sam' had arrived, turned up unannounced at Downham. It still worried me.

As I've told you, Sam was my servant, a black African given to me by my friend and mentor, Doctor Hunyades. He was gentle, intelligent, always with a smile. My friend as much as a servant, he had been cruelly tortured and murdered by the devil Kendall. I treasure his memory. This new lad, age unknown but likely to be around fourteen years, whilst every bit as black as Sam, rarely smiled, always looked worried, and appeared scared of even his own shadow. He seemed to understand little and he puzzled me greatly.

His story was that he was Sam's brother, also called Sam. This seemed a nonsense but perhaps it was some African thing. When I returned to Downham, I found everyone referring to him as 'New Sam'. This simply wouldn't do. Excepting colour, they were as different as chalk is to cheese and it felt like an insult to let him assume my poor friend's name.

I had asked him if he had been christened. He did not seem to know.

I took him into Sir Ralph's church, baptized him (though by rights I am now barred from officiating at such ceremonials) and gave him the name of Cas. I must admit that this was a joke on my part, giving him a diminutive of Charles as an insult to the King, but I must also admit that I didn't really like him. Neither did I wish to give him any real standing in my household until he could gain my trust. He slept in the stable and was effectively under the care of little Pod, barely 10 years old.

Pod was a shy orphan, son of another of Kendall's victims, who was gradually gaining in confidence since he had assumed the care of the stable whilst Nate had been with me in Preston and beyond. He was diligent and gentle with the horses and, more importantly, reliable. Something that I couldn't yet claim for Cas.

Cas started as I passed him. He rose, frightened, and gave a tentative bow. 'What are you at, Cas?' I asked in a not ungentle fashion.

'I be, sir, here.' His skill with language seemed limited and I had ceased to wonder at his strangulation of syntax.

'Where's Pod? Go and help him.' I waved him away with a flick of my hand and walked on. When I looked back, he'd returned to his stone, holding his head in his hands.

I knew I must do something about him but could not think what.

Three

'A Vile Brute...'

SIR RALPH WAS WORKING ON HIS PAPERS AS I WAS SHOWN INTO his study. Tall, in his sixtieth year or even more I think, with a spare frame, previously dark hair and beard now mainly grey and cut shorter than the present fashion, his blue eyes sparkled with energy and intelligence as he rose to take my hand.

'Glad to see you so well, Doctor,' he said with a smile. 'Almost regained your strength?'

'Aye, thank you, Sir Ralph. Unfortunately, I'm starting to regain my girth due to Slater's daily possets.'

'The widow Slater is one of life's great assets, I believe.' He smiled broadly. 'Should you wish to part with her, I would have her command my household in a flash.'

Courtesies over, we got down to business.

'The School, Doctor. We have finally persuaded Mr Usher Brierley and his sister to return to Clitheroe, as you know, and reopen the Grammar School for new pupils.'

Amos Brierley, Usher of the Grammar School under me as Master had been as diligent in his job as anyone might wish until he removed, with my household, to Downham. His sister, something of a shrew, had been Matron to the boarding pupils of the school. Since our remove here, the pair of them had assumed airs and graces that did not become them and, from having had a good measure of my respect for them and considering Amos to be a friend, I was now disappointed with them almost to the point of disgust.

'Yes, sir, and I believe it is not before time. I must say that I've been surprised at his laziness whilst under your protection. We have all been most grateful for the way you welcomed us all to Downham during our, as we should say, difficulties, and am disturbed that he hasn't shown his thanks in a more positive way.'

'Not at all.' Sir Ralph brushed away my thanks. 'You have been of great help and the Usher has been of some utility in teaching the younglings number and letter.'

'I have been thinking, sir,' I began, 'First, I am intending to ride over to Clitheroe in the next day or so and see how the school is progressing. Second, I must see to my house and look to my reception back in the town, pending arrangements to move my household back…'

'Ah. That may be a little premature.' He held up his hand. 'I think there is still some disquiet in the town over you and the unfortunate incidents caused by Kendall. Even though he is now gone, we must take care.'

'It's right that you should wish to attend the School and, as and when you are able to make the ride, I will happily send two men with you for your safety and to stop any possible insult to you from the people. At present, though, I would wish you to remain here.'

I must have looked downcast, for he continued. 'I can understand that this may be something of a blow but, even with Kendall gone, some of his men are still around. That Tench, whose brother we hanged, has a band at large. He has continued to collect the rents on the School's property.' This was unwelcome news indeed.

In his defrauding of the School, Kendall, by nefarious means, had had himself appointed as collector of rents on the extensive land holdings gifted to the School since its chartering by Queen Mary in the year 1554. These rents were collected by his band of near brigands, led by the violent and evil brothers Tench. I had been instrumental in exposing Kendall's fraud, proving his creation of false documents and other calumnies. One of the Tench brothers had later been found guilty of murder and I had watched his execution at Lancaster. I had thought all this was now over.

My mind returned to that awful day. Little Pod had been by my side, for his testimony had been useful against the murderer of his father. It had been a terrifying few days for the mite. To enter the forbidding citadel of the Castle, endure the oppression of the Court, and then witness the hanging of the brute, on the hillside outside the town, affected the child terribly. Sick all over my boots if I remember correctly. Slater said he had nightmares for weeks after our return, and who could blame him?

I should have known better. Wherever there's money involved., you can be sure there are men who will take advantage. The remaining Tench had been the instrument of collection of the School rents for Kendall and there was also the question of the Salt Tax monies. Kendall had used at least some of the monies from the School lands to purchase, from the King, the office of Collector of Taxes on imported salt. Our duplicitous and benighted Monarch, always short of cash, received ready money for sale of such offices, and Kendall gained a knighthood for his contribution to Charles' coffers.

Our own Nantwich salt being insufficient for the country's needs, salt was brought through the Lancashire ports of Lancaster, Skippon Flue, Preston & Liverpool, some directly from the Americas and some imported from France, the Low Countries and Spain, but how the taxes then found their way to Kendall's purse, I didn't know. The monies would keep flowing, but whose pockets were now being weighted down with silver since Kendall's demise? Tench again?

'If I'd been able to keep a watch on Kendall's house at Waddow,' continued Sir Ralph. 'we might have been able to apprehend the remaining Tench brother. With all men needed because of this stupid war, that wasn't possible, but we have heard from our friendly innkeeper at the Dule upon Dun that he has been seen near there on a number of occasions.'

'He is a vile brute, sir,' I said with some feeling, remembering the almost demonic leer Tench once gave me at a visit to Waddow Hall. Would you believe that I once shared a bed with him at an Inn? Not that I knew it at the time, of course, but the thought still makes me shiver. 'Can he not be stopped from collecting the monies?'

'That would be good indeed, but each time I've sent men out to collect the rents, Tench has been there first. The school is losing even more money than before, but with it having been closed, that hasn't had any effect in itself, though that is not really the point, of course.' He paused. 'It leaves us - me - in something of a quandary. There is little enough money left to pay the Usher and, I fear, none for you.'

'However, you and your household are still welcome to the fruits of my land and, after communication with Sir Richard Shuttleworth, who praises your care of his men to the high heavens, he agrees to a small stipend from Parliamentary coffers to retain your services.'

I bowed my head in acceptance. This was all generous stuff and who wouldn't be pleased to be held in high regard by such men? Sir Ralph continued:

'Let me come to the point. As soon as you feel well enough – and there is no rush, I want you fully fit before any exertions,' he stressed, 'I do have an assignment for you, if you choose to take it. The charcoal makers and lime-slakers down by the Ribble river have resisted calls to arms and I don't have to tell you that they live on the very edge of, or perhaps even beyond, the rule of law. I do feel, however, that they could be a source of help to us in the apprehension of Tench and his band. I would set some of my men to the task if most were not away with the army in Yorkshire.'

'My problem is that it might be unseemly for me, as a Justice of the Peace, to enlist their support directly. Grent from the Dule has been of some assistance to you and indeed to all of us in the past. Could I prevail upon you to negotiate with him to provide a band to seek out Tench and his men? I'm sure you see my problem, Doctor. I might be seen to be encouraging one lawless band at the expense of another, with no certainty of outcome.'

It was an easy decision to make and I agreed immediately. 'Innkeeper Grent I can work with, certainly,' I said, 'and you want a more formal arrangement than we had when he attacked Waddow for us?'

'Yes, indeed. I can make a purse available to him. I want what we might call an irregular army. My man Will can work with you and help you if you wish.'

Will Cummins is a grand fellow who had helped me in the past. He had been rated as a Sergeant-at-Arms in Sir Ralph's first muster of troops but had proved his worth in a multitude of capacities since then. We had already survived a number of capers together over the last year or so. In his early twenties, tall and well-built, he always seemed to have a smile on his face and a ready quip on his lips. You could always rely on him when in a difficult situation and he had no airs and graces whatever. Whether talking to Colonel Shuttleworth or a mean beggar, he was always the same.

I hadn't seen Will for some weeks and believed that he had gone off on his own account. We had received sanctuary at the farm of a young widow when trying to avoid the Royalist army before the Battle at Read Bridge and I thought he had taken a shine to her. Hadn't he returned to that farm? No, here he was, grinning as always, meeting me with outstretched hand.

'I hear you're going to stir up some trouble again, Doctor. Do you need me to bring a big spoon?'

'So, your lovely widow has spurned your advances, has she, Will?' I quipped.

'Ha ha. No, I'm not ready to settle down yet, sir. Not when you need looking after. Though I hope there's a little less blood and gore this time.' Will had stood in as my assistant when Nate was not to hand, despite his aversion to surgical procedures.

Sir Ralph gave a small cough. 'Will has been fully apprised of the scheme. I have authorised him to gather some arms for Grent's men, if need be, from the haul that Lord Derby's men abandoned in their flight from Read. I wish I had witnessed that rout.' he said wistfully, 'Derby and seven thousand flying from a couple of hundred of our men. A miracle indeed.' That rout had proved vital in keeping most of Lancashire in Parliament's hands.

A modest repast having been provided by Sir Ralph, it was mid-afternoon before I could take my short ride. The rain had stopped, the clouds passed, and the sun lit the scene charmingly. Little Pod had harnessed my horse ready and held her whilst I climbed the mounting block to drop gingerly onto her broad back. She's a steady, good-natured beast with an even coat of darkish brown and sporting black tips, as good a bay as you'll find. Good intelligence too and a fine turn of speed when asked for.

Nate was at the stable and suggested that he and Pod accompany me, and I waited whilst they saddled their ponies before setting out along the road to Chatburn.

I looked at Nate on his small mount, long legs dangling down almost to the ground. 'I think it's time we found you a bigger beast, Nate.' He looked at me with enthusiasm. 'I don't think your pony is keeping pace with your growth.' Indeed, I didn't think she'd grown at all, odd little thing that she was. 'Dob can be yours for the present.' Dob was my spare horse, slightly smaller than Bay and not as perfect in her colouring but still a good animal. His face lit up. 'Thank you, sir,' he said.

Both boys were good and kind with horses, keeping them well brushed and exercised but, other than me, Nate was the only person I would allow to ride Bay. My mind went back to that damned Major Sparrow who had stolen Bay for a time, when we were fighting in the Fylde. Sparrow might have been on our side, but he was a blackguard and a coward, later being dismissed from our forces after failing to face Lord Derby's troops as ordered. Chasing after Sparrow had led me into a number of adventures, but I would part with Bay for no one.

It was now as fine a day as you could wish, the rain departing with the clouds and a warm sun quickly drying the puddles. I could hear mistle thrush chattering and, as we passed the track to Rimington, a pair of them started from the stand of trees. Beyond, the regular flash of light from sharpened blades began as scythes made their regular to-and-fro, like the pendulum of a clock, a few old men and some of the women from the village having returned to the fields with the sun to cut and gather the long grass, an early cut for winter fodder for the cows and sheep. And then there were the sheep, a modest flock being driven back up the road to Downham and temporarily stopping our path. On such a day, with such a scene, how could you ever believe the country was at war with itself?

It was only a mile to Chatburn and I was feeling good. We took the road over the hill towards Clitheroe but, as we reached the top of the rise, I found my arm aching a little. Not wishing to push myself too hard on this first outing, I reluctantly signalled our return. Still, it had been good to ride out and I knew I could manage a greater distance without too much discomfort.

We were retracing our path, had reached the hay fields again and were passing the abandoned wreck of a cottage called Greenside when I thought I saw movement in the dark of the doorway, just a flicker of colour that disappeared as I looked. It seemed so odd that I reined in Bay and peered into the gloom under the low eaves, the boys stopping close behind me. I was reluctant to dismount as I wasn't sure I could regain my saddle without a mounting block, so I sat and waited for a few seconds. One wall of the cottage seemed to be part collapsed but, despite the harsh sun, no light penetrated the building.

Putting it down to either a trick of the light or perhaps the movement of some animal, I spurred Bay on and rode back to the Hall with the boys, giving no further thought to the matter.

Robb, gatekeeper of the Hall, touched his cap to me as we passed through, and I stopped to ask him how he did.

'Gradely, thank you Doctor, 'cepting for me feet...'

'Aye. The only cure is to rest them, Robb,' I interrupted. For a Doctor, the problem with asking folk how they fare is that they tell you every little ache or pain. If you don't stop them immediately, this often develops into a history of their entire family. I have yet to learn not to ask.

'Tell me, that hovel down at Greenside. How long is it since anyone lived there? It's a ruin now but it would make a tidy home for someone, I should say.'

'Bin a ruin as long as I can remember, sir, maybe ten year or more. If it were Sir Ralph's, he'd a sorted it out. But it isn't his, you see. Just that little plot. All around it is the Master's, but not that.'

I don't know why, but the cottage intrigued me, and I continued to puzzle over it during supper before putting it from my mind.

Slater accosted me as soon as I entered the kitchen. 'Why did you not tell me you were riding off, and with no hat under this wicked sun?' She was in one of her shrewish moods. 'Am I to have to nurse you through an apoplex or overheating of your wits? Here,' She held up the replacement for the hat lost in my flight to Whalley before the battle at Read Bridge, 'Better than the old and I have sewn ribands beneath for you to tie it under your chin. You will not lose this one...'

'And you would have me looking like a damned Puritan, woman?' I had taken an instant dislike to her recent purchase. My lost hat had been low-crowned, wide-brimmed leather, a perfect fit. The new article was felted wool, had a higher crown, narrower brim, and was too large for my head. I sat on the bench at the table, set the hat down beside me and, after reaching across for the jug of ale, contrived to sit back upon the offending article. That earned me a strong rebuke. 'It won't stay on my head even with your ribands.' I retorted peevishly.

'I could see it was too big and so I have sewn a band inside to fill it out, which you haven't even noticed, nor thanked me for. And no-one would take you for a Puritan, using such language to a poor woman…' She swept from the room, holding the edge of her apron to her face.

'All right, I will wear it.' I called after her, beaten once again, 'Thank you.' I looked at the offending article and determined to sit on it as often as possible to destroy its shape.

The following day I rode again, reluctantly wearing the hat, down through the village, turning right along the track to the hamlet of Worston before turning right again and on down into Chatburn. It was the afternoon of another fine day, drowsy under a hot sun that had quieted the birds, causing us to take it slowly. The boys accompanied me yet again but lagged behind a little, chatting to themselves. As we climbed out of Chatburn and back towards Downham the wrecked cottage again came in view. There was a thin trail of smoke, a mere wisp all but invisible, rising vertically from its smoke-hole in the breathless air but, halting outside, I could see no other sign of life either within or without.

I started to ride on when something stopped me and, telling the boys to wait for me, I dismounted carefully and walked back to the hovel. There was no gate to the tangle of weeds that had no right to call itself a garden, and the door stood ajar. I hallooed into the dark of the interior.

Crossing the threshold I found myself in near darkness, despite the brightness of the day, the only light entering from behind me and from the feeble glow from dying embers in the open firepit in the middle of the stamped soil floor. An acrid, fetid smell filled the room and, though it was bad, I've smelt worse. From the droppings it looked like bats were in residence.

As my eyes adjusted to the dimness of the place, I saw that it was empty but, as I turned back to the door, something caught my eye. The edge of a polished bone button caught the sun. It looked incongruous, sitting on the dry soil of the floor. I picked it up, dropped it in my pocket and returned to Bay and the boys. Using a large stone from what had been the garden wall and with a push from Nate, I remounted with difficulty.

As we rode on, a horse approached us at speed from behind. Pulling into the side of the road, the buff-coated rider swept past us with a brief wave of acknowledgement. My immediate thought was of a call to arms. There was a small band of Royalists holding Clitheroe Castle, too small to bother anyone, but were they being reinforced perhaps? Were troops on their way from Yorkshire to reduce the whole valley and bring retribution for our victory at Read? I was worried. In such uncertain times, the sight of a flying messenger brings many negative thoughts to mind. We returned to the Hall, but all was quiet.

Four

A Summons

'I've had a letter and a summons, Doctor.' It was the following day and I'd put the sight of yesterday's messenger out of my mind until Sir Ralph appeared at the door of our cottage.

Slater showed him in with a curtsey. I lay down my book, offered him a chair and a mug of beer, which he declined. 'I also had a letter from my son saying all is well, thank God.' A touch of amusement then showed about his mouth and eyes. 'Do you know anything of Kendall's wife?' he asked.

This was an odd question indeed, I thought. I'd never seen her in the flesh, nor did I know anyone who had, but I did remember the portrait of the small woman paired with a picture of Kendall in Waddow Hall, when that evil fellow tried to bribe me. The image came back to me of a petite, clear complexioned woman, around thirty years of age perhaps. Her light brown hair was combed back, excepting a short fringe in front. That helped frame a face which carried no readable expression. Her part-lidded eyes stared straight out but with an unfocussed look. She wore a pearl necklace and earrings above a yellow dress with slashed sleeves showing lace beneath. A rich lace collar covered her shoulders and a blue ribbon, formed into a cross, sat at her breast. I beautiful image indeed, I must say.

'I know nothing about her save the image hung at Waddow, sir, where she is or even if she's alive or dead. Why do you ask?'

'Well, the oddest thing – I don't know whether to be insulted or amused – I've received a summons, issued by Aspinall of Standen Hall. She has accused me of theft and destruction of property and, under his powers as a Justice of the Peace, he must investigate.'

'Where has she been all this time and why appear now?'

'I suppose, if Kendall is dead, his estate falls to her and she wishes to take possession. We do have some of the contents of the Hall here, including that haul of silver plate. As you know, I have it in store from when Waddow was abandoned, simply to ensure it was not stolen. I wrote to Aspinall at the time to apprise him of that, as much to cover myself as anything, so why he should proceed to such action as this,' He waved the letter, 'I do not know.'

I cleared my throat. 'We did believe that Aspinall was in Kendall's pocket. Perhaps Lady Kendall knows about her husband's hold over him and forced his hand. Aspinall has always appeared to be gullible at the very least.'

'I've written to him, a simple response, stating that I am happy to meet the Lady either at Standen or at a place of her choosing to arrange the handing back of the effects under my care. I'll be interested in the response. In the meantime, I've asked Will to make some enquiries about her. We shall see, Doctor, we shall see, but this is something of an insult, I believe.'

Over the next few days I extended my riding and by the end of the week rode the few miles into Clitheroe, pressing Bay up the steep street to the Church. Few people were abroad and they paid me no mind, excepting the woman illegally washing cow hides in St Mary's Well, who looked at me in fright as if I was the town bailiff. Washing of cloths and beasts in this water was a regular occurrence, despite the fines for such acts, and was the reason we never used this source of water when we lived here. I didn't go down into the marketplace, thinking I'd leave that for another day, until I could be sure that my presence would not cause a scene. I had Will, sword at his side, and Nate with me just in case. I remember thinking that there was, in fact, little to entice me back to Clitheroe.

It was my aim to see Amos at the Schoolhouse, which sat in the corner of the Churchyard. Next door, just over the stone wall, lay my house, now abandoned. I could feel its presence but didn't have the heart to look. I think I'd been at my happiest there but now that seemed to be over.

The school had just two day-pupils as yet and I wondered if it would ever return to the modest but bustling institution that it had been less than two years before.

Amos was downcast. He could barely meet my eye and there was a coldness in his manner as we stood outside the battered oak of the Schoolhouse door. 'I have been thrown out of something akin to heaven, Maister, to come back to what? We have but two pupils and my sister and I now feel like strangers in this town.'

'You must remember, my dear Usher,' I used his title as a reminder of his position, 'that you are paid for this employment. We cannot remain in Downham forever. Indeed, I hope to be moving back here in the near future...'

'But it was because of you that we had to move away!' he said with a petulance, staring at me in a way that I could not tolerate.

'Usher. You are forgetting yourself and taking our friendship too far. Are you saying that I should have ignored Kendall's crimes, that I should have covered his embezzlement of school funds, an embezzlement that could well have finished the school forever?' I was incensed. 'I would remind you that you are paid for your job here and that, at present, I am unpaid, essentially out of a position.'

'I mean the move back here from Downham!'

'That wasn't my decision. But I do think it was time. I suggest you do the job you are paid for,' I responded, angrily.

He dropped his gaze and turned away.

I reflected on how he had changed over the last year or so. Balding for as long as I'd known him, he'd now lost all but a small band of hair running behind his ears. He still stooped slightly but had gained weight and no longer had that habitual near emaciated frame that I once knew. He'd experienced an easy life at Downham and, I think, come to view it as his right. His sister, once a harridan who ruled his life, had lost her spirit since being spurned in love and so he now had no controlling influence over him. He wasn't the Amos Brierley that I had known.

'My sister and I are living in a sty that would disgrace a pig,' he muttered, darkly.

'What do you mean?'

'Our rooms are uninhabitable because there are holes in the roof; my sister has a permanent cough because of it.' He was counting each point on his fingers. 'We have to sleep in the schoolroom; Our only two scholars refuse to bring water from the well. We see no-one. It is no way to live.' He seemed close to breaking.

'What can I do to help, Amos?'

He shrugged his shoulders, walked into the schoolhouse and closed the door behind him.

I'd left Bay in the charge of Will and Nate at the Churchyard gate and as I returned to them I looked next door at my abandoned house. There was a desolate, uncared for look about the place with weeds growing tall between the cobbles of the yard. It matched my mood, sad and frustrated as I was after the altercation with Amos. The fire damaged laboratory that people called my Study had just half a charred door to it, though the building, built into the Churchyard wall, still looked solid. Fleetingly, my mind went back to that awful night when Kendall's men attacked us, but I quickly shook those bad thoughts from me.

'I see you've got tenants,' said Will with a grin as I rejoined them.

'What do you mean?'

'I just had a scout round, saw a chap come through the back gate and into the stable, so I lifted Nate up on to the wall. Tell him what you saw, Nate.'

'There's a pig with squealers in the sty, a cow in't field, and a good few hens,' Nate vouched eagerly.

'This I must see!' I cried angrily and, pushing wide the yard gate, strode up to the stable door, hammering it with my fist.

Feet clattered on steps as someone ran down the stairs from the hay loft. The door was flung open by a large unkempt, ruddy-faced young woman in a surprisingly clean apron, her hair hanging loosely beneath a dirty coif.

'Give o'er with that banging. You'll wake the babby!'

'Don't give me that,' I replied sharply, 'Tell me what you're doing in my property.'

She narrowed her eyes and looked at me accusingly.'Are you this doctor people tell me of, the one as abandoned the town? Why shouldn't we mind it and seek shelter if you don't want it?'

'It's not a case of not wanting it!' I was taken aback and put on the back foot as they say.'It's my land. Don't I have the right to say what goes here?'

'Hey!' she called over her shoulder, as a baby started to cry in the loft above. 'Come and sort this out.' And from behind her came a youngish chap, slightly smaller than his wife in girth and stature, wearing a rough leather apron over an open shirt.'Tell him, John, whilst I feed the babby.' And she turned and climbed back up the stair.

Like most red-haired people, his fair skin had been burned in the summer sun, but his eyes were quite gentle, his voice even and modest in tone.

'Sir. We had nowhere to go and then the child came. Thrown off our land over by Bashall, though we'd done nowt to warrant it. This stable was empty and we could keep our animals behind and thought you'd not mind. We've looked after the place. Are you now returning? I'll work for thee if we can stay,' he urged.

My first thought was to tell them to go, I must admit. Parents with nowhere to go and a child born in a stable? That story sounded too familiar, too glib, but I let him persuade me and show how he'd kept the place.

The area in front of the stables was free of weeds, unlike the rest of the yard, and the stables themselves had been swept clean. The kitchen garden was full of vegetables and herbs and beyond, in my back field, this John had rebuilt our old sty to house his pig. He certainly seemed a straight-forward fellow and, though he must have been worried that we would indeed throw him and his out onto the road, there was an openness to him that I liked.

As we returned to the stable, he called to his wife who came down with the baby in her arms. This time she was more gracious and gave a slight bob. She tried to show me the infant, to take it in my arms perhaps, but I was having none of that. I can't abide babies and wish that children were instead born at the age of seven or so, when they can be of use.

The woman, Sally by name, also entreated me to let them stay.

'I can cook and keep house for you if you're returning and...' I held up my hands.

'I have a housekeeper and stable lads and need no addition to my household.' Her shoulders drooped. But something had occurred to me.

'It is true that I am not moving back yet. I will remain in Downham for the present and until this place is needed I will let you remain,' Her face cleared and John placed his arm around her shoulder, 'and I will charge you no rent, provided that you will keep house for the guests that I may be installing.'

I knocked again at the Schoolhouse door. Opened this time by Amos' spinster sister, looking thin, grey and rather shrewish, she dropped her eyes.

'I'm sorry for my brother, sir. It's just that we are in such a poor state.' She seemed near tears, but I wasn't going to make this easy for them.

'Ask your brother to come out here.' I said brusquely. He came to the door, all defiance gone, an apology ready on his lips.

'Mr. Usher. When you present to me a problem, do not think that a sullen attitude is needed before I try to solve it. You tell me that your living accommodation is untenable?' He nodded. 'Can you still teach in the schoolroom?' Again he nodded. 'If I find you good rooms, can you do the job that you are paid for?' Another nod.

I held out the key to my house.

I left Amos and his sister hugging themselves like children who have received a present at New Year. With no cost to themselves they now had not only a dry and comfortable house, but also something they'd never had before – a housekeeper. At least until I was able to remove back from Downham and the Schoolhouse repaired they would be safe. True, their meagre furniture and chattels would fill only a small part of one of my rooms, but I felt good. Two problems solved at the same time. I made it clear that they must treat John and his Sally with some respect and not lord it over them, for I knew Amos' tendencies in that direction and, though this arrangement could only be temporary, was sure that a long-term solution would present itself in due course.

Five

'I Simply Don't Understand Him...'

'YOU'VE DONE WHAT?' SLATER WAS OUTRAGED. 'GIVEN OUR house away and let goodness knows who have our stables?'

'Perhaps you'll think me a pedant, Slater,' I said with equanimity, 'But, though I value your work, commitment and even, most of the time, your company, I must point out one small fact - it is *my* house. Not that I don't encourage your belief in our joint future back there someday. In the meantime though, this seems a fair and equitable solution to a problem. It even gives me a sanctimonious glow. I feel,' I said, clasping my hands across my belly, 'like the Innkeeper in the story of the Nativity.'

She huffed at me and returned to scrubbing her pots in an overzealous way, mumbling under her breath that she'd never called me a peasant.

'I though you preferred living here at Downham.' I cried. She scrubbed even harder.

'When are you going to do something about that idiot boy?' she said angrily. If she couldn't win in an argument about the house, she would attack me from a different direction. I could read her like a book.

'What boy?' I asked carelessly, 'Pod? What has he done now?'

'Not Pod, who is as near an angel as lives round here,' she blustered,

'Don't you say anything about him. He's a treasure.' This from the woman who huffed and puffed when I told her he would stay with us after his father's murder. She accused him then of being riddled with lice and foul diseases and bringing evil into our household. 'That *Cas*, as you call him. He's not like our old Sam. He's no understanding, idle, and is planning to murder us in our beds.'

'Don't be ridiculous, Slater. He is a problem, I admit, and now I'm better I will do something about him, though I don't know what...'

'Send him back where he came from.'

'We don't know where he came from,' I said with a measure of frustration. 'I wish we did. I can't just turn him out.' Though I'd like to and, in truth, should do so, I thought to myself.

'I keep finding him where he shouldn't be. Trying to get into the Hall. Nate told me he was trying to open the door to the cellars.'

Slater was an unusual woman in many ways. She had never seen an African until I brought Sam back with me from London all those years ago but, unlike the rest of Clitheroe, she had embraced him as a man, taking no regard of his colour. Though others might cross the road to avoid him, Slater took Sam about town with her as often as possible and would scold anyone who insulted him. Though I might try to convince all and sundry that Sam was just as human as anyone, few believed it, yet Slater did and showed a Christian charity for which I applaud her.

I therefore realised that her dislike of Cas was not due to his blackness. Neither did it relate to his lack of education nor his language difficulties. I couldn't put this aside any longer, I must do something about him. I had thought of gifting him to Amos but that might have caused more problems than it would solve. Clitheroe had almost revelled in the murder of Sam. Why should they treat Cas any differently?

Was his lack of acceptance mainly down to me? I certainly had no affinity with him. But then I recalled that he'd arrived whilst I was away and that most of this apathy or dislike of him had surfaced in my absence.

Thinking that I'd first ask Nate and Pod about him, they being the ones who saw him most, I started off towards the stables. I'd barely left the door when I spied Cas at the corner of the house. Seeing me, he turned and ran. I called after him, but the stupid creature didn't return.

Pod was turning hay in the stable. 'He don't talk to me. I ask him things, but he don't answer,' said the boy sadly. 'I'd make him my friend if he'd let me.' Pod is such a gentle, kind lad.

'Does he help you in the stables as he should?' I saw his hesitation. 'Come on, Pod. I need to know, else how can I help him?'

'No, sir, he doesn't help. He don't really care for the animals, and they don't seem to care for him. He stays in the loft much of the time, but I hear him moving about in the night. When Mother Slater calls us for food he comes and takes it, then moves away, not even eating with us.'

'Well, well, Pod. Good boy to tell me.' I put my hand on his shoulder. 'Can you understand him at all?' He shook his head.

'It don't make sense to me. Sometimes he calls out in his sleep, but it is no words that I know. He just seems affrighted of everything.'

Nate looked up as I approached. He was in the field below the hall, helping old Tom repair a fallen stone wall.

'Careful of those hands, Nate,' I called, smiling, 'You never see a one-handed surgeon.' He spun the irregular block in his hands, slotted it in the wall between two others, and adjusted it until it followed the line of the sloping face.

'Tis a puzzle, Doctor,' said Old Tom, 'You have to understand how the stones can fit and grip each other, so none can fall out and bring the wall with it.' He nodded at Nate. ''E understands. E's the feel for it.'

'Excellent, Tom, glad he's of use to you. How long before I can have him back?'

'Oh, tha can have him now. I can finish this off. Just another course and the coping.'

I indicated that Nate should follow me back up the field and, as we walked back towards our house, asked him too about Cas.

'I want you to find him some jobs around the house and barn and try to keep your eye on him. I need to know exactly what he does, and if he wanders off, follow him. Don't make it obvious, though. Make it look as though you're ignoring him, if you can.'

'That's not a problem, sir, for he takes no notice of any of us.'

'Good. I'd also like you to sleep in the stable for the time being. Pod says that he moves about, and I wonder what he does. Try and stay awake and find out, if you can.' Nate nodded.

'I need to change his behaviour, Nate, 'else I must get rid of him. He's no good to man nor beast as he is. I simply don't understand him.'

'Neither do we, sir. Not one bit.'

Six

'Knitbone, Boiled and Applied Hot...'

WITH MOST OF THE YOUNG MEN OF FIGHTING AGE AWAY WITH SIR Richard Shuttleworth's Parliamentarians, the women of the village had to do even more of the work in the fields. It was proving difficult to gather the grass and many were wondering how they'd manage at harvest time.

We'd had notable success against the King's men, with most of Lancashire now in our hands, and it was said that the Royalist leader, Lord Derby, had abandoned his position and fled to his estates on the Isle of Man. We therefore hoped that at least some of our fellows would now return. But apart from four, mighty weary with their exertions, it was not to be. Most had been marched quickly over into Yorkshire and put under Lord Fairfax and his son Sir Thomas, and we wondered how they were doing. I was especially concerned as Sir Ralph's son, also called Sir Ralph to confuse things and who I was honoured to call a friend, was now at the head of our local men. This younger Sir Ralph, Colonel Assheton, had his own estate some miles away at Whalley.

His father had remained in Downham for the most part and taken little or no part in the fighting to date. This wasn't down to a lack of courage, you understand, but to try and keep control over the local area. He was now to administer the sequestration of local Roman Catholic and Royalist estates, remitting the monies raised to pay our troops.

Then came his accident.

'Doctor!' Will came running in to our kitchen. I was just sitting down to some bread and cheese. 'Sir Ralph's had a bad fall. His horse started as he was getting on. He's hit his head on the mounting block and broken his leg.' I grabbed my bag, shouted for Nate, and hobbled after Will, towards the Hall.

'No, sir, it's not broken, thank the Lord,' I comforted the patient. Sir Ralph was in great pain, lying ashen and sweating on his bed, but he made not a sound as I felt all along his leg and manipulated his knee and foot as gently as I could. The side of his head had been badly gashed where he'd hit the stone block but, though there had been a great effusion of blood as often happens from such a wound, it was inconsequential. He'd been momentarily stunned and, as I checked his eyes, he confessed that his vision was still blurred.

It had been difficult to remove his boot, and the leg, already blue-black from ankle to thigh, was starting to swell. I took Nate to one side.

'You know what's needed, Nate?' I queried. He nodded.

'Knitbone, boiled and applied hot, then tightly bandaged, sir.'

'That's right, lad. Not too hot, though. But first, whilst it's being boiled up, just take some of the leaves, brush them together to remove the hairs, and rub, almost caress, his leg with them. We will also exhibit Borage as a drink. Why?'

'To reduce fever?'

'Yes, but more importantly here, it will act as *sedativus,* Latin for calming.' I turned back to the patient. 'I must turn you onto your side, Sir Ralph. More pain, I know, but I must just check your spine, which will have been badly jarred, I expect.'

'I won't nod, Doctor, for it hurts like hell,' he murmured. 'Do what you must.'

Asking Lady Assheton, always calm, to let him drink lavender water as often as possible and assuring her that with care and rest her husband should do well, I left Nate with him and returned to my bread and cheese, Will joining me.

'A bad fall, Will. Not a light thing at his age. His horse started and pitched him off, you say? She's usually such a well-behaved beast. Do you remember when the men were at practice with the cannon when they were first mustered? All she did was snort and toss her head a little.'

'Aye, Doctor, and we were to be off to Colne, hoping to find some of our men today. How long do you reckon he'll be out of play?'

'I wouldn't like to see him about for at least a week. If no fever and the bruising fades he should be back on his feet by then. I may know better by morning.'

I wasn't quite as sanguine as I sounded. Such a fall at Sir Ralph's advanced age could not be considered lightly, so I returned to sit with him late that evening, dozing in a chair for most of the night, if truth be told. He slept better than I had expected, waking only in the small hours with the rest of the house as usual and, as they all returned to their beds for their second sleep, he too returned to the arms of Morpheus.

Next morning, with no sign of fever and with his vision no longer blurred, I let his manservant, Bill, old as the house and almost fully deaf, help him with his bodily functions before giving him a full examination. His piss looked normal. Under my palm, his heart beat steadily and strong. The grazing to his head was crusting over nicely and, opening the wrappings, the leg looked no worse than on the previous day.

'I'll ask Nate to give you a new poultice of knitbone and renew it every few hours. I know you are still in much discomfort, sir, but rest is the thing.'

At this Sir Ralph became quite agitated. 'Hell's teeth, Doctor! I can't just lie here. There's too much to be done.' He tried to throw off his covers, but I held his shoulder and looked him straight in the eye.

'Do not try to rise or I cannot answer for the consequences. You must rest easy and realise that you will be incapacitated for a few days at least.' He looked at me furiously. 'And when you'll be able to ride, I cannot say.' His body quite rigid, I told him that he must relax or perhaps do more damage to his aching muscles.

'Then send Will in to me, will you?' he asked, taking a deep breath and with a degree of acceptance. 'This couldn't have happened at a worse time.'

'Right, Doctor, are you up for a trip?' Will had been with Sir Ralph for less than a quarter hour but, apparently, much had been re-organised. 'He wants to promote you.' There was that infernal grin again. 'I should now call you Colonel, I think.'

'Give over with your nonsense, Will Cummins. You wear me out. Am I to go back in?'

'Aye. He wants us both.'

I'd gone down to the kitchen for a mug of ale. Slater was there, 'Helping out Lady Katherine's cook,' she said. It's a good job that her ears flap more than her tongue. I downed the beer and followed Will back upstairs to Sir Ralph's bedroom in my shirt sleeves. I'd doffed my coat as the fire had been kept up in the room and the windows fast shut at my insistence, for despite the high summer sun there's nothing like heat and sweat to keep out a fever.

'If I'm to be an invalid for some days,' Sir Ralph sounded a little petulant, but I understood his frustration, 'and in the absence of anyone of rank, I must ask you if you feel capable of riding out with Will and my few able-bodied men?'

'If I can assist, sir, I will.'

'I know you're not yet fully recovered...' began Sir Ralph.

'No, sir, I'm fine,' I interrupted.

'Good man. This is the picture...'

Our Parliamentarians might well hold Lancashire but, with the Queen set in York and gathering troops to her, Yorkshire was as near fully Royalist as one could imagine - except for the town of Bradford, still held by us. Lord Fairfax and our men failed to make any inroads in the Ridings and a message received the previous day revealed that his near 7,000 troops had been routed by 10,000 or so of the enemy at a moor called Adwalton, somewhere near Bradford.

'The message came from my son. He has come off the field safe, along with most of his men, God be praised, though many prisoners have been taken. He apparently held the middle ground, the only part to stand fast, which is of great credit to him. Now I know not where this Adwalton is, but Ralph says he will try and cut to the northwards, which may bring him across the moor by Wycoller and on to Colne.' He paused.

'Here's the thing, Doctor. We know there are Royalists holding Colne - not many perhaps – but we don't know if they have cannon. If our men come through there, it could be hard on them. And yet Ralph will expect Colne to be ours. My friend Shuttleworth was intending to reduce the town before he decamped into Cheshire but, at the last minute, it was decided that it had so little value that it wasn't worth the time and effort.'

'Now,' he continued, 'Will is perfectly capable of taking what few men I still have, bypass the town and try to meet up with my son – I have full confidence in him.'

Will nodded his acceptance of the praise.

'But I think it not beyond us to persuade Colne to surrender, if their defences are not too great and they are led to believe that the might of our army are on their way,' he gave me a tight smile. 'You understand me, Doctor? But it needs someone with - what shall we say - gravitas.'

I gave him a wry look.

'I don't expect you to fight, of course.'

I put that comment down to his condition, saying 'Thank you' in quite a sarcastic way, though he didn't appear to notice. 'What about talking to Grent at the Dule upon Dun? Should I attend to that first?'

'No,' he said, 'Colne comes first. Colne comes before anything. Where's the pannier from my horse? There's a map in it. You should take a copy.'

Given the successes we Parliamentarians had had in Lancashire, I had wrongly assumed that King Charles would have come to his senses and peace would shortly ensue. In reality, things were worse than ever. According to the information available to Sir Ralph, almost two-thirds of the country was still of Royalist persuasion, and we must look to defend the borders of the County Palatine. Our mission against Colne wasn't just to help the younger Sir Ralph, but to be a bulwark against the enemy.

Seven

'Not Fit for War...'

TO SAY I WASN'T LOOKING FORWARD TO LEAVING THE comforts of home, even for what I'd hoped would only be a short time, is an understatement. I'd hoped that the worst of my adventures were behind me, along with my wounds. I may be prepared to knock the odd couple of heads together, but I'm certainly not made for warfare. The thought of traipsing round the countryside again in these uncertain times wasn't high on my list of things to do.

The enforced idleness during my recent recovery had allowed me to re-enter the treasured world of my library, still mainly confined to chests since our equally enforced removal from Clitheroe. Sir Ralph and Lady Katherine had allowed me full use of the Hall's modest library and some of my most favoured volumes were, for the time being, now on its shelves, but it wasn't like sitting in my own room, surrounded by my treasures. One tries to make the best of things, though.

My library is my favourite child. I have amassed hundreds of books, including many ancient works, most by purchase but some, I'm ashamed to admit, by theft. I justify the latter by telling myself that they are of more use to me than anyone else.

From the bottom of one of my book chests I'd recovered an unbound tome by one Gerard Honricks dated 1581 about the making of saltpetre.

I think this Honricks must have been a Hollander and fortunately (for I cannot grasp their utterings and don't understand why they don't use Latin for their treatises as any civilised person would) someone had translated his evil language into English. As you know, saltpetre is a main constituent of gunpowder and I was musing on how we could create our own source of powder, for we have no such manufacture in the immediate area.

It wasn't just because of the present war, you understand. I had long been working on a history of metals, their sources, uses and potential, and I'd used gunpowder in many of the experiments in my *laboratorium*, the building adjacent to my house in Clitheroe that most called my study (even though it wasn't – I would never keep books, paper, pens and inks in what was little better than an outhouse, for goodness' sake!). Gunpowder was a useful elixir, a starter if you will, for certain processes. The other volume I had consulted often was one of my most recent purchases, *Pyrotechnia or a Discourse of Artificiall Fire-Works*, by John Babington. I'd met Babington when I was in London, a most interesting and enlightening fellow, and he kindly gave me an introduction to his bookseller, close by St. Paul's. In turn, the bookseller was good enough to sell me a copy of the work that had already been promised to another.

It was due to the occasional, but colourful, uses of Babington's mixtures in the study that wasn't my study that the locals were persuaded that I was probably in league with the Devil. Bangs and flashing lights in the dark mean only one thing to those idiots. In fact, there was only a single true explosion and that only blew out one of my windows. I tried to tell them what I was doing but, like the simpletons they are, they wouldn't listen.

Reading these two books, I'd started to sketch out in my mind the possibility of creating my own gunpowder works. After all, two of the main ingredients, lime and charcoal, were readily to hand. Limestone was still being quarried on the edge of Clitheroe as it had been since time immemorial, and turned to lime in the kilns, fed by fuel produced by the charcoal-burners of the Brungerley woods. Saltpetre, Honricks affirmed, could be brought, by extraction, from the soil of old middens and latrines, with the use of piss, neither product being in short supply. With the two large crucibles that I'd brought from my house, and that had been languishing in a barn since then, I was just about to instruct Nate to build a base of stones on which to sit them and re-commence my experiments when this new call to arms came.

I'm sure you can understand my frustration. Besides being pulled from my work, I had a number of problems to solve. I needed to organise some force against the Tench gang, as I might call them; find a way to repair the School-house; sort out the problem of Cas; and try to improve my reputation in Clitheroe, though this last part was of least concern to me.

Goodwife Slater fluttered round, pleased that Nate was to be left behind this time but saying that I wasn't, as she put it, 'fit to be going to war again'.

'I've never been fit for going to war,' I exclaimed, 'And I'm not doing that now, you silly woman. I'm going to persuade our enemy to act like reasonable men and give up Colne to us. I shall use words as weapons, not swords.'

'Then why are you buckling on that blade, that very bilbo, may I ask?' She had me there, I suppose. 'What about your daily posset, which is needed to build your strength? What about me, left here to worry,' she fussed around, gathering bread, cheese and the remains of a cured ham, '... and you've not dealt with that Cas, who is no good to man or beast...'

At times it is just best to let her chatter on. She was still talking as I took my medicine bag and two blankets out to Bay, placing them in the leather panniers that Will had already arranged behind her saddle.

Ten of us mustered in front of the Hall, a real motley bunch. Will and I were both well mounted. There were three asses. Two of these were carrying our equipment, several muskets, powder and ball, and were to be led by the third beast being ridden by a different kind of ass, if you get my meaning – not quite a village idiot but certainly a lad of very modest intelligence. Four of our remaining troop had only recently returned from the West but at least they were, as one might say, battle-hardened. The best that I can say for the remaining three was that they had all their limbs.

I led off through the gate after a crust of bread and a can of ale to keep us going. It was late morning, another sultry late summer day, with Pendle slumbering before us as we progressed down into the village. As we crossed the stream, a young lass, bonny too, ran out, flung her arms about one of our soldiers, kissed him mightily and then ran off in tears. 'Don't worry, Bill,' said one of his companions in arms, 'I'll look after her if you don't come back.' The others burst out laughing, Bill with them. We began the steady rise up the sheep track onto the lower slopes of the hill and, as I looked back, I could see the heat haze rising from slumbering Downham.

Though I'd lain my coat across Bay's neck, my back was wet with sweat before we'd gone a mile but at least I was riding. Our small Troop of Foot, as you might call them, were in their shirts too, their buff coats being carried by the asses, but they were obliged to carry their pikes, freshly cut down from the standard sixteen feet to a more manageable ten. There was no shade except for beneath the broad brims of our hats, thank God for them.

That first two miles must have taken us at least 2 hours by my reckoning. The wide heath they call Black Moss stretched out before us. My heart sank. We had another six or seven miles to go at least. On we plodded.

Finally dropping down from the high moor we reached a bank of trees which flanked the track for at least a further mile. Stopping for a drink in the coolness of the shade, Will had to help me off Bay as I was already a little stiff though, fortunately, I had no real aches or pains.

'What's your plan then, Doctor?' Will was sat by me as we rested against the trees.

'Haven't got one, young William. I don't really know what we're supposed to be doing,' I responded bitterly, 'I've never been to Colne, don't know its defences or how big a force holds it. Have you been there?'

'No, but you'll think of something. You always do.'

'Ha. Like when?'

'Like when you got us out of that cell up at Rossall with Kendall snapping at our heels,' he said with a laugh, 'What a night!'

'I did that without thinking. We were just lucky.'

'Then don't think. Let's just see what happens.' He turned to the men. 'Anyone know Colne?'

'Aye,' said Bill, pointing his thumb, 'Adam here was born there.'

'Well...I 'aven't been there for a long while. It might have changed.' Adam said with reluctance, but I was more bothered about getting an idea of the terrain. Was there a castle? Town walls? Gates? We all gathered round Adam.

Eight

'Is the Town for the King?'

RIDING ALONG BESIDES ME, LOOKING RATHER INCONGRUOUS on his ass, Adam and I jogged up the rise and into Colne, Doctor and his erstwhile servant.

Adam was small and wiry with long grey hair, a straggly beard, and few words. A farmhand from Downham's Home Farm, he was older than me at near fifty years or so, his face dark and lined from years out in the fields. His wife having died long ago, he lived with a widow and her daughter in a small cottage at the bottom of the village. Some looked askance at their relationship, but Adam and she had done the old thing of giving each other a token and to most this meant they were married. He had a son who was away with the younger Sir Ralph, and prayed he was safe. He therefore had, as you might say, a vested interest in our quest.

The town looked to advantage, sat on a hilltop between two deep valleys, good stone houses lining the wide main road. There was no barrier, no challenge, as we carried on, with the lowering sun behind us, into the town square. The Market had finished for the day, the usual detritus of rotting vegetables, offal and horse shit being swept to one side by a couple of ragged urchins. In one corner, by large piles of fleeces, stood two prosperous looking fellows, traders for sure, and as I watched, two carts lumbered in from the right, their pairs of heavy horses snorting and blowing, ready to take the wool away.

The only indication of the town's apparent allegiance in this current war came in the name of the main inn. A badly painted sign over its wide front door gave the legend "The Crown". Two stout, well-fed men, sat outside with tankards of ale, touched their hats as I gingerly slid from the saddle and handed Bay's reins to Adam.

'G'day, sir.' The innkeeper came out to meet us, wiping his hands on a stained apron. 'Ale, feed, bed and stable is it?' I smiled.

'A fine and exact list that gladdens my heart. Tell me – is it cooler in or out?'

'In, sir, and I have a fowl sitting ready and even half a fish, caught only this morn.'

'That fits the bill. Have you a boy to see to our cattle?' I turned to Adam, 'Bring in my bags.'

'He'll want the stable. There's room in the loft…'

'No,' I interrupted, 'My man stays with me.'

'As you wish, sir, as you wish.' He shepherded us into a cool, dark parlour, full of chatter from farmers and traders who gave us quizzical looks as we were led to a quiet corner by the unlit fire.

The room gradually emptied as we devoured the welcome victuals and downed tankards of near cold ale, constantly refilled. The landlord, as landlords do, gently quizzed us.

'A Doctor! I thought as much. In my job you get to recognise a gentleman from the common herd,' he smiled knowingly. 'You are very welcome here, sir. I am always a picture of health, as you see, but my wife, if you have a moment…'

'Perhaps, before we leave in the morning…'

'Oh! So soon. I'm sure there is much work for you in the town if you could stay. People here are not rich but I'm sure many would pay…'

'I'm afraid I must go.' I paused. 'Do you know of the recent battle over in Yorkshire? Lives of the wounded are at risk and I must attend them.'

'What side do you act for?'

'There are no sides for a doctor. I will attend any and all who need me.'

He furrowed his brow and nodded his head as I added, in as casual a fashion as I could, 'I will receive pay from Parliament, I must admit, but all are God's creatures...' Another nod from him and I thought I'd chance my arm.

'The Parliament men may well be heading this way as they try for home. How will you face them?' Sitting by me, Adam's jaw was steadily dropping as the conversation progressed. I kicked his shin under the table, and he shut it with a jerk.

'I don't think they will be any worse for us than the fools up the road,' the innkeeper intoned. 'They treat us as shit, coming in here and demanding food and drink without payment.'

'I was referring to your sign, "The Crown".' I gave a wry smile. 'Parliament men may resent it... But you have soldiers here?'

'Aye, sir. Set just outside town. They were all right whilst they had a commander, but since his death they've been worse than brigands.'

'So, no commander. And ... there are how many?'

'There were forty or so, but some have returned home. What's left are no good to man nor beast, sir. They were bullies in the town before the war and they're bullies still. I doubt they'll stand up to proper soldiers, though. Worse than useless they are.'

I feigned horror. 'And will I be safe, passing them as I leave the town? Will they fire on me?'

'They've no cannon and I don't think they've muskets... They may demand a few shillings off you for passage, but I doubt they'd harm you.'

'Ee, that's good,' said Adam, and I kicked him again. I didn't want him butting in. I didn't know what he might say. I took a long swig of ale and as I replaced the tankard on the table the Innkeeper immediately refilled it from his jug. Adam greedily thrust his tankard forward too.

'Have you looked to my horse?' I said to him, pointedly. Sulkily he sloped to the door muttering 'I were enjoying that ale...'

'Is the town really for the King?' I turned my attention back to our host. 'All of Lancashire - except, It seems, this place – is for Parliament..' He interrupted me.

'They – we – are for any and all, if truth be known, not knowing what it is all about. It was all down to one man, Captain Spence, who raised this troop. They never did anything, though. No fighting, except in the town. Would have run a mile at sight of a battle.'

After an uncomfortable night sharing a loosely strung bed with a snoring Adam and a stranger who farted, I rose early to another fine day. If I'd thought, I would have bribed the Innkeeper for a room to ourselves. I think Adam had it worst as I'd placed him in the middle, so he had both me and the farter rolling into him, though I seemed to spend much of the night clinging to the bedside to avoid crushing him. But if the bed was bad, breakfast was a fine affair, with baked eggs and milk plus bread fresh from the oven. I gave a shilling for food, drink and stabling, which I found very fair. If I should pass this way again, I vowed to stop here. Providing, of course, that the bed was properly tightened.

I'd left Will and the others below the town of course, and now had a something of a plan. With a quiet word to Adam, I sent him to bring up the others to the Inn whilst I quizzed the Innkeeper further.

'I have the merest outline of a map.' I laid out the rough sketch I'd made before leaving Sir Ralph's bedside, 'Have you pen and ink? I want you to show me the lie of the land…'

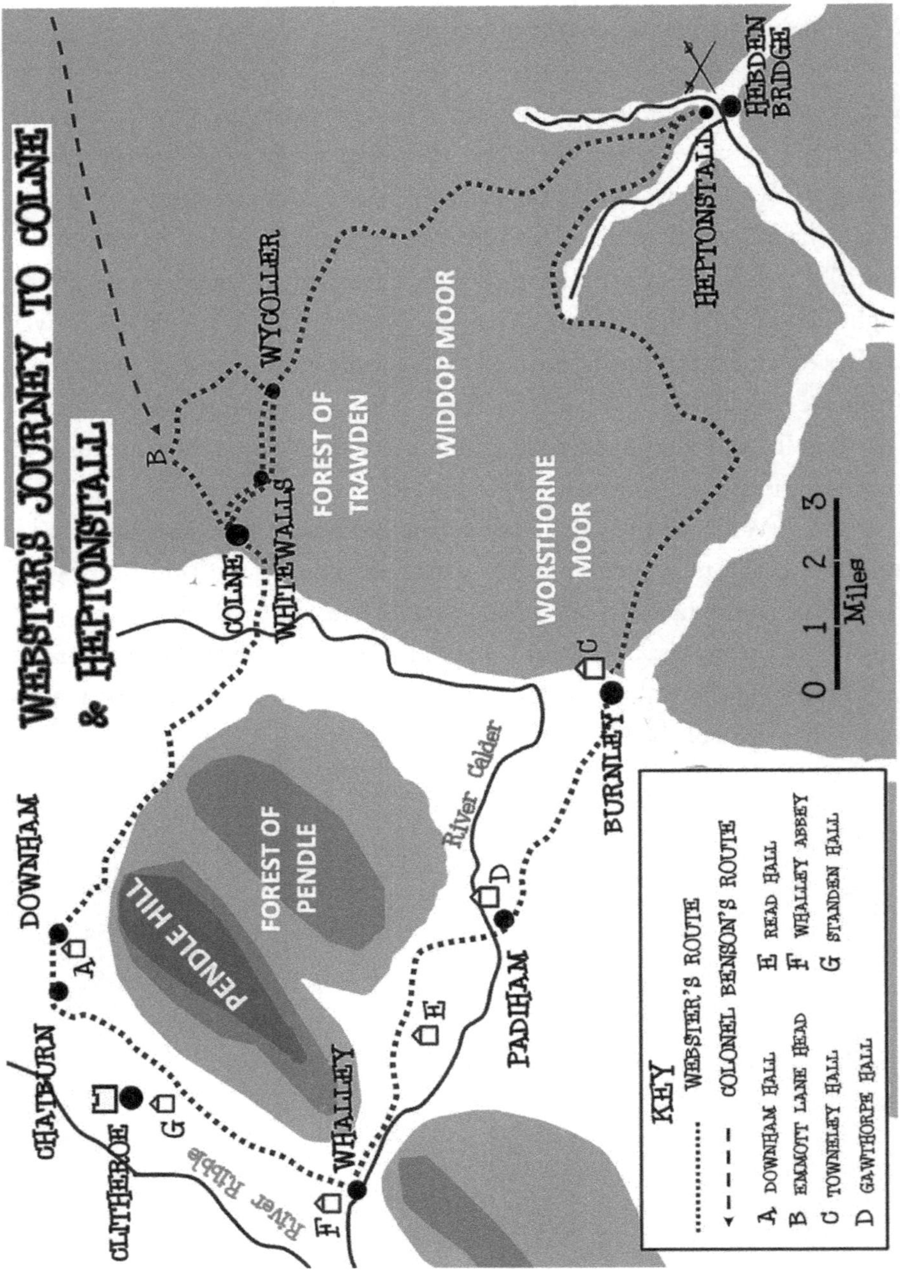
WEBSTER'S JOURNEY TO COLNE
& HEPTONSTALL
DOWNHAM
CHATBURN
CLITHEROE
WHALLEY
PADIHAM
BURNLEY
COLNE
WHITEWALLS
WYCOLLER
HEPTONSTALL
HEBDEN BRIDGE
FOREST OF PENDLE
PENDLE HILL
FOREST OF TRAWDEN
WIDDOP MOOR
WORSTHORNE MOOR
River Ribble
River Calder
0 1 2 3
Miles
KEY
WEBSTER'S ROUTE
COLONEL BENSON'S ROUTE
A DOWNHAM HALL
B EMMOTT LANE HEAD
C TOWNELEY HALL
D GAWTHORPE HALL
E READ HALL
F WHALLEY ABBEY
G STANDEN HALL

Nine

'Persuade them to Keep Going'

'… AND THEIR PICKET IS HERE,' I POINTED TO THE MAP AS THE men jostled Will to get a better look, 'a mile and a half from the town.'

'Well, the town has no fortification, that was obvious when we walked in with no by-your-leave. There's no garrison at all?' Will mused, 'Then we've taken the place. We can just sit here and wait.'

'Yes, but that's not really the point. The few Royalist men are at this point,' I jabbed at the map, 'because it guards both routes coming out of Yorkshire.'

'Guards. Phuh!' The Innkeeper pushed through to set another pail of ale on the table. 'They'll run off at the first sight of trouble, you mark my words…'

We were gathered outside the now un-named inn, the sign of the Crown having been diplomatically removed by our host, who was happy to provide ale for our small but thirsty band when I produced the required coin.

It was still barely seven o'clock, but traders were already bringing their wares into the market square, and a line of carts was pulling up the main road. I was eager to start before too much of a crowd gathered as I didn't want any awkward questions, give anything away, or allow a warning to reach our quarry. Will had already sent one of the boys to the far edge of town to warn of any approach, and the rest had yet to put on their soldier's buff jackets. I had asked them to look as ordinary as possible as they came into the town, not assume a martial air, but it barely mattered for more than one of the locals stopped and asked if we 'were the lads to get rid o'they ruffians down the way?'

'Adam. You can ride a horse and not just an ass?' He nodded. 'Good. I've hired a beast from the Innkeeper because we need to move quickly.' I scanned the other faces and tapped my map again. 'I'm going to take the track to this place, Whitewalls, across here to Wycoller, join the main road and turn back northwards to Emmott Lane Head, where the picket stands. It's about three miles. I'll tell them that Parliamentary forces are a few hours behind me and I'm fleeing the carnage they're causing.' I flapped my hands about, emphasising that 'I might have to extemporise.' I looked about me at the blank faces. 'I mean work out what I say at the last minute.' There were a couple of "Aah's" and more nods now.

'Will, I want you to take the north track through this place…' I peered at the map and tapped the name, 'Heyroyd. Bring the men as near as you can to the crossroads without being seen, have the muskets ready to fire so that, if they break up the lane as a group, as I hope they will…' I paused for emphasis. '… you can persuade them to keep going. No need to kill or wound them.' I smiled. 'Especially not wound them, or I might have work to do…'

Despite Adam's horse almost unseating him on several occasions, it was an easy ride, as most of the way lay across rough pasture. In less than a half-hour we had reached the trees in the deep valley that contained the few houses that made up Wycoller, a temporary relief from the ever-rising sun in its cloudless sky. We ignored the modest Inn with difficulty, our thirst gaining on us, crossed the narrow stone bridge, and passed the Hall. Extensive work was underway, with new mullions being inserted. The stonemasons stopped to watch us pass. I nodded but they just stared. Then I realised we had missed our road, so had to turn around and repass them, trying to look as if our retreat was intentional.

Climbing sharply for a few hundred yards we reached the right path, turning North under trees edging the stony road, coming on the crossroads suddenly, more suddenly than expected.

I pulled Bay up sharply, Adam's mount running into her rear, which made her jump. I'm sure the colour drained from my face as my heart pounded fit to burst. What had I done? There, filling the road, were hundreds of fully uniformed and armed soldiers. Their pikes stood in three sharp pyramids, sun glinting off the blades. Most sat or sprawled against the roadside walls, some passing a bladder of water between them. All looked weary but I – we – couldn't take on such a force. They might look well-worn, but this was little less than an army, for God's sake.

They had been talking quietly amongst themselves but, noticing me, they turned in silence and just stared. Adam hissed at me: 'What do we do now, Doctor?', his hiss loud enough for all to hear, the idiot. I was just about to turn to the left as if to take the road to Colne, when an officer pushed through the crowd, grabbed Bay's reins with one hand, rubbed her nose with the other, and turned to me without smile or expression asking 'Doctor? We've been expecting you. Please come this way.'

I slid off Bay. I was trembling. Trembling as much for Will and our men as for myself. A burned-out building that had probably been an Inn stood at the crossroads. The barn behind was intact though and as I was led inside, there was Will in conversation with an officer. He turned and beamed at me. 'Ho, Doctor, what do you think of this?' And then it dawned on me with such relief that my knees almost gave way. We'd been beaten to the game by our own forces.

'Here's Colonel Benson.' Will motioned to the officer, who advanced and held out a hand. He was short of stature, little over five feet and his bald pate, surrounded by long brown hair, gave him a monkish look. He too looked tired and worn but exuded an air of command.

'Good to meet you, Doctor. Colonel Assheton has talked much about you.' He gave a tight smile. 'Your man here told me your scheme. It would have worked, I'm sure, but the picket fled as soon as they saw the cloud of dust we kicked up on the road.'

'Aye,' broke in Will, 'A couple ran up the road, throwing down their jackets. Seeing us coming down, they shot across the fields faster than a pair of March hares.'

'I thought I'd run straight into the King's men as I rode up,' I spluttered. 'I could see no colours...'

"Ah yes. I suppose we do all look alike in buff coats. I instructed the men to remove all their sashes to perhaps give us a few moments advantage should we meet any Royalist pickets,' explained Benson and then straight to business. 'What about the town? Your man says it is unguarded?'

'Yes, sir. Just walk in and it's yours. I can recommend the Inn in the square...'

'I'm going straight on with most of my men. We're for home. Many have had enough and need rest and comfort,' he interrupted. 'I shall leave enough to man a picket here and to hold the town.' and, turning to a captain stood close behind him, 'they can interchange between them so that they can have the comfort of the Inn by turns. Make it so.'

'May I make two observations, Colonel?' I asked. 'Well, one observation and one request?' He gave a sharp nod. 'The town will welcome your men, I think, as long as they respect the people and property. The picket that were here played merry Hell and paid for nothing. If your men pay their way, it will help all.'

'Agreed. Captain, make it so. Was that your request?'

'What has happened to Colonel Assheton? Is he far behind? How fares he? Have you lost many men?'

'Let's move on to your Inn and I'll give you the full story, or as much as I know. In the heat of a fight, much is confusion you know.'

We were back in the parlour of the Crown, sat over tankards, a jug of ale and bread and cheese on the table, whilst our host put a chicken to the fire. Beside us lay a map, much better, much larger than the one I'd copied from Sir Ralph, covering most of the west of Yorkshire and into Lancashire.

'We were placed under Sir Thomas Fairfax, with his father, Lord Fairfax, as commander-in-chief, holding Bradford,' began Colonel Benson, tapping the map, 'But the town was difficult to defend. Hearing that Newcastle's forces, including a train of cannon, were on their way from the southwards, we mustered as many as we could and determined to meet them at a more advantageous place. We knew the Duke's forces would be sizeable but couldn't risk a siege, for provisions were already running low and we were having to forage wider and wider, which didn't endear us to the surrounding farms and villages.' His finger slid across the map.

'The Royalists captured Batley, taking Lord Saville prisoner, and came on towards us. By the time Assheton arrived with his men we stood at over 7,000 and thought we'd a good chance. It was Assheton too who met the first skirmishers, easily turning them back, and then the rest of us came up and took positions across a front. Given a choice, we'd not have picked this place, Adwalton Moor, for the fight, but we were amongst enclosed land at this point, so did have some cover from field hedges. Lord Fairfax took the centre with us and Assheton, Sir Thomas commanded the right flank and Major General Gifford the left. At this point, we had, I think, more infantry and pushed the enemy back.'

'Now, though, we came to the open moor, where they had their battery. Their cavalry were harassing our sides, yet we charged and, by God, nearly won the day right then. But their pikemen started to turn our left wing, their cavalry swung round to the north and hit Gifford's men right hard. His men ran, not that I blame them, poor sods. Next, Newcastle's men hit our right hand and, seeing his son couldn't hold the line and was being cut off from our main body, Lord Fairfax sent to him to retreat. I don't know how they fared.'

'Our Yorkshire men simply hadn't been trained enough. They'd mostly only done garrison work and not been in battle. Us Lancastrians were better drilled, better disciplined, had seen battle and held. We fell back towards Bradford, and it was only when the enemy put their full force to us and split us down the middle that Assheton, Colonel Blakestone and I were pushed off to the westwards.'

'We lost a lot of men on the field, a good number dead and wounded but many more prisoner. I don't know how the poor buggers will fare. They'll probably do as most have done and sign for the King,' he said with resignation, 'no prisoner lasts long, else.'

He downed a full tankard without stopping, wiped his stubbly face and continued.

'We were harassed all the way to a little village named Denholme.

Assheton had sent scouts before us and they told us that a Royalist troop was coming down from the north. By now it was near dark, we'd been fighting and marching all day and were near exhaustion. Assheton took the rear, sent us north and west to Oxenhope, Stanbury and on, and declared that he would persuade our foe to follow him to the south towards the bridge at Hebden. It was the bravest thing,' he refilled his tankard, "and I honour him for it.'

Ten

Tempest Toss'd

I studied my rough map then turned to our guide. 'And you're sure we carry straight on?'

'Aye. We've passed Steeple Stones.' He pointed forward to an outcrop of rock. 'Them there's Rigging Stones and yon high fell is Grey Stones. Beyond is Cow Stones.'

"I'd like to see a cow get up there," I muttered peevishly.

We'd already come some three miles from Colne, difficult riding up little more than a sheep track onto the high fells, following a line of bare black peat, hard and cracked from the blistering summer sun. No sun now though. No breath of wind, the air stifling and heavy under huge black thunderclouds that had swept in from the west.

'We can turn back if tha wants,' our man called over his shoulder, 'but the going gets better in another mile. The path widens and evens out.' I waved a hand at him to keep going.

I don't know why I do some things. In particular, the course of action that I was now taking seemed more and more unpromising. Despite, rather than by, our efforts, Colne was secure, a post on Lancashire's frontier to hold us safe against the King, as was the aim, and it would have been so much easier to just ride back home with the rest of our small band. But my contrary nature took hold.

You know I read much (some would say too much) and I find I have a good memory for what I've read. Perhaps, though, memory is divorced from understanding at times. I feel, when I have studied a book, that I understand, I ingest, the lessons printed before me. Now I believe this is not always the case.

I have a book containing all the work of a playwright of the last age, one Shakespeare, and I have especially devoured his histories, read them time and again. But has understanding followed? No. In a number of his plays he has the venerable, though divisive, Sir John Falstaff, a larger than life character who, without his buffoonery and boasting, I think I should try to mirror. Of course, he is much stouter than I, I decry his drunkenness and I have much more wit about me, but he has one tenet that I would do well to keep at the forefront of my brain. If I remember rightly he says, in one of the King Henry plays, that "The better part of valour is discretion, in the which better part I have saved my life." Why should that have come into my mind now and not before we left the comfort of the Inn?

It was just me and Will now, guided by a wizened old fell-man on promise of a whole sovereign, in what seemed an increasingly vain attempt to cross the moors and hopefully intersect with Colonel Assheton and his men. It seemed likely that some of that gallant band would be wounded and, if so, I was the one to help. I felt I owed it to the Asshetons – the father for his protection of my household and son as much for friendship as anything, for we'd gone through a lot together in the recent past.

There were, it seemed to me, three possibilities: First, that they'd progressed to the Hebden bridge; second, that they had passed on to a town shown as Todmorden on my map; third, that they hadn't even got as far as Hebden but perhaps taken prisoner by their pursuers. I tried to put that last idea out of my mind.

You know how hard a summer storm can hit? Just as we had got off the peat moor and on to more stony ground, we were surrounded by an ear-splitting blast of thunder, a mighty bolt of lightning struck a solitary tree to our right, and day disappeared in an instant. Rain hit with the force of a thousand spears, which seemed to pierce my very back, forcing my head down under the onslaught. Bay staggered but kept her feet though I barely retained my seat. My hat was whisked off by the accompanying gale of wind. Where it went I couldn't say, for I could see nothing before me. It was as if I was inside a boiling lake of icy cold.

We were completely in the open – no shelter at all, not even a low wall to hide against. All I could remember was that I'd seen the merest rooftop away in front of us just as the heavens opened. I kicked at Bay with my heels, but she didn't move. I smacked her sharply on the neck, which brought her back to sense. Jerking her head, she cautiously began to step forward. I could see no sign of our erstwhile guide. He had been just in front of me on his rough little pony but had disappeared just like Will, just like the day. All I could do was keep Bay moving as the thunder echoed round us and the air crackled with lightning.

The Ancients in Greece, as I read in another of my books, said that lightning was spears thrown by their god, Zeus; the thunder, when those spears hit the ground. Men will always try to give meaning to any and all phenomena, but why should a God do that? I cannot think that our God, the Christian God, would form a storm just to hit us at that point, when we were to all intents on a mission of mercy.

If I believed that Hell exists, which I don't, I should believe that this storm was a vision from there. What I do believe – and I say this from long study of storms – is that thunder and lightning result from the collision of black clouds. Where these clouds come from, I couldn't say but, to turn to the old Greeks again, it was *physis*, something of nature, something physical.

Through the tempest, which seemed never ending, I gave Bay her head as she tottered forward, trusting her to keep her feet and get us to shelter, for she's certainly a sensible beast. After what seemed a lifetime, she shuffled to a halt and I found that we were part sheltered, from wind at least, by a rough stone wall. My hands were near frozen to her reins and it took me a while to release one and slide from the saddle, the rain still beating down. I fell between Bay and the rough wall and she near crushed me between it and her sodden flank. I managed to drag myself up by her stirrup. A vague hint of light, nothing more, was returning to the sky, showing the wall to belong to a low barn and I now stumbled along it, dragging the horse with me. I lurched against a pair of doors and I tried to heave one open. At first it failed to move but I moved back and crashed my full weight against it, when it banged open so easily that I fell inside. As I tried to rise, Bay pushed past and sent me sprawling again. I could do nothing but laugh with, I must admit, a touch of hysteria.

Seeing a large pile of dirty straw, I crawled over, pulled it around me, and slept.

I think it was a rat running over me that first woke me. I felt warm and as though I was immersed not in the icy stabbing cold of the storm but in a heated vat of ale. Not wanting to move I kept my eyes closed, again luxuriating in delicious relaxation. Then something warm and wet slid up my face and a hot breath made me sneeze. Bay, nuzzling me with her nose, brought me to my senses and, as I sat up, the smell of damp horse and damper clothes was overwhelming.

Climbing out of the straw, the cold hit me. The very warmth about me fled. It was as quick as the blowing out of a candle flame and I began to shiver. I barely noticed the sheep huddled in the far corner of the barn, or the other horse, unsaddled and tethered to a post, but headed out the door and into the light of a new day. I thought the sunlight would warm me, but it was only just past dawn, perhaps five o'clock. The bright orb not yet showing above the fell top had yet to spread its heat, and I was instantly aching with cold. But the world had changed.

The sky was now almost clear of clouds and there was a soft breeze, the air fresher as is usual after a clearing storm. But water poured off the fell into the track, turning it into a very river, and just below me, in a stand of trees, I could see several of them had smashed, splintered and fallen.

I crossed my arms and rubbed hard to gain some warmth, though my shirt was sticking to my skin, and pain started to rise from my shoulder where, I suppose, I was bruised from the barn door and my fall. I heard a door open, turned, and there was Will. His mouth dropped open in surprise and then broke into a smile.

'There you are, Doctor! I was coming to look for you and fearing the worst.' He looked puzzled. 'Wha… Where? You've been in the barn? All night? Why didn't you come in the house?'

Now I could see that the barn was just one end of a longhouse, and the barn door just feet from the door to the domicile. I didn't know whether to be angry, to laugh, or to cry.

'Let me brush this straw off you, sir… why, you're still sodden,' he said with concern, as out of the house now came a young lass who stopped and gawped at me.

'Poll, this is the Doctor,' exclaimed Will, 'Too polite to disturb you, he's slept in the barn, would you believe...' The wench bobbed to me. 'Tell your Mam to poke up the fire. He's still soaked and will catch his death out here…' Turning to me, he had the audacity to tell me that, if I'd chosen – chosen, mark you – to come into the house, my clothes would now be as dry as his, the infernal fellow.

A warming fire, a dry blanket and hot broth is a great reviver. I'd stripped off my clothes with difficulty and now they steamed on a hanger above the hearth. Poll had absented herself in her modesty. Not though her mother, who sat rocking in a chair examining every inch of my shame as if sizing me for the pot. I felt even more gross than usual, my skin white and wrinkled after long immersion in water. I remembered once examining the bloated body of a girl, fished out of the Ribble river, days dead, and tried to excise the image from my mind.

My breeches were still damp as I re-dressed. The man of the house was away fighting – I hoped for our side, though thought it best not to ask – and I was given an old shirt of his. It was rather small for me but at least it was dry. Will went to discover our guide but could find no hide nor hair of him. He returned carrying my panniers, upending the contents that fell in a sodden mass on the floor.

Water had penetrated everything except the phials and bottles of ointments and linctus in my medical bag. My spare cloak was covered with some sort of white paste that I could not at first recognise until I realised it was the remains of the bread I had taken from the Colne Inn. The accompanying cheese was the only other thing untouched by the flood.

After brushing down the horses as best he could, Will quizzed me.

'I must have reached the barn before you, Doctor, though I saw nothing of you in the downpour. Did you not notice my horse, tied and unsaddled as you entered? Did you not think there must be a house to such a solid barn? Why...'

'Will, just do one thing for me, will you?' I felt stupid, resentful and in no mood for chatter. 'Just shut up.'

Eleven

Heptonstall

It was with great reluctance that I left the fireside warmth of the farmhouse, though the sun, now high in the bright blue of the sky, was hot on our faces as we navigated the very stream bed of a track. The weather this year had been most odd. If Colonel Benson was to be believed, the East of Yorkshire had been cold and wet, whilst for we in the West it had been hot and dry all summer. Even now as the calendar reached mid-September the heat was excessive. Perhaps the storm just passed marked the change to Autumn.

There was no option before us but to continue on to a village called Heptonstall and the Hebden bridge, though I doubted that we'd ever find Colonel Assheton and our men. I expected that, if they had indeed come this way, a fact that wasn't guaranteed, they would be well past by now. Possibly they would have progressed even past the next place on my map, the town of Todmorden. Ah, well, I thought, yet another wasted journey.

I fell to musing about Will and his luck. It really is beyond my understanding how he always comes out on top of any situation. Wherever we've been together (and we've been through some worrying times, let me tell you!) he always finds some comely lass to look after him. In the middle of this wild, bleak moor, in the depth of a storm and deluge that puts Noah's flood in its place, he finds a warm bed and, I believe, a warmer wench. It is beyond belief. Am I jealous? Of course.

'Will?' We'd descended a dip, crossed a stream and were now passing across pastureland, he some yards in front of me.

'Aye, Doctor?' he responded over his shoulder.

'Do you know the year, day and time of your birth?'

'Year, yes, and I think the twentieth day of February. I'd have to ask my mother for the rest. I doubt she'd remember for she can't even remember our names right.' He chuckled.

'You have brothers?'

'And sisters. I think they still live but haven't seen them for a goodly while. Why do you need details of my birth, sir?'

'I was just musing on your luck. Was thinking to make a chart of your life to see if it reveals where the luck comes from that seems to surround you,' I said. 'But the month and day of your birth is almost the same as mine, so why do I not have the same luck as you?'

'But you're much luckier than me! You have money, learning and skill. All respect you. As for me, I take each day as it comes, pray I don't get killed before my true time is up, take what is given me with thanks and don't think of the future.'

Well, I thought, that isn't a bad philosophy. He called back again. 'I've told you before, Doctor. Clean living and an open heart. That's my secret but I'm happy to share it with you.' His laughter came back to me on the warm breeze.

With a wooded and ever deepening cleft on our left, down which a foaming white cataract of water roared, we passed a couple of desolate farms before meeting half a dozen small cottages gathered round a fork in the road. The pathway was deep in wet mud, stones and rocks, ample evidence that a torrent had passed through. Bay picked her way cautiously. A child tried to sweep water out of a flooded hovel, poor mite. I hailed him for the way to Heptonstall and he pointed us on without a word.

A further quarter of a mile, cresting a small rise, we saw a large yellow flag flying bravely above trees and shortly saw the church tower from which it flew. As it fluttered in the breeze, we made out a line of black stars running diagonally across it but knew not to whom it belonged. Nevertheless, it urged caution, indicating martial forces were in possession of the town.

I pulled Bay abreast of Will and, as the first cottages came into view, I could see tents and soldiery to our right. Many looked to be drying out clothes, steam rising, around a number of large bonfires and paid us little attention as we passed. 'They'll have had a hard time in the storm' said Will thoughtfully. Most were wearing light-blue jackets and wide-brimmed black hats.

On into the town, the numbers of soldiery growing, many sat outside the houses or crowding in the narrow street. All looked weary and some, slumped against walls, looked asleep. But then the way ahead was entirely blocked by a sea of blue jackets, a crowd of men listening to a ranting Puritan, and it became clear that we were in the heart of fellow Parliamentarians, which was a relief. Will bent down to ask a soldier who was in command.

'Colonel Bradshaw. House by the Church is his Headquarters. Who wants him?'

'This is the Doctor, come to help and seek news of Colonel Assheton and his men.'

'They Lancashire men?'

'Aye' responded Will.

'They're just beyond the church. Good lads despite not being Yorkshire.' The soldier gave a cheeky grin. 'Been here two days, I think. Rather beat up, some o'em.'

'Thanks. Any way through this crowd?'

'Nay. Tha'll have to push tha way through.'

'Doctor! Are you here? How did that happen?' Colonel Assheton jumped up, clasped my shoulder and held out his hand, pumping mine with vigour. 'And Will. Good man.' His hair was unkempt, some grey now showing in the brown, and his coat stained. Still, he had kept that great energy that had driven him from battle to battle with our enemies, and his smile was almost radiant at our appearance. He did look somewhat careworn, but who wouldn't be under the circumstances, for Adwalton had been his first defeat.

'Let me name Colonel Bradshaw.' Assheton had been sat round a table with a number of officers and now one, tall, grizzled, darkly handsome I would say, stood and flicked long hair out of his eyes but proffered no hand. He simply said, 'Welcome. Your arts are needed, I believe. Assheton, I presume you wish to show him your men?' and with little more than that I was dismissed.

'He's rather abrupt but an excellent commander.' Colonel Assheton sounded apologetic at my less than fulsome welcome by Bradshaw.

'That's fine, Sir Ralph. I take no offence. He has his job and I have mine. I'm just happy to find you.' I was in the Church, now taken over as an infirmary. 'I don't need special treatment, I'm happy to find a corner in here.'

Bradshaw had insisted that there was no room for me with the officers and that I'd have to fend for myself. It wasn't gentlemanly, but he was, first and foremost, a soldier.

'Should he need my services at any time, of course, he can join the end of the queue.' I gave a tight smile. 'In any case, Will can find me somewhere.' Sir Ralph looked puzzled and I looked across at my assistant, who was re-bandaging a patient's leg. I spoke louder, so Will would hear.

'Will always finds a comfy bed wherever we are… usually along with someone to keep him warm' He didn't turn but I knew he was grinning.

Colonel Assheton had done his job well, shepherding his men along unknown roads since the retreat from Adwalton and fearing ambush at every corner. He well knew that Royalists were on his tail. Indeed, he'd laid a trail to pull the enemy after him, giving time for Benson's and Blakestone's forces to escape towards Colne. This was bravery of the first order, deserving of a reward or acknowledgement, though we all knew there would be none.

They had reached the Hebden bridge just before the heavens opened, met a heavy picket of King's men, and had to fight their way through.

'It took an hour, a whole hour, with rush after rush before they were battered into submission,' said the Colonel, 'That's where most of these wounded came from, though we had many with cuts and scrapes already. I think we lost six on the bridge. Then we climbed to our present airy position.'

'I had an old man from Downham with us when we went to Colne,' I said. 'Adam was his name. He said his son was with you. Do you know if he's here?'

'I couldn't say. You must ask your patients. I sent forty or fifty men away this morning, to give them a chance of getting home in some semblance of safety. They've gone through much and need rest and recovery. You could almost have seen them as you were riding in. You came through a hamlet, some mile up the road?' I nodded. 'The road forks there and will take them to Burnley.'

'As you see,' he continued, 'There are too many troops for this town but, whilst our position is easily defensible, fresh numbers of the enemy have been arriving below us at the bridge and trouble is expected. Their delay in attacking us is down to that storm, for the river is above the arch of the bridge and, if we're lucky, it may just bring it down.'

Five hundred men descending on a town of less than a hundred souls is a burden that is difficult to bear, but the townsfolk had done their best until supplies had been disrupted by the storm. Nevertheless, most of the soldiery was now fighting hunger and foraging at will across the near plateau, to the edge of which Heptonstall clung. Though Bradshaw had issued warnings of the dire consequences that would be visited upon any of his men discovered as thieves, offences did occur, and the cellar of a nearby house became filled with the culprits.

Though supply carts did restart their run across the moor behind us, the evening after we'd arrived at the town was one of rumbling stomachs and misery for many. Will and I fared better than most, having been well fed at our farm sanctuary, but a bowl of gruel and a crust would have been most welcome as midnight came and we made the last of our patients as comfortable as possible.

We had a dozen, all laid on straw in a line on the left side of the church, some of the box pews having been knocked down to clear a suitable space. The vicar, a young man though nervous, helped as best he could, whilst I sent Will out to gather what suitable plants and flowers he could to supplement the salves and lotions from my bag. He returned with Marigold, Rosemary and feverfew which were all of use, the first for cuts and swellings, the last for pain relief.

Lady's Mantle was there too, which I thought may also be of use, its properties going beyond its use at women's monthly bleed. Indeed, I'd used it in my alchemical experiments, it being long said that it was a help in many illnesses and that dew collected from within its leaves is of use in turning base metal into gold. I'd never before used it as a cure-all but was happy to try it.

'We have three desperate cases.' I was sitting with Will and the Vicar, Reverend Martin, around a flickering candle in the choir stalls, keeping my voice low. 'For ease I number our patients, one being nearest to the door. One, two and three have deep cuts in their arms, I presume from pike thrusts. They will all do well, providing fever doesn't take hold. If it stays away, they must be gone tomorrow; up, out and on their way home. I recognise number two, Will, he's one of ours from Downham.'

'As is number four. Three wounds here and he is in a bad way. His leg is swelling badly, I am not sanguine about his head wound, and fever has already set in as you know. He is malnourished, emaciated even, and I do not think he will be with us long.'

'Five. I cannot save that leg and, in truth probably cannot save the man, even from his fever. How he got here is a miracle for it is from an old wound in the foot, not attended to. The infection has spread up the calf and you will recognise all the stink of gangrene. I must cut in the morning, when I have light and a steadier hand.'

'Six and seven. I cannot tell what ails them. I see no evidence of wounds and yet there is stupor to a high degree. *Non compos mentis* I would say, though not, of course, with the influence of any devil or demon as that term may suggest.' I nodded to the Vicar. He bowed.

'Eight is the son of our Adam, Will, and this pains me. as he will be gone by morning. Reverend, you will stay with him?' Martin nodded and crossed himself.

'Give him all the comfort you can. His father will take the loss badly, but if I can say that his passage was eased by your good services, it may help.'

'What do you think to Nine, Will?'

'That I can't see anything wrong with him, Doctor.'

'I agree. A sluggard and idler, I believe, but why remain here when he could be on his way home with those who left earlier? Anyway, we will have him out tomorrow if no sore or injury present.'

'Ten. Another cut. The arm must come off.'

'Eleven and twelve will both have left us by morning I expect and, for their sake, hope.'

Twelve

'Removal of a Damaged Limb can Allow the Body to Survive...'

LITTLE REST FOR US THAT NIGHT AND, AS FIRST LIGHT brightened the windows, we set to work. Just one window of stained glass remained in the church, all others long replaced, probably due to Puritans, but as the sun hit it, a rainbow of colour prettified the sordid scene.

In that first light, Adam's son had breathed his last. It was as if his soul had waited for the sun's rays to carry it aloft. As peaceful a passing as one might wish under the circumstances, I thought. Knowing his father, the son's death moved me but there was no time to linger.

Two others had also passed over in the night and a fourth was so far into fever that it was clear he would follow shortly.

I pressed Sir Ralph to commandeer three of his men, and they laid parts of the demolished pews across the top of some still standing. Even as they lifted the gangrenous patient onto my makeshift table, he expired. It gave me little concern as I had doubted his survival.

That left the arm amputation. Writhing and screaming he was brought to my altar. Will punched him hard on the jaw but it did little good. If I could have treated him shortly after he had been wounded, when he was still in shock, it would have been easier, but after two pain-filled days he was filled with fear, thinking of what must come. Our pale-faced helpers held him down as best they could and, fortunately, after the first cuts that caused the Vicar to slump to the floor, he too fainted away. I'd tightly strapped his arm with a leather belt as normal and was hoping to tie off each vein with ligatures as described by the Roman Celsus, but he was losing far too much blood. I had to use the iron, heated in a brazier by my side, to cauterise the wound as I would do in the rush of battle. He never woke. I think the strain on his heart was too much and he was dead before he left the table.

Our erstwhile helpers threw up at the door of the church before returning to remove the corpses. Will and I walked to the end of the yard and stood silent for a few moments, breathing deeply. 'Hungry, Will?'

'Er, no Doctor, I don't think I am...'

'Well, I need to first find some sustenance and then get some sleep. And if you can still find no injury, throw that idler out, will you.'

Colonel Assheton's remaining men were all camped or billeted to the right of the Church with a kitchen close by under some ancient oaks. I grabbed a bowl of thin soup, with which I could have used some bread, but there was none. It went down well enough. It was only when Sir Ralph approached and offered me one of his shirts that I realised there was space all around me, a kind of no-mans-land, and that others were staring at me in horror. I sometimes forget how the sight of blood worries people, even those who have been in the midst of battle, and I was liberally covered in gore.

The one benefit to all this was that I could rid myself of the shirt, several sizes too small in all truth, given to me after the deluge. Sir Ralph was rather closer to my size than the farmer's wife's husband, though the fabric still stretched tight across my belly.

'How have you fared, Doctor?' he asked cautiously.

'We've lost six. I could do nothing for them. The rest can go, though two are in stupor still and will need a cart. In fact, a cart would be best for all, if possible.' I continued, 'One seems to have been just idling. I can find nothing wrong with him at all. He can rejoin your band.'

'Can't say I've any use for him if he's not willing to fight or support his companions, sir. You know, companionship is so important in a fighting unit. If you have a bond 'twixt you, it gives a better chance of surviving any encounter. One weak element can doom a whole corps in a battle. We're better without him.'

'It can be the same in a single carcass, Colonel. The removal of a damaged or diseased limb can allow the rest of the body to survive, even thrive. Left alone, the opposite is true, the bad part destroying the rest of the body. It is well reported, even by the ancients, and is the natural way of things, I believe. If I could have attended two of my patients earlier, before ill humours had passed from the bad to the good parts of the body, I may well have saved them…'

We were now leant over a wall, on the edge of the steep slope down towards the Hebden bridge, though the structure itself was hidden by trees.

'How many are down there, Colonel?'

'More every hour. A considerable force, I believe, come in under command of Sir Francis Mackworth. I know nothing of him. He will attack, I have no doubt, but he's on a fool's errand if he thinks he can shift us from here. Shall I show you our defences?'

The town stood on a promontory, almost a projection out from the flat moorland behind, and with deep valleys on either side. For two hundred yards in front of us, the narrow road ran straight and steeply down towards the valley bottom, before gently curling away to the right. Though we couldn't see down to the bridge, half a mile away and five hundred feet below, there would be a clear view of any approach. Above us, watchers on the Church tower could give plenty of warning, despite trees hampering their view.

No need for the Colonel to point out the body of musketeers, who would be our first line of defence, for they were sat quietly chatting in the sun, most with helmets by their sides. Two small braziers, red hot and shimmering and from which slow matches would be lit, stood by. Below us, by the bend in the road, a number of large boulders, held back by baulks of timber, had also been prepared, to be sent charging down the road onto an unwitting enemy. Behind us, a similar set of stones had been prepared. They would do as much or more damage as cannon.

'Nobody,' said Sir Ralph, 'be it troop or cavalry, can hope to force this path whilst we hold the top. Though obviously we don't hold the bridge, it too is useful to us, being so narrow as to impede the flow of men and horses, plus it may well be unsafe since the storm. Around us on three sides are the steep wooded slopes that you see. The only clear attack could come from behind us, but we hold that land and it would take a week for them to even reach us from that side.'

'I wondered why there were no pickets out to challenge us as we approached from the North,' I remarked.

'In the normal course of things, we'd have a post out there, but there's no danger. We're as safe as houses here and the watchers on the church tower would notice any advance from behind, as you might say. They even reported your presence from near a mile away. Not that we knew it was you, of course, just two riders approaching and with no martial air about them.' He smiled. 'I doubt we need to stay, Doctor. The town can't support so many of us and I believe that two or three hundred can hold it. We're not needed. Bradshaw says he could hold the place with just a hundred men, so we agreed that I'll march my men out at two o'clock this afternoon. You will join us?'

We were saddled up and ready to move out when the first attack came. Shouts from the watchers on the tower alerted us, Bradshaw rushed out, sword in hand, his captains behind him. The musketeers formed their lines; behind them pikemen gathered; a small party ran down to the wedged boulders. All held their breath.

The first indication that battle was joined was the shouts of the forward party and the deep rumble as they set free their boulders. Musket shot followed, for I didn't know but that Bradshaw had cleverly hidden a party of gunners in the trees lower down. Of the enemy, I'd yet to have sight.

Minutes went by. Two of Bradshaw's captains walked cautiously down and peered round the bend. They seemed satisfied with what they saw, waved back at their Colonel, standing at the top of the slope with his arms folded and who, in turn, began to issue further orders to his other commanders. Sir Ralph walked across to him, a few words were spoken, Bradshaw shook his head, to indicate we were still not needed, proffered a hand, and that was the last I saw of him.

Though the enemy made a further, larger attempt on Heptonstall, they never came close to taking it. Rocks knocked them off the path and muskets rained havoc on them. The garrison chased them down, aided even by villagers wielding pitchforks. The horses of the enemy cavalry, who had thought that they could easily gain the day, panicked, crushing others behind them.

In the rout, that continued right down to the bridge, a goodly number drowned in the Hebden brook and the equally violent river Calder, but by then we were already well across the moor and making our way along what was left of a Roman road to Burnley. We later heard that, in that last rush, Bradshaw had been wounded and subsequently died. I wondered if I might have saved him had I stayed. Though I thought him rather arrogant, he proved himself a good and brave leader.

Thirteen

The Boy, Richard

IT WAS, I WOULD SAY, EIGHT O'CLOCK THAT EVENING WHEN WE rode, tired and dusty, onto Towneley land, and found our way to the Hall. There it sat in the warmth of a late summer evening, an imposing manor house built on three sides of a square with a large portico and oaken door dominating the yard.

We'd been met by a Sergeant-at-arms who we knew, in charge of a small party of Downham men holding the place since the estate's sequestration, which had happened in the few days I'd been away. Jim Siddows was a jolly soul, dark and thickset, and the way he welcomed us you would have thought he owned the Hall.

Sixty weary travellers there were, including Will and me, arriving all at once, a small army needing food, drink and bed. Elsewhere, we might have had to forage for ourselves or go without, but the expansive Siddows greeted his Colonel like a long-lost friend and had already pushed the cooks to put hens and a lamb to the fire. He himself had been living like a lord as his men collected rent and goods from the estate farms, but with good grace he gave up the fine bed in which he'd lain.

Will and I commandeered an adjacent room in the south wing of the Hall containing a wide, posted, richly draped bed with a feather mattress, no less. My companion, for I no longer considered him anything less than my equal, set to tightening the bed strings, as I arranged a separate room for my patients and checked their wounds. They'd been jostled about badly in their cart - two had got out and walked much of the way – but all were healing well and one of the two stentorians was showing signs of coming to.

The bulk of the men was spread about on the floor of the stone-flagged Great Hall, a wonderfully high structure with long bright windows and fire-grates at either end. Some were already asleep.

There had been much money in this estate, built up by the Towneley family over more than 300 years it was said, but their unavowed Catholic bent was slowly bringing them to ruin. They had been fined and imprisoned for recusancy many times during and since Elizabeth's time, and there was still a thinly disguised chapel, showing clear signs of their faith, in the north wing of the building. Siddow's men had sought to plunder some of the rooms, looking for gold and silver, but though they found no valuables a number of hiding places for priests were uncovered, some of great ingenuity.

I can understand people clinging to faith like a drowning man to a branch, but not to invite ruin upon themselves and their family in such a way. Surely it would be easy to appear to comply with the given doctrine of the day as passed down by King or Government, whilst holding your beliefs close. Why could they not do that? For myself, I abhor the Roman's doctrines and could never follow them. Equally, despite - or possibly because of – my previous tie to the English Church, I despise some of its teachings also. But then, that's why I am no longer a curate and have more in common with Grindletonians or even the Puritans than I like to admit.

Would that more people would see sense and decipher the bible in their own way and not simply cling to ancient ritual.

This family continue to support the King though, and Charles Towneley was with the force that threw us out of Preston earlier in the year. No matter, we'll get the town back in due course I wager.

A meal, a very banquet, was served to us in style on a long, narrow, black oak table. Sir Ralph took the middle and sat me on his right, one Captain Wood to his left. Sergeant Siddows was pushed further down, to remind him, I presume, of his true place. Salad leaves and good bread were set down and then hens in their juices were brought in hot and hot, followed by two ducks and then a lamb. I couldn't remember when, or if, I'd ever eaten so well. Towels and water bowls took the brunt of the grease, but I for one was liberally covered with juices when we pushed our plates away.

I took a leisurely stroll around the kitchen garden with the Colonel in the twilight, bats fluttering as they will in the quiet of end of day. He asked me again how I did, and I was happy to reply that I was well and realised that I was free from my previous aches and pains. My old wounds had ceased to trouble me and, as I considered this, I began to think that they had disappeared since my damp night in the hay after the deluge.

I remembered that, even before the onset of the storm, the oppression of the *atmosphaera*, as we call it, had caused my arm and side to throb with deep, deep pain. After that blighted night, when Will did his usual trick of finding a fair bed and shelter and not considering my plight, the Devil, I never felt the slightest twinge or hurt. Why should that be? Then I recalled Celsus.

Aulus Celsus was a great physician of ancient Rome, and one of his books, *De Medicina,* is one of my greatest treasures. Years ago, my teacher, Doctor Hunyades, had pressed me to find a copy, from which, he said, he had learnt the best part of his treatments, and it has guided me since. The one part of his treatise for which I had little regard had been his description of bathing and how the old Romans practised this every day, would you believe?

He said that they immersed themselves in pools of very heated water, then again into cold, followed by warm, before being washed down with fragrant oils. I had considered that very strange practice, almost as odd as the story of Emperor Nero's wife bathing in milk, and so much against our current habit.

I had thought that perhaps such ideas might work in the fierce heat of Celsus's southern clime but not in our country. Now I was not so sure and noted it down for further experiment. I had been swaddled in wet, sodden, clothing and within a heap, a carapace even, of hot straw, further heat being supplied by the horse at my side. There I had steamed, in delicious, comforting heat for several hours before instantly chilling when I rose. Then I had been rubbed, scarified almost, in a coarse wool blanket till dry.

Though I didn't have aromatic oils burnished into me, of course, it could be that this process had removed the pains from my body, helped balance my humours more than any bleeding could have done.

I must investigate the matter further I thought, as I fell into a deep sleep.

A sudden alarm, a shout, and I was instantly awake.'A light, a glim!' shouted Will from the far side of the room as I jumped out of the bed in confusion. A commotion in the corridor, and a sentry crashed through the door with a sputtering lanthorn. In the flickering candlelight, there was Will tightly holding a small wriggling boy who, as I watched, bit my man's hand.

'You little bugger!' shouted Will, giving the child a mighty slap that threw him across the room.

Dressed in dirty satin doublet and breeches of blue, shirt with a lace collar, no hose or shoes, the lad stood staring defiantly out at us, the side of his face glowing red where Will had hit him, my man holding him loosely by the arm. Colonel Assheton, one of his sergeants and myself sat in front, with two guards at the door.

Sir Ralph regarded him closely and then spoke gently and with a smile. 'So. hiding in yet another priest's hole. You were lucky Sergeant Siddows didn't find you. He thought he'd uncovered all the secrets of this place. Perhaps you'd tell us your name and what you're doing here?" The boy dropped his eyes but didn't speak.

'Come on, lad, we're not going to hurt you. Do you need a drink?' That received the merest nod and Sir Ralph signalled one of the guards to attend to this.'Give him a stool, Will.'

Refreshed, the boy seemed still reluctant to talk. Though some fire had gone from his eyes, there was still a measure of arrogance about him which led me to a simple conclusion.'This is your home, is it not, Master Towneley?' His head jerked up at this. The defiance returned to his face.

'Why are you here? Why have you taken my property? You have no right. My father...'

'... Is against the rule of Law, young man...' started Sir Ralph.

'My father, sir, is loyal to His Majesty, as am I'.

'I'm glad to hear it. We wish to be loyal to the King also, but he has broken his contract with Parliament and the people. When he sees sense, this unnecessary fighting will end, and no doubt your family's property will be returned to them. But let that rest for the moment.' Sir Ralph's voice had a gentleness to it, willing the young Towneley to respond. 'Where is your family and why have they left you here?'

'My father is fighting for the King, and I was not left here. I went with my mother, but returned for the sake of my books.' My ears pricked up at that comment.

'Your Mother knows you are here?' asked the colonel.

'I left her a note. I can look to myself, sir.'

'How old are you and where is your Mother?' I interrupted.

He straightened, looked straight in my eye and said 'Almost twelve years and my mother is in Lincolnshire.'

'Tell me about your books.'

Richard Towneley. I quickly took to this very bright young boy. His ingenious hiding place was entered through the centre of a wainscot panel in the bedroom which Will and I had commandeered. At first sight it appeared to be just a hidden cupboard, no bigger than three feet high and wide and just eighteen inches deep, certainly not big enough to conceal a person. But when the left-hand side of its roof was pushed in a particular place, it allowed the side below it to swing open, revealing a short ladder. Will reported that this led down to a space no more than six feet long, five feet high and three wide, my size denying me entrance, I'm sad to say. That Richard had been ensconced in there for some three weeks, only coming out at night for food and water, was attested to by the rank smell that wafted up from the doorway.

Together, he and Will handed up the books. They made a surprising collection, far more advanced than I would have expected from a young child, but the most astonishing were the records, by Richard's own hand, of the weather compiled daily for what appeared to be the last two years or more. They seemed complete excepting for a few months when, presumably, he had been taken down to Lincolnshire.

Even the amount of daily rainfall was noted, and he later showed me the marked vessel behind the house where measurement was taken. Whilst the house was occupied by our men, he had crept out and back each night to complete his records. From a security point of view, it appeared to me that Siddows and his men deserved a good thrashing for dereliction of duty in not catching the boy, but from my own philosophic position, I was glad he'd escaped their clutches.

His whole tale was a record of resilience and fortitude. Taking a horse and making his way through a war-disrupted countryside, he'd returned here to continue his studies. It almost took my breath away in its audacity. This boy would build himself a place in the firmament of philosophers if war did not claim him, I thought, and though I would have been very ready to take him under my wing, I knew we must try to return him to his family.

Colonel Assheton was of my mind, and it was quickly resolved that Richard Towneley would return to Downham with me until arrangements could be made to return him to his family.

Fourteen

An Angel to an Old Fool

As we rode out next morning, I was almost sorry to leave Towneley, even though we were soon to reach home. Sergeant Siddons, having enjoyed his post too much, returned with us, being replaced by Captain Wood. We also carried the monies gathered from the Hall's tenancies which would supplement our army's pay. Young Richard rode at my side.

Bay seemed happy to be going back to Downham, holding her head high and with a slight bounce to her easy gait. My spirits were less high. I had to tell Adam of his son's last hours; I had to do something about Cas; Innkeeper Grent had to be canvassed for forces to find Tench and his band; and something was niggling me about the sudden appearance of Lady Kendall.

We parted from Colonel Assheton at Whalley. As we had ridden over Read Bridge and the site of my wounding by Kendall, I shivered, though there was now little visible sign of the trauma of that day, except for two stone walls that had been toppled and still awaited repair. However, there were signs of the damage done by Derby's Royalists at Sir Ralph's home in the old Abbey grounds, where a couple of his servants were still trying to raise a fallen stone cross. The last time I'd seen the place it was in the panic before its abandonment, as the enemy closed in from along the riverbank. Now it lay tranquil in the sun.

Hearing our arrival, Sir Ralph's fair wife had mugs of ale brought out and I was pressed to stay for dinner. It would have been a pleasure but, with less than five miles to home along a decent road, it seemed a mere delay to the inevitable, so I declined with thanks. I was also concerned to see how our Colonel's father was progressing.

The day, though sunny, had been less oppressive, fresher indeed, and we trotted home with ease. As we passed above Clitheroe, I pointed out the landmarks to young Towneley. Standing clear was the Church, by which lay my property and the school, and I thought of Amos, hoping he was now faring better since I had lent him use of my house. A quarter mile before the church, and higher on the limestone ridge, sat the Castle with its squat, dark Keep. No flag flew over it and I wondered if it was still held by the same few Royalists in their conceit. It had no real value in the current way of things, and they had been left to their own devices. If they thought that what they did was of use to the King, let them.

Not wishing to delay, I left Bay with Will and the boy at the gates to the Hall, instructing him to take Richard straight to Lady Katherine, and walked slowly down through the village to Adam's cottage. He bore the news of his son's death stoically and it was I who nearly broke down as I told my sorry tale.

'I'm glad you were with him, sir. It gives me comfort that a friend was near,' he said quietly, his woman pressing the apron to the corner of her eye, 'for you must allow me to call you friend. God bless you, Doctor.' I took his hand. The lad was Adam's only son.

Slater, as usual, bent my ear as soon as I entered. No welcome, just a fierce banging of pots as she bustled round the kitchen. 'You've brought home another stray? And you wouldn't deal with that Cas,' she fair spat out the name, 'So I've done it. He's gone and good riddance. You wouldn't have it, but he WAS going to murder us in our beds, exactly as I told you, so I had him thrashed and put out.'

'Don't give me half a tale, woman! Sit down this instant and tell me exactly what has happened and what you've done.' After my sad errand, I wasn't up to her antics and fair lost my temper. 'Don't check if I am well, will you? Don't ask if I'm hungry. Don't ask about my visit down to Adam...' Will and Nate looked in through the open door and quickly beat a retreat.

'What? Adam Seddon?' her face dropped, 'Oh! Not his lovely lad?'

'Aye,' I said quietly, 'But we were with him when he went, which he did easily.'

'I'll go to them. They're good people.' She began to shed her apron, but I caught her arm.

'Give them some time, first. By all means go down later. Indeed, I would wish you to do so, but let them catch their breath at least.' She nodded and I continued, 'Cas is gone, you say? Then let's call a truce. I'll just go and see how Sir Ralph does, speak to his lady, and then you must give me the full story.'

'Which Sir Ralph is still in bed. He tried to rise but the pain in his poor leg was so bad that he fell again...'

'I'll give him a full examination,' I promised and got up to leave. She looked at me suspiciously.

'Where's your hat?'

'Later, later,' I said, hurrying out the door.

'I believe it was serious rupture to a muscle of your lower leg, sir.' I turned to Nate. 'You remember Galen, the physician of antiquity I told you of? He refers to it as the *gastrocnemius,* which to my mind is a stupid name as it literally means 'the stomach of the leg.'

Sir Ralph had borne my examination with patience, but I caught a touch of exasperation in his voice. 'I'd find it kind of you to pursue this discourse later and instead, tell me when I can get to it' was how he put it. I forbore to point out that if he had stayed in bed as instructed, he would now be well on the way to getting 'to it'.

He was obviously still in some pain and there was still a swelling to his leg that might indicate a crack in the tibula or, more likely the fibula. 'I am sorry to say,' I shook my head, 'that rest is the only thing. Keep the leg raised upon this soft cushion as much as possible, and we will use the blessed Poppy for pain relief. I think comfrey paste should continue also.' He grimaced.

'You hate the smell, I perceive. I understand, but it's that which does you good.' I tried to bring some cheer. 'Look on the bright side, sir, you can sit and direct all to do your bidding.'

The patient took me at my word, and I was given my orders for first thing on the morrow. It was time to catch up with our friend at the Dule upon Dun Inn, though first I needed to find out about Cas.

Walking down the wide, shallow staircase, I was deep in conversation with Nate, discussing our patient's injury, telling him to take out Vesalius and look to his pictures of the leg and its muscles. 'Examine the diagram and see this *gastrocnemius*, that has been damaged, strained or ripped, and how it braces the leg bones and acts in conjunction with the other muscles. The text is in Latin, of course, but the image is the thing.' Lady Katherine entered below with Richard Towneley in her train and I almost stumbled.

Her hair was unbound, the first time I'd seen it so. Long and auburn it cascaded across her shoulders, lit by the sun. And here I must confess it, to me she is the exemplar of womankind. If I could but find another like her for my own… But such a one doesn't exist.

She is moderately tall, and still willowy despite her years, perhaps ten years younger than her husband and thus more than ten older than me. But the way she holds herself, the way she moves has never yet been described by any poet, I believe. I cannot explain her look, the enticement of her lips, the gentle brown eyes that always hold the glimpse of a smile.

Yes, stupid fool that I am, I must think I love her. How ridiculous is that? And I think she knows this and pities me. When she looks at me I can't hold her gaze, though I wish to. I want to spend the day in her company yet feel the need to flee. I throw my arms about and walk into things in her presence. I am, in total, a ridiculous figure with all the lack of grace of a village idiot. And yet she is never anything less than gracious to me.

I felt doubly bad this day, as I still carried all the marks of our ride, hadn't washed, and carried several days stubble on my face, but she held me in conversation for some minutes whilst I squirmed in shame at my appearance in front of this Venus, this angel.

'This young man, Master Towneley, has been telling me that you have taken him from his books, Doctor. That doesn't seem like you,' She said with a smile, 'and that he is your prisoner. Is this true?'

I gave an embarrassed laugh. "Not exactly, my Lady, but we simply couldn't leave him at Towneley. He has a great deal of spirit and is ingenious indeed, but we can't let him fend for himself in these troubled times and I'm sure his family would welcome news of his safety.' Richard gave a slight bow to me, and I continued.

"He is welcome to stay with me but, though I don't wish to press him upon you and Sir Ralph, perhaps in view of his family, you might feel that he should stay in the Hall? I'd be happy to talk with him further and he may wish the company of my boys, but he might take more comfort with you until we can find a way of returning him to his mother? I have not yet mentioned him to your husband.'

We spoke for some time and concluded that he should stay at the hall till the morrow, when I would collect him, introduce him to Nate and Pod before bringing him back by evening, by which time we might have a plan for his immediate future.

So, from this vision I returned to my own personal harridan. I jest, of course, for though Slater has none of the Lady's grace or visual beauty, she has a heart of gold and, had she money and position, would prove better than most. She is an uncut gemstone and though I don't lust after her, I suppose I love her too.

Again I say, don't tell her that. I'm just an old fool.

Fifteen

The Weather as it Turns

THE FOLLOWING MORNING, I WALKED ACROSS TO THE HALL TO check on Sir Ralph and collect master Towneley. As I was led in I could hear young voices, and there were Nate and Richard poring over a book. I had wondered whether the two of them would get on together, given their different standing in life, but here they were close as thieves already.

'Hello, youngsters. You've met already. How are you, Richard, and what are you about?'

'I'm well, sir, and your son is showing me of his surgery.'

'Not my son, Richard, but I treasure him nevertheless.' I beamed at Nate and pointed to the book that they were examining. 'Is that Woodall's *Surgeon's Mate*, at all? You can't do better than start with him.'

Nate spoke up excitedly and reached for a second book laid close by. 'Richard was showing me his book of travels and we were talking about some of the monstrous peoples found around the world, with no heads or just one large foot...'

As he continued to chatter, I noticed the book was the third volume of Hakluyt's *Principall Navigations* and interrupted. 'I saw you bring this from your hideaway at Towneley. I have all three volumes. You may borrow the other two if you wish, but I would take care over some of the descriptions within. I think some are fanciful and mere sailor's tales. A man with no head would be a sad figure, would he not? His eyes, nose and mouth might be pressed down towards his chest and present as though he had no neck, but those organs and a brain he must surely have, else he is not a man.'

We chatted on for some time until I remembered our patient above. 'Have you attended Sir Ralph already, Nate? How is he?'

'Comfortable, sir, but agitated. Should we give him more Borage?'

'No. It is a good enough sedative when the patient is first injured as it also helps with the pain of a wound, but loses its efficiency when used too much, I find. I'll go and see him. Why not leave your books for a while and take the air. Take Richard, see Pod and the horses and let him meet your mother.'

'Oh, must I?'

I gave him a sharp look.

'Ah, Doctor!' Sir Ralph was propped up in bed, surrounded by papers, quill in hand. I noticed the ink-horn, sat on the coverlet, had part spilt, a dark stain slowly spreading at his side. 'This Towneley lad, what are we to do with him?'

'Can we get a letter to his mother in Lincolnshire, sir? It will take some time to arrange his passage back there, I believe.'

'Yes, I'm concerned at sending him such a distance across country at present. It would be too easy for any brigand to take him as a prize. Even some of our own commanders would not hesitate to hold him hostage, I fear."

'He will take no harm here until the matter can be fixed,' I said, 'providing you are happy…'

Sir Ralph brushed my comment aside. 'Oh, he may stay as long as he wishes. I know his family. Though they are Romans, and his father is for the King, I'll do what I can to help. You may not know, we are related from some generations back.'

A week went by, a letter being sent to Lady Towneley with our sincere hope that it would get through. Autumn had now truly arrived, the trees turning their colour, but still with little rain or high winds. The few reports seen had suggested that we'd had better weather throughout the year than elsewhere in the country. Last winter had been harsh, to be sure, but Scotland had seen terrible storms and floods whilst harvests failed in the South of England. Meanwhile, our fields flourished, rainfall was modest here and our summer had seemed to stretch on and on. Excepting of course for the biblical tempest that hit me crossing the benighted moors beyond Colne. God save me from another such storm.

I asked the young Towneley about his weather notes. He was still recording each day in a small calf-bound notebook, his writing so incredibly small and precise that I needed a glass to read it. Why had he started this work?

'I noticed that, after a hot and dry summer three years ago, the following summer was so wet that all our streams overflowed. My nurse also told me that if the sky is red at night, a good day will follow; that a fruitful year is followed by a long winter. I wondered why God should make things so. I wished to see if I could know what the weather might do in advance of the day. My father did say that such would be akin to necromancy, though I think he was joking.'

'And have you formed a theory?' I asked.

'Not yet.' He paused, then said, in all seriousness 'Do you think I am mad, Sir?'

'In no way, I assure you. It is on such observations that knowledge is progressed. I am sure you will go on to great things, great discoveries that help to uncover the mysteries of this world, if you continue this work.' I proffered my hand. 'Take this, young man, as one seeker for truth to another. We may not hold the same views of religion, but I can see we will agree on much else!'

Sixteen

Fighting Like a Ruffian

NOW CAME A DAY OFF FROM NURSING OUR FRUSTRATED Knight. Nate accompanied Will and me on our mission. As we reached the outskirts of Clitheroe, we turned right and down through the woods towards Waddington. Before the river even came in view (and its ford of bad memory to me), we could hear raucous voices murdering an old song that I recognised, about how local men had beaten the French at Agincourt, a battle that was still celebrated every October, on St Crispin's Day.

'...and the Billmen of Bowland swore never to yield....' Blackened from the smoke as ever, a half dozen charcoal-burners sat outside the Dule upon Dun Inn. Despite the customers, the Inn looked rather better than I remembered, with newly painted shutters to the windows and a repainted sign. There was the Devil, sitting backwards on his horse, now in bright red and with wide staring eyes, as though screaming curses at the world.

It wasn't just the name and sign that caused most people of the town to shun the place. The woods around were a netherworld, semi-outlaw, where only charcoal-burners and lime-slakers held sway, but though gentler folk might stay away, there was plenty of custom for the Dule from the woods.

The company fell silent as we tied our mounts to the gatepost, as if resentful of losing the opportunity to cat-call us as we passed, like they would usually do to passers-by, because they knew who we were. As the bear-like landlord, the inestimable Grent, emerged from the door carrying pitchers of ale, his face broke into a wide smile. Slamming the jugs on a bench, the contents slopping and soaking his customers, he wiped his hands on a filthy apron and held out a paw.

'Doctor and company!' he exclaimed in delight. 'Welcome, welcome.' He looked at Nate, pretending puzzlement. 'Do I know this brave fellow though? It can't be that mere babby that I knew. What was his name? Nate, I think. But you look more like a Nathaniel, I believe.'

Nate looked puzzled, pleased, embarrassed and proud, all at the same time, as we were hustled towards the cool darkness of the Inn. 'Mind your noggins,' warned Grent as we entered, but the only one who needed to duck under the lintel was him. 'Come through to the back, I've someone for you to meet.'

The back room was little altered from the last time I saw it. The rather grand oak table, looted, no less, from Waddow Hall after our battle with Kendall's men last year, still filled the place. I shivered slightly, remembering the time when I lay in this very room, near drowned, after antagonising that same enemy. Grent grinned. He understood.

'Not thinking of another tangle with yon Boggart at the ford, are you Doctor? I don't want to play Jesus again, bringing you back to life like that chap Lavender.'

'Lazarus.' I corrected him and let go the blasphemy. 'I'm glad to see you well. And thriving, I believe.'

'There's a reason for that, Doctor. A reason that keeps me in bed much longer than should be right. I want you to meet my pride and joy.' He opened the back door and hollered, 'Hey, Beth, come and meet the gentry!'

In from the garden, now well set out and not just the patch of weeds that I remembered, came a small but pretty lass. Her bonny face coloured up as she rubbed the earth from her hands. Grent introduced us and she bobbed to each of us in turn. 'This is the Doctor, a great man I would say. Here is Will and this young warrior is Nathaniel, who goes by Nate.'

'The Doctor,' he continued, 'did everything he could to save my first wife after those bastards in the town called her a witch, which she never was, and I honour him for it.'

Another memory came back to me of that silent woman, driven to self-destruction out of what? Jealousy? Hatred? Fear? Who knows, but Grent was right in labelling the townsfolk bastards and I could think of other, worse words he could have used against them.

Sitting to mugs of ale, Beth brought bread and cheese, becoming chatty and gay as her husband looked on adoringly. Have you heard the phrase "a force of nature"? It could justly be used as a description of these two. We drank to their health, wealth and happiness before getting down to business.

'So, a few men to try and discover Tench and his gang, you say?' queried Grent. 'Not easy at present though I'll do my best. The woods have never been busier, for there's such demand for lime. More is being carried to Manchester, Oldham and the like than ever before. It's the gunpowder works in this time of war. We've more men coming in to work the woods too, for the money gets better and better.'

Will interposed. 'Tell us the rate and we'll pay. We have arms too, if need be. It should only be for a short while anyway. Mostly, it just needs your men to be on the lookout for these robbers and give us the information. It'll be just before next Quarter Day, when they try to take the rents, that force may be needed. Even so, we might have our own men by then.'

'We have five days until Michaelmas,' I said, 'and I believe Tench and his party will try to collect the rents just one or two days before, to thwart us again. If you can get some men together for tomorrow, we will have the arms delivered to you, together with a map of the specific farms to cover. You can decide which place is best suited for an ambush. What do you think?'

'Leave it to me,' said a determined Grent. 'Shall I send word to you or will you call here again?'

'Will will be here before evening tomorrow.' I responded. Will pulled out the purse but the Innkeeper shook his head.

'No money now,' he said, 'let's see what we can discover first.'

I took the opportunity to ask Grent if he knew anything about Kendall's wife but he said that he'd never seen her and had heard no real talk of her. He might know someone who did, though. He'd been told that an old chap who had worked for Kendall several years ago and who had occasionally drunk at the "Dule", had been seen again in Clitheroe.

'Can't remember his name, Doctor, and you can tell how long it is since he was last in here 'cos we've hardly been pally with Kendall and his men for the last six or seven years.' He paused. 'No, it's come back to me. Perkins, Perkins it was. He left when the Tench brothers came into play. Probably wasn't vicious enough for Kendall then. He'd worked for Kendall's father before him but then just flitted off. I'll keep me eye open on him."

With that we took our leave of the happy couple, first trotting down to the river to gaze across at the stark and eyeless façade of Kendall's Waddow Hall, and then back towards Clitheroe.

Up the hill to my house we went, for I wished to see how things progressed with Amos and the lodgers, and Sally came out to meet us with a curtsey, calling John to hold the horses. All looked well and tended, better even than at my last visit.

Hearing the voices, Amos' sister came from the house, asking me if I wished to inspect. She looked less harassed and careworn, for which I was glad. 'My Brother is in the School,' she said, and with a smile, 'Two more scholars now, Maister.'

I walked round to the Schoolhouse to find the Usher giving the first rudiments of Latin to two bright looking new boys, the other two students with slates and chalk silently copying something from a book. Amos looked pleased to see me, he too seeming much improved and, though he was a little hesitant in my presence, I could see that our past friendship would soon be restored.

I left him feeling much was still right with the world and rode down into Market Place with Will, leaving Nate talking with John and his Sally. I thought I'd see if I could find out anything about Grent's "Perkins", though now I wish that I'd left it to Grent.

We rode up and into the yard of the Swan, site of the altercation that had led to Pod's father's death, now a couple of years back. Tethering the horses, we entered the Inn, the smell of stale beer assaulting us. It was never the best of Inns but now looked even worse than I remembered. The floor was strewn with filthy straw such as I would not allow in my stable and there was a fug of woodsmoke and tobacco that hung about the low ceiling. Several men sat with pipes at long trestle tables, their chat dying as we entered. We sat down, the bench creaking as we did so.

The landlord, a tall, thin, stooping man with long unkempt hair, and who looked none too clean, slopped a jug of ale on the table before us, together with two cans. He gave no greeting. I was just about to enquire if he knew someone by the name of Perkins and where he might be found, when a man close to us rose and said he 'wouldn't sit by and sup with the devil'. I suddenly recognised him as someone whose wife I'd treated for dropsy only just before we'd left the town. I wasn't going to sit by and take that from such an ingrate.

I jumped up, oversetting our trestle, and lunged at him. He was turning from me, but I caught his shoulder, spun him round and pinned him to the wall with a hand around his throat. 'If you can say that after taking my charity, then you are worse than a Devil!' I shouted, my face close to his. 'If your wife still lives, then it's by my hand and charity, you drivelling, lousy, pox ridden bastard!' I let go his neck and punched him straight in the mouth with all my strength. 'Defame me again and I'll take a warrant against you and pursue you to the full extent of the law.'

This rascal's drinking companions had risen and, to prevent them helping their comrade, Will had drawn his sword. They backed to the door and fled. Will grabbed my arm. "Doctor, enough. Leave him and come away before we're taken for affray." I gave my slanderer a sharp kick, threw a couple of coins at the landlord, and allowed myself to be hustled out to the horses. 'I didn't know you could fight like a ruffian, Doctor!' commented Will. I sensed a touch of admiration in his tone as we rode out of town. I however was in high dudgeon.

That feeling lasted almost until we got back to Downham. Instead of hearing out Slater and her story of Cas, I shut myself away with a book, trying to calm myself down. Will had been right to usher me away from the fight. I could have had us both taken for affray and with no-one to take our side. But though it might have been a stupid thing to do, I was sick and tired of having ignorant idiots treat me in such a fashion. Too long have I left such insults unanswered. I tried to turn my thoughts to the vision of loveliness that was Katherine Assheton, but instead I found that damned boy Cas clouding my thoughts, and finally I went to find my housekeeper.

Slater was, at least, more composed than she'd been on the previous day, though she was still a little upset, but more with herself than with me. She disliked herself for her near instant dislike of Cas, from the moment that he turned up in Downham asking for 'Sir Doctor' and saying he was another Sam.

'And those were his exact words?' I queried. 'Did he say how he'd found us, how he's got here?'

'The more we asked him, the less we understood. He can speak English I'm sure, not well, but he can speak it and knows more than he lets on.' She looked at me earnestly. 'Doctor, you know I look for the best in everyone and don't care whether they come from Africa, America or even Scotland, God forbid. I care not what colour or shade they wish to be. I don't even care if they worship a stone or a log of wood rather than the true God, if truth be known, but that boy worried me so much. There was something not right in him and it frightened me.' She was now almost in tears. 'Even that innocent, Pod, couldn't get near him. I think he was frightened too.'

I reached across, touched her hand, and said quietly, 'You are a good woman, Joan, few better. I know your feelings, but if he's now gone, he's gone.' It was the first time I'd ever used her first name, I think, but it didn't seem to register with her.

'But I don't think he is gone, Doctor,' she said, plaintively, 'He's still around. I can feel it.'

I was more worried by the time she'd told me how he seemed to disappear for hours on end, and that three times she had seen him sitting by the door on the side of the Hall that opened into the cellar, shooing him away each time. Finally, she'd found him there trying to open the lock, which was when she finally beat him, marched him up to the very gates of the Hall and pushed him out.

I made my way round to look at the cellar door that Slater had mentioned. There were scratches and marks round the keyhole and, as I turned, I noticed an iron nail on the ground. The end had been bent over, probably after being hit by stones, for there were rough marks and scratches where the end had been turned. It looked like a crude attempt to form a key, which more than confirmed Slater's suspicions.

Now I looked to the boys for information. Days before, as I was leaving for Colne, I'd asked Nate to watch Cas, so now called him and Pod in to find out what they knew.

'I saw him once only before Mother threw him out,' said Nate, 'but then I was with Sir Ralph much of the time. He was stood by the back of our stable, looking over the fields. I shouted to him, he ran, and I couldn't find him.'

'I think he went out in the dark each night,' Pod confessed, 'for the horses were shuffling about as they do when he's about and I don't think he was still in the loft, for I never heard those odd noises he makes.'

'And neither of you have seen him since he was thrown out?' They both shook their heads. 'Tell me if you do so, will you? Come and find me straight away.'

What in Hell's name had been going on?

Seventeen

The Ancient, Whittle

THE FOLLOWING MORNING, IN A NEW LEATHER HAT, LOW crowned, just as I wanted, and purchased by Slater for the price of two hens – 'Good laying birds too' she'd grumbled - I walked with her down through the village to see how old Adam was faring. His woman met us at the garden gate, saying he was in the fields. I left the two women chatting and went off to find him, continuing on with the brook on my right.

As I passed the last cottage before the open fields, a mere hovel it seemed to me, I noticed an old crone sat by the door. I don't recall having seen her before but, even before I could bid her good day, she addressed me with 'I wondered when you'd pass, Doctor. Too busy to notice an old lass like me, I suppose.'

'How are you, Goodwife?'

'Same as ever. I don't change, though the seasons do.' She gave what I can only describe as a cackle. 'And Goodwife, is it? Not many call me that.'

I was about to walk on when she asked 'Do you seek change, Doctor, with your books and learning? You delve into the secrets of the ancients, do you not?'

'I do.' I said in surprise.

'But you don't see what is right beneath your nose. How's your blackamoor?'

'What do you know of him?' I asked sharply.

'I would ask you the same question. You never wanted to know about him until now, I believe.'

I could feel my temper rising. Who was she to question me in this manner? 'Look, who are you, woman, and what do you know of the creature?'

'I keep my name quiet that it doesn't identify me as a witch. But you don't believe in such things, do you?' This time her laugh sounded like the opening of an old door.

I was annoyed and perturbed by this bag of bones, no more, but something held me. All hinted that she knew much about me and, even more importantly, about Cas. I'd been studying her deeply lined face during this exchange and now something occurred to me. I softened my voice a little and asked 'Are you blind?'

'My eyes are dark, but I see all I need to.' She patted the bench beside her. 'Why not come and sit a little.'

I hesitated, but something told me that this was more than just play. I sat down beside her on the old and warped grey oak bench, leaning back against the cottage wall, warm in the sun. I didn't look at her, just stared straight ahead as we talked.

'Do you live here alone?'

'For nigh on twenty years, give or take. Came over from Roughlee. Not far, but far enough to be away from my relations.'

'Why's that?'

'My name is Whittle. Same as my Great-aunt who ended up on the end of a rope. You'll know of her.'

'I will?'

'Oh aye. Though you'd call her Chattox.'

Now that was a surprise. A name from the past, still used to frighten children hereabouts and send them to bed in a quiver. Chattox and her rival, Demdike, haggard female heads of two families from over the hill, sat long in the imagination since that day, now more than thirty years past, when they and their seemingly cursed broods had been hanged at Lancaster, found guilty of witchcraft. Their shadow still hung heavily about Pendle.

She'd rightly said that I don't believe in witches. I could be called a witch by some fools, for didn't I make potions and poisons like so many Cunning women who have been so titled? Many of those borne or raised with such crafts and resource were, indeed still are, consulted and used as doctor to the poor, just as I might be by those who could afford my services. What's the difference between their simples and my concoctions? If some Cunning persons should come to believe that they could use their knowledge for evil, that they could summon devils perhaps, it doesn't mean that such belief was real.

That infernal side, attributed to some, was certainly not real to me, though that bastard Kendall had held the title of Witch over me in forcing me out of Clitheroe, and the idiots of the town, of which there are many, believed him.

'You then settled here. And who looks to you?' I asked, for she looked helpless enough and I couldn't see how she could manage on her own.

'I have coped well enough so far. It's by our Lady's leave I stay here and can eat.'

'You are a Roman?' I queried, thinking that she referred to Saint Mary.

'Our Lady Assheton,' she said with a touch of irritation. I should have realised. There was another feather for the sainted Katherine's cap. 'She sends me bread and meat and her kindness has caused a few others hereabouts to help me also.'

'What do you really know about me?' I asked carelessly, breaking a moment's silence.

'I listen to the currents about me, and it tells most of what I need to know. It's how I know of you and how I knew you would pass today. I would have sent you a message before this if I had one to take it to you.' She put a hand on my arm. 'My time is almost run, so listen…'

It was more a skeleton of a hand than any I've seen, the skin loose and translucent with bones and tendons clear below. For her age, if I was told she was a hundred years or more, I would have believed it, and I wondered at her survival. Surely, the way a body clings to life or life clings to a body is a miraculous thing, especially when our human temperament can be raised to destroy it in an instant, if so desired. There is an easy violence around us, it seems, to allow one person to kill another with little thought, as we see in the present war. It is a wonder that any live to old age in these blighted days.

'In this year, I've had two visitors,' the old woman continued, 'One who calls himself my nephew, though I would not admit it, for he is a brute. My sister, his mother, is long dead, but she had despaired of him and his brother, setting them from her house.' She waved a thin arm dismissively. 'In turn, they set themselves up with an acquaintance of thine, but who's name I shall not give.'

Thoughts that I didn't wish were beginning to flood into my head. I found I had almost stopped breathing. The sun continued to shine, the birds to sing. I could even hear some children splashing in the brook nearby, but I was hooked to the woman's words like a fish on a line.

'The other visitor was your Blackamoor, whose visits came and went but occasionally met with those of my nephew, usually at night.'

I took a deep breath and asked, quietly, 'What passed between them? Do you know?' She gave a thin laugh and continued.

'My hearing is a much greater power in me than I expect it is in you. The loss of my sight is nothing to me, when sound and touch tell me so much more than my eyes ever did. I can recall colours to my mind when I wish to and can infer them from what I sense around me.' She continued. 'I could feel the darkness around my nephew as he spoke to your boy in his gentle whispers; I could hear the threats beneath his words as he told the lad that he was his only hope of salvation and that you were the true source of evil; that you were a great pretender who would, in due course, take his soul.'

I felt bound to ask, even as I knew the answer. 'Your nephew… Is he called Tench?'

'Shaddock was his father's name, but he and his brother spurned it. Might even have killed their sire if rumour is right. I believe it, certainly. The two were alike as peas in the pod. And equal in darkness. The pair were poachers, first caught with a haul of tench when they were barely out of swaddling. So, yes, that name fit them like a glove.'

'So, what connects the Blackamoor to Tench?'

'Just a line of evil, I fear.' She hesitated. 'The boy is not as stupid as you believe, you know. He is afraid of you but much more afraid of my nephew. I found him by the door one night, weeping and almost frozen. I thought he had been beaten but, as I felt for wounds, could find none. I touched his face and, as I laid my hands on him, felt his fear. Since then, he has often come to me, laying his head in my lap and I comfort him. I could feel the darkness of his skin but no darkness in his soul, just despair and fright.'

'Was he brought here by Tench? And if so for what? To destroy me? I wasn't even here when the lad arrived.'

'I think your destruction was the first reason, or at least to disrupt things and leave you open to destruction, but there is something other now, I believe. Cas has been told to get into the Hall and to search for something. That I am sure of, though I know not for what. Destroy Sir Ralph, perhaps?'

That made little sense to me, but I needed to try and find Cas. 'So where is the boy now?' I enquired.

'I'm not sure, but not far off, I believe. Holed up somewhere and hoping for safety. He has nowhere else to go. What would you do in his stead? My nephew will come again at the next dark of the moon, expecting to see him. Is that in four nights? I believe it is. Perhaps Cas will turn up then.'

Eighteen

'Once a Witch...'

'DINNER HAS BEEN READY SINCE TWO O'CLOCK, DOCTOR.' Slater looked vaguely annoyed. 'When you are at home, we eat at a Christian hour, I'm sure.' She dropped a bowl of stew on the table and bade me sit in peremptory fashion. I was in something of a daze, trying to clarify matters in my head, and was in no mood for chatter but she wittered on just the same.

I had barely raised the spoon to my mouth when something occurred to me. I had a hunch. Letting the spoon clatter to the floor, I sought my coat. 'And is my food not good enough for you now?' she shouted after me, but I was quickly back.

'What did Cas wear?' I asked her.

'That devil again. What does that matter? He is gone, he is gone. Just sit and eat or you will waste away to skin and bone as you did when ill with those nasty wounds...'

'Slater, dear, I have never been down to skin and bone, not even before you inserted yourself so successfully in my life. Your excellent food and care has seen my waist grow to an unrequired size.' I patted my belly. 'My enforced fast, as I lately recovered, merely re-adjusted my weight to a more comfortable measure, giving me a more sylph-like figure. Which, I might add, I would like to retain.'

'Inserted myself! I never inserted myself in this or any other place in all my life. What do you mean, inserted!' She set to, fiercely wiping the table with the bottom of her apron, this being the usual way of showing her delight at our verbal jousts, and I laughed.

'Laugh, is it?' she cried, 'If my boy should say such things which he won't do being brought up to have more manners than many I could speak of I'd box his ears and you think that I wouldn't do the same to you if you throw down insults upon me day after day and then laugh at me who never does anything but for the good of someone who would never think of looking after himself...'

'Slater, Slater. You know that I jest and that you are one of the great treasures of my life. You are right, without you I would be skin and bone. I'd even trade my library for you, if I had to...'

'Well. Now I know that you are lying like the Devil, God spare you. Nothing nor no-one would part you from that pile of books, most of which no right-thinking person can understand.' She was now trying her best not to smile, to pretend she was truly mad at me, but I know her too well.

'I formally acknowledge you as my true guardian angel. Saint Joan. I don't know who the female equivalent of the biblical Gabriel is, but you have taken her crown...'

'And now blasphemy! May the good Lord save you from the fire.'

'Will my Angel allow herself to sit with an old sinner for a moment? Come, take this stool.' I applied myself to the rapidly cooling broth. 'I really do need to ask about the clothes Cas was wearing.' I placed the button that I'd found in the wreck of the Greenside cottage on the table. 'Could this be from his shirt?'

She poked it with a finger then picked it up and studied it. 'You know....' she said with a frown. 'Yes, I'm sure!' I raised my eyebrows in anticipation. 'I'm sure... that I have no idea!' and the wench grinned.

'If I were younger,' I said, 'I'd chase you round this table...'

'If I were younger, you'd not catch me.' We both laughed.

After the tension that followed my talk with the spinster Whittle, our laughter was a great relief, just what was needed. We were still laughing when Nate and Pod came in. They looked at each other, Pod shrugged and broke out his lovely smile. That set us off again and now both boys joined in, laughter being so infectious.

The moment passed, I returned to a more serious frame of mind and asked the boys about the button. Pod didn't know but Nate thought it could be from Cas.

'It's just an ordinary bone button,' said Slater,'and could be from anyone. Look at Pod's shirt. His has just the same'

'Yes, I do know, but it may just have been that one of you noticed him with a button missing?' I sighed, 'I know I'm clutching at straws... Nate, if you're going back to the Hall, can you look for Will? If he is at large, tell him I need a word, will you? And give Master Richard my good wishes. I'm sorry not to attend him today.'

Will arrived and sat, Slater passing him a mug of ale. Hot and bothered, he jerked a thumb over his shoulder, declaring with irritation 'I've sat with our Lord and Master all morning. He's wanting to get up again and firing orders left and right. Can you not tie him down, Doctor? Give him one of your sleeping draughts?'

'I'd better go and have another word with him I suppose,' I condescended. 'What's he after now?'

'He only wants to go and fight Squire Aspinall for some insulting letter he's received.'

'Oh, this will be about Lady Kendall, I have no doubt. I suppose she is as big a scoundrel as her late husband. Aspinall is only slightly better.' I placed a finger on the bone button. 'I think we've got a bigger problem than that...'

'... and so we have, I believe, a few days till the change of the moon...' I was giving the full story, as I knew it, to Sir Ralph. He had stopped his fidgeting as my tale unfolded, but whether he had fully digested my repeated warning that he should not try to rise for a few more days yet, I didn't know.

'I think we can readily guess what your black was after,' said Sir Ralph. 'Most of what we brought back from Kendall's Hall is stored below us. Tench must have told him that, but how did that blackguard know, I wonder?'

We shook our heads.

'Should we bring mistress Whittle here for protection, do you think?' Lady Katherine had been taking down a letter to the dictation of her husband as we arrived in the bedchamber, and still sat with her paper, pen and ink. She looked concerned.

'No, I don't see that she is at risk,' responded her husband, 'for if she is removed, Tench may not come. First thing is to find that boy and then set an ambush for the beast. Will, set everyone on it.'

'Aye, sir. The Doctor's boys are already combing the woods as best they can, but I'll call in our fellows and organise them. Then I'll get those swords and pikes down to Grent. Some muskets too?' he queried. Sir Ralph nodded and Will then nodded at me. 'Come, Doctor.'

'If Grent's men see Tench first, we may have no problem anyway,' I said to Sir Ralph as I crossed to the door.

'Keep me informed by the hour,' shouted the invalid as we left the room.

As soon as Will had given out instructions for the men to search the village, I asked him to walk up to the Greenside cottage with me. There was no sign of Cas, but then I didn't expect to actually find him there, in residence so to speak, and I didn't know if there really was a connection between the place and our missing boy. It was just a feeling, no more, but every time I'd passed the place in recent days, it had drawn me to it.

Let me describe the building as it stood in that evening sun. The plot of land, that sloped upwards to the right hand as one looked at it was only small, perhaps sixty feet square, the overgrown garden barely big enough to provide for a family, I would say, suggesting that the owner would work at some additional occupation rather than rely entirely on his ground. The remains of a pigsty stood in one corner. The slope of the earth allowed the right end of the cottage to be part buried in the slope, or so it seemed. The walls were of random stone, out of true on the left side as though it might soon collapse, the stone slabbed roof probably too heavy for it. Despite this, the building would have been near weathertight had the bent and warped door been secured. It now barely closed and any lock that might have once adorned it was long gone, possibly smashed off by the look of the door's edge.

I asked my companion to walk round the building, examining every piece of ground for anything, anything at all, that either looked out of place or gave any indication of who might have been there. I went inside to do the same, noting the thickness of the walls. The place had been built to last.

There were no windows to the single room, which was no more than fifteen feet by ten. The only light came from the door, which I propped as wide open as I could, and the hole in the roof above the firepit for smoke to escape. I stood stock still, letting my eyes adapt to the gloom, until I could peer into the corners, look into the dust of the floor. I could see nothing except for footprints, which could have been my own from my last visit, plus bat droppings on the floor. I looked up at the roof beams, warped by the weight of the stone roof, but couldn't see any of the creatures. The firepit was, of course, stone cold. A few half-burnt logs remained in the ashes and I stirred them with my foot, uncovering one or two white objects that I deduced were bones. No surprise there - one could imagine a fowl or even a lamb put to the fire to feed whatever occupants had lived in the cottage – but then I noticed a few singed threads, no more, in between a couple of the fire-stones. I pulled the fibres out, felt them between my fingers, and put them in my coat pocket as a shadow filled the doorway.

'Come and look at this, Doctor.' I could tell nothing from the tone of Will's voice but followed him out and round to the back of the building, trying to avoid catching myself on the undergrowth. 'It looks like someone's been sheltering under the eaves of the sty. See the pile of grass in the corner and these footprints in the dried mud? Small feet, I'd say. Could be Cas?' I shrugged.

'Also,' he said, pointing to the back wall of the cottage, 'there's a near path through the brambles – you can see the broken branches and thorns leading to yon pile o'stones right under the wall.'

'I can't see that Cas could hide behind them, Will, though he may have used the sty. Can we get someone to watch the place tonight?'

As we walked back to the Hall, I pointed out to Will that the cottage, though small, was well built. 'The walls are mighty thick and, though part of the end wall looks near collapse, the building is sound. I think it's just the weight of the roof that has caused some of the outer stones to fall from the wall.'

'Aye. I'd want a window to the place, but it would tidy up well, Doctor.'

'So why would anyone desert the place? How long has it been derelict? Several years, I'm told.'

'Since before I arrived for certain, Doctor, and that's five years or more.'

We stopped as we reached the Hall gates. 'Two things then, Will. Someone here must know something about it. Ask around the village - go from door to door if you have to – and get a couple of the men to watch the place tonight. I'll ask Sir Ralph.'

'A sad tale, Doctor, a sad tale.' I sat by Sir Ralph as he recounted the story of the cottage. 'I knew of them. It was some fifteen years ago, I think, when my father was still alive. A couple with a single child – a daughter who disappeared. I was away in London at the time but was told that our men helped search for her, to no avail. I think the girl was said to be very forward and had been seeing a boy, so it was thought that she'd run away, but her mother would neither believe it nor accept it.' He shook his head, slowly. 'Perhaps the mother lost her wits, I do not know, but then both parents disappeared. I don't think anyone realised they'd gone.'

'And the cottage just sank into disrepair?' I asked, 'No one claimed it?'

'Oh, a few people took it – with no legal right, I must say – but they left quickly. It might look welcoming, but people believe it has an evil atmosphere about it. Some say that they've seen lights around it on dark nights.'

'Who would tell me more about the people who disappeared?'

'Lucy, maybe? She's the oldest here. Lives in the cottage nearest the church Lyke-gate.' He looked at me quizzically. 'Why this interest, Doctor?'

'Only that we think Cas has used the place from time to time. And two weeks ago, I found the remnants of a fire....'

'Beggars or vagrants, perhaps?'

'Oh, that could well be, Sir Ralph,' I replied, 'but I'm hoping it's Cas and that he returns there.'

'She ne'er went off with nobody from here,' said the old woman, scornfully. She could almost have been sister to old Whittle at the other end of the village: little flesh on her bones, heavily lined face and the same near transparent skin, though she wasn't blind, and her voice was, gratefully, less of a broken reed. Neither was her cottage a hovel but trim and modestly furnished with table, two chairs and a small dresser. A pot of stew sat on a low fire, the smell from which made my mouth water.

'A bonny, modest lass, I remember. Mother pleased when she found a place with a Butcher in Clitheroe. Home each Sunday and came to Church with her parents, then stopped. Never seen again, would you believe?' She smoothed down her smock. A thin lock of white hair hung down from under her coif and she pushed it back with a bony finger. 'After two weeks, the parents raised hue and cry, though no-one took much notice. Asked for help from the old Squire Assheton, who sent them to Standen...'

'Standen Hall?' I interrupted, 'To Aspinall?'

'Aye, as Justice for Clitheroe. Another week or so and their cottage was abandoned, they never seen again!' She ended, triumphant.

'As quick as that? Did anyone search for them?'

'No.' She wrinkled her nose. 'They were never very friendly and not much liked. They were neither of here nor Chatburn, if you get my meaning. We were sorry their daughter was lost to them, of course, and at first many of us went from house to house to discover her.' She fell silent.

'So, nobody looked for the parents?' I ventured.

She looked at me from under furrowed brows, 'And nobody went near that cottage after, for it's cursed. Strange apparitions seen at night my daughters tell me.' She jerked a thumb towards the end of the village. 'It's her brood. They're still around...'

'You mean Mistress Whittle?' I queried, 'But she renounces her family! She has the Bible read to her I'm told. And she's blind and near helpless...'

'Once a witch, always a witch. She don't need eyes to move about. She can send spirits to do her bidding. She pretends, sir, she is a pretender and works with the Devil...'

I could stand no more, bid her good day and quickly left. I've said it before, the old ways, ideas and prejudices are still here, just below the surface and many are those who are deaf to all reason. In a sense, the spirits of those witches, Demdike and Chattox, do still fly around, for they poison the minds of the credulous, blind them to rational thought. I blame the

Church, and most of the Puritans are every bit as bad, who seek to keep the multitude in the dark with tales of Hell-fire and damnation.

Thoughts were now whirling around my head. I remembered the rumours of girls missing from Clitheroe and their possible connections to Kendall and his men. In particular, I recalled the sight of the drowned lass, pulled from the river at Eadsford a year ago, that I knew beyond doubt had worked for Kendall. Her distraught father had confronted Kendall and, in the ensuing affray, was himself killed. Could this story of a girl and parents missing from Greenside also be connected? Through old Whittle, I now had a connection twixt Tench and Cas, together with a likely link twixt Cas and the Greenside cottage. More important yet was the thought that it was now just three days to the dark of the moon when Cas and Tench were due to meet. It made me shudder to think that such a brute could move about the village almost at will.

Will caught me as I returned to the Hall. 'I've checked with the men,' he said, 'No sight of the Blackamoor as yet but will keep searching, Doctor.'

'I think we need men watching Greenside all night, plus a couple posted within sight of Whittle's cottage,' I responded. 'Surely he can't avoid being seen when we're aware that he's likely to be there?'

The dark of the moon coincided with the feast of St Michael and the Angels and, with the usual presentation of geese to Squire Assheton, it was his tradition to give his villagers a feast and a bonfire. With many having their wits deadened by drink, Tench might think he could move with impunity, but we had to ensure that couldn't happen.

Nineteen

'A True Martial Band'

THERE WERE NOW A NUMBER OF ENQUIRIES HAPPENING simultaneously and I, for one, was praying that at least one would bring results and soon.

We had Grent and the men from Brungerley woods searching for Tench and his Band, though in reality that beast might be close at hand; There was a search on for the mysterious Perkins, who had apparently worked for Kendall at some point, to find out information regarding the mysterious Lady Kendall; We were searching too for Cas, who had some yet unfathomed link to Tench but who now, if Mistress Whittle was to be believed, appeared to be more sinned against than sinning. Perhaps I was just too simple in thinking that the removal of Kendall would see everything right in the world.

Grent we could leave to his own devices for the present. He knew what his job was and would, I was sure, send word as soon as he had found anything. Perkins would have to wait, as would Lady Kendall, though Sir Ralph was eager to be up and about and off to beard Aspinall in his lair. We had every available man out searching for Cas, with two watching the abandoned cottage each night.

The country being at war with itself was still at the back of my mind, but just at this moment it almost seemed the lesser of our problems.

In fact, things were going well for our side. As soon as he'd recovered from his return from Heptonstall young Sir Ralph, Colonel Assheton, marched on Wigan, gathering men on the way and meeting up with a large detachment from Manchester. By the time they reached the town they were 2,000 strong, more than a match for 700 Royalist foot-soldiers and a troop of horse under one Colonel Tyldesley, who chose to retreat westwards to Ormskirk. Our Colonel took the town without loss, demolished the fortifications, burnt the gates, made the townsfolk swear never to bear arms against Parliament again and pushed on in pursuit of the Royalists.

That news, brought by a blue-sashed rider, put a smile to his father's face. 'Ralph is now moving on Lathom, Lord Derby's seat. He will soon have them all surrounded.' He turned to me. 'Would I were there, Doctor. I can't lie here forever. You must let me rise.'

I examined his leg. All the swelling had gone but a slight bruising remained. 'No pain, sir?' I asked.

'None at all. That is what is so frustrating. Come on, man, I must be up and doing.'

'You must use a stick, sir. Rest the leg whenever possible and, if you should try to ride, must promise me that you will be lifted on and off your mount. If you will do that, You may indeed rise.' In reality I was very pleased with his condition, having first thought that he might have occasioned permanent damage to the limb. Comfrey is a wonderful cure-all.

Will Cummins was the first to solve one of our problems. He still had friends in Clitheroe, and they send him word that Perkins was living at the rear of one of Kendall's burgages on Castle Street. A number of the burgage plots, though narrow, stretched back and down a long way from the street and had cottages and hovels associated with them, bringing in extra income to the burgage holders. Perkins was persuaded by Will, on the promise of safe conduct and a small purse, to meet me at the Dule upon Dun. In the meantime, Sir Ralph prepared to ride over to Standen Hall and confront Aspinall over his impertinent summons.

I was not happy that Sir Ralph should ride the mile to Standen so soon after I had allowed him to rise from his bed, but he agreed that I should go with him and turn him back if he began to struggle. We were to be a party of seven, including Will and four of the fellows who had been with me at Colne, armed and helmeted. Each had a light-blue ribbon tied round their upper left arms, the current sign of our allegiance. Sir Ralph was lifted onto his steed as I demanded and, though he looked rather paler and more gaunt than usual, he sat easy on his mount. Rather than an armband, he was wearing a blue dyed feather in his hat.

'It's good to be in the land of the living again, Doctor,' he said as the horses walked gently down into the village. It was a bright, warm autumn day with high Pendle free of cloud and swallows fluttering from woods to cottage eaves, though they would be gone within the next few weeks. The few villagers about smiled at their Master and touched their caps or curtseyed as we passed. Bay was pleased to be out on such a fine day and frisky, though I don't think she was in season. I had to hold her hard to her job until we left the village behind. The trees had turned colour, though many had already shed their leaves in the previous day's high winds. Two or three lay toppled close to our path, but none blocked our passage.

We seemed to be a true martial band, and that was no mistake. When travelling alone or with Will and Nate, I felt that we could generally pass not un-noticed but as common travellers, which gave me some comfort. I could play "The Doctor" and move freely, generally without let or hindrance. But this armed escort and the sword at my side now comforted me when we believed Tench and his band could be somewhere close by. Will was at my side and kept up a flow of idle chatter as we passed between high hedgerows, but I barely heard him, my eyes flitting from tree to tree, bush to bush, and the heights of Pendle, looking for the first sign of trouble.

There was none. The countryside slumbered in a gentle warmth and before the sun reached its height we gained the gate of Standen and swept down to the imposing entrance of the Hall. Two guards stood by the gate as we rode past and, though they didn't try to stop us, I noticed they both had daggers at their sides and pikes leant against one of the gate posts.

This was a grander building than Downham Hall and, though more modest than Towneley, had a similar plan to the latter, a central hall flanked by wings on either side, all in grey stone. Two servants rushed out to take our horses, but the sight of our armed party seemed to both surprise and frighten them. One ran back into the house to tell his master of our arrival and as two of our men slid off their mounts to assist Sir Ralph to dismount, Aspinall, short and fat, bustled out in a lather to welcome him.

In the normal way our escort and the horses would have been led round to the stables or the kitchen entrance of the house, but Sir Ralph had already instructed Will to keep our party by the entrance porch and to be on his guard. Passing a walking stick to Sir Ralph, I kept at his side as we approached the door. Aspinall gave something of a smile but seemed unsure as to whether he should proffer his hand. Sir Ralph's brief nod and business-like good day settled the matter.

'Welcome, Sir Ralph.' Our host stuttered. "I wasn't expecting you, because of your leg. I hope it gives you no trouble? How is your lady? A fine day for a ride. Please come and take your ease. I shall call for food and drink...."

'Thank you, but we will just attend to our business, Aspinall, if we may.' Sir Ralph, though there was no edge to his voice, cut our host short in his babbling.

'Yes, yes, indeed, please enter, enter.'

We were led through the main hall, dominated by a large oak table and an imposing fireplace at one end, decorated with Aspinall's armorials, to the room that I expect he uses when sitting as magistrate. It was heavily panelled with two wainscot chairs standing by and a large inlaid coffer chest filling the space under a latticed window. A modest trestle table in the centre of the room stood in front of a most ornate armchair. The tall back of the chair was most delicately carved, though it was difficult to see the full detail as it was in part shade, whilst its arms curved out as if to welcome the sitter, perhaps even to enclose him. I found it both remarkable and intriguing. The only other thing of note was a tapestry screen in one corner masking a door.

Aspinall circled the table and sat in the ornate chair, offering us seats against the wall. Sir Ralph declined the offer, preferring to lean against the table. His presence, looming over the much smaller man, caused Aspinall to rise from his seat, not to be at too great a disadvantage or appear less than courteous.

Sir Ralph came straight to the point of our visit. He kept his voice quite even and without anger but there was a touch of steel there as he said 'I was rather taken aback by your recent summons, Aspinall. Only the damage to my leg prevented me from riding here immediately and demanding to know what the devil you meant by it. I would ask you to explain yourself.'

'I – I beg your pardon, sir. No insult was intended, I assure you. I am simply seeking to ensure that the goods and chattels taken from Waddow Hall are returned to their rightful owner.'

'Then a simple request would have sufficed. You could have had the courtesy to visit me and deal with the matter, rather than send such a summons, man.'

At least Aspinall had had the grace to redden and I must say that I was enjoying his discomfort.

'I don't think my letter was a summons, per se, sir…'

Sir Ralph thrust his hand into his bosom and pulled out a paper. His jaw was set, his eyes narrow, but yet he held his temper. 'I have your very letter here. You clearly say that you must demand – Demand, note – that certain goods and valuables, being held by me against the wishes of the owner, must be released and due restitution made for damages, and you sign it as a Justice of the Peace. How else should I take it? Except that your understanding seems astray, I would fight you for such an insult.'

I was so engaged with the matter that, although I felt something of a draught enter the room, I didn't hear the door in the corner open or notice the tapestry flutter, but from behind the screen flew nothing less than a Harpy.

Twenty

'Take Care and Watch Your Tongue'

IT HAD BEEN MANY DAYS SINCE I'D HAD CHANCE TO CONSULT MY library. Most of it was still packed in wooden chests since our flight from Clitheroe. It is an extensive collection and in amongst the volumes written in Greek - and there are a few, even though I am not completely proficient in that tongue and can only read them slowly and with difficulty – there is one that give stories of their Gods. I would say "Ancient" Gods, but they are a benighted people, now under the thumb of the Ottomans, and though some are believed Christians, the Apostle Paul having tried to convert the Thessalonians at least, I expect that many still worship the multiplicity of Gods headed by one Zeus. I suspect that Zeus is to be considered like our own single God, as he is the chief of their pantheon of Gods and spirits, but why one would believe that God needs eternal demi-gods to assist Him is beyond me. Mind you, the Catholics have a myriad of so-called Saints and angels that they pray to, so I suppose it is all one. I am with our non-conforming sects and even the Puritans (God help me!) here. There is but one God and all else is just stuff and confusion.

Actually, I must correct myself. The book in my possession is written in English, a translation from Greek by a man called Chapman. The original was by a Greek called Homer, who described a long journey by a man called Odyssey or some-such. It tells us that the Greek's Zeus had some handmaidens, half woman, half eagle, that were named Harpies. They were his Hell-hounds and wrapped themselves in storms and whirlwinds. It was just such an apparition that now appeared in Aspinall's room.

'You've ransacked Waddow Hall and left it a shell.' She fair spat her words out. Standing as tall as Sir Ralph, her hair unbound and flying back from her face, she flew towards us. Aspinall was pushed to one side as she faced us, her clenched hands pressing hard down on the table. Rather gaunt and common-looking I thought, a poor complexion and her speech flat and hard, so that one could not believe that this was a Lady.

She was dressed well enough in a yellow dress, embroidered with small flowers and green ribbons. The high white collar was surrounded with delicate lace that fell down and around her shoulders. Whether it sat well on her is not for me to say but if she was common, her dress was not. Her look was of thunder and her eyes flashed fire at Sir Ralph. 'You've allowed all and sundry to pick what they want but you have embezzled my treasures. You have stolen what is mine by right.' She wiped a hand across her mouth.

'Lady,' said the Knight, slowly and evenly, though one could see he was taken aback, 'I would take care and watch your tongue. I will not take such insult from you or anybody.' She opened her mouth to retort, but he stopped her with the raising of a hand. 'You have lost your husband and, though it is now more than several months since and it appears that you are out of mourning, I give you my condolences and will forgive that unwise and unwarranted comment this time.' Her eyes seemed to flicker at the mention of Kendall and her back straightened, but I thought little of it at the time.

'You are fully mistaken in what you say.' He continued, his voice rising as she attempted to respond. 'Let me make the position clear. I believe, as many do, that Sir Christopher was a thief and a scoundrel and probably much more. You may take that statement as you will. You may regret his loss - I do not - but he abandoned his Hall.' He leaned forward to emphasise his words. 'And yet I would not condone the laying waste of a knight's true property. More than enough mischief surrounds that place.' She now looked more shocked than tense and angry, and her shoulders drooped slightly.

'What remained of your goods was collected and placed in safe keeping by me, and I gave an inventory of the items to this Justice of the Peace.' He turned to our host who was squirming in embarrassment. 'Is that not right, Aspinall? You still have it?' The man nodded.

'Give Lady Kendall that document and she may make arrangements to wait upon me at Downham with, I suggest, two large carts, and I will release the items to her. You will have the courtesy of giving me a few days notice of your arrival.' He nodded briefly to the woman, said 'Madam, good day', turned, asked me for my arm and we walked, without further ceremony, from the room and out to where Will and the men were waiting. We left raised voices behind us, or rather we heard her voice berating her host, and Aspinall did not come to see us off his land as politeness should demand.

As we rode back along the quiet track to Downham, I could tell that Sir Ralph was still furious at his reception and so kept quietly in file behind our knight. Will brought his pony alongside me, raising his eyebrows in question, but I gave a slight shake of my head in dismissal.

If our master was angry - and who would blame him for such a show – I was both puzzled and perplexed. Something here was very amiss and not just with Lady Kendall's savage and unwarranted accusation.

Twenty One
The Portrait

As I watched Sir Ralph being assisted to dismount his steed with great care at the door of his Hall, and with Pod and another groom ready to take the horses, a small deputation of two men and two women rose to meet us. I recognised the men as those who had been put to watching the abandoned cottage.

'We've seen the savage, sirs, and Betsy and her friend,' the fellow I knew as John pointed his thumb to the two women over his shoulder, 'say he's down at the old lead workings past Twiston and by Ings beck.'

'Don't call him a savage,' I exclaimed crossly. 'He has been baptised.'

'Yes, but he's black and they say has been consorting with the witch Whittle...'

'His blackness matters not, and Mistress Whittle is an old blind woman and is no witch.' I was incensed, angry and even wounded at his ignorance. I took a step towards him to give him a clout, but Sir Ralph stopped me with a hand on my arm. 'So, what have you done about it?' he asked.

'Well... Nothing, sir. We thought we should wait for you...'

'You have effectively let him go, then? Who knows where he'll be now?' he said sharply. Turning to Will, Sir Ralph addressed him with the title he had before being detached to my use, 'Sort this matter will you, *Sergeant* Cummins. Take as many as you can and comb the area around the beck. Ensure your prey is not harmed, will you?' Will gave a sharp nod, turned and pushed the two disgraced watchers towards the gate as Sir Ralph, leaning heavily on his stick, limped into his house.

Pod tugged at my sleeve and with an eager look asked if he should get Nate and help the search. 'Aye, lad. You go and make sure they don't hurt Cas if they find him.' I looked with fondness at the sweet boy. 'Tell Cas that all will be well, and you and Nate bring him back safely, will you?' I followed Sir Ralph into the Hall.

I found him sitting sideways to his table, one arm on the dark oak and holding up his head. He looked tired after the day's ride and the lace cuffs of his shirt were dusty as was his blue hose. It was gratifying to note that he was resting his bad leg on an adjacent chair.

'What do you think about today's episode, Doctor?'

'It was…' I struggled momentarily for an appropriate word, '… Illuminating?'

'Illuminating! What on earth do you mean? It was a much as I could do not to strike that harridan. It was a disgraceful show.' He scowled. 'I'd like to know what she was doing at Aspinall's. Yet he's a weak man, no good to man or beast, and the least wench, never mind a Lady, could bend him to her will, I believe.'

I had been going over every element of our meeting as we rode the road back to Downham, and there were a few things that I wished to put to Sir Ralph. Firstly, there was something that I believed was still stored with the cache of items brought from Waddow, and which this 'Lady' was keen to get her hands on, that I wished to see. 'May I retrieve an item from Kendall's goods, sir? I think it may be revealing.' He looked at me quizzically and, as a servant boy came in with a cold ham, bread and a jug of ale, gave me a set of large keys. Without a word to me, he ordered the lad to show me down to the cellars.

We clattered down a flight of stone steps into a dank corridor. If the Hall above was cool, down here it was rather chilly despite the warmth of the day. There was little light. The servant boy left me to get candles from the sconces above, and alone I could hear odd echoes from the life going on in the kitchens over my head. The boy returned and, with our hands cradling the wax-fuelled flames, we trod the passage accompanied by flickering shadows. To our left came a door and I fumbled with keys, dropping them on the flagstones with a clang. After finally getting the right key in the large lock, the door opened with only the merest hint of a groan. I now found myself in a low, barrel-vaulted room that stretched further than our candles could penetrate but, three or four feet inside, the way forward was stopped by heavy iron bars.

It was the servant who pointed out the grill that gave us entry into the store. As we got past, first through piles of barrels that I hoped were not gunpowder, we could see recesses filled with rolled tapestries, chairs, candle-stands and the like. A number of chests also stood by. I lifted a couple of lids, and found one was filled with pewter and the next with silver that brightly reflected our candlelight despite its tarnish. These were Kendall's goods, I knew.

It took some time to locate the items I was looking for, for it had been placed behind some high-backed chairs and two heavily carved doors and, by the time I carried them triumphantly out of the cellar, I had broken into a sweat from the effort I'd expended.

Lady Katherine, looking as graceful as ever, had joined Sir Ralph. She sat by the window with an embroidery whilst her husband had closed his eyes and dozed.

'Doctor.' She smiled. 'You are dusty and worn. But there is a look of achievement in your eye, I believe. Do you find something useful in our cellars?"

'My lady.' I gave the briefest bow. 'I must admit that I scarce know what I've found as yet. It could either solve a problem or create a larger one, but it is something that I must show your husband.'

She rose and touched Sir Ralph's arm. He started up, blinking his eyes, looked about him and then swore he'd not been asleep but just resting his eyes. How often have I done and said the same thing.

"Right, Doctor. Show me what you're about.'

Under each arm I carried a roll of canvas. As I placed them on the table, they both shed dust, flecks of colour and two or three spiders that I quickly brushed onto the floor. I unrolled the first, clumsily holding it down with both hands. It was an image that I'd last seen in an ornate frame on a wall in Waddow Hall. It had been cut from its frame and also sported a number of tears and slashes across it. It had been a portrait, and its subject was still readily identifiable, even though the face had been defiled. Sir Christopher Kendall, my arch enemy, last seen in the aftermath of the Battle of Read Bridge as he badly wounded me, would have gazed up at us if his eyes had not been cut out of the picture.

Sir Ralph and his Lady both looked at me with their eyebrows raised yet said nothing. I could sense that they were questioning my sanity. Why would I spend time and effort to recover a damaged image of my nemesis? As I lifted my hands and reached for the other canvas, Kendall disappeared, rolled up as I'd found him. I held the second canvas for a moment before placing it before us. My exposure of Kendall's picture first was quite deliberate. It certainly gained their full attention.

'Two portraits were removed from Waddow when we brought away Kendall's other goods and chattels.' I said, trying to keep any element of triumph from my voice, 'But though his portrait had been damaged, that of his wife was not.' I unrolled the next canvas, revealing a lady in a yellow dress, decorated with small flowers and green ribbons. Her shoulders were covered by white lace that reached up to her neck. Her hair was light auburn held back from her face, with a short fringe of curls high on her forehead. It was a lovely image, I have to say, and it had rested in my memory since I first saw it.

Sir Ralph looked up and stared at me. I knew what he was thinking. We'd seen that dress earlier that day. But the person wearing it today was not the person shown in the portrait.

Twenty Two

'I'll Take my Boot to Them'

'Hell and death, Doctor. What is going on?'

We continued to stare at the portrait. Placed next to that of Kendall in Waddow Hall, it had purported to be that of his wife but, if so, who was the woman that Aspinall seemed to be supporting as the rightful owner of both Waddow and the goods held in the cellar below? Both this and the damaged Kendall image were painted by the same hand, that was certain, for the background was identical in both instances. I knew Kendall's had been a very good likeness and could therefore assume that this was also a good image of the sitter. Kendall was of modest stature, no more than 5 feet 3 inches I would say, and this lady looked no taller. The "Harpy", as I had named her, that accosted us at Standen was as tall as Sir Ralph, close to 6 feet; her skin was coarser and darker than that of the portrait; her hair was darker also.

'We can be assured that we are being misled in some way, Sir Ralph, but at present we cannot know which is the real Lady Kendall, though we might believe Aspinall's woman is an imposter.' I ventured.

Lady Katherine spoke up. 'Perhaps the portrait is of a first or previous wife and that Kendall re-married. Surely that is not beyond reason?' We could both see the logic in that.

I hesitated. It is said that the naming of the Devil brings him into existence. I'd taken this to be figurative only: If you talk about the Devil, then you believe he exists, therefore he is real. I do not believe in the Devil, only in evil persons.

'I noted something else today, though I may be reading more into it than is really there,' I said. 'You noted that the woman was not in mourning for her husband, Sir Ralph, but, more than that, when you gave her your condolences, her eyes flickered. It was as though she didn't know what you meant.' I paused. 'Kendall's body wasn't discovered after the battle. You don't think he is still alive?'

'I cannot believe that is so, Doctor. You know I spoke to the man who saved your life, the one who shot Kendall? He said Kendall was so close that he was hit full on. Nobody could have survived that. No, let us not divert ourselves down that path. What you saw may have been nothing. You could have been mistaken.'

I hoped to God he was right.

It was now more important than ever to speak to the man Perkins, who might be able to help us understand this latest turn of events. If Will, who had met the man and persuaded him to speak to us, had been to hand we could have sent him to arrange an early meeting. Will, however, was out with the men trying to discover Cas.

Sir Ralph decided, with my full agreement, that with the dark of the moon now just a day away, we couldn't let ourselves be diverted from trying to catch the hated Tench, should he be around. If we got past the dark of the moon without sight of him, then we could return to the problem of Lady Kendall.

There being nothing more I could do for the present, I returned to the cottage and tried to interest myself in trying to replicate some notes lost in the burning of my Clitheroe study, or workshop, now many months ago. At that time, I'd been working on a treatise regarding metals, including their discovery, history, and utility, together with the prospect of finding more. It was no good. I couldn't concentrate. Slater was at her stocking frame, having added more spinach, and sorrel to her seemingly perennial pottage and, in addition to the heat from the hearth, the warmth of the day had me drowsy.

At some point Nate must have returned from the search for Cas as he was there when I opened my eyes. The sun was now much lower in the sky, and I guessed that it was near evening. 'No sign yet then, Nate?' I asked.

'No, sir. Pod said he'd stay with the searchers until they got back here.' He said. 'There was excitement when something ran through the woods, but it was just a deer. We went up the Ing beck, then down, and they are now in a line, beating the woods back towards Twiston. I thought I should report back and then set to watch the derelict place until the men got back.'

'And I suppose the thought of food was an encouragement?'

He gave a sheepish grin.

Another hour passed and the sun had dropped below the treetops when I heard a commotion over towards the Hall. Nate appeared at the door. 'Pod's found him, sir. He's holding on to Cas as the men are taunting and frightening him. Will you come?' I was out of my chair in an instant, and not waiting to put on my hat, rushed off towards the noise.

Pod was shielding a cowering Cas, hiding as best he could behind one of the pillars of the Hall's portico, and holding out a stick in lieu of a sword, trying to hold back the men who were taunting the Blackamoor. Before I could shout them to stop, Will emerged from the Hall and set about two of the idiots with the flat of his sword. 'Bugger off, you arsewipes,' he shouted, 'and come to order by the gates!' He saw me.

'Sorry Doctor, I left them to report to Sir Ralph.'

'Aye, sort them out will you Will, or I'll take my boot to them.' I needn't tell you that I was again angry. This was just what I didn't want to happen. If we were to get anything out of Cas, we must make him feel safe and protected, and not like a trapped and baited beast. I smiled at Pod, gave him 'Good lad, none better' then turned to Cas. He looked utterly dejected, dirty, thin with worry, and with tears running down his cheeks. I felt sorry now for my previous aversion to him.

'Come, Cas. Let's take you home.' I said as gently as I could and, putting my arm around him and with Pod at his other side, we walked him slowly back to our cottage.

'Goodwife Slater,' I said as heartily as I could, 'Look. We've found our Cas! Let him sit by us and bring him a bowl and bread.' Even she smiled at him encouragingly. Quietly, I said to her 'Make him a bed here tonight and the boys should sleep in here also. We must make him feel safe. He needs a wash.' She nodded. I let her take charge as I now turned to Nate as he entered. 'Give my compliments to Sir Ralph and tell him we will keep our fugitive safe tonight and look to find out what he knows on the morrow.'

Twenty Three

An Understandable Antipathy

I DIDN'T TURN TO MY BED THAT NIGHT BUT SAT IN MY CHAIR AS the boys bedded down by me. It was hardly comfortable, but I did manage a few hours of sleep until early dawn bid me rise. The cock crowed, answered by another in the distance. Pod rose first, instantly awake, and gave me a generous smile, then Nate, stretching and yawning and with bleary eyes. Cas was still fast asleep. No doubt he was exhausted and, though I was with child to interrogate him and find out what he knew, I thought it best to let him lie as long as possible.

Slater roused the fire, the new logs so dry that they cracked and sparked furiously, then sent Pod off to see what bounty the hens would allow us whilst Nate looked to the cow. It seemed a day like any other.

A knock at the door. Will looked in and beckoned me out. The early morning chill made me pull my cloak tightly round me. 'What's up, Will?'

'Grent's been up. His men caught some of Tench's brigands at Nolland's farm over by Bashall. Bit of a battle. Four enemy dead, two ran. No dead or injured on our side.' He took a breath. 'No Tench. He weren't with 'em.' That was disappointing.

'He's sure? Was Grent with his men?'

'No, he wasn't there but his men know Tench well enough. The bastard wasn't there.'

Mid-morning and Cas slept on. The boys let the horses out for exercise and brushed out the barn. The sun was already well above the tree line, giving us another warm day. Will came from Sir Ralph, eager to hear of information from Cas. 'I will let him sleep on till mid-day,' I said. Will looked at me askance.

'Yes, I know it's the dark of the Moon tonight, Will, but he has been mentally wounded, I suspect. We will do better from him if he is fully rested. It's good,' I said, "that he can sleep so sound now, for he must feel safe in our care.'

He was still asleep as mid-day came and went and, finally, I felt we could wait no longer. Slater woke him and, as he came to, passed over a bowl of milk that he drank voraciously. "Give him more if he wants it,' I said. He took two more and a hunk of bread before settling with his back against the wall. As gently as I could I suggested that further sleep would be a fine thing after his ordeal, but it would be both a great help to us and help to ensure his safety if he would speak to me first. He nodded. I thought it best to start at the beginning.

'Do you feel safe with us now, Cas?' I first asked. Another nod but I could see he was on the verge of tears. 'When you first came here, you told Goodwife Slater that you were the brother of Sam. Do you remember?' His breath quickened and his eyes widened a little, but he gave another nod.

'Did you know who Sam was?' A shake of the head now. 'He was like you and very dear to us.' I turned to Slater who was stood just by me with her arms folded across her bosom. 'We loved Sam, didn't we?'

'Oh yes, sir, we truly did.'

Turning back to Cas, I asked who had told him to say he was Sam's brother and he started to shake. I pulled a stool to the table. 'Don't worry. We didn't trust you at first because we didn't understand you, but we now know you are not bad. Come and sit by me and let us be friends.'

As he did so, Slater put a stool next to him and sat with her arm round him. 'He's still shaking, Doctor' she said, but I could see that with my own eyes. "We do want you to stay with us as part of our… family,' I said and Slater confirmed this with 'Oh yes, indeed we do.' and hugged him even closer.

He had yet to speak but this brought more tears that caused Slater to wipe her sleeve across his eyes. I asked my question again.

'Big man.' It came out like a whisper.

'And he brought you here?'

'Yis.'

'From where, Cas?'

He looked confused. 'Not know.'

'Was it near or far? A day's ride?'

'Two and more.'

'And you had a Master before you were brought here?'

'Yis.'

'So, the man who brought you here, the big man, was he called Tench?' He nodded vigorously. 'And the master you served, what was his name?'

'Not remember, sir. Have two masters. Both with King. One master then two.'

That confused me a little, but I thought best to leave that to one side. And asked: 'So Tench brought you here and told you to say you were Sam's brother and to stay with us?'

'Yis.'

'And what did he tell you about us?'

'That you were bad, sir. That you very bad. With Devil!' His eyes were wide.

'Do you believe that I am bad?'

'No. No. I see you good but I must do what he say.'

'You don't believe I'm bad? That Mistress Slater is bad? That Nate and Pod are bad?' He shook his head at each question. 'But he told you what to do or..?'

'He hurt me.' He stood, peeled off his shirt and showed his back. That caused me to sit up sharply, for there were signs of old bruising and substantial patches where the skin looked as if it had been burnt. Slater too looked shocked.

'He did all this?'

'More, sir.' He moved to take off his breeches, but I stopped him. I didn't really want to see more. 'And said more still if I did not help him.'

'What did he want to know about me?' I queried.

'Where you were. I said ill, ill, ill, then he say it not matter. What was in house.'

'What, this house?'

'No. Master's house.' And he pointed in the rough direction of the Hall.

'What did he want there?'

'To get in. Draw house in dust for get in.'

'I don't understand. Where was this?' Then it came to me. 'Did you meet him in the old cottage up the road?'

'Yes. And he make like this." He leapt up, grabbed a piece of kindling from the fireside and began to make marks on the floor.

'He drew a plan for you on the floor of the cottage?' I was now getting excited. 'Mistress Slater found you by a door into the bottom of the Hall. You were trying to open that door? He told you to open it?' He started to shake again as fright took hold of him once more. 'Don't worry.' I took his arm and looked him square in the eyes. 'You are not in trouble, I promise you. I want to do everything I can to keep you and us safe, and the best way to do that is for you to tell us everything.'

Beyond Cas I saw Will approaching the doorway. I gave him the briefest shake of the head, he waved in acknowledgement and turned back around. I expect Sir Ralph had sent him to find out what was going on, but I wasn't going to disrupt my questioning at this point. I turned back to Cas.

The sun was still high when I walked over to the Hall. I'd called Nate and Pod into the cottage, told them to stay close and not venture out beyond the estate walls. I left my sword on the table with a meaningful look at Nate, though I didn't expect anything to happen until after sunset.

Will was leaning against the portico. I asked him how many men he could muster and how quickly. 'More than twenty and in minutes only,' he said with his usual grin.

'That quickly?' I was surprised.

'Well,' he answered, 'I have a system. I tell the two nearest, they each tell the next two. And they have to keep a pike or billhook close to hand wherever they may be. Shall I give 'em a call?'

'Good lad!' I was impressed. 'Don't call them yet though. When did you put that in place?'

'This pretty face conceals a lot, Doctor. You saw how easily I picked up surgery when we were at Preston…'

'Aye, and I saw how green you turned at the sight of blood.'

'Just a lack of ale, that was. I could now even set myself up as a Colonel, having digested all of that book, *Exercise of the Militia*, that Sir Ralph lent me.'

'I've seen it. Did that include your system?'

'No. That was my own idea.'

'Well done. Very well done.' I really was very impressed, though as much by his boasting as anything. 'Just stand by for orders.'

'Yes, Captain.'

I gave him my most sarcastic look as I entered the Hall.

'So, Cas was brought here by Tench, and you think this was with the intention to do you harm but is now something else?'

'That's right, Sir Ralph. I am to blame in not attending to Cas. I knew something was wrong but failed to sort it out. My antipathy to the lad…'

'… Was entirely understandable. Don't beat yourself over it.'

'If it had been me, I would have fled as far as ever I could. I wouldn't have stayed in the area as Cas has done.'

'But where could he run to? He's hardly un-noticeable, is he?' Sir Ralph paused. 'Let's concentrate on tonight. Do you think we can have the situation under control?'

I hesitated. 'I am not sure at all. Tench seems to know the layout of your Hall. We don't know how, and neither do we know how many might attack.'

'Yes,' said Sir Ralph, 'How does he know about the Hall? Has he a spy in our midst? I'm sure I trust all my men...'

'I believe the most pressing element is that Cas said things were being stored at the Greenside cottage, but he didn't know what.'

'Arms, I expect.' He looked thoughtful. ' Do you think that he might make a full attack on us?'

'I wouldn't preclude it sir.' He drummed his fingers on the table for several seconds.

'I think we must proceed on that basis. Now, If Tench's band have muskets, they wouldn't want to risk being seen coming this way already armed. It's a simple matter. We'll just go and demolish the cottage, find whatever it is and...'

'Sir, I'm sorry to interrupt you but if we do that, Tench and his men might just fade into the scenery. If we even approach Greenside at this moment...' I paused. 'We might not get a better chance to capture or destroy him than tonight.'

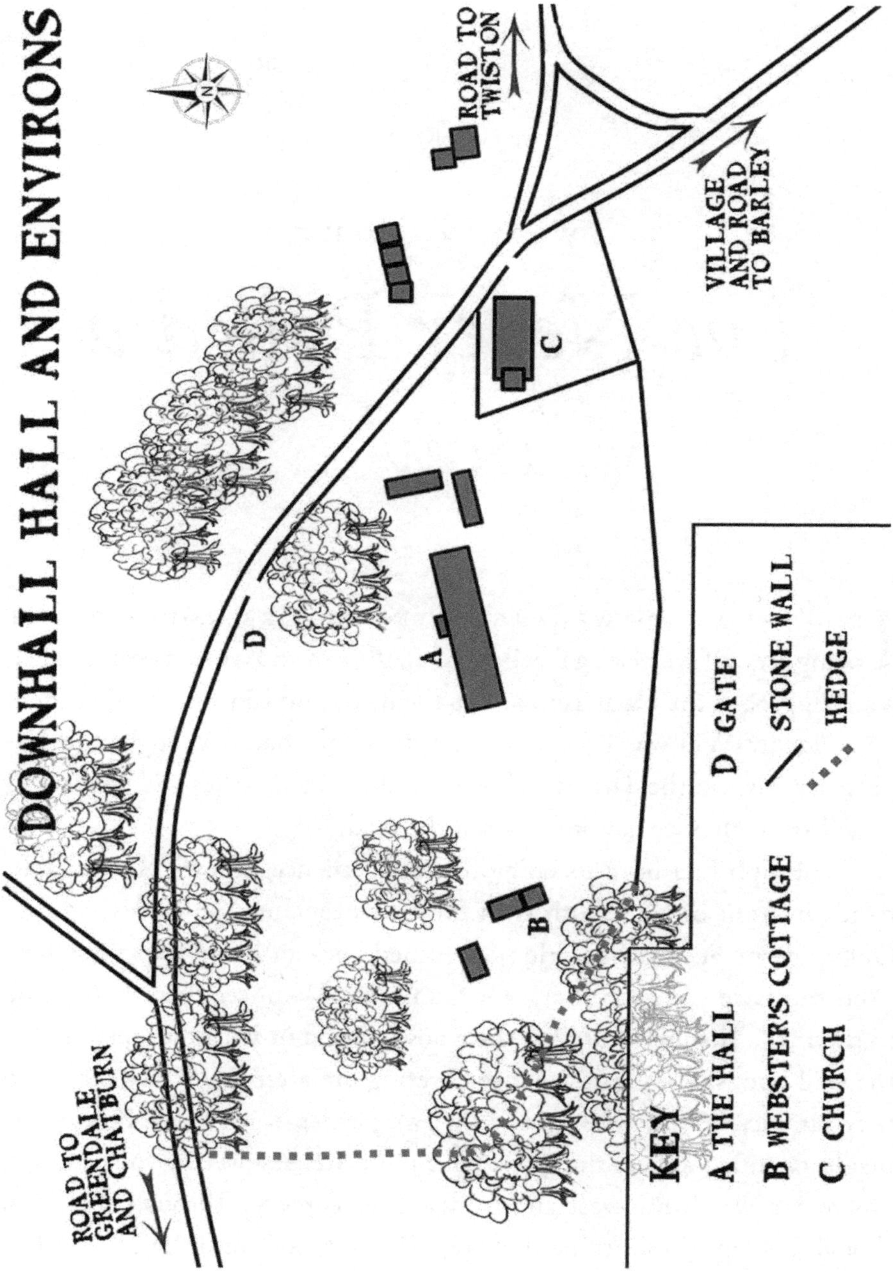
DOWNHALL HALL AND ENVIRONS
ROAD TO TWISTON
VILLAGE AND ROAD TO BARLEY
ROAD TO GREENDALE AND CHATBURN
D
A
B
C
KEY
A THE HALL
B WEBSTER'S COTTAGE
C CHURCH
D GATE
STONE WALL
HEDGE

Twenty Four

'I've Never Pulled a Bow'

'I DON'T KNOW HOW WE CAN GET MEN UP TO GREENSIDE WITHOUT being seen! If we place a few behind a wall, how do we know that Tench won't approach the place from across the fields and come up behind them by accident?' Will was incensed and rightly so. I hadn't thought this out properly. 'Also, in the dark, the glow from the slow matches will be seen, so they'll know that we have muskets at the ready.'

Sir Ralph had been listening to this in silence, elbows on the table, hands in front of his mouth with fingertips touching, still insisting that Greenside be approached. He now leaned back in his chair and sighed. "You can have your way, Sergeant Cummins. We meet them here, close to the Hall. The men still have their bows. Put four with muskets behind the wall opposite my gates to give covering fire after any attack starts, so they can pick off any who try to run. Two parties of four with bows to be inside, on either side of the gates. Four more archers over by your cottage, Doctor, to watch the west and in case they come up through the trees, though I doubt they'll come that way. The rest close into the Hall. All to have swords. Pikes are likely to get in the way, but lay them close to hand, just in case.'

Will was unsure. 'We might end up shooting across at each other.'

'Then ensure that none of our parties are directly across from each other. Can we obstruct that part of the arc of fire where our men are? And can we give each party some cover?'

"I can try,' sighed Will, 'I just wish we'd more time to prepare.'

Sir Ralph shrugged his shoulders. "We must make the best of the time and resources that we have. Total silence until the blackguards are within our grasp. Password is *Downham*. White ribbons on right arms, but not until the last minute. Bring the men in through the kitchen garden singly, not as a whole.' He looked at Will. 'You bring them in, but don't use your calling system, and make it quiet and relaxed.'

I cleared my throat. 'In the meantime, shall I put Nate on the Church tower? He can view the area and may see some movement before full dark?' I also wanted to keep him out of the way.

'Good idea, Doctor.'

'What about Master Towneley?' I asked.

'We must certainly keep him out of harm's way. What about the church tower with young Nate?' I nodded.

'In addition, perhaps everyone should eat, sir?'

I wasn't there as Sir Ralph spoke to the men. I went back to tell Slater and Pod what I expected of them, which was simply to keep out of sight and safe behind a locked door with Cas. Nate was to stay up on the Church tower with Richard and only come down if he saw anything before night fell. Otherwise he was to stay up there till morning, unless I called him down. I wanted no heroics.

I brought a musket back with me from the Hall, loaded it with a ball as I'd seen done, and left it by the door. I kept a piece of slow-match by the fire. I picked out a book and tried to read, but it was no good. Taking a smooth stone I sat sharpening my sword, slow strokes along the blade, but still the sun refused to go down.

Will brought two of his lads over and I suggested that, instead of putting them behind our cottage, they might as well come and sit with us. Though I'd seen them in church, I didn't really know them as they were from outlying farms, and they were concerned that their homes were left undefended. 'The attack will be on us, lads,' I explained, 'I'm sure your places will be safe. It's the Hall they're after.' They were still unsure.

The second two fellows arrived, one being Tom, uncle of one of the boys who died at Heptonstall. They propped their bows by the door, put maybe twenty arrows on the table and Slater brought ale for our party. The bows still looked fearsome weapons and, though muskets had replaced some in the general line of battle, I had heard that our archers were still a force to be reckoned with.

At one time it had been law that every able man should have a longbow and practice each week. That was not now the case, but the weapons were still used for hunting from time to time. Tom picked up one bow that was much shorter than the rest. 'Still playing wi' a child's bow, are you, Rich?'

'Ah can still stop a buck at two hundred paces with it.' his friend said with a wink.

'Well, I wouldn't wager against thee.'

'Tom,' I said. 'I've never pulled a bow. Come, show me.'

'It'd play havoc on thy fingers after a few pulls, Doctor. You keep your hands for that fine sewing work that you do.' Then he looked horrified. 'I didn't mean women's work!'

I laughed heartily at that. 'I well know what you mean, Tom, but hope that I don't need to use that skill much tonight.'

'Amen to that, sir.' He looked at the string of another bow. 'I think I'll just change this for thee, John.' He deftly bent the bow, unhooked the old from its horns, took a length of linen cord from his jacket and quickly bent on the new. He gave it a few pulls. 'Aye, that'll do.'

I went over, picked it up and was surprised at its weight. Lifting it as if to fire, I pulled the string back as far as I could but couldn't get it even as far as my face. Tom grinned, took it off me and easily pulled the cord back as far as his ear. 'Take you a week or two to learn that. And it's not just strength. Stance is important as well.'

'I take your point.' I raised my hands in submission, 'I'll leave it to you.'

The man Rich was trying to raise a smile from Slater with silly grins and failing, whilst John was running his fingers along the feathered flights of the arrows. Pod and Cas had long since climbed the ladder into the loft. We all fell into silence. I went out and round the side of the cottage, the sun was now below the horizon, leaving a pinkish tinge in the West. I returned to the men. 'I think you should get into position now, with as little fuss as possible. Go to the end of the cottage and barn. Lie down as long as possible, but one of you try and keep a watch westward through the hedge behind you. I don't want you surprised from that direction.' They rose quietly.

'Remember: No talking. Tie those white rags round your right arm when you get in place. Only shoot if you are sure of your target and not towards our men that are set twenty feet on either side of the gate. Look for them now, as they should have some cut brushwood to hide them. If you hear the cry *Downham,* then you sing out as well and we are out and fighting. God protect you.'

Splitting the arrows between them and picking up their bows, they moved to the door, but I noticed something missing. 'Where are your blades?'

'Which Will was to bring them.' Said Tom.

Twenty Five

'Not One of Ours'

IN THE TWILIGHT IT WAS EASY TO PICK MY WAY ACROSS TO THE bulk of the Hall. Full night was on its way but, even with no moon, I swear I could have read under the starlight had I brought a book with me. As I reached Will, Nate appeared beside me.

'I told you to stay atop the tower.' I hissed at him furiously,

'Yes sir, but I've seen some movement to the Northward,' he said urgently. 'It's difficult to see through the trees, but I'm sure there's two or three gone over towards Greenside.'

'You can see so far?'

'Aye, sir.'

'Right. Sorry Nate. Get back to your perch now though, will you. Is Master Richard all right?' He nodded and ran off round the side of the Hall.

Will sent one of his men, crouching low, across towards the gate to give warning to the men there. I grabbed some blades and, cradling them in my arms, loped off back to our cottage. Tripping over a stray stone, I fell, the swords clattering as I hit the ground. Beginning to rise, I saw three bodies come from the hedge. 'No, no. Get back.' I hissed as loudly as I dare, 'Not yet, not yet!' Fools, I thought, who can't follow simple instructions, but then they started to run towards me. Two stopped and dropped to the ground and it was only as the third was within a dozen paces of me that I realized these were not our men.

Still on my knees, I scrabbled for one of the blades as he came on with sword raised and, before I could do anything, he fell on me. I collapsed backwards under his full weight and I could taste blood. The wind had been knocked out of me and I struggled to take a breath, fighting for air.

I was on the edge of consciousness, I believe, when the weight was lifted off me and I was dragged, literally dragged back across the field, with two men holding me, one under each arm. As I was dumped down without ceremony, I heard a muffled voice. 'He's all right. Just leave him here.' I had just realised that it was Tom's voice when there was a flash of light with an almost instantaneous bang, like a cannon shot, as the gates to the Hall were blown in. I gulped in a lung-full of air, rolled over and rose on my elbows. Two bodies lay face down a few yards away, arrows sticking straight and true from their backs.

There was no shouting and no sign of assailants, but I heard three musket shots, the sound echoing between the stone walls.

As I tried to regain my feet, I saw movement to my left. More men were pushing through the hedge much closer to the hall. I shouted '*Downham, Downham, Downham*' over and over, pointing at these new intruders. Will must have seen me because he repeated the cry and strode straight and steady directly towards them, holding a pistol in front of him. Tom and his men came out from behind my cottage, their bows at the ready, but dared not fire as Will was now in their line of fire. His pistol cracked, and one man fell with a cry. Tossing the pistol aside, he drew his sword and stood ready to take their charge. It was the bravest thing.

I looked from side to side and, spotting a blade close by, made a dive for it. As I bent down, I heard a whoosh as several arrows flashed out of the night and into our attackers, our men having opened the angle 'twixt Will and the enemy, who now had had enough. I think I might have glimpsed Tench among them as they retreated with speed, but I couldn't be sure.

Will was shouting, gathering our men, and quickly dividing them into a chasing party with some to stay and guard the Hall. Despite my injunction, I found Nate at my side once again. I cuffed him round the head for his disobedience. He barely flinched. 'I couldn't see them for the trees. I don't know which way they went..."

I banged on the locked door of my cottage. I could hear the scraping of the table across the stone floor and shouted 'Slater dear. It's me, we're all in one piece I think.' In reality I hadn't waited to see who was injured or dead, being more concerned to see that she and the boys were safe. The lock clicked, the door swung open, seemingly by itself, and there was my housekeeper pointing the musket straight at me.

'Hell's teeth, woman, put it down!' I cried, ducking by instinct. Loaded guns have that effect on me, I have to say. Then I noticed that there was no match-cord in the serpent. I took a step forward and took it out of her hands. 'If I didn't think that you'd end up by turning it on me, I'd show you how the instrument works.' Instead of the musket ball, she shot me one of her withering glances.

'Why do you always make jokes at the wrong time? Here am I near defenceless and trying to protect these boys from death and disaster and… and murder and killing and maiming…'

"You've done well. You've done well, and I think we are safe again, Joan. Now let me get my bag as I must check that everyone else is in one piece.' I picked up the tools of my trade and told her to lock the door again behind me just in case, and that I'd give four raps on the door when I returned, so she could be sure it was me. I could see Pod and Cas peering down from the loft. 'Back to sleep for you two,' I barked.

'Back to sleep, says you? Which they've not closed their eyes once this night…'

Even the shadows cast by starlight seemed sinister as I walked across the open ground. I kept my head low as I realised I'd forgotten to mark my arm with a ribbon. Glancing at the bodies, I could tell they were dead without examination, and though I had an itch to investigate the damage done by one of our arrows, I continued past. Sir Ralph limped towards me, leaning heavily on his stick.

'Well met, Doctor. I don't think we've sustained more than a scratch, excepting of course for my gates. There's at least one more body in the lane.' He looked over my shoulder and grimaced. 'I may have spoken out of turn, for here's one injured.'

Through the hedge came two men supporting a third between them, but as they came closer it became clear that the injured man, dragging a leg, was not of our band. 'Live one for you here, Doctor, I believe.'

Sweating and only half conscious, the wounded brigand was laid on the stable floor. He'd been found hiding behind a tree as Will's men chased after the felons. Lady Katherine, coming in to check he wasn't one of ours, quickly left me to it, and I slit and ripped his breeches around where the remains of an arrow shaft stood proud. I could tell it was against the femur from the grating and vibration as I pushed it through and out the other side. It had probably scored the bone but had not broken it. Possibly it had cut a chip from it and, if so, that might give the man further pain, but as to that, I couldn't care. Nate put a bandage round the wound, the fellow was fettered and chained to the wall, and I left.

Twenty Six

Undeserving of a Christian Burial

I WAS DEAD BEAT AND WOKE LATE. THE SUN WAS ALREADY OVER the treetops as I rose, another fair day. Slater was scrubbing the floor but rose to prepare me a posset. 'Well done on your defence last night, lass,' I said, in what I thought was a winning style.

'Don't you poke fun at me,' she cried, 'You're always poking fun at me and me doing my best to save those poor lads from those Devils whilst you put my Nate in danger which I'll not forget...'

'Dear Slater, laughing at you was the last thing on my mind. I mean it. I admire your courage.' I declaimed. 'And, I assure you, Nate was only in danger from disobeying my orders to stay on the Church tower. Yet he came down just to impart information that he thought important.' She set a bowl down before me and sniffed in that way she has.

Will was surveying damage to the hedge with Sir Ralph as I left the cottage. I was eager for news of the chase and to confirm that we had no men injured.

'We tracked them as far as we could but lost them in the woods,' said Will, still looking fresh as a daisy though he could scarce have had a wink of sleep. 'All ours well, six o'theirs dead and one injured.'

'We got six!' I exclaimed. 'Of how many?'

'Couldn't truly say. Mebbe a dozen or so.'

Sir Ralph spoke up. 'It was lucky you saw them come through the hedge, Doctor. I placed those men by your cottage as I thought an attack might come from that side. It seems the attack on my gates was just a diversion.'

'Aye,' said Will, 'Gunpowder did for the gates. They must have hidden a barrel at Greenside. You should raze the cottage, Sir Ralph, then it can be of no further use.' The Knight seemed unsure.

'I'll put a claim on it as abandoned, but let's keep to the Rule of Law as best we can.' A wry smile crossed his face. 'We might seem to be falling towards anarchy, but I'd like to keep our legal standards intact as best I can.'

We crossed first to the gateway, where two men were already loading the debris of the night onto a cart. 'We can put hurdles across until new gates are built. I want four men on guard here at all times for the present. At least two muskets here every night, Will. That'll be a cost in slow-match, but it can't be helped. I doubt there'll be a further attack tonight though we must be vigilant. With luck such extra precaution won't be for long.'

Sitting now in the cool of the Hall, we went over the events of the night once again. The second attack through the hedge had been almost at the nearest point to the west end of the Hall as could be made. 'I think that tallies with what Cas had told Tench,' I said, 'He was made to show him where the outer door to the cellars was. He drew it in dust on the floor at Greenside.'

'I'll have that doorway bricked up,' said Sir Ralph, 'It's of little use anyway.' He paused. 'There are two things that occur to me. Firstly, that the blast at the gates could have been much worse. It appears to me that the powder might have been rather decayed, either damp or needing regrinding perhaps. A prime barrel could have taken part of the wall with it. Secondly, though we anticipated a secondary attack from the west, we didn't foresee two separate parties entering that way. I thank the Lord that they didn't come through at the same time. If they had done… But let's not dwell on that.' We let this sink in.

'Perhaps Tench didn't train them properly' mused Will. 'or they can't follow instructions.'

'If Grent's report was correct, he might already be short of men. Four dead reported at Bashall, and now six and one captured here. That's eleven down now. He's probably no more than six or seven left.'

'Still makes him dangerous, Doctor.'

I took a drink of ale. 'What of the dead? Can we identify them? Do I need to examine them, Sir Ralph?'

'They are now of no consequence, Doctor. They don't deserve, and neither will they get a Christian burial. Tench is not amongst them, that is both certain and unfortunate but…' We mused over this unpleasant fact. Somewhat later, I did take Cas to see the bodies, in the hope that he might recognise them, but he did not.

'The archers were a great stroke,' I continued. 'I didn't know we had such adepts at that ancient art.'

'Yes. They can do some damage. As my deer can attest, incidentally. Tom and his like know that I will turn my eye from their occasional poaching, provided they keep within bounds and do not let it be brought to my notice officially,' he said. 'Their skill has its uses as you see. My son still keeps a company of archers with his force. I'll best not tell him of Tom, or he'll be sequestered.' We smiled.

'Sir, let us get news to Grent, immediately,' interposed Will. 'His men may now join us to track Tench.' I nodded in agreement.

'Yes, but first, Doctor, you may do us further service. Call the men together by the gateway Will, and let the good Webster give us a prayer for our present salvation from evil.'

I didn't choose to join in the interrogation of our prisoner. He was given a choice: The gallows or turn evidence against Tench. He chose the latter but, in reality, could give little of use. Our enemy's band had been a dozen strong, which confirmed our supposition that it now stood at less than half that number. They had first taken a farmstead over in the Riding beyond the Ribble, bound in by forest. From there they rode out to extract rent, food and the like from Kendall's holdings and the Grammar School's lands. They only moved before sun-up and returned by mid-morning. Tench didn't always accompany them on their forays, but his Quartermaster, one of the dead at Bashall, was given instruction. Not to comply was likely to have meant death.

A week ago, the band had been told to move to the woods on the edge of the wild moor above the hamlet of Pendleton. There they were schooled ready for the attack. When the gunpowder had been left at Greenside he didn't know, but he did know that Tench was furious that an informer within Downham had failed him. Was that informer Cas or someone else? He didn't know.

Will prepared a band of ten to ride the two miles to Pendleton and see if any trace of the brigands remained but, just before they set out, Sir Ralph called to him. 'If you find Tench, do not endanger your party unless you can be reasonably certain of success, Will.' He handed over a sealed paper. 'Before you return, please to deliver this note to Aspinall, for Standen is close to your search. I have told him that we've been attacked *by Royalist forces*. I don't wish to disclose too much to him. I've told him that Lady Kendall's goods must therefore stay with me for the present as otherwise they may fall into the King's hands, which I cannot allow.' He hesitated. "Tell him, should he ask, that we had no loss but that the action has inflamed my leg and I am confined to bed, would you?'

That last was a good move. Such a weak and easily frightened soul as Aspinall would probably be scared half to death at the idea of troops marauding through the district. It would delay any move by the woman purporting to be Kendall's wife to obtain the goods stored in the cellar, which would give us further time to investigate her claim. In addition, it might make Sir Ralph seem at a disadvantage that in truth did not exist, and that might be to our advantage.

Twenty Seven

Loss of a Barrel

THE VILLAGE WAS STILL IN UPROAR, IT BEING IMPOSSIBLE FOR anyone to have missed the noise of the attack. Rumour abounded. Lady Katherine walked through the village radiating calm, but the consensus was that doors and windows should now be barred each night 'just in case'.

St Michael's Day was upon us, and a further concern was whether that celebration, as greedily looked forward to as Harvest Festival, would go ahead. The villagers need not have worried. Sir Ralph would not disappoint them, all were welcome to the Hall though he did say that all able-bodied men must carry their arms with them in case of trouble and that there would be a parade down through the village so that the men, with blazing torches, could see everyone home safely.

Though Cas still showed signs of nerves at any sudden noise or movement, I could see that the knowledge that we had beaten off Tench's men with no loss to ourselves was something of a comfort. I told him and Pod that they may go with the parade if they wished, but Cas shook his head and Pod said he would therefore forgo the pleasure also.

The boys left to clean out my cattle and let them out into the field. It was interesting to see how Cas, age unknown but likely to be fourteen or even fifteen years, was happy to be directed in all things by little Pod. Nothing but good could come of that, I thought.

Not long after noon we went to Church, where I gave prayers and a benediction on the village, Sir Ralph and his Lady, and for our salvation from the attack. Richard Towneley processed with the Asshetons but, immediately before that, when we entered as a household, there was some murmuring at the sight of Cas. I ignored it and Slater put an arm around his shoulder, shepherding him into the seats behind the Assheton family box. Later everyone ate their fill, played games and, unusually, drank modestly of the beer supplied. As the sun went down Sir Ralph gave his thanks to all for the work done, Nate went off to join the parade whilst the rest of us returned to the cottage, the boys to sit in the corner where Pod taught knucklebones to Cas, and I sitting companionably with Slater behind a locked and bolted door. I saw no reason to take chances.

The next day again dawned bright and fair with nothing new having happened – or so I thought. None of us had taken to bed, Slater and I dozing on chairs, the boys sleeping where they were, but birdsong stirred me, and I sat out on the bench by the door.

I ran my hand across my face, noting that I hadn't shaved for a week or so. I've never been one to keep a beard, having been in Holy Orders until thrown out by an idiot of a Bishop. Would you believe that being now nominated as a surgeon for our army, I've sometimes had people asking me to shave them? Not that I would, as I class myself more in the physician category. I thought about fetching my knife, my *scallpellus* as the Roman Celsus called it, but I simply couldn't be bothered. I dozed off again where I sat.

Still dozing when Slater nudged me awake with a bowl of warm milk, I felt as relaxed as I had done for some days. Some of the workers, looking bleary eyed, filed past to complete work on the hedge and gave me a good day. The boys went off to the barn, Cas almost giving me a smile as he passed. I was sure now that I'd got the lad all wrong.

By mid-morning I thought to bestir myself. If Will was free, I would have a look at Greenside.

'Not on our own, Doctor,' said Will. 'Let me see if I can get another two to go up with us. And we go armed.'

'Surely that's a bit much, Will?'

'Let's just be safe. I don't want to be scrubbing round in the dust and somebody come at me without warning.'

Four of us walked the quarter mile on the now leaf-strewn road to where the cottage lay under a warm sun. Will drew his sword as he and I entered the garden, leaving John and Adam on guard outside. Nothing had changed inside, no sign that anyone had been there since I last looked in, but there had been activity round the rear of the property.

'Look here, Doctor.' Will pointed to where we'd last seen a pile of stones. They were scattered wide and the undergrowth around them had all been flattened. 'I think we were luckier than we thought. That's where the gunpowder was hidden, but it wasn't just one barrel.' I peered into what was now a shallow hole. The staves of a barrel were scattered about and the black of powder coloured one side of the depression. 'They had two barrels but one fell apart or perhaps was crushed by the stones placed on it.'

'Lucky for us, as you say, but it's unusual for a barrel to collapse like that, isn't it?'

'Well, yes, but I'm not complaining, are you?'

'No, not at all,' I said, 'but let me just work through this. Tench sends a few men to disinter these barrels and move them down to our gate. We don't know when they were put here.'

'No, we don't, but that doesn't really matter does it?'

'True, Will, but humour me. They find one damaged but can't tell Tench, because he's over beyond my cottage with most of his men for the main attack. So, they only took one barrel. But it still did a lot of damage, didn't it?

'Not really, Doctor. I'd have expected more. I know how they did it, though. They took the barrel down on a handcart, put it against the gate with the cart on its side behind it so as much force as possible would hit the gates. It's what I'd do.'

'So, the loss of a barrel made no difference.'

'Oh yes it did. Two barrels at full power would have knocked our wall down, possibly onto some of our men. And it might have taken down the wall opposite, where our fellows were hiding. We'd have rushed over and left the way open for Tench.'

I'm sure Will was right.

Twenty Eight

'An Untimely Death, I Believe'

After many months of questioning my faith, I was beginning to think that God was on my side after all. Despite the fiendish murder of my man Sam, despite all Kendall's doings, despite Tench and his attack, despite the very war itself, I was still alive and well. In my ministrations to the wounded, in support of the cause of Parliament against a duplicitous and intolerant King who wishes to turn us back to the Church of Rome, I felt sure I was doing God's will.

Despite my noises and complaints about Puritans, I'm sure you realise that I do share most of their tenets, though their belief in the Devil and demons is anathema to me. In that, they are as superstitious as King Charles and his father before him. If I believed like them, then I wonder if I could find the fortitude to battle the forces of evil as I do. I've said before that evil walks amongst us, as I can attest, but I don't believe that there is an opposite to God. Excepting perhaps the Bishop of Rome...

Back in my Kildwick days, I spent many nights in conversation with Roger Brearley when he came to teach in my Parish. He believed that the power of God's Spirit alone is sufficient to bring a person to salvation, that a true Christian who has the Spirit within them does not sin and *ergo*, is not bound by the laws contained in the Bible. I argued that, if a person was without sin, they automatically kept to the biblical laws and would be brought to God through them, but then I was and am in love with the Bible that the last King left us. Brearley and his Grindletonians said the book was so misused by the established Church that for most it had become useless. I would accept all that he said if I didn't believe that I wasn't such a sinner. I'd been mulling this over for the millionth time as we walked back from Greenside. Will was in front with the two others, chatting and laughing, as I dawdled along behind.

The cause of my main sin or, rather, sinful thoughts, was just leaving the Hall's gate as we returned. Lady Katherine, looking as lovely as ever and with her maid behind her, stopped and spoke to Will, who turned and pointed at me. I hurried forward. The blue of her eyes always un-nerved me.

'Doctor, I've been looking for you.'

'I'm here and at your service, my Lady. Is something amiss?' I said nervously.

'Only that there has been a death, and no-one will touch the body. I hope you will come and allay their fears.'

'The fever has reappeared? We are to be visited by the smallpox again?' My heart fluttered. The village had been free of disease for several years, avoiding the plague that had run through Clitheroe in the years before this war.

'No, no. It's the old superstition, I'm afraid,' she said, and I breathed a sigh of relief. 'Mistress Whittle's soul has left her and her neighbours, though not repeating the old tale that she was the Devil's creature, will not attend her body.' Katherine Assheton always speaks in a calm and measured fashion, ever the lady, but I could sense a touch of exasperation in her tone. We saw eye to eye on the question of witches.

It didn't surprise me that Whittle was dead. She was old and frail of body and well beyond the normal span of three score and ten. I was sad though, having only recently made her acquaintance and she having put me on the right track with Cas, helping me see that we had judged him wrongly. I was also intrigued with her senses, having been blind and yet seeing things others didn't. Her relationship to the Pendle Witches, and in particular to Tench, must have made life hard for her.

A few women were gathered near the gate to Whittle's hovel, chatting. They curtseyed to Lady Katherine as we passed through, past the oak bench by the door where I'd spoken to the old woman for the first and last time, and into the dim room. It was cool inside, the sun's heat failing to permeate the stones. To my right was the corpse, laid out on a plain, hay-filled bag that served as a mattress, a coarse wool blanket carelessly thrown over it. I crouched down and lifted a wasted arm, the skin loose under my fingers and noticed that her eyes were already closed. 'A gentle passing, Doctor. Taken in her sleep as we can all wish.' said Lady Katherine quietly. I was not so sure.

'No-one has attended to her, Madam?'

'I believe not, sir.'

'And who found her?'

'My maid. I sent food down to her. If my maid called her, she would acknowledge and say her thanks. Mary would then lay the food at the door and come away.'

'Mary never usually entered?'

'No, Doctor.'

'How then did she find her dead?'

'This day there was no answer, but the door was open. She peeped in, saw Mistress Whittle was still abed, realised she was past care and called an alarm.'

'And did no-one then enter?'

'I do not believe so.'

I rose and escorted Lady Katherine back outside. Her girl, Mary, was stood by the gate, her face pale and with an appropriate touch of sadness. I spoke to her, confirming that no-one had entered the hovel apart from her.

'I don't think so, sir. I called for help and though plenty opened their doors they didn't come. Which is why I went for my Lady.'

'Did you touch the body, Mary?'

She hesitated. 'Only to close the eyes, sir, in respect.'

'That's good, lass,' I said gently. 'And you saw nothing else?'

'I don't rightly know what you mean, sir. Everything was just as you see it now.'

'Except for the eyes?' She nodded.

I addressed the few villagers still looking on. 'Mistress Whittle has left us. She was no witch, but even if you believed she was, she can now do you no harm. I will say a prayer over her, I will bless this house and all around it and you can then feel safe in the protection of Our Lord. It will serve you well with Him in his Glory that you should attend our poor sister in her final needs.' Under my breath, I cursed them as fools for their stupidity. Again I say, the old ways linger on around here.

'Nicely done, Doctor.' Lady Assheton put a hand on my arm. 'Though you think something wrong here?'

'I'm afraid I do, Madam. It was an untimely death, I believe.'

We passed back in and I stood over the body. 'I saw many bodies in my studies with Doctor Hunyades in London.' I said. 'Something that we studied was the stiffness, the *rigor* as it is called by some, that affects the body a few hours after death. We saw that it disappears over the course of a day or even more. You will recall that I lifted one of the poor woman's arms. There was little resistance there. We did notice that both in children and in the wasted bodies of old people that stiffness is sometimes barely noticeable, but I believe that Whittle could have been dead for more than a day.'

'Is that of any real importance, Doctor?'

'Well, perhaps not in itself.' I looked at her and said quietly 'But she did not have a natural death.' Lady Katherine was shocked.

'If you look at the neck.' She leaned forward, holding a hand across her mouth and nose, 'You will see some bruising, and if I lift her head... Yes, I feel certain that her neck is broke.'

'Oh, my Lord, Doctor. Who...' She stopped herself, the question becoming a statement. 'You think this is Tench's work.'

'I do.' I opened one of Whittle's eyelids. 'It is the breaking of the neck that caused her death, not choking, as in the cases I have seen, strangulation causes blood to show in the eyes. She has none. Additionally, even with such a meagre body, I would think that great strength is needed to simply snap a neck. At least,' I said, 'it will have been a quick death."

'Why should he do this, Doctor?' said Sir Ralph, 'As a warning that we were still not safe?'

'I can only but think that the brute believed that she had told Cas to give him no further help, or that she had helped thwart him. It must have been clear to him that we were prepared to meet his attack.'

'And you cannot be more sure of when she was murdered?'

'No, sir, I cannot. It could have been the night of the attack on us or last night.

'Well then, for our sakes, I would hope that it was not last night, for the thought that the monster is still about us and can move with impunity makes me shudder. Even to think that he might even have doubled back on the night of the attack to take this poor creature's life leaves me cold'.

'Amen to that.' I said.

'If only the majority of our men were here and not with my son's forces, I would order a full sweep of the valley to find him.' He paused. 'There is one stroke of luck that I'm thankful for, apart from our success against the attack of course, and it is that we have quite possibly cut his evil band down to just a few supporters.'

'Let us hope we can keep it so, sir.' I responded, 'Have Grent's men agreed to continue to help?'

'They have. Let's hope they have quick luck'.

If Cas had thought Whittle his only friend, I foresaw that he would take her death badly, and so he did. Slater sat him at our table and put her arm round him and I gave him the news as gently as I could. He burst into tears. When he had recovered his composure, I told him I believed it was the work of Tench and to remember both that Mistress Whittle had kept him safe and we would now do the same.

To the end of keeping all of us safe from that evil and vengeful bastard, Sir Ralph had set two men, our friends John and Tom, to billet with us, and I was instructed that I must not leave the confines of the village without an armed escort. I needed no persuasion to agree to that.

Sir Ralph now intended to ask Aspinall to attend him in a matter of business, on the pretext that he was bedridden. Unless Aspinall could fully answer our concerns over the woman purporting to be Lady Kendall, she would be arrested, and proof of her standing demanded. In the meantime, I and my lifeguards would visit Grent and try to meet with the man Perkins.

Before I left, Nate appeared. 'Our prisoner's feeling sorry for himself, sir, but his wound is prospering.' he said. I'd left him in charge of the villain.

'Hmm,' I exclaimed. 'No sign of fever?'

'Not really. Don't think he'll walk properly again though.'

'Serve him right.' I said dismissively, watching Pod as he brought Bay out of the stable.

'Yes, sir, you are probably right, but I think you should hear his story. I don't think he knew what Tench was about. He'd been told he was fighting for the King to get hold of secret documents. I think he's short of understanding.'

'Aye, short of a lot of things I'm sure, but certainly short of brains, siding with that monster. I'll give him no countenance.' I was feeling less than charitable towards him as you could well understand. 'Tell Sir Ralph if you wish, but I'll not plead for him, the plague sore.'

Twenty Nine

The Idiot, Perkins

THE BACK ROOM OF THE DULE UPON DUN WAS PLEASANTLY warm, something of a relief as, though the sun still shone, its warmth was waning with the year. Grent listened intently and without comment to my story of the raid on Downham Hall. As I finished my tale and reached for my ale, he grinned. 'So, Tench has had most of his teeth drawn, has he? Not before time.'

'We've cut his force down, but he is still dangerous, and we don't know where he is. Even after the attack, he may have got back to the village and disposed of his aunt.'

'Aye, Doctor. And was she another that wasn't a witch, just like my last wife who you tried to save?'

'You know my feelings about this. "Witch" is just a name to cover envy, hatred or simply the unknown. Mistress Whittle was no witch.'

'Even though her family produced her nephew and his brother?'

'Even so.' I replied. 'But this isn't the point. Sir Ralph is now offering six gold sovereigns for the capture of the animal. Your men haven't seen him but are still searching, are they?' he nodded. 'Now there is more urgency. He may be hiding above Pendleton, but we haven't enough men to do a full search...'

Grent interrupted. 'I don't think my men would feel happy working over that area. Some have had problems above Standen.'

What those problems might be I didn't wish to know. The men of the Brungerley Woods often worked on the very edge of the Law and sometimes beyond it. They saw themselves akin to the Robin Hood of legend, though in truth they were nothing like. Never mind robbing the rich in favour of the poor as the story said, they would rob each other if needs be, though all of them be poor. I did ask for the news of Tench's losses and Sir Ralph's reward be spread as far as possible, and to make it clear to all that to assist or harbour the brute would lead to the gallows tree.

'Could Sir Ralph do anything to persuade your fellows to cover Pendle? Give them a letter confirming you are working for him, perhaps? It is vital that the area is searched.'

'I'll see what I can do, Doctor,' He sighed, 'but I doubt even that would answer.'

Will had gone to bring the man Perkins to parley but returned without him. 'I'm sure he was there but wouldn't come to the door.'

'How sure, Will?'

'Well, the door was bolted from the inside. I'd have broken it down if I'd thought it would cause no stir, Doctor.'

I rose, roughly pushing my stool back. 'I'm not waiting further.' Turning to Grent, I asked how quickly he could get a few men up into Clitheroe to create a brawl or some like diversion. 'A half hour, I believe, sir.' he replied.

"Then do it.' I threw a handful of coin onto the table. 'Tell them to make plenty of noise and make it seem real. We'll have a jug of ale whilst we wait. Will, bring your two in to drink, then we go for Perkins.'

Grent provided a half dozen men who seemed more than happy to cause some trouble in the town.

Near halfway between the Town's marketplace and the Swan Inn that I have mentioned before, lay the long burgage plot that had been Kendall's, and Kendall's father's before him, at the bottom of which was the hovel inhabited by Perkins. Down the side of the plot ran a rough lane. Our Tom would ride up into Clitheroe, stay close to Grent's men until they started their disturbance, then ride down the rough lane and give us our signal.

It worked perfectly, excepting that we didn't need Tom's signal, for we clearly heard the commotion. Will, John and I pushed through a gate, the hovel leaning against the surrounding wall to our right. I tried the rough-hewn door. It was still bolted. Stepping back, I nodded to Will, who rammed his shoulder into the door. I winced.

'God in Heaven!' Will shouted, grabbing his shoulder and with his face contorting with pain. 'The fucking thing!'

'Perkins,' I called calmly though the undamaged door, 'if you don't unfasten and come out, I will have this place burned around your ears. You have damaged one of my men and, if you should escape the fire, I will irreparably damage you. D'ye hear me now?' I drew my sword, ever at my side these days, and tapped the blade against the door. There was some movement and a small wizened old man came from round the side of the hovel. 'What's going on? What's going on?' said the apparition, suddenly looking both surprised and scared at the contingent by the door. He looked from me to Will. 'Oh, it's you. Are you back?'

Will looked ready for murder. 'Why was your door bolted, you silly old fool?'

'What?'

'Your door. Why was it bolted?' yelled Will.

'Which I were asleep. Why didn't you just knock?'

I took over from Will, realising that the man was more deaf than foolish, though I'd seen some fools with more wit about them. 'We did knock. Have you another door?'

'Door is it? Yes, another on the side. You could have just walked in through there.'

I was about to ask why, having taken the trouble to bolt the front door, did he leave his other door unlocked, but the thought processes of the local blockheads are a closed book to me. Will was quietly exercising his arm in no little pain as I asked Perkins to tell us of his connections to Kendall and what he knew of his wife.

'I worked for his fayther, do you know,' he said. 'Right through to his death. He were a hard man, tha knows, but he did right by me. Used to beat his son, sometimes badly. To harden him, says he, and he were right, for that Christopher turned hard as nails.'

'But you still stayed on and worked for him?' I enquired.

'Aye, for a few years at least. I had nowhere else to go and, though I knew him to be bad to most, he was civil to me and paid me enough.'

'You must have heard stories of what he was up to?' We were still stood outside Perkin's hovel, he leaning against the wall.

'Look, sir' he said, 'I told thee I knew he was bad, but what was I to do about it? I didn't listen to the tales. It weren't my business. He had the money. He could do what he liked, couldn't he?'

'What, thieving off folk who couldn't stand against him. Cheating every which way? What about the girls who went missing from his employ? What about the Tench brothers?' I was getting angry.

'I could do nothing, man. He could have snuffed me out like a candle if he so wished.' I had to admit that that was true. Perkins was just one of many who couldn't stand up to Kendall on pain of their lives.

'Come, Perkins. Come down to the Dule with us, I'll buy you food and drink and you can tell us your full story.' He looked wary. 'I give you my word that you'll be safe, and we'll return you here by nightfall. John will take you behind him on his horse.' John looked affronted at the suggestion, as Perkins did look as filthy as a beast, but that wasn't my problem.

Bread and cheese went down well enough and I refilled his ale as often as he quaffed it down. Again, we were in the back room of the Inn, sitting at what had been Kendall's dining table till it had been sequestered by Grent in lieu of past losses. Grent himself leant against the wall behind Perkins.

'So, you stayed with Christopher Kendall after his father's death?' I asked.

'It were the right thing to do. I needed the work. I continued his dad's butchery until the son ended it.'

'Why did he end it?'

'He'd made enough money and saw himself as moving into the gentry, I'd say.' responded Perkins. 'As anyone with sense would do if they could, don't you think?' There was now a touch of insolence in the man's manner. I might not have accepted this, but I needed his information and made allowance for the man's advanced age. 'He gave the butcher's business to another of his father's men and took rent.'

'He didn't give the butchery to you. Were you not annoyed by that?'

"No,' said he, almost with scorn, 'because he said I could move with him to help run his Waddow estate.'

'Trusted you then?'

'Knew I would keep my mouth shut about whatever he did.'

'How did he manage to accumulate such wealth so quickly?'

'He'd taken on the Tench brothers, who put the fear of God into everyone, including me, and he set them to visiting the small yeoman farmers who paid to be left alone.'

"You knew this and did nothing?'

'Again, I say,' he thrust his face towards mine, 'sir. I could do nothing.' He was turning surly.

He had already denied knowing anything about missing girls, and I didn't expect he would say anything that might incriminate himself in any wrongdoing. I needed to change the subject. 'Why did you leave his service and where did you go?'

'My brother died, and I went to live with his widow over by Burnley. She had his Inn. Thought I'd be made for life, running an ale house.'

'And did you have an easier life?'

'I did. For a few years it was good but then she died, and her sons threw me out.'

'Ah, that's hard.' I tried to sound sympathetic. 'So, you came back to try for your old job? Did you really think that Kendall would take you back on?'

'Had no choice. It was that or starve.' He gave a grim laugh. 'But the bastard had gone, hadn't he? Word was that he were dead, so I installed myself in that hovel. Mashiter who rents the land said I could stay if I worked the garden. It wasn't much worse than where old Kendall had kept me, so…' He tailed off.

Perkins had now drunk plenty, and the ale was making him drowsy, I could tell. My questioning could now go either way, either he'd shut up, or his answers might become befuddled. Not wanting to have to tackle him again on another day, I brought out my main question when, I hoped, he was at his weakest.

'Tell me about his wife.' He started to giggle.

'He could see a good bargain could Kendall, you've got to give him that. A chance to build his fortune further.'

'There was a portrait of her, next to his own in Waddow Hall.' I said. 'She looked a fine lady.'

'Aye, looked is right.' His smile made him look younger than his years. 'Should have been too, if he hadn't been cheated.' He began to laugh, long and hard, which turned into a violent coughing until I thought he might choke.

'Oh, dear, dear,' he said, slapping his heaving chest and wiping his eyes, 'That did me a power of good. Yes, Sir Christopher thought he had a quick way to join the gentry, get in with one of the oldest families round here.'

'Through marriage, you mean?' I asked.

'Yes, but his bride were not what she seemed. A bit away in her head in truth, but that was the least of it.'

I sat back. He was now fully alert again and would now tell his story in his own time, I felt sure.

'If a man of property and fortune, who is descended from Noah, says you can join yourself to his cousin, even you'd do it, I expect.' continued Perkins. 'Would you care what she looked like if she brought a dowry? I wouldn't.' He paused for effect, staring straight into my eyes.

'If she looked nice, like, then that would be a bonus, I would say, a real gift from God. And she did look quite fine. She could have shared my bed, I tell you.' he said with a leer. 'I didn't understand why they married so quietly. I thought he would wish to parade her around, because that was the kind of man he was – plenty of show, you know.'

'Quietly it was, though. We were told to hurry with rebuilding Waddow, money was no problem, though it became a problem because he threw it about as if his purse had no bottom. Then the damned Tenches were sent out to press more from whomsoever they could. I know they took money from the Catholic families, large sums I believe, so they would suffer no public censure for their faith. Like to keep such things from the public eye, they do.'

'So, what was your job at Waddow?' I asked.

'Which it was to keep the building going. But I were a butcher's man, not a builder! I laboured with the others, but when the panelling was put in wrong - which I didn't know – it was me got beaten.'

'What was wrong with the panelling?' I asked, remembering the main hall and the hidden room where we found the missing papers relating to the frauding of the Grammar School and, later, the trove of treasures that now lay under Downham Hall.

'Part was pine when he'd said oak, but money for oak wasn't there when needed, and a door had been covered over that should have been left. We had to rip it down and do it again. I couldn't see properly for a week after the beating and my hearing now is bad. I still had to work, though. But that's why, when I got the chance of my brother's widow, I took it.'

'So,' I said, 'You prepared Waddow ready for his wife.'

'Well, it weren't ready when they married. He stayed with her. Her picture arrived before she did.'

'The painting that paired with one of Kendall?'

'Aye.'

'And was it a good likeness?'

'Well now, I only saw the lady once, but I would say so, yes.'

'Small, light brown hair, rather pretty?"

"Aye.'

Thirty

A Lady, Suspect

I NOW HAD SOME PROOF THAT ASPINALL'S SO-CALLED LADY Kendall was a fraud. The painting was of Kendall's true wife. There was, however, more to come from Perkins that would account for his laughter. 'Who was his wife then, and of what family?' I asked eager to move the conversation on. Perkins smiled broadly.

'She were one of the Nowells,' he said triumphantly and, noting my surprise, 'I knew you'd like that.'

He was right, that almost stunned me and, whilst it potentially answered some questions, opened up even more. 'So why was that news not spread around? Surely Kendall would want that trumpeted far and wide?' I exclaimed.

Perkins laughed again. 'Well, she was only part Nowell, if you take my meaning.'

'A natural daughter of one, you mean? How did you hear this, man?' I asked quietly. Will's lips were pursed but his eyes were shining, trying not to laugh, whilst Grent, still leant against the rear wall, was quietly chuckling.

'I were in the house when he came in, shouting fit to raise the dead and smashing things. The Tench brothers were with him. He was calling the Devil down on Nowell, saying as he'd been told she were his cousin, not his bastard sister, and the Tench brothers should go and rip Nowell's head off.'

'And he found out, how?'

'As to that, I cannot say, only that he knew.'

'So, what happened then?'

'You'll have to ask others that, for I do not know. I kept quiet and hid myself away. I wasn't going to say anything that might get me killed.'

I studied the man. There was no reason for him to lie, and his story made sense. Nevertheless, he could be mistaken in the detail. Did that matter? Not really. It might explain the hold that Kendall seemed to have over Nowell, who had proposed him for Governor of the Grammar School and who, with Aspinall, allowed him charge over its finances. I now had what I needed - proof that Aspinall's "Lady Kendall' was false.

'Can you tell me anything more about Kendall's wife?' I asked Perkins, 'Where is she now?'

'I don't know, and neither do I care.' He was becoming insolent again and, in truth, I'd had enough of playing the inquisitor.

'Thank you.' I said, rising stiffly from my bench, for we'd been sat some few hours. 'My men will see you home.' I tossed a shilling on the table. 'If I need to speak to you again, you will come here at my call?' I was thinking I might need a signed statement from him but had no paper or ink to hand. The coin was to keep his goodwill.

'If you pay, then yes, but I don't know anything more.'

Will and I rode home together, and though his shoulder was still aching, he was in high spirits at the revelations. I was thinking what a story I had for Sir Ralph. The fate of the real Lady Kendall exercised my mind, especially in the hint from Perkins that she was "a bit away in her head."

'It is an odd story indeed.' Sir Ralph rested his jaw on his fist. He, Will and I were sat around his dining table, upon which the portrait of Lady Kendall was spread.

'There could be other explanations here,' I said, 'We've only Perkin's word to go on, though it does have the ring of truth. The Lady we see in this painting may or may not have had a touch of insanity. She may have been put away, died, killed perhaps, and Kendal remarried to the woman we saw at Standen. That is all conjecture at present, as is her being a Nowell. I think the first step is to beat some truth out of Aspinall, to be blunt. He is either in league with or under the thumb of the woman who confronted you, sir.'

'I might not go so far as a beating, Doctor. Aspinall is a Justice of the Peace, after all. But you are right, let's start with him. He still thinks I am confined to my home, if not my bed. I will write him to come to attest the signing of some documents. We get him here and put him under pressure.'

'What if he won't come?' asked Will.

'In that case we will attend him in force, but I doubt we shall need to go so far. And,' Sir Ralph smiled, 'that would uncover my pretence of incapacity.'

'But you still do have a measure of debility, sir,' I broke in, 'another month will see full recovery…'

'I've never seen you as an old woman, Doctor! Stop your fussing. Will, find me a man to take my letter to Aspinall whilst I write – or rather, you write in my name Doctor, and I will simply sign to confirm my frailty.'

A day had passed and, with a verbal assurance that he would attend, we awaited Aspinall's arrival. We didn't know how many men might accompany him, but they would be kept outside. It had been decided that Will would meet him at the door, looking suitably grave, I would be awaiting in the hall to escort him into the parlour, where the window drapes would be half drawn and with the rolled-up portrait of Kendall's lady on the table. Sir Ralph would then enter behind the seated Aspinall. Two of our men with swords drawn would also enter to give a menacing air to the proceedings.

Will came in. 'He's here. Just two with him.' We took our places.

The seated Aspinall near jumped out of his skin when Sir Ralph's heavy hand grasped his shoulder from behind. He'd already been looking slightly worried with Will and me standing silently before him with our arms folded. He had tried to engage us in conversation as the minutes ticked by, asking how my patient was, how his lady was. I simply said it was not my place to say and that he'd see for himself momentarily. His hands fussed about and more than once he pulled out a cloth and wiped his brow.

He now half turned to look up at Sir Ralph, who simply stared at him for a few seconds, and he began to stammer a greeting, saying he was surprised to see the Knight more improved than expected. Sir Ralph let go his shoulder, walked round the table to stand between Will and me as our two guards positioned themselves close behind the now quaking Aspinall who, making an attempt at bravado, sat up straight in defiance, though his eyes gave him away.

'I would like you to look at something, Aspinall.' Said Sir Ralph quietly. He pushed the rolled painting towards him. 'Just hold that bottom edge as I open it, would you?'

The canvas was unravelled part way till nought but the face remained undisclosed. 'Do you recognise this dress?'

'No. No, I don't think so. Why?'

'Well, I recognise it as being upon the woman you introduced me to in your house a short while ago. And if I can recognise it and my good Doctor can recognise it, why can't you? It is most distinctive, wouldn't you say?'

Our victim, if I might call him that, made no verbal response but his lower jaw began to shake. I enjoyed his discomfort. Slowly, Sir Ralph now revealed the face in the picture.

'You said that the woman at your house was Kendall's wife. This is the same dress but not the same woman. We have witnesses who confirm that the woman here,' and he pointed to her face, 'is the real Lady Kendall.' And now with menace, 'What game are you playing, Aspinall?'

The man was a wreck. He seemed incapable of speech, his mouth opening and closing without a sound. We waited.

'Would you like a drink?' He nodded and a tankard of small beer was poured for him and slid across the table. So fast was his drinking that he near choked. Coughing fit now over, he seemed to shrink into the chair. Then, having composed himself somewhat, he began to speak in a tremulous, reedy voice.

'The lady in the picture is indeed Lady Kendall but she is now not of sound mind and is confined for her own safety.'

'You know this how?'

'Sir Christopher told me some time ago. I had no reason to doubt him.'

'What was her family?'

'Of the Nowells, I believe.'

'Where is she confined?'

'I know not.'

'So, who is the woman demanding Kendall's possessions and where is she?'

Sullen now. 'Her name is Margaret, and she says she is now Lady Kendall. I don't know where she resides.'

'If she takes that title, would that not mean the original Lady Kendall was dead? What proof have you of this?'

'I don't know!' Aspinall shouted, now clutching his head. 'She came to me knowing things about Kendall, about me, and about the goods you hold. She came with Kendall's man, Tench, and I was frighted for my life. Don't you understand?'

I interrupted. 'But you have your men around you and have the ability to get more, I wager. You could have solicited our help…'

'The men around me are controlled by Tench. Even those with me now are his animals. This meeting alone might kill me if Tench hears anything about it other than a mission to witness the signing of deeds. I had to seek his permission to come here. He is a devil, a witch, and can come or disappear at will, as can that… that woman!'

Here we go, I thought, back to the supernatural, back to witchcraft, and said 'We have just dealt Tench a major blow and he has only six men or so with him. How many has he at your Hall?'

'Four. Two here with me and two at Standen.'

'Just four and you couldn't stand up to them?' Aspinall shrugged his shoulders.

We left him under guard and convened in the dining hall. 'We can't let him go,' said Sir Ralph. 'Not only are there more questions to be answered, but he is our prime witness, and his safety is compromised. Will, disarm the two men outside and lock them up, will you, whilst we consider what else must be done.'

'We need to eliminate Tench's men still at Standen.' I said and a further thought came to me. 'I wonder if Tench himself is holed up there?'

'Good God, Doctor! That is a thought. It makes sense for him to have gone to ground, and where better!'

Thirty One

Lancashire, Yet for Parliament

Whilst we were mired in our own problems, the war dragged on across the country and, apart from broadsheets casting both sides as villains, claiming their forces were raping and pillaging at will, we could only get a sketchy picture of how the country stood. News was coming out from Lincolnshire of success for our forces and there was much talk, so Sir Ralph said, of a cavalry leader called Cromwell who had formed there an 'Eastern Association' of Parliamentarian troops. That London still held for Parliament we knew, but Wales and Cornwall clung to the King.

Most of Yorkshire also was still for the King. The redoubtable figure of his Queen must take credit for this and, if Lord Derby hadn't failed her, her troops would have invaded Lancashire. If the Royalists had come, then Downham's peace would have been upset, I'm sure, and it would no longer be a safe haven for us.

The cowardly Derby had never recovered from the rout of his troops at Read Bridge, and the latest news was that he'd ignored the orders of Queen Henrietta Maria and fled to his holdings in the Isle of Man, leaving his wife to hold Lathom House, near Ormskirk, against the forces of Parliament. So much for chivalry, though that itself is considered an old-fashioned concept by many. But to think that our little engagement at Read Bridge and the routing of several thousand Royalists by a few hundred men should have had such an impact! I say 'our engagement' as, though I was only there by accident and took no part in the action, the wounds I received there give me some right to brag, I believe.

Lancashire was yet for Parliament in the main, and Colonel Assheton, Sir Ralph's son, had taken Warrington, Manchester, Nantwich, Liverpool, before turning north to re-take Preston. He had now continued on to roust the few remaining Royalists holding Lancaster.

But it was now, when we in Downham were in the desperate search for Tench and the fraudulent Lady Kendall, when we felt danger near at hand, that I was asked to join Colonel Rigby's forces due to an outbreak of the bloody flux.

Thirty Two

'A Poor Hand to Play'

'It is ridiculous in the extreme, sir. We have a major problem at hand and Rigby instructs, nay orders for goodness sake, that I travel through the country because he has a few soldiers ill?' I couldn't believe what Sir Ralph was telling me. 'May I see his letter?'

He handed it to me with a level of forbearance. 'I can hold him off for a few days, Doctor, but…' He could have made the point that I was receiving regular monies from Parliament for my medical services, which I couldn't deny. But the thought of being placed under the command of the over blunt, overbearing Rigby made my blood boil. I'd been on a mission to Hoghton Tower the previous year, when his tactlessness, whilst surrounded by Sir Gilbert Hoghton's men, had nearly brought us to blows and a thousand Royalists about our ears.

I sighed, knowing I had a poor hand to play, and would have to go. 'Sir, I know I'm not in a position to make demands, but I have real concerns over leaving at this point. We must strike at Standen now. We've held Aspinall overnight. He'll be missed. If Tench is not there himself we know two of his men are, and even just depriving that monster of them will be something…

'I have that in train as we speak, Doctor. Will is already away with twelve men. He's taken a small cart upon which is placed a shrouded body, purporting to be that of Aspinall…'

'You mean he is to try the Trojan Horse trick again? We did that in the attack on Waddow Hall. Surely it will not work a second time?'

'But this time there really is a dead body on the cart, not attackers ready to jump out. One of my tenants died the day before yesterday. He had no family. He will do me one more service before we inter him. He was much the same build as Aspinall and has been dressed in his clothes. Will believes it will work.'

I think my jaw dropped but Sir Ralph continued. 'He has three men with him to approach the gate, where there are two sentries. Two parties of four will enter the grounds on either side. They are good poachers all, as I know to my cost. Their stealth is guaranteed, and we expect them to contain all others there. They have instructions not to enter the house itself but send word. At that I will ride out with Aspinall and all the men I can muster. Then we can search the house.'

'I must have Bay saddled and be ready to ride.' I exclaimed, turning for the door.

'No, Doctor. You must stay here. Guard my household and your own.' I opened my mouth to respond but he held up a hand. 'I'm aware of the risks. You remain here. Bring your people into the Hall if you see fit.' He gave a wan smile. 'All may be over by evening.'

I was not convinced. I just hoped my services would not be needed in the next few hours.

Lady Katherine worked quietly at a tapestry. Slater sat knitting with Pod and Cas at her feet trying to untangle a skein of wool. Nate and Richard Towneley were chattering, rather loudly I thought, over a book at the dining table. I paced the floor, waiting for the sound of horses. I had placed a sword by the main door. Adam and another from the village stood outside. Nobody seemed worried except for me, but I was in a sweat, not least by the Lady's presence, as the minutes slowly passed.

'Doctor!' hissed Slater, 'For goodness' sake, sit down. Read a book. You'll disturb the Lady else. You're certainly disturbing me.' I glared at her but then grinned. That was the first time she'd ever encouraged me to pick up a book rather than muttering under her breath that I was wasting my time again, and how much knowledge did anyone really need.

Suddenly there was a noise outside and I sped to the door, grabbing my sword. In my agitation, I flung the door back with a crash and there was Will, grinning once again.

'I surrender, Doctor. Here, let me give you my sword.' He slid down from his horse.

'Where is Sir Ralph?' I said, ignoring his insolence and looking past him towards the gate.

'Just behind, bringing back Squire Aspinall. All are safe but no Tench or false Lady, I'm afraid. We did take two of Tench's men, but that's all.'

'Everything went to plan then?'

'Better than the plan. We didn't need Bert, the pretend dead squire.' I looked at him confused.

'The dead body?' he said, 'As we've brought back unused, so to speak, for Christian burial?'

'I didn't know his name.'

'Yes, Bertram it was. And he was no more use in death than he was in life.' He said, crossing himself.

Sir Ralph entered the grounds with the rest of the men and, as a much reduced and diminished Aspinall, wearing clothes that were too long in length but too short in girth and obviously not his own, was escorted into the Hall and seclusion, a motley band of ruffians, headed by Grent of the Dule Inn, came through the gate.

'Sir Ralph, and Doctor! Here comes the army of Brungerley Wood. For just a little, a very little, of your coin, these fine fellows, having been abused and assaulted by the brute Tench, undertake to pursue him even to the top of Pendle. Give them ale and bread beside and they will be like your finest hounds at the hunt.'

Smiling at Grent, I leant towards Sir Ralph and quietly whispered. 'What have we started now?'

He laughed, walking forward to grasp Grent's arm.

With Will now trying to coax our new force into a semblance of order, and to give them instruction, I sent Slater and my boys back to our cottage. I wanted the fine detail of the late expedition, but Sir Ralph said little. There was no sign of Tench or the imposter, and some of our men had been left at Standen to keep it secure, so that was that. But he did want to discuss my service to Colonel Rigby. He had given it thought on his way back home.

'You must go, Doctor. There is no choice. My son marched from Lancaster to Hornby and began the siege of the Royal forces in the castle there. He is now returning southwards and will leave Colonel Rigby to bring this matter to a close. A last push here and I believe Lancashire will be secure.' He paused. 'Understand, Doctor, it is more important than ever that we consolidate our position, for the Irish have made a peace with the King and will now fight for him. We expect troops from there within the next few months. Rigby must finish his task, and quickly, but his men are falling ill, he fears a plague and there are no spare troops to bring to his assistance. You are their surgeon, and he calls for you.'

I felt defeated, backed into a corner, but he continued. 'I'm sure you can see the point. We need to support Rigby at this time. Hornby must not be seen as the point at which control of Lancashire begins to crumble, and you have a duty to our men.'

'But Rigby…' I exclaimed, lamely.

'I know you don't see eye to eye with him,' said Sir Ralph, 'and he tells me to put you under his command. What if I make it clear that you are under my son's command entirely but, with his blessing, will attend his men for a short time?'

'Kind of you, sir. That may help but you should know that there is little, nay nothing, in my physician's bag to remedy the bloody flux. The only efficacious thing is blood-letting and to remove people from the immediate area to avoid the noxious emanations that cause the complaint.'

'That may be, but you must attend, I fear.'

So that was that. I could have Will and two men to travel with me, he said, but I wasn't keen on that. Will, yes, but other armed men might give me more problems should we meet any royalist troops on the way. That was unlikely I realised, but myself, with a covering letter of purpose and two assistants, Nate and Will, was a safer bet. To be true, I'd rather leave the two men to guard Slater and Pod in our absence. However, as I walked back to my cottage to give Slater the news, I realised that, although I felt able to rely heavily on Nate as usual, I didn't want to expose him to any great contagion. It would be me and Will alone. We would travel swiftly and light on the morrow.

PART TWO

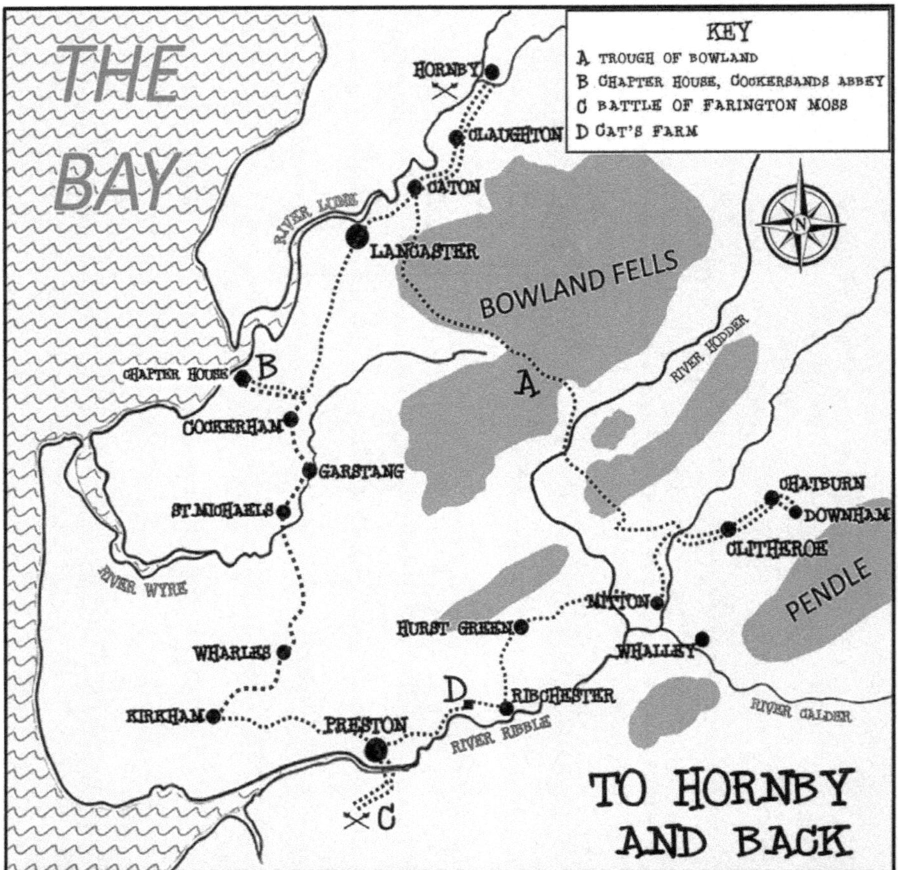

THE CHAPTER HOUSE OF COCKERSAND ABBEY

Thirty Three

'Rum Place, This...'

We got underway shortly after dawn, Bay being sprightly and ready for an outing. Will seemed bleary-eyed and barely awake, from carousing or whoring, I did not ask. I had little to take excepting my usual medicines and blood-letting bowl and knife.

The flux is a terrible illness, death often occurring within a day with uncontrolled and bloody shitting. It is, of course, an intense imbalance of the humours. I have heard others say that the blood of a fresh-killed hare mixed with stale ale can be efficacious, but I doubt its use. That, I think, would increase the imbalance, add to the wet humours. No, unless yellow and black bile, the dry humours, could be increased, early blood-letting or tobacco smoke is the thing.

The weather was changing. Behind us Pendle was wreathed in cloud and before us there was a greyness. A cold breeze blew from the west. It had rained during the night and damp leaves dulled the sound of our horses' hooves as we trotted down into a deserted Chatburn and up and over Horrock's Hill. The Brungerley Woods, showing a few trails of smoke from the lime-burning being dashed away to the East, lay to our right as we rose once again up towards the Church and my Clitheroe home. We didn't stop.

A few traders were setting up in Marketplace, looking at us quizzically as we passed up to the Castle gate, then right, down the steep incline of

Maluesgate, out into the wastes and on to the Eadsford Bridge. We had no conversation, Will now looking more alert but still rather glum, matching the day.

We made a short stop at Nolland's Farm, by Bashall, where Tench lost four of his men only weeks before. Nolland himself was out in the fields, but his sturdy wife gave us a welcome drink of small beer whilst we put the horses to the trough. She wished to talk but I gave her our apologies and we quickly moved on, itching to get past the great defile through the Bowland fells to the north.

Past Browsholme Hall, home of Squire Parker we went. There was no-one about and the house was hidden by trees. The family were romans and I wondered why there had been no attempt by our Parliamentary friends to sequester their property as we had the Towneley's. Perhaps they had paid us off, as Sir Ralph had hinted that they had a letter of waiver from disturbance. Within the cache of Kendall's things, taken from Waddow Hall and now held in Sir Ralph's cellars, was a communion cup and other items marked with the Parker crest. I believe Sir Ralph had informed Parker of this, but nothing had been done about its recovery. I still wondered if there had been some connection 'twixt Waddow and Browsholme.

We slowed the horses down as we climbed over the moor to drop down into the valley of the Hodder, but Bay at least was still in spirits, and we fair cantered along the riverside towards the hidden gap through the high fells that would see us towards Lancaster.

I'd last ridden this way with a small troop taking Tench's twin to Lancaster for trial and hanging. That was more than two years since and it had been a terrible journey through heavy rain, which delayed us so much that we were forced to spend the night in a dreary hovel. Little Pod, as a witness to the crimes of our captive, was with me then, and he had a particularly hard time at the assize and following execution, bless him.

Near thirty years since, those poor half-wits from Pendleside, accused as witches, had also travelled this very road to their deaths, and if the terrible path known as the Trough of Bowland wasn't itself dread enough, the thought of the evil that continued to haunt us, in the shape of Tench, weighed on our spirits. Only a few days ago, hadn't that vile creature murdered mistress Whittle, right under our noses in Downham? It's almost enough to make me believe in witchcraft.

The path led us along the fell side, with a deep drop into a gushing stream on our left and there were signs of recent rock falls. Thankfully we could rely on the sure-footedness of our beasts. We saw no-one and I could see no sign of the hovel that sheltered us the last time I passed through. On and on the road rose, Bay lowering her head not, I believe, through tiredness but from the feeling of the countryside. A blasted tree, some stunted saplings and gorse or some such covered the moors. The cloud lowered, touching the fell tops and, though it looked like we would meet with a downpour, the rain thankfully kept away.

Cresting the first height, the road dropped away before us, the way being even more treacherous now, with the horse's hoofs slipping on loose stones, and then we were in a mossy defile, the harsh skeletons of trees rising about us, aside a foaming stream. Some of the trees had been toppled, as by a storm, their roots ripped up and open to the sky. Twiggy nests of rooks and crows hung in the topmost branches of those that still stood, but even these social birds were near silent as we passed. It was a melancholic scene, to be sure.

By the time we had climbed out and onto the next and final height, it was past noon and we had done sixteen miles or so. Good going I thought. Now out of that blighted place and with the cloud lifting like our mood, travel would be easier. Lancaster and its castle lay below us, ten miles or more away, with an arm of the sea beyond it. Again, Pod came to mind, with his wonder at the sight of such an expanse of water. I had tried to explain the tides to him as we had seen the water flood the bay, but I fear he could not grasp the concept.

Lancaster was not my concern this time. Leaving it to our west we struck out due north on a gentle downward slope into the green of the Vale of Lune, to the hamlet of Caton, past Quernmore with its large park, once owned by King Charles himself but now in the hands of yet another roman family I believe, of whom I knew nothing. Caton was empty, or so it seemed, two cottages had an abandoned air to them, and we could neither see nor hear any animals. Knowing that Rigby's forces would have passed this way from Lancaster, I wondered if this was down to their foraging. We stopped by a stream to water the horses and ourselves and ate a little bread and cheese.

'Rum place this, Doctor.' said Will quietly. 'Do you get the feeling we are being watched?'

I hadn't but, with an attempt to look casual, I slowly looked about us. 'No, Will. I see nothing.' He shrugged. We hadn't unsaddled the horses, so we remounted and moved off.

Our horses were tired now, as was their right after such a day, but at least the true hardships were behind us, and the road now passed through gentle, undulating country. The River Lune was to our left but near invisible, with a low wooded fell beyond, and the Bowland fells over which we'd passed were now away to our right. Two miles on, a further hamlet of a farm, ancient chapel, and a half-dozen houses of no account, again seemed deserted.

But as we passed through and rounded a bend, there was a shrill whistle from behind and out of the bushes before us came several soldiers, two with muskets. Though they showed no colours, I felt sure they would be Rigby's men as they wore grey coats, and I believed that most Royalists had been cleared from the area, with most now in Hornby Castle. One never knows, though. It is as well to be cautious in these tempestuous days.

We stopped some yards from them and waited for their challenge. One fellow, in a dirty coat and grey bonnet, approached us with drawn sword. 'Password?' he queried.

'Not known.' I replied, 'We are not martial. I am the surgeon and this,' pointing to Will, 'is my assistant. We have been asked to attend an outbreak of the flux?'

The soldier turned back to his fellows and a short discussion followed, with the occasional glance in our direction. I chanced my arm, as they say, dismounted and walked towards them, the two musketeers tracking me down their long barrels.

'I have letters of safe conduct and, as it has been supposed I will meet with Colonel Rigby's men, I have a message for him.' I held out my pass which they peered at but didn't take. Illiterate all, I expect.

Will brought our horses slowly up and, not without some hesitation, we were pointed forward with 'Two miles to next picket. At the bridge.'

Long before we reached the sturdy stone bridge, we had seen an impressive castle rising above the trees, a large purple banner atop the Keep. A sergeant-at-arms commanded the road here and I recognised our light blue colours both ahead and to our right. He gave my letter little more than a glance before detaching two men to escort us to the Colonel. I wasn't looking forward to our meeting. Immediately to our right, and some two hundred yards away, was a small encampment, two tents only, part sheltered from the castle by a bank of near-leafless trees and a beech hedge, only one soldier in sight, leaning against a tent and looking to be asleep.

Before us the road stretched between lines of wattle and daub houses roofed with thatch. Beyond and to the right stood a church tower but before we reached it we heard the crack of a musket and our guards turned swiftly to the left between two hovels. 'Best dismount,' said one guard over his shoulder, 'Th'enemy hold the church.' A further, larger tented camp now revealed itself on our left, beyond two solid houses and barns, and we were told to leave our horses. I wasn't happy with this, so told Will to stay with them and try to find some feed, as I was led on a track, through some cultivated plots, parallel to the road.

'Keep your head down, sir. Them Royals are poor shots, but I don't think the Colonel would be happy was you to be hit.'

'Well, I wouldn't be pleased either.' I said huffily. "Where is Colonel Rigby?'

'In what passes for a Town Hall, should this dump ever be given such a name. It usually supports a weekly market, but our presence seems to have frightened the people off.' He grinned. 'Tis only across the road from the church, near a hundred yards only, but we take shots at them as and when their heads peak over to fire on us. It keeps us all interested, that I will say, sir.'

I was led to what, apart from Church and Castle, appeared to be the largest stone building in the place, an odd, two-storey edifice with a high gabled roof in some decay, attached to an assorted range of buildings. Its main room was set above us upon squat stone pillars of seeming antiquity, with its ground floor open on two sides, a curtain wall to its frontage on the road, the attached buildings closing in the left side. I presumed the true entrance to the room above was from the front of the building, but that would be in clear sight of the Royals in the Church tower. The only entrance from this side was by a crude wooden ladder on the right reaching up to a window, through which a soldier was climbing out. This open space between pillars and walls was barely fifteen feet by twelve, but there, leaning over a simple table was Rigby with his officers. Slightly below average height, his weather-beaten face looking as angry as usual, he barely looked up as I approached and proffered Sir Ralph's letter. Another musket boomed above out heads, with an answering crack from the Church tower, which made me flinch.

Frowning as he read the message, he glared at me. 'Why does this still put you under Colonel Assheton's orders and not mine?'

'I simply act on his orders, sir,' I replied without expression, 'which are to attend your men and, as quickly as possible, join him to the South.' That last was a fiction on my part. I didn't have such orders but wasn't going to remain here for any longer than I had to.

'Colonel Assheton is not in the South. He remains here.' My spirits rose. With a withering look, Rigby near threw the letter back at me, which I ignored, and instructed a captain to take us to the commander.

In a barn some way back from the Town Hall, Colonel Assheton greeted us warmly, his open countenance in marked contrast to Rigby's scowl. Not as tall as his father, stocky, and with his mother's look in his face, he was washing as we entered but quickly dried himself and proffered a hand. 'Good to see you, Doctor. Are you well? What news from Downham?' We chatted for a while until a messenger came in.

'I am called away, Doctor. I'll leave you in Captain Fossett's hands.' He grabbed his sword and steel helmet and was gone.

Fossett seemed very efficient. Tall and darkly handsome, he wore his hair unusually short for an officer A clean lace collar lay over his buff coat, tied with a blue sash. 'Keep your head down, Doctor as we proceed,' he said. 'Don't want to lose you to a shot from the Church. It's only yards from the front of our headquarters. A great nuisance but we can't dislodge them. Unless we burned the church, of course, and some of us would be for that.'

Puritan, I thought, and queried 'You are taking me to your sick tent, Captain?'

'Well, I would if we had one, but these men are dying before we can give them any attention. And, of course, no one wishes to touch the poor devils and catch the illness. Pits are dug and the bodies rolled into them, prodded with sticks, which are then thrown in after them. We've already lost thirty-odd, so are down to near two hundred and seventy men, so far.'

'So where are your men positioned?'

'We have twenty-man pickets to the north and west of the castle, just ten left to the south, and outliers up the road towards Yorkshire, from where any relieving force might come to the Castle's aid. I doubt they will receive any help, though, and if we can sit tight, we can starve them out.' He gave me a thin smile. 'Unless we lose many more men, that is.'

'How many oppose you?'

'A few hundred in the castle, perhaps. It is unclear. But we must evict them. Enemy troops are mustering in Furness, and we can't afford to leave a Royalist toehold here to give them comfort.'

'So how goes it?'

'Not well, if truth be told. When we set up our positions and thought ourselves well set, they launched an attack on us, would you believe, and might have pushed us back had we not been at watch. It was brave and audacious, and I give them credit for it. But we lost no men, thank God, and now sit here and must starve them out, I fear.' He paused and looked directly at me. 'Providing we don't all die from the flux in the meantime.'

It was more of a question than a statement, but I had no answer at that point and just nodded, saying 'If you lift the siege, you will march on northwards?'

'I doubt it. We will be happy to keep what we have till next year. Then, who knows?'

'I must find my man and medicines.' I said, 'I left him to attend to our tired horses. Where will we sleep? We must have stabling for our cattle.'

'A tent only, I'm afraid, and I doubt stabling. Everywhere is full and I can do nothing tonight.' My spirits sank. Things were getting worse and worse. I cursed Rigby in his arrogance.

Fossett still wanted reassurance from me. 'Can you stop this plague do you think, Doctor?' He looked earnestly into my eyes, and I could see a touch of fear. 'I have a wife and children who I would wish to see again, Sir. I've not seen much real fighting, I'll admit, but this worries me more than the thought of battle. That a pestilence can creep up upon you without you knowing...'

'I think I must bleed the men on the morrow. It is the only thing I can do to balance the humours.'

I started to walk away but turned back and called to Fossett. 'Captain, did I hear you right? You said you had just ten men left to the South. Do you mean most of the men were lost there?'

"Yes, Doctor,' he called over his shoulder, 'all of the dead are from that picket.'

Thirty Four

'Any More Ill Yet?'

It took a time to find Will. He was beyond the tents somewhat to the west and sitting on his saddle with our bags whilst our unharnessed horses quietly grazed nearby. He seemed to be keeping his distance from a group of soldiers gathered round a well.

'Just been some trouble, Doctor. Two Sergeants-at arms, came down, beat one of that group and hauled him away. Seems he refused to go to the picket up by the river.'

'The one where the sickness is happening?'

'Aye. They're all grumbling about it.' He nodded over towards the well. 'Should I be worried?'

'I might be able to tell you later,' I replied. 'I'm going see what's happening over there.'

'Well, I hope to see you again. I don't fancy being stuck here on my own.'

I walked back towards the road, then almost ran to cross the bridge, not wishing to present a target to the enemy in the church. I doubted that they could spot me and fire with any accuracy from five hundred yards or so, but I didn't want to test that theory.

Immediately after the bridge I turned left on a narrow, muddy path between the river and a long burgage plot. It was dusk and I stumbled once or twice as I entered a line of trees. I could make out the shape of the castle's tower against the sky, with a couple of lighted windows below, but little else.

'Who goes?' A challenge before me.

'Doctor. Any more ill yet?' I could just make out his face, swathed in a cloth that he pulled over his mouth and nose after he spoke.

'Not as I knows.'

'Have you food and drink, enough? Don't let anyone else join your party and tell the rest to keep their mouths and noses covered just as you are. It's getting too dark for me to do anything now, but I'll return in the morning.'

'Not much food but a keg of ale came up earlier. Tomorrow you'll come? We might all be dead by then.' He laughed harshly.

A bad night in a draughty tent with nothing to break our fast did little to lighten either of our moods. I rose, cold and weary, to another overcast day and prayed that it would again stay dry. My Bay and Will's horse, tethered to a tree, looked equally downcast. I set Will to foraging for food and drink and walked across the small camp, stopping every man I saw to ask if they'd any signs of the bloody flux. None had. I found Captain Fossett to confirm that there had been no cases in the camp or pickets overnight.

'No. Excepting the soldier from the south picket who was brought back here before he died.' Fossett declared.

'And even then, nobody here that came near him succumbed to the flux?'

'No. All are fine.'

That gave me hope. Whatever was causing the illness, it wasn't a true contagion but some noxious thing living by the River Camp. 'Why keep men over there if they're falling ill?' I asked.

'We don't want them bringing this plague to the rest of the men, God forbid.' He crossed himself. 'And we must ensure that the enemy cannot be re-enforced or supplied from that side, of course.'

Back across the bridge and up the river's bank I went. A different sentry accosted me, and I asked how the night had gone. 'Most of us are still shitting loose but not with blood or continuous like the others did,' he said, 'but we're sore frighted, sir.'

'Have you seen or smelt any miasma or noxious gases around your tents?'

'What do you mean, a mist or the like?'

'Yes, anything like that. Or a foul smell?'

He scratched his head. 'No worse than anywhere, I reckon.'

'Does the main camp supply all your food and drink?' I asked.

'Some, but we've mainly to fend for ourselves. I can write, so I've been told to make record of what we take from the cottagers on this side of the river, mainly eggs, poultry, and the odd sheep, and tell them they'll be paid in time.' He shrugged. 'They don't like it, but…'

An idea was already beginning to form in my mind. Immediately in front of me were two round tents and a smouldering fire, round which sat a few dejected figures, comprising the whole of the River Camp. Through the trees I could see that the river flowed from the northwards, close by the castle, changing course to the west at this point.

'Don't show yourself at the river, sir.' The sentry cried a warning as I pushed through the trees toward the water. 'The castle might fire on you else.'

I crouched down by the water, watching its flow for a few minutes. It was a busy stream, but the water carried foam and was murky with detritus as it passed. I turned to call to the sentry and as I did so, I heard a crack and a few splinters of wood fell about me. I was under fire from the castle. Scrambling back into the trees, I put one between me and the castle whilst I tried to calm my beating heart.

'I told you that would happen.' The sentry gave me a smug look which I ignored.

'Do you take water from the river?' I snapped.

'Yes.' He said, as though I was mad. 'Where else?'

'See the castle? How it sits just a few yards from the river? All the shit from the Royalists up there is flowing right into the stream, it then flows down here and you're drinking it. The water smells bad from it.' He looked at me with little comprehension. 'You're getting the flux from them in the castle, you idiots.' I was near shouting at him. 'They're killing you with shit and who knows what filth!'

'Captain Fossett.' He was stood by Rigby round the table under the Town Hall as I called him over. "A word with you, sir.'

'Do you wish to start bleeding the men, Doctor? Can't say I look forward to my turn.' He gave a slight grin.

'I'm not sure even that will be necessary. That River Camp or South picket are using poisoned water from the castle which is giving them the flux. It's a simple matter.' I said bluntly. 'Either withdraw or move that camp or give it a constant supply of ale for drinking and order them not to use water from the river.'

Fossett looked aghast. 'Poisoned you say? A deliberate act? I must tell the colonel.'

'Not deliberate, sir. I do not believe even the Royalists would stoop to that. No, it is a simple matter. There's a few hundred men in the castle and all their effluence, excrement and other wastes flows from the castle into the river below and your men drink it. Why they should do so when turds can be seen in it and it clearly smells, I cannot say, but I feel sure that is the cause.'

'I will attend to it at once.'

"I will stay here two days, provided you can find us a room, bed and stabling for our horses. If no further illness have arisen by then, I will leave in line with my instructions.'

Fossett looked worried. 'A tall order, Doctor, a tall order indeed but I will try. What shall I say to the Colonel?'

'Just what I've told you, sir, no more or no less, I suggest. If any need treatment whilst I am here, please send them to me and I will attend them.' I began to turn away but stopped. 'In fact, Captain, though I said I wouldn't bleed all the men, I will bleed those of the River Picket. It may relieve their remaining symptoms. I will attend them tomorrow.'

Thirty Five

'To Cleanse Them and Balance Their Humours'

A COMFY NIGHT, THOUGH IF IT HAD BEEN LEFT TO RIGBY WE would have had nothing but the open ground to sleep on. Thank goodness for Colonel Assheton, I say. At his instruction, Captain Fossett billeted us at a smallholding some three hundred yards south of the bridge and on slightly higher ground. I expected the farmer to be resentful towards us for this imposition, but I was wrong. When they heard that it was a physician that was to be placed with them, not just a surgeon, we were treated with respect, the goodwife even dipping a curtsey to me as we entered.

Thomas and his wife were country folk, plain and sturdy certainly, but could both read and write, possessing a bible, almanac, and a psalter, as I could see from their table. I didn't press them on their religion. There was little of the roman about them, but we were in their hands, and I'd take bread and shelter from a Catholic, Musselman, or anyone after the night we'd last experienced.

It was a modest house, to be sure, but clean and with fresh straw on the floor, and a loft reached by a ladder. It even had a chimney. We were pressed to mutton stew and given their own bed in the loft, a proper bed indeed and tightly strung. This last we did protest at out of courtesy, but quickly agreed.

'Two grown sons, sir.' said Thomas in response to my question about family.

'Away with an army?' I asked innocently and, though he said no, I sensed that he didn't wish me to query the matter further. Perhaps they made themselves scarce when they saw troops arriving in the area. If so, who can blame them. I forbad to enquire as to their own affinities. They probably took no side in this conflict, just wishing to continue their lives in peace, like most folk.

'Are our troops a big drain on your resources?' I queried.

'Aye. They say a note is taken of what we supply and that we'll get paid, though when or at what rate I know not.' He looked grim. 'T'will be a hard winter for us I fear.' His wife nodded. 'They haven't taken our pig yet and I pray to God they don't, and that their war is over soon so we are left alone again.'

Amen to that I thought.

Being a fair way from the river, I asked where they got their water from. 'We have our own well.' was the answer, which pleased me greatly. 'What of the properties closer to the water?' I enquired.

'Most of them do use the river in normal times,' Thomas replied, 'but that water's turned foul since so many troops crowded into the castle. One or two fell ill, so we let them take some from our well.'

'Well thought out, Thomas,' I said and reached to shake his hand. 'That's exactly what I thought.' So, there were people using common sense, men after my own heart: see a problem, give thought to its probable cause, and take suitable action. If Rigby and his officers had thought like that, I wouldn't have needed to come here.

I woke up in comforting warmth. Will was out already, looking to the horses I guessed. Pulling on my boots and with my cloak under my arm, I gingerly descended the ladder to find bread, cheese and warm milk waiting for me at table. I exchanged a few pleasantries with the goodwife, and she asked me to look at Thomas' back, he suffering with the rheumatics in cold weather. I suggested use of Black Henbane, but she'd not heard of it and doubted it grew in the area. 'It may be called Stinking Nightshade or the like in these parts,' I suggested, but it still meant nothing to her. The only thing that I had with me that gives some relief, was juice or extract of poppy, and I promised to attend her husband when he came in from the fields.

In the meantime, one limping soldier, thin, pale and clearly racked with pain, arrived on the arm of another in the mid-morning. 'Our sergeant sends his compliments to the Doctor, and can he do summat for this man,' declaimed his companion, dropping to a near whisper for 'his name's John, sir,' before returning to his oratory, 'as he is no use to man nor beast.'

Despite his obvious discomfort, this John was reluctant for me to examine him. With difficulty, I pulled off his boot as he pleaded 'Don't cut my boot. Don't cut my boot.' With the boot off and his toe-rag unwound, revealing a swollen foot and blackened toenails, this changed to 'Don't cut off me foot. Please don't cut off me foot.'

'Shut up and let me examine this appendage.' I hate people who moan in such fashion, especially when I'm sure they're lice-ridden and probably poxed. He winced and whimpered as I poked it. I pressed it hard to determine if it was broken and he yelled out. It wasn't. It smelt, but not of gangrene. 'What caused it?' I asked, 'Horse?'

'Aye, sir. Stepped back on me three days past.'

'Bad bruising that's all. Two choices for you – either three day's rest and continuous application of comfrey, or...' I paused for effect. 'I could remove it for you.' He looked horrified but I like to have a joke now and again.

'Comfrey, comfrey, sir. I'll eat all the comfrey you wish…'

That made me grin and just then Will came in. He looked at me and at the ashen face of the wounded soldier, knew exactly what I'd done, and his face broke into a smile, the first I'd seen from him for two days. I turned to Thomas' wife. 'You have comfrey, I don't doubt?' I asked.

'Aye, Doctor. Knitbone, as we call it. Some boiled down, even to a paste.'

'Even better, Goodwife. You'll not begrudge some for this fellow, I expect?'

'I'll get some this very second.'

'What's the situation with the River Camp now, Will?' I enquired, once we were alone. 'Have they done what I asked?'

'Camp pushed up the river beyond the castle. New men put in place, but...' he paused, 'the old guards from there won't be accepted back into the main camp until they're cured, so the officers say.'

'So where are they?'

'On their own, muttering that they're being treated like the enemy when it's not their fault that the true enemy was poisoning them.' He grinned. 'They're just on the other side of the bridge and to the left, where we took the back way to the Town Hall.'

'I'll go down and bleed them all to cleanse them and balance their humours. I'm going to tell Rigby that they must have ale aplenty for their full cure, which will annoy him, no doubt.' I felt smug at the thought. 'Two days at most and we should be on our way home.'

Thirty Six

A Spaniard's Help

'Up, Doctor, up.' Will shook me awake. 'We're assaulting the castle.'

Groggy from sleep, I tried to pull my senses together. Grabbing my boots and cloak, I near fell down the ladder and onto Thomas, holding a pitcher of milk, some of which slopped on the floor. Will was itching to get going, so I gave a quick 'Sorry' to our host and followed him out the door.

It was barely light, cold enough for me to draw my cloak tightly around me, no wind, dry but wet underfoot. We walked quickly to the undercroft of the Town Hall, but there was no-one there. Above us came the crack of a musket. 'Up the ladder, Will, and see if someone up there can tell us what's happening.' I instructed, but before he could move, a trooper with two muskets began to descend.

'How goes it?' I asked. He shrugged his shoulders.

'Don't know, sir. We've just been told to keep them in the church tower occupied. The rest have gone round it and up to the castle. That's all I know.'

I looked at Will and he nodded, knowing what I was thinking. 'Back to the bridge and up this side?' he asked. We set off.

Three hundred yards away stood the castle's outer wall, stark on its high mound, with the tall keep behind. We stood in a bank of trees at the foot of the rise as our troops retreated at speed, back from a modest but well-fortified gatehouse. A mere glance showed that our attack had failed, but with what even I could see, there had been very little chance of success. Why then had it even been attempted?

Further to our left we saw a group of officers and I quickly recognised Colonel Assheton, even though his back was to me. I hurried over, Will in my train.

'Why, Doctor. Come to see the fun?'

'But it looks like bedlam, sir. Is this not a repulse?'

'I hope it looks so to the defenders,' said the Colonel, 'for that's what we intend.'

'Have we not taken large casualties? Do I not see stones and other debris raining down on our men?'

'Not a single man truly hurt, I believe.' He grinned. 'But we will try them again in a moment. For what you don't see, Doctor, is that Rigby and his men are on the far side of the castle preparing to surprise the enemy.'

He continued. 'We had a stroke of luck just before dawn. The River camp that you wisely made us move, captured an enemy trooper trying to escape the castle, and he gave us some very useful information. You might like to talk with him yourself, for he is a very odd royalist.' There was a twinkle in his eye as he pointed further back, 'You'll find him under guard yonder.'

I found a sorry looking fellow, dressed only in a shirt and torn breeches, sat with his head on his knees. He didn't look up. He was loosely guarded, you would say, as three of our men were happily chatting and pointing out details of our retreat from the gatehouse whilst smoking stubby pipes and giving their man no attention whatever.

I shook his shoulder. 'Are you injured?'. He looked up but with matted black hair covering his face, I couldn't make out his features. He jumped up, taking me fully by surprise, grasped me round the chest, and in a heavily accented tongue gleefully cried 'Medico, Medico, Doctor!'

I literally fell back and, if Will hadn't caught me, would have landed flat on my back with the fellow still clutching me. 'Get off him, you fucker,' Will cried, pulling him away, and this even caused the prisoner's supposed guards to at least take the pipes from their mouths, the idiots. But I recognised something in the wretch's voice. '*Dios me salve*. it is I, Miguel, from the *Santa Anna*. *Ayudame por favor*, Doctor, *ayudame*!'

I can't say I really recognised him or his name, but I remembered the two sailors from the Spanish ship that came to grief in the River Wyre early in the year. They helped us destroy the ship to prevent Lord Derby's troops getting its cannon. In charge of our band had been the good Colonel Dodding, who in the spirit of mercy had sought a place with a local catholic family for our two Spaniards, in the hope that they could be sent home in due course. What had happened to change this? Why was this Miguel here?

'We were sent away, Señor. The country was killing my friends. Hungry all. Nobody wished good for us.'

'So how come you here?'

'Soldiers find me, say they will feed me if I fight for them,' He shrugged his shoulders. 'or I die.'

'You were brought here and were in the castle?'

'*Si*. But they beat me, piss me, and laugh. So, I climb from window to run. I tell it your Colonel.'

'Don't worry, you're safe for the present. Let me see what I can do.'

Telling the guards that Will, as a sergeant-at-arms, was in charge and that they must take Miguel back to the main camp, find him a coat, food and water, I returned to Colonel Assheton's party.

'What about that, Doctor? An interesting find, don't you think?

'I do, sir.' I replied. 'I know the man, would you believe? He is no threat to us and might even join your army if he is well treated. I believe he has already been of use?'

'He has, poor fellow. Tell me what you know of him and then I'll give you the picture here.'

It had been obvious to all concerned that the castle was near impregnable and only by starving the royalists out would we gain victory. But with details given by Miguel, a plan had been hatched.

Here at the front of the fortress and on its left hand, the ground sloped quite gently up to the walls. On its right side, the slope was much steeper, falling into the river. The rear elevation was steeper still, a true climb up to the masonry of the very Keep that, at a high level, included large windows to illuminate the castle's Great Hall. It was from a smaller window close by that Miguel had escaped.

Rigby, commanding fifty or sixty troops armed with scaling ladders, ropes, and mauls or great hammers, was on his way to the rear of the edifice, whilst here, at the front of the castle, the rest of our troops kept the royalists busy.

'We have simply circumvented the church tower, leaving a couple of men to fire the occasional shot at them. They pose no danger to us and, if our attempt on the castle is successful, they will have to give up the fight.' explained Sir Ralph, 'We will make a renewed attack on the gatehouse here as soon as I receive word that Rigby is in place.'

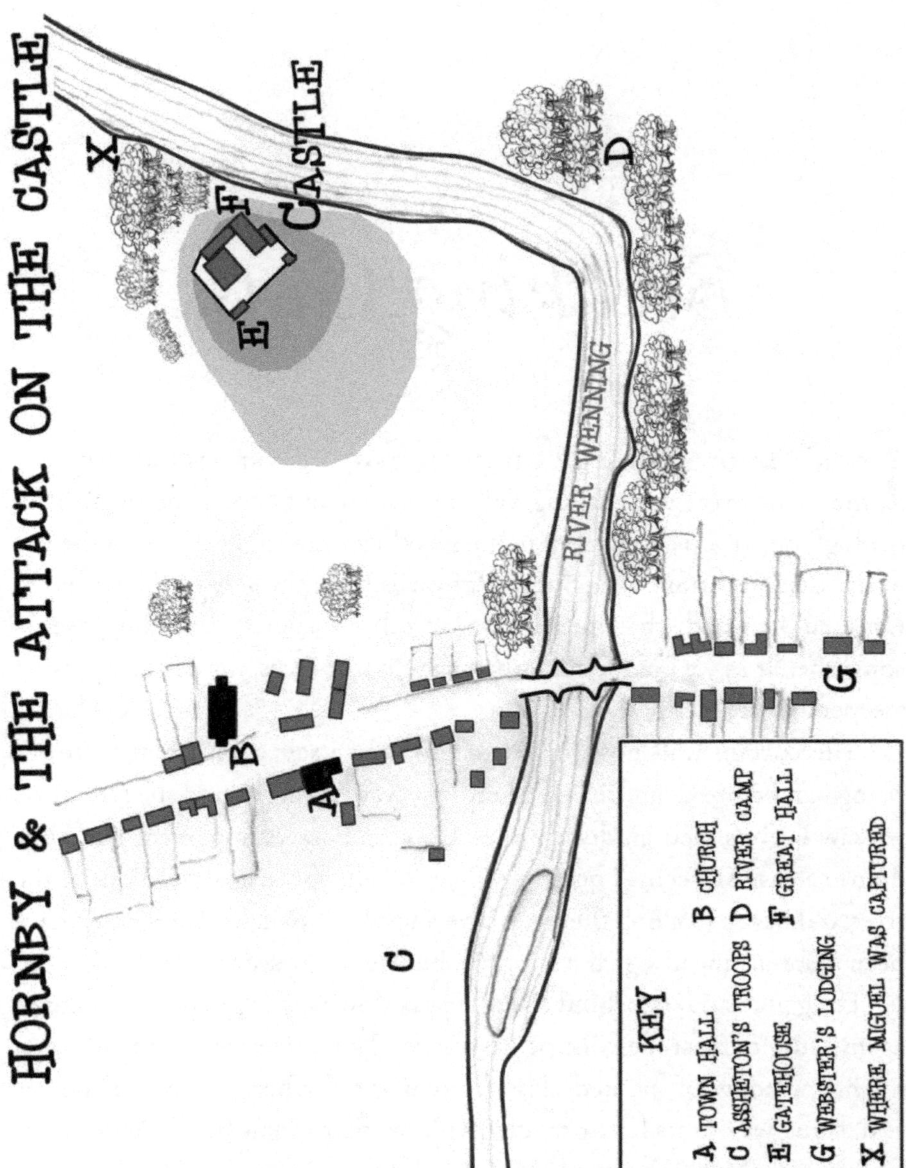
HORNBY & THE ATTACK ON THE CASTLE
X
F
CASTLE
E
D
RIVER WENNING
B
A
G
C
KEY
A TOWN HALL
B CHURCH
C ASSHETON'S TROOPS
D RIVER CAMP
E GATEHOUSE
F GREAT HALL
G WEBSTER'S LODGING
X WHERE MIGUEL WAS CAPTURED

Thirty Seven

Breaking Glass

I DON'T KNOW WHY, BUT I HAD AN URGE TO SEE THE ACTION AT the castle's rear and, calling Will to me, set out across the open field, through our troops, drawn up in lines as they were, and passing to the left of the castle's curtain wall. Some fifty yards from the side of the structure ran a sunken path that might have once been a moat, and this gave us some shelter as we ran forward, then up and into trees, the castle hill rising steeper and steeper here.

The curtain wall now joined to the keep itself, with its main tower rising just before us and, as we found our way further round the structure, we saw Rigby's men hidden in trees. Captain Fossett was of the band but didn't see us. All seemed quiet. As we watched, our men started out of the trees and began to climb the steep bare slope before them. There must have been a pre-arranged signal, I suppose, but we didn't see it.

Dragging ladders behind them, it was slow work but soon they stood against the dark stonework of the castle. Thirty feet above them was a mighty window of painted glass stretching a further twenty feet higher and, some way to its left, a smaller window that might have been the one from which Miguel escaped. Minutes dragged on as three ladders were tied together and raised with great effort to be placed, near vertical, against the wall. More delay now, as the foot of this construction was fixed, before the first man began to climb. A rope tied over his shoulder dragged a large maul after him. We could hear little sound from here but suppose that the renewed assault on the gatehouse had begun.

The climber had almost reached the sill of the huge window when his mallet caught in a rung below him, nearly jerking him off the ladder. He stopped for a moment, to steady his nerves I suspect, and started to descend. But another brave fellow near ran up the ladder, which visibly shook as he did so, unhitched the offending article from its rung and, as it swung free, the first soldier raised it by its rope, tied himself around the ladder, released the hammer, leaned back, and smote at the glass. We heard the crack and the sound of tinkling glass, but the blow had disturbed the smiter and he lost his footing. His maul fell, crashing to the ground and on down the slope as he swung precariously, held only by his rope. The second man darted up, scrambled over him, onto the window ledge and threw himself bodily through the shattering glass. Without delay, the rest of the band, with the good Captain Fossett in the middle and Rigby following, ran up the ladders, over the initial attacker still struggling to right himself, and out of view into the building.

Will was all for following the troops, but I quailed at the thought of ascending that frail ladder. I left my companion to help the struggler above us and, with a firm order not to join the attack but to follow after me, began my return to the front of the castle.

In a line before the gatehouse our musketeers fired at the battlements, forcing the enemy to keep their heads down. It was near continuous firing as loaders kept up the re-supply of readied weapons. Under this cover others had reached the very gate and, throwing bundles of straw and wood before it, set them alight. Smoke and flames were already rising as we rejoined Colonel Assheton's party.

He stood with his arms folded, his gaze, flitting from gatehouse to the flag atop the Keep, being the only sign of nerves. A servant approached with a lump of bread, cheese and flagon of ale which he declined. One of his officers, who I didn't know, leant in towards him and muttered something, receiving a short shake of the head in response.

Then, suddenly, came confused and muffled yelling from within the castle's curtain wall followed just minutes later by a white shirt waving above the parapet. A head showed and, above the now sporadic firing, came the shout 'Quarter. Give us quarter.' Sir Ralph gave a smile, slapped his officer on the shoulder, out went the cry 'stop firing' and, with difficulty the charred gates were pulled open, men now trying to clear away the flaming debris.

The royalist officers first surrendered their swords which, upon their parole, were returned to them, and they now stood in a dispirited band as their men filed out, dropped their weapons in a pile and were led away under guard. I wondered how many would elect to join our forces, rather than face imprisonment and likely starvation, for it was always difficult to find enough food just for our own men. A good many of them had little understanding of who stood for what in this conflict and the promise of some pay, even if deferred, and a morsel to eat would persuade them to fight for us. The flag came down from over the castle.

It was time to find the butcher's bill. Rigby had exited the castle and was in discussion with Colonel Assheton. He looked my way and waved me towards the gatehouse, so I guessed that I had some patients to attend to. Inside the courtyard were four royalist bodies, Will checking that they were dead. A number nursed sword cuts, none looking very serious at first glance, but in the Keep's very doorway I could see a slumped body sporting the light blue sash showing it to be one of our officers.

Captain Fossett, face almost serene, was held by one of his men. His right leg was obviously shattered, the foot at an odd angle, and there was blood soaking his left sleeve. His helmet had been removed and his man was wiping the captain's face almost tenderly. He was clearly in shock and, as I've noticed before, the pain from his wounds had not yet impinged on his conscious mind. His eyes turned to me. 'Ho there, Doctor,' he said weakly and then passed out.

My bag beside me, I quickly cut through his hose and even managed to cut away much of the upper part of his boot, but it was clear that there was nothing to be done for the leg. I bound it around the thigh to prevent further loss of blood, looked briefly at the wound to his arm, which was a mere scratch, Will and two soldiers carried him in and through to the Great Hall, laid him on a long oak table, held him down and I set to work.

It didn't take me long to remove the leg and my patient stayed unconscious throughout the operation, thank God.

Now I looked around me. Much of the huge window at the east end of the hall was shattered and there was little to tell me of its original design or pattern. The cold, dark walls must have had coverings or tapestries at one time but were now bare. With long tables at either end of the space, a fire still smouldered in a central hearth. Around the walls were piles of dirty straw where many of the troops must have slept. It was a sad, sad place made even sadder with the task I'd just performed. How I hoped Fossett would live to see his family again.

Thirty Eight

'Let Him Work His Passage'

My hopes were soon dashed. The brave Fossett never even woke from my surgery. Fever set in quickly, his soul leaving his body in the small hours of the morning.

He was the last of just three losses for our side, with six lost by our foes. There were a few minor wounds and bruises, but nothing to delay our departure for more than a day.

In view of the now worsening weather, and with cold rain threatening to come in from the west, I decided it would be foolish to return home over the high fells. It would take longer, two days in all probability, but we would have the safety of numbers by taking a different route, as Rigby had detailed off a troop of men to escort prisoners to Lancaster. And so we left the comfort of Thomas's home with grateful thanks to him and his wife, leaving what coin I could spare for our care.

Colonels Assheton and Rigby and their forces pressed on the few miles to nearby Thurland Castle to take its surrender before following us back to Lancaster.

The Spaniard Miguel I sequestered as a temporary servant, with the blessing of Sir Ralph, and Will found a nag for him to ride, from where I didn't ask. With a blanket as a cloak, he was mightily pleased to ride with us when both prisoners and most of the guards were to walk. Before us Will was laughing and chattering to one of our mounted captains and I conversed with Manuel as best I could as we travelled behind the wretched captives.

'When we first met,' I asked Miguel, 'you were with another, were you not? What happened to him?'

'*Si*. With Diego. He die. Hunger and cold.'

'And your countrymen, the other sailors?'

'Many die also. Some join army, to eat, as me. The rest, I do not know.' He shook his head wearily. 'I want to sail ship to anywhere. Maybe get home to España.'

'Then maybe Lancaster is for you.' I said brightly, 'It is a port, and ships come here from all over the world, I believe. I will do what I can once we are there.'

'And all others from the *Santa Anna*, they too?'

'I can't work miracles, Miguel.'

'*Si, si*. You are *Santo Doctor, Santo Medico*. You save me. You save them.'

I turned from him with a small measure of disgust and urged Bay forward. Papist talk, I would have none of it, and neither would I waste my time gathering this group of sailors from far and wide in the vain hope of finding them all a ship.'

The rain held off and we continued on to the city. With a little sun, it would have been a pleasant journey, but the road was bad with mud and deep ruts where many carts had passed. The squat bulk of the fortress came into view long before we came to the first hovels. Down to our right, the muddy banks of the river could be seen, but of the water nothing, for these were in the reach of the tide, which must have been out.

St. Lenord's Street was flanked by burgage plots. Many looked prosperous, though an earthwork ran between two of them, earth and stone thrown up into a low bank that led away to our left, a defensive line, I believe. We reached the Stone Well and beyond it ran a line of burned-out buildings, men pulling timbers out of one. There were many townspeople about, attending to their business, I'm sure, and a Gentleman being carried in a chair by two black servants dressed in green satin. Little notice was taken of us as we passed. We turned into Church Street and I shouted for Will, who dropped back for me. 'All are going to the castle, Will, but let's leave them to it. I've little wish to join them in that forbidding place. Find us an inn if you can.'

'No sooner said than done, Doctor,' he grinned, 'here's a very one, right by us.'

The sign of this hovel, no more, without even shutters at its window, showed a bare man, crudely painted, sat cross-legged, with a huge pair of scissors hiding his parts. The legend below it read 'The Naked Taylor'. 'You do have an eye for all the best inns, Will' I said sarcastically.

'If that don't please, sir,' said he, 'I can try The Mare, or The Maid. Both are just further down.'

How he always seems to know every inn and alehouse wherever we go is another of life's mysteries, the primary one being how he is never without a comely lass to share his bed. Except, of course, when he has to share with me.'

I thought he would try The Maid for its name alone, but we settled at The Mare, a big improvement, which promised me a room to myself and 'blankets washed that very week'. Normally I would have had the room for myself and Will, but I didn't want Miguel there too. His place was in the stable with our cattle and, as I didn't like the look of the inn's other customers, Will must lie there also. My Bay is such a fine creature that everyone covets her, and I didn't want to find her gone by morning.

Having pushed our way through to the fire and commandeered a table Will asked, in what purported to be a whisper but could, in reality, be heard by anyone, 'What are we to do with the Spaniard?' Heads turned and, as we were already under some scrutiny simply for being strangers, all attention was focused upon us. I gave Will a pained look and he grimaced as if to say sorry. Manuel, already a little short of medium height, sunk even further into himself. I turned and looked each man directly in the eye for a moment and they soon looked away.

For food the landlord, fat as a butcher, could only give us cold buttered chops, but it sufficed. I settled for a pint of wine, fresh brought from Portugal I was told, Will had ale and Miguel was given small beer.

'The town looks well and prosperous.' I said to the landlord, looking to engage him in conversation, for a thought had come to me. 'The war doesn't trouble you much, I see.'

'Oh sir, you jest, surely? We are lucky to be spared here, for much of the town has been fired and laid waste by the King's men. They asked our Mayor for help to remove Colonel Shuttleworth's men from the castle, but he wouldn't give it, so they wrought fire and pillage and other despoilation upon us. Just this very street behind us is destroyed even. And sparks rained upon my roof but was put out in a God-given rainstorm.' He crossed himself.

'We did see one or two properties burned, certainly, but no great destruction.' I was shocked.

'Half the town gone, sir, I do assure you.' He put a hand to his heart. 'It will take years to put things right, I believe. Providing, in course, that war does not visit us again...'

'But you have good wine, ale and food.' I was astonished. 'There is no sign of the misfortunes of war in here.'

'Just God's protection and luck, sir. I can't believe that I am still here with my house intact. A miracle, sir, a miracle.' He shook his head. 'It is also as well that we are a port, for the ships still come in, war or no, and so my trade continues.'

'Yes. And this is indeed good wine. Fresh in from Portugal, you say?'

His aspect changed. He now looked a little worried, furtive even, and a bead of sweat ran down the side of his face and into his whiskers. 'All duty paid, sir, I can assure you. I have no trade with smugglers, your Honour, I do assure you...'

I laughed, remembering that Parliament now levied a tax on beer and ale to pay for our army. 'Have no worry. We're not here to claim duty. In any case, do you now have to pay on wine also?' That was a development I hadn't heard of. 'I care not how you came by the wine or what you paid. I am interested in any ships to and from Portugal, however.' I pointed at Miguel. 'This man is a Portugee.'

Ignoring Miguel's pained, affronted look, I continued 'He is stranded here and wishes to return home. Do you know who we may talk to and discuss his passage?'

The Innkeeper relaxed. 'Not I, sir, but I can direct you to someone who might help.'

It was mid-morning on another grey and oppressive day, and we were standing close to the bridge spanning the grey-brown waters of the Lune, the city and castle behind us. I had paid handsomely for someone to guard the horses and, with the Inn's fees also paid, my purse felt much lighter. I felt quite well. I had been shaved, rather clumsily it must be said, but with a comb having been dragged through my hair and my face washed, I was ready to face the world anew.

We had been there some time, watching the tide reach its zenith, and waiting for a small boat. There was plenty of bustle along the quaysides with some small ships tied up, some loading, but one unloading salt. Small wheelbarrows of the near white stuff were being pushed up a brow from ship to shore, and I wondered who collected the salt tax here. It had been Kendall's main money-spinner, after buying the office from the King. Two large fellows, shabbily dressed and with large wooden shovels over their shoulders, walked past, one kicking and oversetting a barrow, the other punching its pusher to the ground. Will ran over and helped the victim to his feet. 'What was that about, Mate?'

'It's them bloody sleechers,' he said, cradling his arm, 'who make salt in the Bay. They're always doing this. Even with higher tax, the salt we bring in is better nor theirs, and the rich prefer it. Says we're doing them down. Bastards. Look at this mess!' he righted his cart and began ladling the salt back with his hands.

'Not all peace and light here then.' said Will, returning to my side.

The bigger ships of more than one hundred tons burthen were out at the mouth of the river, too large to brave the Lune's muddy and shallow waters, I was told. At a warehouse close by us, merchants were haggling over bales of tobacco.

The previous evening, I had been called from my room to meet a swarthy fellow, heavy set in his shoulders and arms and in the skirts of a sailor, from one of the out-anchored ships. I was familiar with such types, having seen many mariners when I was in London. They are a peculiar lot, throwing their money about when they have it, drinking to excess and often needing treatment for various ailments, usually the pox, costiveness, or hernias. Yes, binding hernias had been quite profitable, helping pay for my studies, I recall.

We sat over a jug of ale, he drinking the most of it to be sure, silently sizing each other up. I waited for him to speak first, having found that this can give one a slight advantage in a negotiation.

'Why do you want passage?' His voice was deep, with a rough edge to it, but not hostile, and something of a lilt like a Welshman.

"I don't. It's not for me.'

He frowned. 'You a King's man or Parliament? If I'm going to carry a spy, I needs to know.'

I laughed. "In this matter I'm neither for King nor Parliament. And there is no spy. In fact, if you're sailing for Portugal, I have a sailor for you. I'm told that most ships always have need of crew?'

'Maybe,' he said, 'It depends. Can he hand, reef and steer small? How much will it cost me? He's not a Sallyman, is he? I won't have no Sallyman.'

'If I knew what a Sallyman was, I might be able to answer.'

'A Moor, a Rover, a Corsair,' he exclaimed, 'Captain will have none o'them aboard us, and quite right too. Vile murderers all, that would set about us if we gave them leave. Chased us many times, fired on us even, and if one rope had given way, then I wouldn't be here now. Either dead or worse.'

'What would be worse?' I was intrigued and fascinated.

'Chained to an oar in a galley-ship.' He shivered. 'It chills me to the bone. You ever seen one o'they galleys?'

'Never, sir.'

'They be hell.' He took a long draught of his ale and stared into the fire for some moments. 'I seen 'em, poor Christians all, like skelingtons, and if they begins to fail are thrown overboard to drown.' I let him stare on for a few moments.

'Look,' I said, 'This innkeeper says you are a fair man, your master is a good captain, and I take him at his word. This is my need and my offer.

Travelling with me is a Spanish sailor. Did you hear of the ship, wrecked in the Wyre River early in the year?' He nodded. 'Then he is from that, just one of those thrown on the mercy of the people and neglected. Many of his fellows are dead through cold and hunger. He is lucky. He gave me some assistance and now I wish to help him. I require nothing from you but to let him work his passage. If you go to Portugal, it is next to Spain, and he may even walk home from there, perhaps.' I paused. 'Will you meet him?' he nodded.

The bargain was soon made.

I never saw the ship *Dainty*. She had been part loaded with woollens, lighters dropping down the Lune to load her, and she lay at anchor off Sunderland Point, waiting for the last of her cargo and crew. I had been assured she was a well-found vessel, stoutly built here on this very river only four years ago. I could only hope that she would safely land Miguel somewhere from which to get home. This was a late last run for this year and, I was told, if the weather was fair, *Dainty* would be in Porto in six weeks, returning either here or to a southern port before Christmas, carrying a return cargo of heavy wine.

I knew Porto was to the north of the country and, though a Spaniard, I expect Manuel would be received well there, especially having arrived aboard an English ship. We have long had a good reputation with Portugal, going back as far as the Crusades it is said.

We saw the Long-boat or whatever one should call it leaving the wharf just up-river and it quickly bumped into the riverbank immediately below us. Miguel was both affected and elated in equal parts, throwing his arms around Will and me in turn, calling me '*Santo Doctor*' in his catholic way. He jumped down into the craft, a sailor pushing him onto a thwart, shoving an oar in his hand, and moving to the stern in one fluid motion. The Mate turned and touched his hat to me, Miguel flashed us a smile, the craft shot under the bridge and was lost to sight.

'Hope the poor bugger makes it,' said Will, 'but I'm glad to see him go. Why can't they speak like us, instead of that babbling noise? Thought you were going to take him in, Doctor, to be honest.'

'I've enough to cope with. Slater, Nate, Pod, Sam and you."

'Me! It's me looking after you, Doctor, and no mistake.' He was laughing. 'The scrapes I've got you out of...'

Thirty Nine

The Chapter House

WILL IS QUICK, I'LL GIVE HIM THAT.

We had left Lancaster some six miles behind, passing the new-looking Thurnham Hall. I believe it was only built five years ago by a roman family, but it already looked deserted with closed shutters. The ground being uneven, we let the horses walk, and shortly expected to meet the hamlet of Cockerham. To our left a line of bare trees flanked the road, to the right a shallow ditch and a few bushes still in leaf opened onto rough pasture.

'How's Bay?' said Will, quietly. 'Will she reach gallop at your bidding?' I looked across at him in surprise. 'I thought I saw a movement just back there as we passed, and I've definitely seen something ahead. Don't look, Doctor.' I'd just begun to turn round but stopped myself. 'If you think your horse can do it, let's make a break to the right. The ground looks soft, but I think it'll take us.'

He knows this stuff better than me. We'd heard tales of bands of deserters turned brigand in many areas and this could be one of them. If we kept our track, we might lose everything, even our lives. I have full trust in my trusty Bay, know she will respond instantly to my urging, and Will must believe in his mount also, or he would never have asked. I gave a brief nod. 'On the count of three then.' he said, 'One, two…' I pulled Bay to the right, she jumped the ditch, and we were off into the open field. If Slater hadn't added ribbons to my hat, I would have lost it.

The ground was wetter than I expected and after a few hundred yards I pulled Bay up and looked back. Will was still some way behind but closing fast, whilst beyond him I could see a group of men gathering, possibly twenty or so, some in white coats, some in dark blue, Royalist colours. 'A close call there, Will.' I said as he joined me. We tried to press the horses to trot but the ground was getting boggier and boggier and dotted with clumps of sedge and rushes. With no sign of pursuit, we reduced the pace back to a walk.

Now arcing to our left, to try and make some southing before re-joining the road, our way was blocked by a deep water-filled drain. This could have been easily jumped if the ground was hard, but not in its current soggy state. For a half-mile we followed its course as it became deeper and wider. I had seen these conditions before, when we'd been chased by other royalists through the marshlands of the Fylde, so I had no doubt that it would lead into the salt-flats that lined the coast, though we couldn't yet see the sea itself. To our right the ground rose slightly, so we made for that.

'Whoa, Doctor!' exclaimed Will as we breasted the low rise, 'I've never been this close to the sea.' Before us, the land dipped away into a broad swathe of mud, with a placid sea beyond. To our right the land swept inwards to a broad river mouth, and almost in the angle between sea and river was an odd-looking stone building.

'You're wrong, Will. You've been much nearer the sea than this. Remember when we rescued Colonel Dodding from Rossall Hall. We ran along the sea wall with the water hissing below us.'

'Ah, yes. But that was at night. I never got a glimpse of the sea then, did I?'

'No, but it was still there.'

'Not if I didn't see it. Doesn't count if I don't see it.' he pronounced smugly. 'Nearest I seen it is from the top of yon fells.'

One can't argue with a sophist. Let him have his little victory, I thought, or this argument could go on all day and drive me to distraction. 'Have you had sight enough now, or are you going to keep staring at this less than wonderful vista till night falls upon us?' I asked. We rode on towards the stone building.

Low piles of reddish stone and scrubbed out walls were on either hand as we came near, whilst the single storey building itself appeared, part octagon, each corner supported by a buttress. Arched windows, roughly bricked-up, looked sightlessly out of walls eighteen feet high and with crenelations above. Topping all was a broken cross. I was racking my brain as to what it could be, and then remembered reading of an Abbey, Cockersand by name, pulled down, as so many, in the time of the last King Henry. Perhaps this was part, I thought.

I cannot judge whether King Henry was a good monarch or bad, but his actions did start to move us away from Rome to a truer faith, if Martyn's *Lives of the Kings of England* is to be believed. That is one of the treasured volumes of my library, of which I have said more than once, is as dear to me as my family. Dearer if truth be told.

The only other thing I remember of Henry is that he had a multiplicity of wives, poor man. Yet most of these he had killed, which would suggest he was less than Christian, though I cannot believe he was as duplicitous as our present king, who would move us back to Rome and has brought us to war amongst ourselves. Still, I think, I hope, I expect Parliament to prevail, God willing. I am with the Puritans in this.

From the side of the building a face appeared, but quickly withdrew before I could tell whether it was a man or woman. No door could yet we see. Circling left but keeping twenty feet or more from the walls in case of ambush, the edifice became more regular, the side a straight wall with no windows. Further, and a sharp corner brought an arched doorway into view. We dismounted, me with my hand to my blade, Will drawing his sword as he cautiously approached the heavy oak door. We could hear nothing from within. Will put his ear to the door itself but then looked at me and shook his head. Silence. We looked at each other for a second and I could see he was waiting for a decision from me. I raised my eyebrows, gave a short nod, and he slowly reached for the handle, turned it and the door opened with a slight creak.

It was the smell that hit us first, a rank odour of decay and sweat but also a sweetness that I couldn't at first place. It was dark inside, the windows being blocked, the only light from behind us and through a small hole in the roof above a few smouldering embers in the centre of the space. As our eyes adjusted to the gloom, we saw emaciated faces, large eyes staring at us. No one made a sound. Then a figure came towards us, an ancient, bald man, badly bent. It looked as if he was wearing a dirty white smock. And then it hit me. Of course, the sweetness was incense. This must be a catholic priest. How could he have survived here? Surely not since the Abbey was dissolved? Looking at him I could believe it, though it would have made him over a hundred years old.

The priest held up a small wooden crucifix and began to mumble what I took to be a prayer. Even in his mumbling I recognised a little Latin. I waved his words away and indicated that he should come outside, where I might breathe freely, and he followed me out of the door.

'What is this place?' I asked harshly, 'and what are you doing here?'

He blinked in the daylight and said quietly 'This is my home and I tend these men.'

'Tend them with your roman nonsense?' I sneered.

'It is their faith and mine. I was taught to minister to poor souls such as these and give what comfort I can. No-one else would help and they made their way to me.'

There was a gentleness about him, a sincerity in his voice and look. I abhor his beliefs but there could be many a misguided person capable of doing a good deed for his fellow man. I would give him the benefit of my doubts.

'I am a doctor. I attend the body as you do the soul. Your attentions do not sit well with me and, to be plain, I think your religion is false and dangerous. But then my ministrations cannot always cure the body...' My voice trailed off as my thoughts ran on. 'Are these men King's men or for Parliament? Are they deserters?'

'Neither sir. They are a dozen poor, beleaguered sailors, cast ashore in a land that will give them no shelter, no succour...'

My spirits sank. 'Don't tell me. Are they Spaniards?'

'Yes. Do you know of them?' he said eagerly.

Did I know of them? I was beginning to feel haunted by them. 'They are from the ship that wrecked in the Wyre River? What are they doing here, for God's sake?'

'Here by God's hands, by all means. Through His goodness and mercy, he has steered them here to me and I must help them as best I can. It is little enough, I fear, for they are dying. But even in that I can help them pass into God's hands.'

I don't believe in Saints like the Romans do. I don't believe that praying to someone who says he has seen God, or to one who has been killed because of his beliefs, or to one who has been said to have performed miracles, will persuade God to help the prayer. I don't believe that, unless shriven, the Devil will take your soul. None of that makes sense to me. But I concede that faith, even a catholic faith, must be a comfort in a time of despair, and I also concede that one does on occasion find a saintly person on earth. To me, this priest, in his actions, should therefore be considered a saint.

'I cannot feed them,' the priest continued, 'and they are dying of hunger. Can you do something for them, in God's name?'

'This isn't our land,' I said, with no little exasperation, 'We are just travelling through. We know no one here. I've been able to help one of their friends, who has just passed by here in a ship bound for Portugal, would you believe. Before that we put two in the keeping of a roman family south of here, but they were eventually turned out.'

The priest shook his head sadly. "Then these men will die.'

There was little I could do. I thought of suggesting that they get to Lancaster in the hope of a ship but realised that would not do. They could not walk that far, no captain would hire such men in their condition, and I doubted that any more ships would leave for Spain or Portugal this year. Would that they had joined an army of whatever colour, as Miguel had done, they would have been fed at least.

Though the atmosphere, in what the priest said had been the Chapter House of the large monastery, was fetid I gave what attention I could to each man. Many had the sores, swollen and bleeding gums of scurvy for which I could do nothing, as I had no vinegar or elixir of vitriol. I suggested a change of air might help, as the noxious fug of the building must cause a worsening of their condition, and a few wearily rose and went outside, to shiver in the cold air off the sea for a moment before returning to their dirty straw. A bleeding might have helped, excepting that it might weaken them further. I applied unguent to some sores, but the little I had soon ran out.

Will touched my arm. 'The light is fading, Doctor.' He looked at me earnestly. 'What are we going to do? We've no food neither, and I can't see a way out of here unless we head north to the river mouth and try to follow it round and back to Lancaster. Unless, that is, you want to throw our lot in with them Brigands that we lately avoided?'

'Not I, Will. I hate to say it but think we must stay here in this terrible place for the night.'

'That's what I thought you'd say, damn it.'

Forty

'No Point Trying Anything Else'

I have possibly spent worse nights, though I can bring none to mind. It was far worse than our first night in Hornby. We cleared a space by the door and slept sitting upright against the wall, our saddles on either side. I say slept, but in truth I did little but doze from time to time, with bugs biting and Will falling heavily against me. There were constant groans from all parts of the room, and the passing of bodily fluids increased the rank stench of the place. Before first light, with the drone of the priest intoning prayers, I could stand no more and rose, jerking Will awake as I got up. Pulling at the door, I stumbled out and took a deep breath and scratched myself.

The moon was still up in a clear sky that was beginning to light from the East. To the West lay the full Bay, small waves rippling across its surface from a cold breeze, the tide still rising, the horizon obscured by a bank of cloud. I pissed against the wall, pulled my cloak more firmly around me and Will joined me, shivering and only half-awake. Our horses stood in the shelter of a wall, looking as disconsolate as I felt. Bay's legs were covered with mud almost to her knees, a thing I would never have allowed, if I had a choice.

'What now, Doctor?'

'All I know is that we must get from this hellhole, Will. How, I don't know, but I need food and drink. And a warm bed.'

We saddled the horses, Bay looking at me with accusatory eyes. The sky continuing to lighten with the dawn, we moved to the other side of the Chapter House and onto the small rise to peruse the landscape. It looked desolate.

To the North was a drain, stretching right across our path and, even beyond, the ground looked marshy and wet. To the South, the drain that we had followed the previous day emptied into the mud of the Bay. To the East, a few stunted trees and bushes stood in low and damp land for a mile or so before reaching true woodland, but there lay the prospect of brigands. Still further lay the Bowland fells, and I now wished with all my heart that we had taken that path instead.

'What if…' said Will, pausing. 'No. No, I can see no clear path.' He again fell silent.

'I think, Will, that the only thing is for us to retrace our steps till we get close to the road and then try and push to the north, back towards Thurnham.'

'You're right, Doctor, I'm sure, except that those cutpurses or whatever, if they are on watch, will have plenty of time to see us and move to catch us as we finally get on the road.'

I realised that, but just nodded and moved off without comment.

'Not going to give your farewells to the priest?' Will asked. I gave no response. There was nothing I could do for any of those here, and I wanted to erase the memory of the damned place.

Again, it was hard going across the waterlogged land, and it seemed to take longer to return to the road than it had taken to get to the Chapter House. The horses were so reluctant to move that we dismounted and led them for most of the way, leaving us wet, mud-caked, and despondent. Neither of us spoke.

We had gone almost two miles, travelling South then East, with still almost a mile to go to the village of Cockerham, when we were stopped by a drain running across our path. "We're going to have to cross this,

Doctor.' said Will grimly. 'No point trying anything else, I'd say. Shall I go first?'

'I'm just concerned that the horses may baulk at it, but I'm sure you're right.' I replied, looking around. 'We must try. Any sign of those bandits?'

Will stopped, peering to our left. 'Not them, but I hear something…' I stood stock still, Bay breathing down my neck, and then I heard it too, the clatter of many people moving along the road.

'Safety in numbers, Will. Let's get going.'

The drain was only five feet wide, its muddy sides sloping into dirty water of an indeterminable depth some two feet below us. If the banks had been dry and sound, both Will and the horses could have jumped it with ease, though I might have struggled to clear it, I fear. I unclipped the reins from one side of Bay's bridle, whilst Will brought his reins and fastened them to the loose end of mine. Holding tightly to this lifeline and with Bay as near to the edge as I could get her, he let himself down the bank and into the murky water. Bay bowed her head with his weight. 'Damn, it's cold.' was all he said, as his boots sank below the surface. He let go the rein, tugged his boots from the cloying mud, and started to clamber up the far side.

'Not so deep, Doctor,' he cried, standing up, the whole of his tunic and his hands liberally covered in mud. 'See if you can persuade Joanie to follow me.' His horse was standing by me as I held her by a saddle strap. 'Give her a belt on the arse if needs be.'

'Bay would be better to take the lead I believe. She's the less skittish of the two I think.' I spoke into her ear, 'Go on, lass, you can do it' and patted her behind. She hesitated, turned and looked at me, then put her feet on the edge of the ditch and slid down into the water in a very undignified way, snorting as she did so. She very nearly fell, swivelled so she was parallel to the sides and started as though to move down the stream, panic showing in her eyes.

'Throw me the rein,' shouted Will, but I could no longer reach it, it too falling into the water. I launched myself down the bank, grasping a stirrup. 'Up Bay, up,' I shouted at her, as Will threw himself flat to grab her bridle. Snorting like mad and with her eyes large and frightened, she pawed at the mud. Then, miracle of miracles, part of the bank collapsed, she gained a grip with a hoof, Will pulled, and she leapt clear. The stirrup was snatched from my grasp, and I fell bodily into the water.

Now it was my turn to panic. I've never liked being immersed, especially after nearly drowning in the river Ribble when trying to escape from Kendall's men, now more than a year ago. Then, Pod and Nate pulled me from the water. This time it was Will. 'Now you've got both of us wet,' he said, as I lay on the ground trying to catch my breath, which I think was meant to pass as humour. I didn't reply.

With Bay safely across the drain, and possibly in fear of being left behind, Will's Joanie seemed more willing to try and follow. She stood on the edge of the bank, nodding her head for some time before we could coax her across, then literally jumped into the stream. Her legs first seemed to crumple beneath her, but she was up and out in seconds to stand, like Bay, shivering and likewise coated brown with thick mud. We led them across the uneven ground towards the road where men and carts were already passing through, light rather than dark blue colours now in evidence.

'They're ours, Doctor. Is it Rigby or Colonel Assheton, do you think?'

'I couldn't care less, Will.' I was feeling less than happy. 'Even if it was the King, I'd bow and scrape with the best of them to get out of this filth and wet.'

We had now attracted some attention, two mounted officers detaching from the line of men to stand watching us as we struggled and stumbled the last few hundred yards to the road. 'I think that's the Doctor and his man,' exclaimed one, 'I recognise that bay horse. What a beauty, I say, and too good for him.' Then he shouted to us, 'Is that the Doctor? What are you doing, sir? You look filthy and wet.'

'Yes, it's us,' I shouted angrily. I was in no mood for their stupid questions. 'Bear a hand, bear a hand, for goodness' sake.'

Colonel Assheton's army was on its way to the south to bolster our forces in Cheshire, where certain Royalist positions were holding out. As his men and baggage train marched on, he and his senior officers had stopped at an inn in Cockerham. It was there we caught up with them.

'Doctor!' he exclaimed in great surprise. 'I thought you'd be home by now.' He looked me up and down. 'But you're wet and filthy…' I nearly swore at him.

'Yes. As you see, sir, we are in some distress.'.'

'Where have you been, has someone assaulted you?'

I was eager for a wash, for food, a bed, care for the horses, but gave a short account of our doings. I have always had a respect for him, but it was sorely tested when he grinned at our flailing about in the drain. He was also surprised when I related the plight of the Spaniards at the abbey.

'I thought Parliament had resolved to help them home. Their condition was reported to them after the ship had been fired.'

'That maybe so, sir, but nothing has been done for them. They are dying of want.' I replied.

'God help them then, for I can do nothing at present. How is the place to be reached?'

That I did not know. Certainly not by the way we had used. I didn't even know how the sailors had found that place of sanctuary, so far from the Wyre.

Forty One

'A Strange and Wonderful Monster'

Bidding us farewell and good luck, Assheton left us to resume his progress to Preston, whilst Will and I stayed at the Inn. Our host found a child to attend the horses, clean them and our tack from the mud, and feed them. Our clothes and boots we dried by a roaring fire and were given basins of warm water in which to bathe. Cheese, bread, and ale we devoured with relish before taking a rest, Will on a palliasse at the foot of my decrepit and loose strung tester bed. Though it was only just past noon, I immediately fell into a deep sleep.

I awoke to the sound of a dawn cockerel and lay in warmth and comfort until the harsh notes of geese under my window persuaded me to rise. I used the piss-pot, noticing that Will had already risen and my dry clothes now lay next the bed. I still must have been a little groggy from sleep, as I hit my head quite heavily on the low doorway before descending the narrow stairway, but a pint of small beer cured that. My hat and boots, still near the fire, were yet damp, despite being filled with straw to draw the wet, but it was of little consequence.

The mistress of the house brought me an egg and a small bowl of gruel as Will came in to join me, telling me that the horses were revived and, though the saddles were near dry, the girths appeared to have shrunk with the water. They would need extra holes to be punched if we were to go straight way. Though I wished for home, I was in no immediate hurry after the upsets of our last two days, happy to wait in warmth and comfort for a while longer.

Under a jug on the table, I noticed a paper, a newsbook, to which I gave my attention. You may be surprised that I, a prodigious reader, should normally eschew such publications, but I'd found that, since the start of the current dreadful conflict and their proliferation, they were devoid of accurate news or information. Both sides were using them to instil a dread of the opposition, reporting on savage treatment, massacre, or devil worship by the other side, of strange apparitions and portents appearing. This tract was no different, claiming the appearance of a monster, and with a terrible image printed thereon. What attracted the most of my attention was that this monster had appeared at a town near Preston.

It read:

A DECLARATION
Of a strange and Wonderfull MONSTER:
Born in KIRKHAM Parish in LANCASHIRE (the Childe of Mrs. *Haughton*, a popish Gentlewoman) the face of it upon the breast, and without a head (after the mother had wished rather to bear a Childe without a head than a Roundhead) and had cursed the PARLIAMENT.
Attested by Mr. FLEETWOOD, Minister of the same Parish, under his own hand; and Mrs *Gattaker* the Mid-wife, and divers other eye-witnesses; Whole testimony was brought up by a *Member* of the House of Commons.

Below it was a picture of the very beast.

The Innkeeper knew nothing of the story, excepting that he believed it, the newsbook having been left by a traveller more than a week ago. I wondered at the coincidence. Only a few weeks ago I had spoken to young Richard Towneley about this very sort of story. He'd been looking at sailors tales of such strange beings in Hakluyt's *Voyages* and I'd commented that they were probably untrue. Now, just twenty miles from here was a supposedly authenticated version. I couldn't let this pass. I could justify myself that just a small detour from our homeward path would take us to Kirkham though, in reality, it might add a day and more than five and twenty miles to our journey. Will would not be pleased.

In a brighter day than expected, though with a bitter wind now blowing from the East, we passed through Garstang and reached the small settlement of Churchtown in time for a late repast. The horses were glad to be out and on a road that, although badly pitted, was a pleasure to them, though all around us were the same dreary marshlands of yesterday. The Church of St. Michael at Wyre was our next waypoint, its stubby tower a pointer for some miles, before crossing the bridge and passing through better drained fields to Inskip and Wharles, both small hamlets with no-one in evidence. We reached Kirkham before dark, quickly finding a good inn in the most prosperous place we had seen since Lancaster, though I knew that armies from both sides had passed through in this last year.

The Queen Inn sat on the west side of a fine market square, well and pump in its centre. My store of coin was dwindling, so I first checked that room, stabling and food was still within my means, and luckily it was, though we had to share a room and beds with others in the attic.

Over a jug of ale, we asked of the Reverend Fleetwood, to no avail. Did anyone know Goodwife Haughton or Mrs. Gattaker? No-one did. Production of the newsbook got shocked looks from some and hearty laughs from others. From one table near the fire two fellows rose, took the paper, and perused it in detail, their close-cropped hair marking them out as Puritans.

'Such monsters are appearing at this time to show the Lord's displeasure and see, it has been born to a popish woman, who had cursed Parliament. It is a sign, a sign of the end of days, before which the Antichrist will reign with terror before the Last Judgement…' In a loud, booming voice the Puritans harangued us all, till a pail of beer was thrown at them and they were bundled outside to a great cheer. Even then, they continued to shout in the square for some time. I thought their speech was rather too much, especially when it was already becoming clear that the story was a fraud, no-one here knowing of the monster or the people named. The event cheered me up immensely, but I did start to have a little, though only a little, sympathy for some of the people who, in their ignorance, clung to the roman ways. You might think me growing weak in my faith but to have to face such ranting fools day to day must be a great trial.

In the chill wind, now even colder, Will and I walked to the church next morning. A few of the stained-glass windows were broken and inside, the altar rail had clearly been removed. All catholic adornment was long gone, the walls roughly whitewashed. There was no-one inside and we quickly left. Outside, we found an old woman tending a grave. Did she know the Reverend Fleetwood? No, she did not. She had lived here for all her fifty years and had never known a Fleetwood. Had she heard of a monster being born here? No, and she would say prayers in the hope that God would protect us from such devilish things. So much for the story, for false it was, I'm sure. Yet people will believe in such things.

Whilst so many of these tales are false, and designed to fool people, I do believe in the end of days and that we will be judged at that time. With all the troubles the country is under due to our deceitful King, it is easy to believe that judgement may be upon us soon.

There was no point in staying further. Leaving now, we might just make home tonight, but we would first call on an old friend in Preston and then press on towards Hurst Green, where Will at least might find us a bed for the night if needed. He would be happy with that.

Forty Two

The Apothecary

PRESTON STOOD BEFORE US AS WE RODE UP STAND PRICK LANE to the Fisher's Gate. The small group of soldiers gathered round a brazier just inside the entrance looked up but didn't stop us. They all wore the short hair of the puritans, Round-heads we used to call them, as a mark of contempt, but I would not now dare to call our soldiers such names.

On and into the Market-Place, bustling with troops, their light blue coats telling us that we had caught up with Colonel Assheton's army. A party of pikemen were lining up to the shouts of their officer, whilst a few desultory folk, mainly women, stood at near empty stalls nearby. Close under the walls of the Town Hall, a dozen horses stood, ready saddled, attended by a small boy wearing a coat that was far too big for him. Down to our right was the house that had for a time, earlier in the year, been my Infirmary.

Leaving Will with the horses I walked the short distance to the shop of the Apothecary, Moshe ben Israel. His alley had fared no better since last I was here, stinking of piss and shit, and even the bonnet shop had closed down. It was quite dark and gloomy, the jettied storeys of the properties almost shutting out the sky, and I had to pick my way carefully through the effluvium. Above the Apothecary's door was a rough sign indicating the property's purpose, but still visible was the scrawl of white across the door saying *JEW*. I knocked and, after a few moments, heard the sound of boots crossing a flag floor.

I nearly fell back in horror as the door opened as, in the half-light, it looked to me as if the dreaded Tench stood before me, but I quickly recovered myself. Just as large and at least as ugly, this was no Tench, and the scarred face held no sign of malice. He simply looked at me, stared in fact, but said nothing. 'I'm looking for the Apothecary,' I said, and he gave a slight nod, stood aside and let me enter.

Two sharp raps on the counter he gave, and my friend appeared from a back room, looking more haggard and bent than I had last seen him. His near white beard now reached almost to his waist. His face was pale and his eyes dull.

'Johannes, my friend,' he cried, and moved to shake my hand, smiling openly. 'You are well? Come, come, and drink a glass of wine with me.'

'I was rather taken aback by your servant, Moshe.' I said. "It made me think that you had left this place, perhaps.'

'No. As you see, I am still here and employ him as my protector. I took him in from the street where no-one would help him, for they thought he was cursed. Rather as they think of me,' he replied with a wry smile, 'In my faith they might call him *Golem*, so I call him Gem. It is my little joke. He cannot speak but he understands well enough.'

'And you still need protection?' When I was last here, I barely prevented his destruction by a band of raving Puritans.

'It is much better, thank God. They realise I have use to them and that is enough. They need my pills and potions, so see me as a necessary evil, I believe.' He picked up his wine. 'I have little need to mix with them in the town. I send Gem out for food and only go out when ships come in carrying useful goods for me.'

'I have just come from Lancaster and see that foreign trade is still continuing, despite the war.'

'Yes. Profit comes first, I believe. I can get almost all I require with some ease. China Root is a problem, but anacardium, verdigris and tobacco come in as usual. Long may it continue. I have some good Spanish Root, which is called Liquorice, from Yorkshire, good for coughs, hoarseness and shortness of breath, if you need it?'

We fell to discussing various illnesses, their possible cures, and new medicines. 'But few potions can help when I'm obliged to amputate.' I said sadly, thinking of Captain Fossett. 'And many bad fractures bring on deadly fevers that we fail to stop.'

'When you treat a fracture, you immobilise the limb with splints, do you not?' asked Moshe. 'Do you follow Rhazes and set the leg or arm in lime and the white of egg? He also talks about the importance of diet in recovery.'

'I have heard of the fellow, and something of his methods, but have no information on how to apply them.' I mused. "He is not in my library. I will consider him. Thank you, dear colleague.'

I rose. 'I wish I could stay and talk but I must away.' I said with a sigh, 'I merely came to see you were in health, still living in fact. I almost hope that I never have to travel this way again, but if I do I will call. If I can be of service to you, please write to Clitheroe or Downham and it will surely reach me. In the meantime, you would oblige me by re-filling my depleted supplies...'

'With all my heart, dear Doctor. Can you manage a large pot of Honey? It is my own, made specially by Jewish bees and therefore sweeter by far than your gentile creatures...'

As Moshe placed various potions into my bag, there came a loud knocking at the shop door, followed by the sound of a child's voice saying, in tremulous tones 'Message. Will says, Doctor come now.' Walking into the shop, I saw a small and filthy waif cowering under the towering Gem. 'What was that, lad?'

'Message. Will says, Doctor to come NOW.'

I grabbed my bag, heavy now, gave a brief farewell to my friend and pushed past Gem's bulk into the alley. The urchin held out a grubby hand, 'Said will give a penny.' I fumbled for my purse, light as it now was, and threw him a two-pence.

'What's up, Will?'

'Message from the Colonel. Which he sees me here, though I think he recognised Bay first, and sends a captain over, saying to follow on. Battle is promised to the South and your skills may be needed.'

'Hell and death. If we'd just ridden on, we might be out of reach by now,' I said in disgust. 'Give me a taste of your beer, at least.' I grabbed his tankard and gulped it down.

The market square was now near empty, but as we passed the church and rode through the town gate, carts were being loaded in the fields to our left. Before the turn down to the Ribble bridge, two teams of four horses pulling field guns galloped past, sending small stones flying from the roadway, and thundered across the bridge. We followed as close as we could, which proved a blessing as, turning to the right, they came up behind a troop of pikemen, hollering for them to make way, and we all passed through without loss of speed.

In less than a half-hour we clattered into a hamlet where one small troop were busy wheeling barrels of ale from an inn, whilst the Innkeeper tore at his hair in distress. Less than a quarter of a mile further on, with a bank of trees on both sides of the road, we found the mass of troops and two companies of Horse. We pushed through them, hoping to find someone who would tell us what was happening.

Standing on the only slight rise in an otherwise flat landscape, the road dipped and continued on before us, with a narrow river to its left. To our right pastureland sloped gently away for two hundred yards, but beyond that, grassy clumps and reed told a story of marshland.

The day was clear, clouds high, and we could see far along the road where, less than a mile away, unknown forces were approaching. Colours were flying but, at this distance, they could not yet be made out. Assheton and his command group were on the edge of the slope under his blue and white colours and looking out over the plain, their horses standing quietly under the trees close by. The Colonel turned, pointed at a few different groups of soldiers, no doubt discussing their deployment, and various captains walked off to put his instructions into practice. He noticed me and gave a slight wave in acknowledgement.

Taking this as a sign that I might approach, I dismounted, handed Bay's reins to Will, and walked towards him, but an ensign, who I recognised from Cockerham, detached himself from Assheton's group and intercepted me. 'If you'd stay back please, Doctor. I think we'll be in action in the next half hour.'

'And who are we fighting, Ensign Tolson?'

'Lord Molyneux. He was thrown out of Liverpool by Colonel Shuttleworth some time ago but has now picked up some of the troops deserted by Lord Derby and comes at us. We received intelligence that they were marching to Preston thinking that we were still engaged to the North.' As we spoke, the cannon were run up beyond us.

'Would it not have been safer to wait for them at Preston?' I asked.

'Excepting that word has been sent to Liverpool, and Colonel Shuttleworth should be on his way. Molyneux will find himself between our two forces.'

I looked round. 'I can see nowhere for me to set up my hospital, except in the hamlet we passed.'

'Then perhaps you will move back there if battle is joined?'

'You say *if*, sir?'

'Yes, Doctor. I think we will be roughly matched in men but have what you might laughingly call the high ground. And we have two cannon. I believe the Colonel will send to Molyneux, telling him his retreat will shortly be cut off and that, for the prevention of bloodshed, he should surrender.'

I looked out beyond him, where the Royalist forces were nearing and spreading out to each side, little more than three hundred yards from us. Molyneux's colours could now be clearly seen, a yellow cross on a pale blue ground. I could even see the man himself, broad hat fastened up at one side and with a red feather in it.

Four companies of our pikemen had been placed across the road at the bottom of the slope and out to the trees on either side, with musketeers immediately behind them, to either side of our cannon. Out of the main view, our horse troops were behind the trees with the remaining companies of foot soldiers. As I watched, Colonel Assheton gave a signal and a party of three detached from his party and rode along the road with a white flag flying bravely, and shortly two enemy cavaliers came out to meet them. There was an exchange of salutes, the message passed over, and the emissaries retired.

Tolson was still by my side. "What do you make of that?' I asked.

'Standard procedure, Doctor. I think our Colonel has given them a half-hour to make their decision. It's now just wait and see.'

Forty Three

Farington Moss

HALF AN HOUR IS A LONG TIME TO WAIT UNDER SUCH circumstances, and it was cold just standing there. More carts arrived behind us, some carrying powder and shot, but more with bread, cheese, and beer to cheer the men, a good and thoughtful idea from our Colonel to keep up their spirits. He, with his command group, had now mounted their steeds. Assheton rode slowly along the line of men, stopping for a word here and there, giving his men further cheer.

I looked beyond the enemy, scanning for an indication that Shuttleworth's troops might soon arrive, but could see nothing.

There was movement in the enemy camp, with Molyneux's horse gathering on the right. With the river on his other side, he must have felt safe there and comfortable with his deployment. There was, however, no sign of a reply to our letter and now, with a shout, his musketeers came through the front ranks of pikemen, knelt down and fired a volley.

A couple of our men were hit, I could tell from the yells, whilst to my right, where Colonel Assheton had rejoined his party, a horse fell screaming, cascading its rider to the ground. In its pain, the beast tried to rise, legs flailing, and neck stretched out, until a sergeant brought a pistol to its head and shot it dead. I heard the Colonel shout to the nearest ensign 'Give the Lieutenant your horse and go find yourself another.'

As Molyneux's pikemen strode towards us, our musket men readied themselves for a signal to fire, whilst our cannon boomed out, the smoke quickly whipped away in the sharp breeze. Our front line of pikemen dropped down with the enemy less than one hundred yards away, and now our muskets fired, doing great damage to the advancing foe. Up jumped our pikemen, ready for the fray.

The enemy's horse charged to our right, but as they did so, our horse came round the trees and crashed into and through their left side and into the side of Molyneux's pikemen. All was confusion, pistols cracking and swords slashing, and I knew I'd soon be busy.

The pikemen were now at each other, their long and deadly weapons being forced up into the air as the men pressed together like an angry swarm of wasps, each side pushing to gain ground. And then our second troop of horse appeared to our left. They were beyond the river, but as I watched, they galloped forwards till they were almost behind Molyneux's troops, leapt the river in unison and careered into the enemy colour party, whose flag went down. It was a brilliant stroke.

From out the back of this melee appeared Molyneux who, with a small group of officers, galloped from the field of battle, whilst his rear-guard desperately tried to recover their colours and prevent our men from pursuing their now defeated commander.

Fighting was continuing below us, but I could see wounded men being helped from the field, so left them to it. There was Will away to my right, trying to commandeer a powder wagon and I quickly joined him, waving and shouting for the wounded to be brought to us. Jumping down from Bay, I gave each one a quick look, set those capable of walking back to the hamlet, and literally threw those who couldn't walk onto the cart.

I saw someone trying to hold Bay and grabbing at my bag and panniers. What he was at I didn't know but, a spare ramrod for a cannon lying just to hand, I grabbed it and swung viciously at his legs, collapsing him in a heap. Bay trampled him as I pulled her to me, jumped on her back and waving to the carrier to follow me, rode back up the lane, the sound of battle fading behind us.

It takes a long time to stop a battle, as most cannot hear orders to lay down their arms, or even hear anything at all if they've been next to a cannon, musket, or pistol. A good number of the injured had some excuse, though, as a surprising number had lost an ear to a pike thrust. Lacerations large and small, mere nicks or deep cuts provide my main stock in trade at such a time, and I can do little except simply bind the minor ones or stitch and bind the worst, perhaps with a little grease to protect the wound. I'm sure I've said it before, but the nastiest are the broken or smashed bones where I can do little but amputate. Fortunately, there were few of the latter this time. Despite this, Will had quickly excused himself from the barn that I had commandeered, and I had little help for the first few hours until a butcher offered his services.

One of the Royalist officers, deathly pale and shivering, had taken a pike head right through his chest plate, the top part of the blade still embedded in the metal. It was obvious that at least three inches had penetrated his chest, and I was uncertain what I would find when his armour was removed, but removed it had to be. He was taking small, shallow, breaths, very quickly, and his eyes fixed on me as we undid the straps. Though we tried to lift the plate gently, the blade in his chest held fast and we were forced to literally rip it away. The spray, the very fountain of blood, drenched the butcher and there was nothing I could do to stop it, the officer dying inside of a minute with a low moan.

Another young fellow (I think one of ours, though I could not be sure) probably not yet fifteen years old, had taken a bad wound to his belly. His coat had been ripped away and he was, quite literally, holding his guts in place with both hands. Again, there was nothing for me to do except try to make him comfortable with a coat under his head and another over his torso. Crying for his mother, I grabbed a passing soldier and asked him to stay by him. 'No,' he said, 'I'm for food and drink…' I grabbed him by the shoulders, stared him in the eye, and in an angry whisper, for I didn't want my patient hearing, told him he would stay and see him through the next hour, or I'd cut him for it. 'He is dying and has no-one near. Wouldn't you wish someone to be there, should you be in a like state?' I was quivering with anger.

'Sorry, Sir. You're right. I'll stay.'

The boy, the mere child, didn't last an hour.

A good number were uninjured, but in shock, something I have seen before. They appear in stupor, awake but seeming asleep, and again, there is little I can do for them. It is usually troops who have not been in action before, but sometimes the most battle-hardened can succumb. Food, drink, and rest seems to be the only answer. Two were brought into the barn cackling like old hags, their wits turned by what they'd witnessed.

After a couple of hours work, I went back to the battle site, in case there were other wounded still there, but I found none. The scavengers were at work, stripping the bodies, of which there were thirty or forty by my reckoning. A few hundred prisoners stood in small groups, some crying, before being herded towards one of our captains to be given a choice, - join us or starve, that was the nub of the thing. If they chose not to become a Parliamentarian in name at least, prison might present a greater risk of death than fighting.

Our troops were either exhausted and showing no emotion in their faces or they were jubilant, but were formed to begin the slow march back to Preston. Will arranged four carts to bring back those wounded who were at all fit to travel. One of our men was a Puritan preacher and, though I was loath to leave the remainder of the injured under the torment of his sermons, I begged him remain, and I returned to Preston with Will and the carts. It was a miserable journey.

It was dark as we climbed through the town gate, but the Market Square was well lit by torches. I tried for the lodgings I'd used before, and the landlady grudgingly gave us a shared bed in the attic, and a small slab of pease pudding, cold of course. Will managed to place the horses under an open sided barn behind the house, though the straw was filthy, and they too had little to eat that night.

Tiredness compelled us to sleep, and despite the discomfort of a yet another badly strung bed and someone vomiting copiously in the corner soon after we laid down, the slattern of a hostess had to wake us. It was an even colder day than last, the wind sweeping down the streets and trying to lift the hat off my head. Thank goodness for Slater's ribbons I thought.

Just along from our boarding was the Oak Inn, formerly the Royal Oak, and there we went for breakfast. A shilling and sixpence for a chop each and a jug of small beer was usury I felt, but we had to have some sustenance, for little had we eaten since the previous morning.

Forty Four

Will, Pure and Chaste

It must have been nearly ten o'clock when we walked across to the Town Hall, where I expected to find Colonel Assheton, it being the usual headquarters for the Army. He wasn't there, and we were sent to his lodging, a fine three-storey house further along the square. Ensign Tolson greeted us and asked us to wait. 'The Colonel hasn't had much sleep and has much correspondence to attend to. It's the bane of a commander's life, I feel. There's only so much that he can pass off to the other officers.'

'Have you heard anything of Colonel Shuttleworth? Do we know why he didn't come?' I enquired.

'I believe that he was detained by some Royal ships appearing in the Mersey river, but whether they've attacked his positions, I do not know.'

Colonel Assheton was indeed looking tired and harassed. If he was jubilant at his victory of yesterday, he didn't show it, but greeted us both with enthusiasm.

"Thank you for your attention yesterday, Doctor and Sergeant Cummins. I'm told that you worked wonders on the injured.' he said.

'We merely did our job, Colonel.' I replied, feeling a little uncomfortable at the thought that in reality I'd done little enough. "I hear the forces from Liverpool were delayed?'

'Yes, and though sight of them might have prevented the fight, we handled it well enough, I believe.'

'Where is Lord Molyneux now?' asked Will, 'Are you to pursue him?'

'I think he'll be hiding somewhere with his tail between his legs. For the time being he is a spent force and I see no real advantage chasing after him. A large number of his men surrendered and have joined us, whilst we have another few hundred captives who will probably do the same.' He shook his head. "You know, it's a sign that many of the soldiers on either side have no real understanding of why we're fighting. Their Lord, whether it's Derby, Essex, or whoever, says to them 'I need you as a soldier', promises them food and pay, and they say yes.'

'I'm sure that's true.' I replied.

'So, though I think some of our Puritan brethren go a little too far with their Hell and Damnation, I've let them loose on my troops in the hope of instructing them in the importance of our quest.'

"I wish you well in that, sir, I really do, but some are of very meagre intellect I fear.' I paused, 'I couldn't help but notice the way you looked after your men yesterday, fed them before battle and then went amongst them to give them heart. I think that is the way to keep them on your side and draw more to you.'

'Thank you, Doctor, thank you. I think you are in the right of it.' He reached out and grasped my hand.

"May we take leave of you? We are for home, if you please.'

'Yes, yes. With my grateful thanks. Please give my respects to my father, love to my mother, and to my wife if you should go through Whalley. God speed you home.'

Leaving Will to see to the horses and try to find them some decent feed, I returned to the Apothecary. 'You are back for more supplies already, my friend?' Moshe enquired with a smile. Though he knew that the Army had run south and us with it, he knew nothing about the fight. As I finished my account he asked about the dead and injured.

'Thank God for your safety.' He exclaimed. 'You will need extra supplies, as I guessed.' He moved to collect various ointments and salves and told Gem to see what herbs were left in the garden that might be of use. I tried to restrain him, saying I was almost out of money, but he waved my comments away. 'Take them, take them,' he smiled, his beard parting like the opening of a flower. 'Though don't tell anyone that I do this for no money, my friend, or they will think me nothing of a Jew.' I laughed at that.

'So, you will remain here some days, I believe, to attend your patients?' he asked.

'No, Moshe, We're for home, before something new arises. I have patched them as best I can and passed the message that you are here if needed, but we must away.'

It was now after noon and, this being late October, we had little more than four hours to travel the 24 miles to home before sunset, a near impossibility. I had something of a plan, though. I knew our horses were strong enough for the task, so I believed that we could keep to a trot most of the way, and that we might even raise our pace in parts. Earlier in the year, we had even galloped part of this same way.

Mind you, we were in fear of our lives from Kendall and his men that time.

Will had had the horses watered and given nosebags, good lad that he is, and was laughing and joking with a couple of rough, two-a-penny whores by a good fire when I found him. 'Not your usual standard of women, Will.' I remarked caustically as we saddled up and rode off.

'No, that I grant you, Doctor, but they were fun to talk with and everyone needs to do what they can to survive, don't you think.' He had a point, and I couldn't disagree.

'I just hope you don't need my services after having their company.'

'No fear o'that, sir.' He replied with a grin. 'You know I keep myself pure and chaste.'

Pure and chaste? May God not strike him down for that. It is a constant annoyance to me, with not a little envy if truth be known, that wherever we travel, Will usually finds a bed with the comeliest girl around. 'Well, young Will, I hope you're pure enough not to disappoint the girl at our next stop.'

He gave a delighted laugh. 'I was going to ask if we could call but feared that it would be too big a delay, given how far we have to ride, especially with this harsh wind in our faces.'

With golden hair, blue eyes, and a figure that one might describe as slender and well-formed, despite the difficulty of running a farm on her own since her husband's death, Cat had given us shelter and sustenance at a time of dire need. Will obviously had an eye for her, and I thought he'd visited her more than once over the last few months, something that he later denied. Already a widow at two or three and twenty, she had no children, only a younger brother who was away fighting.

In well under two hours, we rode into what had been her farmyard. It was deserted. Even as the place came into view we could see that the barn, that had once given us sanctuary, had been burned to the ground and, as we searched the shuttered house with its cold hearth, I could sense Will's growing worry. No-one had been there for some time.

Cutting across the fields to Ribchester, a village with ancient ruins, we clattered through the street to the White Bull Inn. They knew of her there.

'Aye. Stayed nearby after her farm was ransacked by troops, but now gone up to Hurst Green,' said the innkeeper, a surly, morose fellow. 'With a soldier she was. Expect be married now.'

Given the suspicion in which grown women without a man are often held, even if widowed, such a marriage wouldn't be unusual. It was different when she had her farm, but with no assets about her the situation was changed.

Without stopping for a drink, we pressed on, Will's mood sinking further. 'These things happen, Will,' I said, trying to cheer him a little. He lowered his head and spurred his mount on.

We near galloped into Hurst Green and accosted the first person we saw, an old man bent under a large amount of kindling. Did he know of a woman from a farm over beyond Ribchester, lately believed to have come here?

'Aye. Fair-haired lass, Catherine by name, brother a soldier?'

Will perked up. 'Where was she? Is she married?' he asked urgently.

'At Cross Gills, the farm about a half mile on. Didn't hear she were married though.'

Will shouted his thanks, smacked Joanie on the rump, dug in his heels and sped away, I following at a more leisured pace.

The farm was before me, and Will was already banging on the door as I came down the rough lane. In a field to my left, I saw a figure stand up and look towards the noise. Though a shawl covered her head, hiding hair and shrouding face, I instantly knew it was her.

Turning towards me as she approached the lane, she gave a slight wave in recognition, passed through the field gate, and calmly walked down towards the farmhouse.

Will disappeared round the back of house as the door opened and a sturdy fellow looked round in puzzlement. He saw me, and with a questioning look, shrugged his shoulders, raised both palms outwards, almost as in supplication, and waited for me as I caught up with Cat and dismounted.

She looked tired, unkempt, and thinner than I remembered, but still a truly bonny lass. 'Hello, Cat,' I said quietly, 'Good to see you. Is this your husband before us?'

Smiling, she said 'No. A cousin, sir.' As I gave a sigh of relief, Will came from behind a barn, saw us and ran. I caught him before he could reach the girl, whispering quickly in his ear 'Not married', and felt him relax.

Forty Five

A Bargain Reached

'You see, Doctor,' said Will, 'I have an idea.'

It was mid-morning, and we were riding back towards Downham, having been obliged to spend the night at Cross Gills Farm. Cat's cousin and his wife treated us to a meal of fresh pork, they having killed two pigs ready for winter. They were pleasant people, though a little in awe of me, but I tried to put them at their ease. Will ate little and then spent the whole evening with Cat in one corner of the modest farmhouse, whilst I made polite conversation with our host by the fire, me being given the best chair and an ever-filled tankard of small beer.

The cousin, Tom by name, lamented the war that had already taken half of his stock, mostly plundered by Lord Derby's troops on their way to be routed by our gallant fellows at Read Bridge. He was delighted to find that I'd been at the battle and wanted the full story of Colonel Shuttleworth's ambush, and declared it a fine tale, fit for a book. He couldn't understand why the country was at war, 'For surely do not we kill ourselves when there are Spanish and French enough to fight?' He was in the right of it, but I told him of the King's duplicity and how he was moving more and more back towards Rome.

'But,' he said, 'I care not if some wish to worship in that fashion. I believe everyone should pray according to their own conscience. Begging your pardon if I speak out of turn, sir.'

'I agree with you in part, Thomas,' I replied, 'But our world abounds in superstitions that our Church and the Romans promote, of which I believe most are false. They would keep the people in darkness, when our world is full of light, if you choose to see it. Do we want to return to the time when no-one could read the bible in his own tongue? Do we want any church to keep us from God and the truth?' I paused. 'For me, this is reason behind the struggle. King Charles thinks that he should control our minds and our purses, and I cannot go with that. Excepting that many Puritans, who are now taking control of Parliament, mean to deny us all joy, I think their opposition to the King is right and just.'

'All I wish, sir, is to live my life and provide for my wife,' he said, 'And for our child who is on the way.'

I congratulated him, wished his wife joy and an easy labour, and we changed the subject.

I praised Tom for taking in Cat in her distress and, having a strong idea that Will was already thinking of a more than passing acquaintance with his cousin, asked how she did.

'Well enough,' he said, 'after the ransacking of her farm and being thrown out for non-payment of rent. That farm had been in her late husband's family for generations.' He shook his head.

'And is she no burden to you?'

'Life is hard, to be sure, and harder with an extra mouth to feed, but we can cope.' He nodded over to where she and Will were deep in whispered conversation. They were both smiling. 'She may not be here long, perhaps.'

I had been offered the bed for the night and, though the offer was very tempting, I assured our host that we would do well enough in the barn. I didn't want Will abusing their hospitality by ravishing the lovely Cat that night. This wasn't due to my puritan leanings as much as envy, I'm ashamed to say, but whether he did stay in the barn all of the night I cannot say as, despite the lack of comfort, I did sleep soundly.

Now, as we rode on to the Hodder Bridge, Will was full of chat. I let him ramble on, burying my neck into my cloak and with my hat pulled down against the cold, eyes watering in the wind. A bargain had been reached and Cat would marry Will as long as he could provide a home for her. As Will only lodged with a couple in a small cottage in the village at present, that posed an immediate problem.

'What's happened to Cat's brother William?' I asked, 'He was a good lad and true.'

'She says he's with Shuttleworth's lot, but where they are, who can say?'

'He knows where Cat is at present? Might have a shock if he returns and you've spirited her way.'

'It'll be right,' he said, 'He'll be a good brother, I'm sure.'

'Will he want to live with you, though, that's my meaning.'

'Aye, well, that's to be decided. Won't be a problem, I don't think.'

In Mitton, we turned left, past the Hall, looking shabby and with one wall half collapsed, and then the Church which, I'd been told, still had most of its Roman accoutrements in place. How long they would last should Puritans pass by, I could not say. Towards Clitheroe we went, the bitter wind still full in our faces, passing the old Leper Hospital above the bridge at Eadsford, and continued up into the town, keeping the horses at a walk as the road was as bad as we'd seen since Cockerham.

The Marketplace was busy despite the cold. Few stalls to be sure, but I could see plenty of meat, some fish, and two barrels of apples. A few people looked up as we rode through and, to my surprise a couple waved and one even smiled, as we carried on up the rise towards the church. Will dismounted, opened the gate and we passed through into my yard. All looked neat and trim. John came from the stable to attend to us, touched his forelock to me and asked how I did. 'Well, thank you,' I replied. 'Doing a good job I see. The yard looks well tended.' As we discussed the field beyond the house and the pigs ready for slaughter, his wife, Sally, came from the house, baby in her arms, gave a brief bob in the way of a curtsey, and hurried back inside to tell Miss Brierley of our arrival.

Amos's sister looked much improved since I last saw her, rather more colour in her cheeks and looking neat in a sober black dress, lace collar and coif. She curtseyed with rather more dignity than Sally. 'Welcome, Doctor,' she said with a smile, 'I am for the school, to attend to the pupils' lunch. We have more numbers now.' She turned to Sally. 'There is food and drink enough for the Doctor and his man, Goodwife, if you would.' And with another curtsey, took the path to the school, saying that she would send her brother to me.

'Twelve pupils now,' said Amos, almost back to his old, spare self after the pounds he'd put on whilst in Downham. 'The School is almost back to what it was before…' His voice tailed off.

'Before our difficulties,' I said tactfully, then grinned. 'Do I need to attend them, Mr Usher, or can you still beat the lessons into them on your own?'

'I can manage, Maister, I do assure you, though perhaps your attention might prove beneficial from time to time.' He paused, and I see in his eye that he was with child to give some news. 'Your *problem*,' he stressed the word, 'might now be close to resolution, I hear.' My heart near skipped a beat.

'We've been away for more than a week, Amos, what's been happening?'

'I know that a large body of men from Brungerley have been combing the land around and been in battle with that big fellow whose brother was hanged…'

'You mean Tench!' I cried. 'And have they caught him?'

'That I don't know, only that there was a fight, and some are dead.'

I pushed my bread and cheese to one side. Will swore under his breath, but I needed no word from him to know that he was now as alert as I. 'We must go. Sally, would you ask your husband to ready our horses?'

'Just one thing, Doctor,' said a worried looking Amos as we swung our horses round to depart. 'You may now wish to return here. May I ask, what must become of me and my sister?'

'I don't count chickens before they hatch, Amos.' We fair galloped from the yard. Yes, Amos might have a problem if my household were to return, but that was for another day. And something of a plan for that was already forming within me.

Forty Six

'It Is the Job of a Natural Philosopher...'

As we rode into Downham and to the gates of the Hall, I noticed a number of men gathering before us, unarmed, and chatting. They turned to us and some waved a greeting.

'Our troops are back,' said Will. 'I thought you said all were needed against the Irish? Not that I'm not pleased to see them, in course.' I shrugged.

Gatekeeper Robb opened our way, and with a few words of greeting, we swept into the grounds, making straight for the Hall and Sir Ralph.

'Grent's men did us proud, Doctor. With the help of a man who came looking for you, a camp was found just beyond the hill. Two were taken and four were killed.'

'And Tench?' I asked hopefully.

'We don't know. Either he wasn't there or got away, the position isn't clear,' My spirits sank. 'but I believe that all his band are accounted for. He's on his own now. Notice has been given to every farm from Roughlee to Read that any who assist him will be treated as outlaws and may hang.'

'Are we still searching, though, sir?'

'As well as we can. Most of Grent's men have now gone back to the woods, but now we have some of our own men back from the fighting, I'll send them out to sweep the area. They've had two days to rest since they returned, and I've asked them to gather for instructions. You might have seen them?'

With a pressing need for a piss, I took my leave, promising to return later. My good mood had been spoiled at the news that Tench was still free, but my spirits were lifted by the welcome from my household. Slater pretended to be annoyed by the length of my absence, and why could I not tell her that I was to wander far and wide instead of returning straight home from the war and her left to worry and what was to become of her.

'Slater, dear, I only delayed to ask how my friends did. And Will and I didn't take part in the battle.' I said with a laugh. 'And I have interesting news for you. Will is to be married, it seems.' All thought of chastisement of me was now forgotten and all work stopped, as I was besieged by her questions.

'I think the bargain is settled,' I said, 'But he has to find a home for her first.' I paused. 'It seems to me that the time is coming when we must return to my house...'

'Which you have given to the Usher and his sister.' She interrupted in high dudgeon, 'And to strangers living in the stables. Which we will have to sleep propinquitous in the schoolroom.'

'No, no. I wouldn't put you to that, woman. Don't be silly. No,' I continued, 'proper arrangements will have to be made, but if we do return to Clitheroe, and if Sir Ralph agrees, perhaps Will can have this place.'

Slater began to bustle about, making plenty of noise to indicate her disapproval of my plan. I went across to the stable, where Pod and Cas were already grooming Bay, to keep out of her way. She would come round in her own good time, I felt sure. She has long held the view that, living close to Sir Ralph and on his land, we are given greater status and privilege than before. She has access to Lady Katherine and is sometime called upon for assistance. Nothing I say seems to disabuse her of the notion, but she must accept that we will return to Clitheroe some day. My household has been kept safe here for most of our time, sure, and I give thanks for it, but I've been kept from my studies and experiments for far too long.

Richard Towneley was still with us, and now embedded even more firmly in our household. Where he had first been sleeping in the Hall, he now spent most nights with the boys in the stable loft. Though Pod was nearest to his age, he had formed a strong bond with Nate, each profiting from the other's particular talents. I hoped that Sir Ralph's letter had reached the boy's mother and that we would soon receive her reply, though how his passage home could be arranged, given the state of the country, I could not conceive.

'Master Towneley,' I said,' You will recall the image of the supposed monster of a man with no head when you were reading Hakluyt?' He nodded. 'Well, see what nonsense I have here.' I showed him the tract found at Cockerham.

"Tis the very same, sir.' He exclaimed.

'It is. And just as fanciful. Will and I went to Kirkham to investigate, and what do you think we found?' His eyes grew wide. 'Not a single person named here is real and this avowed *monster* does not exist. This paper is worthless and designed to trick the ignorant and unlearned. Always read such things with a sceptic's eye, I would advise.'

'I shall, sir, I shall.' He frowned, 'So is all Hakluyt's writing false?'

'Not all, by any means,' I smiled, 'but he is of an earlier, simpler age. And he was just reporting what he'd been told by travellers and adventurers, who might have enjoyed playing a trick on poor Hakluyt, of course. I believe that he himself travelled no further than France.'

'It is the job of a natural philosopher to question everything, is it not, sir?'

'You have it exactly, young Richard.' A lad after my own heart, I believe.

Cas was now under Pod's wing, his speech and utility improving each day, according to Slater. Part of me was still unsure of him, in that I couldn't see him remaining a permanent part of my household should we return to Clitheroe. I would have to put that problem to one side for the present, for there was still a number of matters of greater import that needed to be resolved. And there was something else niggling at my brain.

"Did you say, sir,' I asked Sir Ralph, 'when we spoke earlier, that someone came asking for me and that he helped in the finding of Tench's band?'

'I did, Doctor. He seemed in a poor way, thin, tired, and somewhat unkempt, but spoke well, as if educated. He had come over the hill from Higham, walked to Clitheroe, found you not there, and then called here.'

'And he brought information of Tench and his band?'

'That was not his intent, which was to see you, but we questioned him, and he told us that he'd nearly stumbled across a band of rough fellows above Higham. He believed them to be bandits and quickly went round them. We fed him, for which he was most grateful, whilst I sent at speed to Grent. That fine fellow called his men together and went round Pendle, whilst I set my men over by the rough pass to Sabden, and the ruffians were found exactly where he said.'

'But not Tench?'

'The two we captured said he had left them with supplies a few days before, saying he'd return, and they knew not where he was excepting he always came to them from the West.'

'Is there nothing more to find out from the prisoners?'

'I don't think so,' answered Sir Ralph, 'They are being held for the Assize and will surely hang.'

All Hallows was upon us and the last of the pigs and sheep were being brought in for slaughter, as was local custom. This eve, the two worlds of the living and the dead would be at their nearest, and many still believed that a portal would be opened between them, allowing those departed to return to their old homes. Witches too would be about and must be '*lated*', candles kept alight in each house over midnight. If the candles burned steady then the house was safe for the season, but if spirits blew them out it was a bad omen. I considered that custom as silly as I do the existence of Witches, but Slater still firmly believed it, so candles we would have. In my youth, we always set a bonfire for All Hallows Eve and kept it burning till dawn but now, even here, that was put off for five days to mark the 'Gunpowder Treason' and the saving of Parliament from the Catholics thirty-eight years ago, God be praised. It also saved the King, of course, and if James had gone, would we be better off now? He had tolerance for every religion, I'm told, unlike his son. Perhaps this war would have begun then? I couldn't say, but if Astrologers of the calibre of William Lilly had been around to divine the future, we might not be in the difficulties we see now and that have riven the country in twain.

It would be on just such a night that creatures like Tench might move about with ease, no-one wishing to confront such a devil on this night, and I knew that the Brungerley Woodsmen would not continue their search. I was for taking Will and others in our own search, but they wouldn't stir, no matter what I said. The boys ran around making mischief in the normal way in the first hours of night, and then we all retired behind locked doors. I cracked open one chest of my books and took out a volume at random. It was Hill's '*The profitable Arte of Gardening*'. I quickly fell asleep.

Slater shook me awake. 'Come Doctor, we're off to Church. You've slept long enough. Too long if you ask me.' The boys stood behind her grinning like fools as I rose from the table, stretched my back, and scratched my head. I felt cold. She bustled round me, wiping the table where I'd slopped some beer and muttering 'Reading your books has so overfilled your head that you can't take more, so you sleep like the dead .'

'And why should I go to Church, Slater?'

'Because it's All Saints and don't you well know it.' She picked up my cloak and shook it. 'When you were Holy and went every Sunday, I'm sure you were a better man.'

'By that you mean when I was part of the Church, *before you knew me*.' I stressed those last words. 'I didn't believe in saints then and I'm not starting now. It's Catholic superstition. I'd be a better man if I hadn't a harridan bullying me and a bunch of youths gurning at me.'

'You can call me a harridan as much as you wish if you'll get on your way. If the Curate doesn't arrive from Clitheroe, You'll have to lead us in prayer.'

It's now some six years or more since I was removed from my living at Kildwick and, on a number of occasions, I'd been told by the bastard Bishop who threw me out that I was banned from preaching in his churches. The last time was earlier in the year, when I received a letter from one of his minions. By that time, I was living here in Downham and, the village church being the advowson of the Asshetons, they having built it, Sir Ralph had asked me to preach in the absence of beneficed clergy, and I did so. I would have liked to respond by telling the Bishop to fuck off, but restrained myself. Instead, I wrote that he should take care that he didn't end up like Bishop Laud, held for the last two years in the Tower of London for treason. Should Parliament prevail, he should expect no less.

The Clitheroe curate, piss-poor, shabby and who was led a dog's life by his lazy vicar, did not come, and so I did my duty. I don't hold with sermons that ramble on for hours on end, such as the Puritans delight in, castigating and damning everyone as they do. I prefer to be more succinct and give a simple message that people can apply to their lives and thus find their own way to God. I don't believe in Saints, it is true, but in saintly behaviour, and so gave them the story of the Good Samaritan. Here, I said, was someone acting like a saint and helping a fellow man as we should all do. It went down well, I think. Some were relieved at its brevity, whilst our few Puritans were disgruntled for the same reason.

The obligatory note was made of those present, as Parliament now required, and as I looked round it appeared to me that only three or four persons were missing from the congregation. Slater was sitting towards the front with Nate, Pod, and Cas, whilst Richard Towneley sat with Sir Ralph and his Lady in their stall.

I was just giving the final prayers when we heard a dull thud from outside. It gave us no concern, but moments later, the sturdy church door was flung aside and in burst Robb, one of Sir Ralph's gate guards. Scanning the crowd, he saw Will, and muttered urgently in his ear. As Robb ran to the Assheton Stall, Will grabbed two others and ran from the church. In seconds all was panic.

Forty Seven

A Creaking Cart

THE HALL HAD BEEN ATTACKED. NOT THE WALL OR GATES this time, but the very building itself. Hearing the creaking of a cart from within the grounds, one of Sir Ralph's sentries, guarding the gates, had gone to investigate and received a musket shot for his trouble. The ball lightly grazed his temple, and he was otherwise unhurt, but it persuaded him to lie low whilst his companion ran for help.

Under the portico, the Hall's oak door stood wide open, three closed chests visible on the floor within. I recognised them immediately as part of Kendall's seized goods, for it was only weeks before I'd been amongst them in the cellars of the Hall. Outside, harnessed to one of the farm carts, stood Will's Joanie and Nate's Dob, throwing their heads up and down, neither being used to being thus fastened. A full field away to the South, a few running figures could be seen, heading to the woods for cover, with Will and others a long way behind but in full pursuit.

Sir Ralph, face like thunder, gathered his men, sent some inside to search the Hall for intruders, gathered the remainder, and shouted for his horse, whilst Pod and Cas ran to our barn to saddle Bay. Nate quickly unhitched his horse from the cart, swung himself up, clutched his ride's mane and set off at speed, bareback. I tried to stop him, but he was gone.

Adam Seddon was looking to Tom, our wounded guard. Sending

young Towneley to fetch my bag, I questioned the two of them, whilst Slater ushered Lady Katherine towards our cottage. 'Four of them, I think,' said Tom, 'and must have come over the fields. We saw nothing at the gate. All armed, swords, two muskets and a pistol.'

You can guess my first thought. 'Was Tench amongst them?'

'The evil one? No.' Blood was running down his cheek and, even with a cloth held to his wound, it fell in large drops onto his jerkin. 'No, he wasn't with them. I recognised none. Showed no colours either.' That latter didn't surprise me at all. This wasn't a random raid by Royalists, or even by a band of disaffected soldiers. It had a specific target, Kendall's treasure. Tench's work, surely?

'What did you see, Adam?' I asked, 'And why were you here? You're not one of the guards. I saw your woman in church, and noticed you were missing.'

'Just keeping these lads company, like.' He looked rather unsettled, rather shifty, and not meeting my eye. 'Just lost the time, so missed church.' To the wounded man he said 'Hope you'll be right now, mate.' Touched his forelock to me and quickly walked off.

A mounted party with Sir Ralph at its head now galloped down through the village and across the stream, to take the rough track towards Worston hamlet, in the hope of cutting off the enemy. Seconds later, with Bay under my heels, I sped directly after Nate, trying to hold a random sword across my lap, and cursing the boy for his impetuousness.

Bay easily shouldered aside the hedge where it had only recently been repaired from the last attack on us. The ground was firm, I gave Bay her head, and she leapt Heys brook with ease. I had just pulled her round to skirt a wood when I heard a muffled cry and seconds later Nate's mount burst out of the bank of trees. I near threw myself off Bay, dropping the sword into a thorn bush as I did so. Retrieving it at the cost of scratched hands and face, together with a torn coat, I walked into the trees, all my senses alert and heart pounding, hoping against hope that the boy wasn't killed.

It was easy to follow the path forced by the bolting horse, and I soon same upon Nate, crouched over a supine body. He looked round as I approached, face white. 'Head wound, sir. Can't tell how bad.' It was Will, laid out on his stomach.

'Does he live, Nate? Tell me he lives?'

Forty Eight

'Did Will's Candle Stay Alight?'

I turned Will gently on to his side. 'You were right not to move him straight away, Nate.'

'You've said to me a number of times to assess the patient fully before turning him,' replied the boy. 'I saw the wound to his head, checked he was breathing, felt round the wound and then his neck and shoulders. He doesn't seem to have any other injuries, Doctor.'

'Good, good. See, I now check his eyes. The black parts, the pupils, are different sizes, which often happens in a concussion. Though there is blood enough from the head wound, note that there is none from nose or ears, which would be bad indeed. We must hope there is no other damage. I wonder how long he has lain here?'

'Hit only seconds before I found him, for I think I caught a glimpse of his attacker running away. It was then only a minute until you arrived, I would say.'

'I will stay with him, Nate. Bay should still be at the edge of the wood. Take her, as quick as you can, bring men and a hurdle or door to carry our brave friend back, and we can attend him further.'

'Doctor,' he hesitated, 'Did Will's candle stay alight last night?'

'Don't give me that silly superstition, Boy.' I said angrily, ' You should know better than that.' Seeing the grief in his eyes, I relaxed a little and patted his shoulder. 'I'm sure it stayed lit.'

Will was still unconscious as we got him back to the Hall. Lady Katherine had a bed prepared for him, an indication of how well he was thought of, but I first had him placed on a table to treat his head. I cut away part of his hair, matted with blood, just behind the crown of his head, and carefully secured a small flap of his scalp with two stitches. Nate smeared the wound with honey and bandaged it as best he could. Cuts to the head always look worse than they are because of the free flow of blood, but I didn't think he had lost much. Into the bed he went, a fire burning brightly in the grate, and we settled down to wait.

It was about an hour before he stirred. I looked again at his eyes. They were still unfocussed, but it can be some time before they return to normal in such cases. He tried to sit up and began to mumble, but what he said we couldn't tell. We pushed him gently back down and I checked his brow for fever. There was none and he seemed to settle into a true sleep, for which I was grateful. I left Nate in charge, and went downstairs, as I'd heard Sir Ralph's voice below. As you would expect, he wasn't in the best of moods.

'It's the damnedest, Doctor. We found nothing. With no sight of the robbers, I continued on to Aspinall's Hall to see if he knew anything or was harbouring any of them. He swore he didn't and wasn't, and I believed him. I left three men to climb Worsa Hill as a lookout. I fear they'll see nothing, but it's worth a try.' He continued, 'It's obvious what they were up to, and chose their time well, with us all in church, but how did they expect to get past the two guards without commotion?'

'There were three at the gates, Sir Ralph. Adam Seddon was there also.'

'What was he doing there? That's no part of his work.'

'He said he was late for church.' I paused. 'What makes me wonder is, even though they might have overpowered your guards, how did they expect to get any distance with a heavily loaded cart pulled by two reluctant cattle, before we could catch up to them. It's not as if they could make it disappear.'

'When I think on it, I don't recall seeing Seddon at church for a long time. His absence should have been noted.' Sir Ralph's brow darkened. 'I want to talk to my two men again. There's something not right about this. They said Tench was not about, but I don't believe he was not involved and, if so, where was he? Waiting for the cart down the road? We never checked for that, just went haring after the men we saw.'

'It's easy to rethink things after the event, Sir Ralph. We reacted to what we did see. The theft was prevented, and we may take heart from that, I believe. There are no deaths. Will is looking promising, it was a minor wound and, providing his wits are not astray, he should be well again in a day or two, albeit with a headache.'

We sat in Sir Ralph's kitchen with the two sentries, going back over the events of the morning. Yes, they'd heard a cart moving, which surprised them as all were supposed at church. Thomas, the injured guard, saw it come from the direction of one of the barns and stop at the Hall's door and went to find out what was happening, leaving Robb, his fellow sentry, still guarding the gate.

'So, Robb, you and Adam Seddon stayed at the gate?' I asked.

'No sir, Adam weren't with me. Don't know where he came from. Just appeared when Thomas fell.'

'Appeared from where?' demanded Sir Ralph.

'Came from by the Hall doorway.' said Thomas.

'From near the door, or from the door itself?'

'I'm not sure, sir, but he was in front of me and shouted 'no' or something to the thieves as I was fired at and ran to me.'

Sir Ralph looked like thunder. 'We need to talk to Seddon. Find him for me.'

Seddon was not at home, and neither was his woman, and a search of the village and surrounds failed to find either of them.

Will woke in the late evening. As he lay blinking, I called his name and he grunted. Looking again in his eyes, I could see they were more focused than before and his pupils had returned to near normal, so brought a candle closer to his face. 'Oh, that hurts!' he said clearly and screwed his eyes shut.

'Are you back with us, Will?' I asked quietly.

'Aye. Have I been asleep?'

'You've been hit over the head.' He lifted a hand as if to touch it, but I pulled it down. 'It'll be sore for a bit, so just leave it, lad. Keep your eyes closed by all means but, if you could just open one a little and tell me how many fingers I'm holding up, that would be good.'

'Hold up as many as you like, but I'll keep my eyes shut yet awhile, I think, for I've a fair thudding in my head.'

It was early morning when he sat up, looking rather peeved but otherwise fine. His eyes seemed fully focussed and I asked him if he still had pain. 'Only in my pride.' he answered.

'He looks like a Turk with his head bound don't you think, Doctor?' said a grinning Nate.

'You'll look like a Turk when I get up,' Will growled, 'if you don't leave off your cheek.'

'Can you remember what happened to you?' Sir Ralph had joined us. 'Nate came upon you just as you'd been hit, and said he saw someone running off.'

'I can remember fully, sir. I ran into the woods, caught up with one of the attackers, grabbed her arm…'

'Grabbed *her* arm, you say?' queried Sir Ralph, 'A woman? You're certain?'

'As certain as I am that Nate deserves a slap for making fun of me. She was dressed as a man and wore a wide-awake hat. Not a pretty girl, or I wouldn't have let go of her.' He gave a rueful grin. 'Tall, she was, and I think I've seen her before but can't call it to mind.' He paused. 'That's all I can think of.'

I looked at Sir Ralph and he looked at me. I knew what he was thinking.

'Keep to your bed a mite longer, young William,' I said, 'and Nate will dress your head. We'll talk later.'

I now spent some time with Sir Ralph, who was in a most philosophical mood. He'd recently received a bundle of letters and newssheets from London. For some time now, I'd had little indication of what was happening in the country as a whole. All I did know was that various armies were rampaging through towns and cities throughout the land.

'I suppose It is something of a miracle that any letters at all have got through,' said Sir Ralph. 'It's a mixed bag, to be sure, some good, some bad. London is still firm for Parliament, of course, and Newbury has been taken, which protects the City from the King's heartlands in Devon, Cornwall and the like. Good news too in Lincolnshire, for King's Lynn has been taken for Parliament and we've won another battle elsewhere in that county.'

'No word from Richard Towneley's mother yet?' I asked.

'Ah, yes. Grateful thanks for taking him in and easing her heart by my letter. Knows he cannot be sent to her at present, will have to wait on God's mercy and so on.' He frowned. 'The most worrying news is that the King has fixed a truce with the Irish. Many think that they will now fight on his side, but even if they don't, it allows him to bring his own troops back from there. The only good thing to come from this is that it has brought all the various Protestant factions together to face this further Catholic threat. We have sent Commissioners to Scotland to ask for their help, and I think they will now back us.

Forty Nine

Thoughts of a Return

THE FIFTH OF NOVEMBER DAWNED DRY BUT BITTERLY COLD. In Downham everyone seemed on edge, and few people were to be seen as I rode Bay to Clitheroe, Nate at my side. The year was fast drawing to a close, and the trees stood stark and bare against the fleeting sky, but it was good to be out. For three days I'd been at my books but, apart from trying to put in order my ideas for producing gunpowder, I couldn't seem to concentrate.

Will was fine. His intellect intact and his head mending well, he had been re-organising defence of the Hall. I felt it was unlikely that we would be attacked again, but Will pointed out, rightly, that I'd said that very same thing after Tench's attack.

When he wasn't actively doing something, Will was now always deep in thought.

'I know I've seen that woman before, but that blow has knocked it right out of my head, Doctor.'

'Put it to one side and it'll come, Will. Don't brood on it.' I had replied. 'Think about your girl. Have you sent news to her?'

'No, I don't need to tell her that I've lost half my wits to another woman,' he said with half a smile. 'I want to ask Sir Ralph if I can have a place, so I can bring her here, but he's been in a foul mood since All Saint's Day.'

'In truth, Will, I think such a request from you, and the knowledge that you're to settle down, might well cheer him. I'd not delay if I were you. Go to it.'

I was right, Sir Ralph and Lady Katherine were both delighted. Though it was yet a mean hovel, he could have the late Mistress Whittle's place straight away, if that would do, with promise of something better as soon as ever possible. He should, in any case, bring her to meet them. For a day he sat about biting his thumb, wondering if his Cat would consider living in what had been a Witch's house.

'I'm surprised at you, young Cummins. I've told you Whittle was no witch.'

'But it's not what you think that matters, Doctor, is it? You might not believe in such things, but Cat might. If that's all I offer her, she might turn her back on me, then where would I be?'

'Only one way to find out, Will,' I said sagely, but he was still undecided.

The ride to Clitheroe was uneventful. I found Amos in the schoolroom, and I briefly questioned some of the pupils about their Latin, though I had no real interest in them or the subject. Nate was talking to John, the self-appointed caretaker of my property, and as I walked round and into my yard, Amos's sister came out and offered me bread and beer, which I gratefully accepted, though it was not yet noon. I sat in the hall, thinking what I might do to the property. The whole building is well built of stone but had had a number of changes and additions since before my time.

It is built at right angle to the street, where a door gives on to a passage, and it is clear that this whole house was a Passage-house at one time. To one side is a parlour, little used, and on the other is what was my library. Further on is the hall, open to the roof, with a great fireplace dominating the left wall, whilst to the right is a more imposing entrance with a larger oak door giving onto the yard. It is obvious that this was meant to be the main entrance. Beyond the doorway is a staircase. The main passage continues beyond the hall to the kitchen, with a scullery to its right, and through a further door into a storeroom and laundry. Above the library and parlour lies my bedroom, or what would be my bedroom if I was in residence, of course, whilst over the kitchen and scullery and reached by a steep stair from the corner of the scullery, are two more bedrooms.

Outside, and continuing the line of the main building, are a stable and a barn of wattle and daub, but solid enough, with lofts over. Across the yard is the churchyard wall and built into its end is the small tower-like building that everyone refers to as my study, though it is, or was, my laboratory, before it was fired by my enemies.

Between the barn and the tower, a gate lets into a field that slopes sharply down to woods. John had improved the piggery, to his credit, and created enclosures for his fowl.

My problem was this. Should I return with my household, I must displace Amos and his sister, who had previously lived above the Schoolroom. With the Schoolroom roof leaking and without funds for its repair, I couldn't send them back there in all conscience. Then there was the question of John and his wife. They had installed themselves in my stable loft, initially without my consent to be sure, but they were thriving, looking after my property, and I would be loath to see them thrown out. I felt sure there was room for us all but couldn't see Slater putting up with Amos and his sister round her feet all the time.

I thanked Amos's sister, bid her good day, and went to find Nate. He was still with John, who was holding a goose by its neck as it hissed and scrabbled madly with its feet. He had one of its wings stretched out and was pointing something out to Nate.

'I could do with some of those fine quills, John,' I said and told Nate to re-saddle our horses. 'Can you mend a roof, John?

'I'm sure I could, Sir, but is there a problem with your house?'

'No. I'm referring to the schoolhouse roof, which leaks. What will it take, do you think?' He gave a sharp intake of breath and shook his head.

'I can't say, your Worship, but I'll take a look. There's not much of the year left, begging your pardon, and I wouldn't like to try anything in ice and snow. And as to cost....'

'I wouldn't want that, don't worry. If it can be mended quickly as soon as winter is past and with little cost...'

In Downham, brushwood was being gathered and stacked ready for the night's festivity. It would be held within Sir Ralph's grounds rather than down in the village, as a safety measure in case of further attack. I saw Pod and Cas helping the men and told Nate he could join them just as soon as he'd stabled the horses.

Richard Towneley was sitting at my table as I entered. He had a serious look about him. 'Will they burn the Pope again tonight, sir?' he asked.

'They may, Richard, they may. I haven't seen an effigy, but it is the usual thing to do on this night.'

'Then I cannot attend, for that is wrong,' he said sadly, 'Though I would like to see the bonfire.'

'You must do as you see fit, young man. Though can you not count it as All Saints and forget who burns?' He shook his head. 'Anyway, I have no stomach for festivities tonight, whether it is to burn the King or your Pope, so I will stay here with you. I'm sure we can find things to discuss.'

As the church bells started to ring we glanced at each other and continued our reading.

Fifty

From Higham, a Stranger

THE MATTER OF THE STRANGER FROM HIGHAM WHO HAD been searching for me was solved a few days later, when one of the gate sentries came for me. I was in the Hall, giving a lesson on the brain to Nate and Richard Towneley, using Fernalius' *Universa Medicina* for illustration. I was just explaining his concept of physiology, with his famous quote that '*The brain is the citadel and dwelling of the human mind, the abode of thoughts and of the reason, the wellspring and origin of movement and of every sense; it occupies the highest point of the body, looking upwards, nearest to heaven.*' The beauty of that phrase constantly resonates with me, and I was annoyed at being called away just at that moment. I marched to the gate impatiently.

A sad young fellow, no more than six or seven and twenty, pulled off his hat and greeted me with a bow. A round face with sunken cheeks was dominated by an aquiline nose and framed by long dark hair cascading on to a dirty lace collar, much frayed. He wore a simple black tunic, brown britches, hose that had seen much repair, and boots so distressed that I might have thrown them out. 'Who are you, sir?' I asked quite harshly.

'My name is Moore, sir. Have I the pleasure of introducing myself to

Doctor John Webster?' I nodded my assent. 'Then I have tidings from your brother, in the heights above York.'

I resolved to take him to my cottage but, even as we reached the door, he near fainted, and it was with difficulty that I prevented his falling. Slater fussed round him, and we sat him at table. 'Apologies, Mistress, but if I might have a small drink and a morsel of crust, it would revive me. I haven't eaten for two days.'

'And how do you know Edward?' I queried, as food was provided.

'He gave me aid when my family was set on by ruffians.' he replied, 'But perhaps I should give you a little of my history?' I nodded my assent.

'My name is Jonas Moore, and I was born over Pendle, at White Lee near Higham. After my education, I was fortunate to be made Clerk to the Vicar-General in the great city of Durham, due to my knowledge of Latin in law. It was a good post and I never regretted leaving my parents or this area, for it was quite an honour, as you will understand.'

'The stipend was good, accommodation acceptable, and my future seemed secure, so five years ago, I married. Eleanor is everything one could wish for a wife, and I now have a son and two daughters. Then came this terrible war. Last year, the income from the diocese was sequestered by Parliament. My income stopped, my house was taken for soldiers. What could I do? I would turn for home, come back to White Lee, where my father farmed.'

'With what little money I had, I bought a cart, hitched it to my horse, and began our journey South. All was well until we left the town of Thirsk, when we came upon bands of troops heading North, so we diverted off the main road. We were approaching the village of Coxwold when we were set upon and almost all was taken from us. Though we were not hurt, my wife was in much distress and the children sore frightened. Then a farmer came upon us, helped us in our distress and gave us shelter for two nights, without which I doubt we would have survived, God bless him.'

'And this was my brother?' I asked.

'It was. I told him we were on our way to Lancashire, he said he had a brother there, Master of the Grammar School at Clitheroe, and I was astonished that we should be so near.'

'So, you bring me tidings of him. He is well, then?'

'He sends his good wishes and that he is well, has three sons living and the farm has yet escaped the notice of soldiers.' He paused for a moment, looking at me as though there was a question on his lips. 'But forgive me, Doctor, I am not here just to pass this message.'

Clearing his throat, he told of his arriving home to hear that his father died some months before, the news never reaching him. His now widowed mother destitute, and the farm near empty of stock, she had tried to sell all, but in the current state of things, there were no buyers.

'I must therefore find work. I have my Latin and Mathematics. I was hoping there might be room for me at your school, yet I see you are not there. Can you not make use of me, sir?'

It saddened me to tell him that there was no place for him, despite his pleading. In the briefest way possible, I told him of the problems the school had faced over the last two years, how its finances were broken, and that I was now in the pay of the Parliamentary army as a surgeon. His face fell, as you might expect.

I grieved for him in his plight. I couldn't take on more additions to my household, not another lame duck and his brood. What I could do was introduce him to Sir Ralph, in the hope that he might know of a position for Moore. After all, he had helped us find Tench's band of miscreants, though if he'd found Tench himself that might have put Sir Ralph under a greater obligation. We would have to see.

I did invite him to take a look at some of my books. As an educated man (and I don't have much chance to talk to such people), we had a lively chat. He was very much the mathematician and was working on a treatise on the subject. He was fortunate that one of the few possessions he still retained was the draft of his book. I lamented the loss of my own notes on the history of metals, lost in the firing of the laboratory that all called my Study, in Clitheroe.

We must have a use for such a bright fellow, I thought, but I would have to leave that in Sir Ralph's hands. In the meantime, I loaned him my mule to spare him the arduous trek home, and Slater filled two panniers with what food we could spare for his family.

Fifty One

A Face Remembered

THERE WAS A BANGING ON THE DOOR. SLATER WAS ALREADY up so I let her answer it whilst I stayed warm and dozing under several blankets. It was Will.

'Is he up, Mistress?'

'No, Will. He's behaving like one of those Shakers in Araby, where it's beyond him to treat with the day. He desires the warmth of the sun and is beyond simple work, I believe.'

'I can hear you, woman,' I shouted, throwing off my covers. 'I'm not deaf.'

'Then come and break your fast like a Christian. Which I've had pottage boiling for the last age.'

Pulling on my boots and throwing on my jacket, I nearly fell down the ladder, now fully alert. "What's ado, Will?'

'I've remembered, Doctor.' He beamed at me in triumph. 'I know where I saw that woman' He paused, dramatically. 'Read Hall.'

It seemed like a lifetime ago, though in reality only seven months had passed. There we were, Will and I, hiding in the trees above the bridge at Read, hearts pounding, nerves on edge, waiting for Lord Derby's army to meet our ambush. A few hundred of us against several thousand, it bore little thinking about except to know that there would be casualties.

I felt a twinge in my side, as I do every time I pass or think of the place, recalling the wound dealt me by Christopher Kendall later that day. A vision of that awful Knight leering at me as I lay under his sword came back to me. I had no memory from that point until wakening in comfort after ten days of fever. I did remember what happened just before the battle, though.

I had been concerned at the lack of medical supplies, bandages in particular. Some half a mile behind us lay Read Hall, home of the Nowells. That ancient family was well-known and feared hereabouts, for it had been Roger Nowell, father of the present head of the family, who had discovered and prosecuted the witches from Pendle 30 years before. But the Hall had since been shut up and left in the care of a housekeeper, Squire Nowell being off fighting for the King. Where the rest of the family were, I knew not, nor could I understand why the estate, which encompassed several farms, had not yet been sequestered.

Before the arrival of the enemy, I'd sent Will to the Hall in the hope of supplies. The housekeeper had been less than helpful, but Will had slapped her out of his way and a maid brought what sheets she could for our use.

'You saw her at the Hall when you went for bandages?'

'That I did, Doctor. She was the damned housekeeper. A true harridan. Said she was in charge, that I should be gone, and near spat in my face. I thought I'd remember hers, so can't believe it's only just come back to me.'

'You had taken a hard knock to the head, lad.'

'Aye, well. I came here first. Haven't told Sir Ralph yet, so are you coming with me to let him know?' I thrust Slater's pottage to one side, grabbed my cloak and followed him out.

'If I might ask, why has the estate not been sequestered? Nowell is leading an army for the King, I hear, and is a roman.'

'That I can't answer, Doctor. Read falls under Colonel Shuttleworth's jurisdiction, I believe.' said Sir Ralph. He turned to Will. 'But you're sure this woman is one and the same?'

'I think I am, sir. I might be tempting fate in saying there couldn't be two such termagants living, when we've had the Tench twins to reckon with, but I believe it is the same woman.'

'Then how does a housekeeper know about Kendall's effects stored in my cellars and have the temerity to mount an attack on us? We've had his supposed but unproved widow claiming the goods, and Tench attacking us for them. It makes no sense to me. What do you think, Doctor? Is Seddon something to do with this?' I had no real answer. 'We need a plan of action.'

Read Hall must be visited and, more than that, without knowing what or who might be found there, a plan of attack would be needed. I watched as Sir Ralph and Will first discussed the position of the Hall. 'Correct me if I'm wrong, Will, but as I recall, the house faces South, large central hall, the main door in the centre, and flanked by projecting wings on each side.'

'That's right, sir. The wings three storey high, with further buildings joined on to the left-hand range that I think are the kitchens and servant's quarters with stables beyond. That's where I called to get bandages.'

'And where you met the housekeeper?'

'As I supposed. The main parts of the house were shuttered up, I believed, though I didn't look closely.'

'What about the approaches?'

'I approached from the north-west of the house through woods that ran all the way back to the road. There is a trackway from the road to the Hall, in course. To the east was more woodland, but immediately to the rear of the Hall was pasture, dotted with trees but little real cover. I think the south aspect ran to parkland all the way to the river but can't be sure.'

'We must have men both to the East and West of the place then. The road from Read Bridge passes behind the Hall. What is the distance 'twixt road and house and can the road be seen from the house?'

'I'd say three hundred yards distant and can be seen from the house, but for much of the stretch the road lies between high hedges.' He thought for a moment. 'The hedgerows are bare at present, so I must say that there is likely to be a clear view of the road, excepting that there also is a high wall round the garden at the rear of the building and so, unless someone is looking from the upper floors of the Hall, passers-by might not be discovered.'

'Let us assume that they can be seen. What about to the North of the road?'

'Runs into trees, though not as thick as the woods on either side, I believe.'

'There is a cart track,' I interrupted, 'running from the bridge along the outer edge of the wood and down to the river, you know. That's from where Kendall's band appeared on the day of the Battle.'

'Good, good,' said Sir Ralph. 'The more we know of the lie of the land the better.'

Planning continued for the rest of the morning. There was little I could do, so I returned to my books, all thoughts of Jonas Moore temporarily forgotten. It was only in the afternoon, when he brought my mule back, that I remembered his plight, though it wasn't the right moment to be asking Sir Ralph's help when he was fully engaged in a plan of attack on Read Hall.

Jonas fell hungrily on bread and cheese and a bowl of Slater's pottage, whilst she put a basket of goods for him to take back to Higham. 'And how are your wife and childer, sir?' she asked. 'Better for your charity, Goodwife,' he replied. She smiled.

We fell to talking about mathematics and its use in Astrology, and I was astonished to find that we had friends in common. Before taking up his post in Durham, Jonas had travelled down to London and even attended a lecture by my mentor, Johannes Hunyades. We could not be sure, but we might have even been at the same discussion. Such strange coincidences do happen in life, but even more surprising, he had met William Lilly and had his chart divined. It showed that he would have difficulties at this time in his life but that he would overcome them and prosper. I shook his hand, telling him that I was sure of it.

'And have you heard anything of William in the last few months?' I enquired, 'for he has become a great man, casting for both King and Parliament.'

'I have not, Doctor, and it sounds to me that you know more of him than I. Do you follow his computations and perhaps read the stars yourself?'

'I have tried, sir, but it does not completely answer. Lilly is a genius, whilst I am a poor traveller in his wake.'

It was a pleasant afternoon and we parted on excellent terms. I promised

I would speak to Sir Ralph as soon as it was appropriate to do so, told him to keep my mule for the present, and that I hoped for his company again within the next few days.

Fifty Two

'I Can't Ignore an Order'

Pod, Cas, and Richard Towneley were out with Nate's horse Dob, collecting wood for the winter store. Nate was busy chopping up the larger pieces, being rather more careful with the axe after once missing his target and hitting his leg. Fortunately, the limb was only bruised, and he insisted on completing the task. It was bitterly cold once again, but dry, and though the sun was out it gave little warmth. Slater had shooed me out of the cottage in order that she could renew the straw on the floor, so I walked across to the Hall in the hope of fresh news.

I had expected all to be a-bustle with preparations for the assault on Read Hall, but it was quiet. Sir Ralph was out, a maid informed me, his wife in the village. I spoke to Robb at the Hall gate, who told me that Will hadn't been by since the previous day, before trying to engage me in a discussion of his feet, but I was not for that, so I walked down into the village to ask after the missing Adam Seddon.

"Will Cummins has already asked me, and I know nothing of them.' said Goodwife Meeker. I was calling on the Seddon's neighbours for more information. 'I seen neither hide nor hair of them since All Saints Day.'

'You did see them on that day, though?'

'She was at Church, but not him. I thought she looked uncomfortable being there.'

'How so?'

'She weren't for talking. Didn't sit with us as was usual and left before we could talk. We usually has a chat as we walk home.'

'Did you see Adam at all that day?'

'Can't say I did. It's a mystery. I thought they'd got over the loss of Adam's son. He were his, not hers in course. She has a daughter in Clitheroe where I 'spect they'll be.'

I wasn't so sure, but I'd ask Will if he'd checked on that. I asked how their cottage had been left. Were there signs of disturbance, things missing? She crossed her arms and lifted her bosoms in the way women do to show they are affronted.

'I'm sure I don't pry into other's misfortunes...'

I interrupted her and touched her arm. 'And I'm sure you are a good caring neighbour, checking that neither Adam nor his wife were lying ill, for instance, as any friend would.'

She looked mollified by that. 'Well, in course I did look in as you say, just to see if they were dead or some such, but no, the house was empty and undisturbed.'

I thought I'd take a look inside for myself. 'She didn't keep the cot as well as I would've done.' Said Meeker with a sniff. So much for good neighbours.

As I climbed back up through the village, I saw Sir Ralph and Will ride back into the grounds of the Hall together and shifted my pace that I might find out what was afoot.

'Ah, Doctor,' Sir Ralph hailed me, 'Well met. Come for a glass of wine, will you?' He dismounted his steed at the mounting block and strode off. A few months ago, he would have jumped off his horse like a young man, but his recent injury had told on him, and I had to remind myself that he was now an old man of more than sixty years.

'And where have you been, young Cummins?' I enquired as I walked into the Hall with Will, who was looking pleased with himself. He grinned at me but said nothing.

'There is a slight complication to our proceedings, Doctor.' said Sir Ralph. Wasn't there always, I thought. 'I have had instructions from Lord Fairfax, telling me to press the few Royalists that are holding Clitheroe Castle to leave. I think the place is of little importance in the scheme of things, but he doesn't want it to become a thorn in the side should the enemy cross our borders to threaten our hold of the County Palatine.'

'Surely our first priority should be Read Hall, sir?' I cried.

'It is, excepting that, for one thing, I can't ignore his order, and for another, I haven't enough men to do either thing at present. I can barely raise a dozen men, bearing in mind that I must leave some on guard here. How foolish would we look, attacking Read Hall without enough troops, when we don't know what we'll find, and then come home to find our own place ransacked.'

'What about…' I started, but Sir Ralph held up his hand.

'Let's just find out what Will has discovered, before we make any decisions.' He turned to the trusty Cummins. 'Well, Sergeant-at-arms?'

I'd almost forgotten that Will wasn't just my bodyguard or, as he had lately been, my assistant. He was, in terms of the men here in Downham, an experienced soldier, though that was due to his innate skill rather than training. As I have cause to confirm, he is the right man to have with you in any difficult situation.

'I take it that you haven't been visiting your lady then, Will?' I queried.

'No, more's the pity, Doctor.' he said ruefully. 'Well, I did call on her before completing my errand, just to reassure her that I'm still alive, as you might say. I'm sure you'll not hold that against me?' He looked at his master, who gave the merest of smiles, and continued.

'I've been scouting out Read Hall. Not too closely,' he quickly added, seeing my surprised look, 'just the surrounds. I know a girl nearby.' Well, that came as no surprise.

'And you an almost married man.' I retorted.

'Absolutely correct, Doctor, the key word being *almost*. I'm still a single man but, despite your poor opinion of me, I didn't go a-courting.' He scolded me with a grin. 'She lives just along the road to Padiham, and her mother worked at the Hall as second cook, so she knows the place. Most of the staff were turned out when Nowell left, and she says that these days no-one dare go near.'

'Does she know the housekeeper?' asked Sir Ralph.

'Only that she is indeed a harridan and beats the other servants. Rules the house as if it's her own.' he said. 'Thinks there are only two others and a stable lad there now.'

'If that's the case, we could almost walk in, though we must assume otherwise. Even Tench could be there. We just don't know and must act with caution,' responded Sir Ralph. 'We'll speak again later, but I have a letter to write.'

The letter was to his son, asking for the release of at least a dozen troops into his command, in order that he could comply with Lord Fairfax' instructions. Though I was itching for action, this would delay things by at least a week, which couldn't be helped. I'd asked why we didn't just ask for help from Grent, but Sir Ralph was afraid that we wouldn't be able to stop his woodsmen from looting the Hall, should we take it. Having seen what they did after Kendall's Waddow Hall had been taken, I couldn't but agree.

Will hadn't looked for the Seddons' daughter, so next day he set off for Clitheroe, with the understanding that he'd also use this as an excuse to continue on from there to visit Cat. I talked to Sir Ralph about Jonas Moore's prospects, and found he was open to the idea of Moore teaching the village children their letters and numbers on two days per week, like Amos had done previously, if that would suit. I then prepared to ride over to Higham to discuss the matter with him, but before I could do so, he came to me.

'It will be a very modest stipend, Jonas, but it's the best I can do.' We were sitting over a bowl of Slater's excellent broth as I outlined the opportunity.

'And most welcome it is.' he replied, 'I will take up the offer, certainly. Our situation is improving all round. The farmer next to our land will pay rent for our fields and has sealed the deal with a slaughtered pig that will see us over the next months, I hope. I'm also dealing with him for a cow against future rent and, with our hens and ducks, we should do well.'

'You are your Father's only son, I perceive, so the farm is now yours?'

'Only surviving son, yes, and on his death all did pass to me. I had an elder brother, but he died several years before I was born.' He looked at me archly. 'He was bewitched to death, they say.'

I don't believe in witchcraft, as I've often said. It is silly superstition that has led to the deaths of many countryfolk since the King's father sent out his call to discover witches, but I was interested to hear more, especially since Jonas is an intelligent and rational man, who would surely question such claims.

'I know few details, but it seems that Elizabeth Southerns, known as Demdike, cursed him and he died a short while after.'

'And do you believe this?'

'My mother certainly does, but no, it makes no sense to me. There are many things we don't understand but, just because someone is a Cunning Woman and knows the cures of the countryside, it doesn't mean that her curses can kill. She might deliberately poison a person, of course, but that isn't the claim here. What do you think, Doctor?'

'My thoughts exactly. Perhaps people who believe in such superstitions can be frightened to death, but that is in their own mind. I do not believe that harsh words or curses from so-called witches can kill. I could think dark thoughts and curse somebody,' I was thinking of Tench, 'but it wouldn't answer. Such is the belief of many folk that an old woman here in Downham was shunned as a witch, simply because she bore the family name of one who was hanged as a witch at Lancaster.'

'One of the Southerns, sir?'

'No, sir, a different family.' I paused. 'Demdike didn't dance on the end of a rope, I hear, but died in her prison cell before trial. If such were the creatures of the Devil, you'd think that he would save his adherents, would you not? I have a mind to write a treatise on this and decry King James' book, which has caused such damage.'

'That would be a brave thing to do, Doctor, though I certainly endorse your views.'

We lapsed into a companionable silence.

Fifty Three

'King of My Own Castle, Doctor'

I am no diplomat. I can be tactful, which is one of the traits of that profession, but most of the time I just speak my mind. Neither can I abide fools, so diplomacy goes out the window. Sir Ralph does not abide fools either, but he is undoubtedly a diplomat. He has been a Member of Parliament, in which there appear to be many fools, but Sir Ralph is not one of them. He weighs things carefully before acting and, though he doesn't shrink from action, looks to resolve things without bloodshed. Our current fight with the King worries him deeply and he deplores the depth the country has sunk to in this dispute, but he knows our Monarch is duplicitous and his word cannot be trusted, and so accepts the war. In his hands diplomacy itself can be a weapon, as he now demonstrated.

We were impatient at the delay in our plans for Read Hall but had to wait for an increase in our forces, though that was ostensibly to further the taking of Clitheroe Castle, currently held by less than two dozen irregular Royalists. I had decried the delay but had to concede that it would be unsafe to attack the Hall with our present numbers and resigned myself to wait. But Sir Ralph the diplomat rose to the fore.

A letter was written to the captain in charge at the Castle, advising him that the forces of Parliament were on their way with orders to besiege and destroy. He intimated that we knew stores were limited, that no cannon were held within and that sappers, using tunnels known to him, could blow up the building with ease. To avert loss of life and, as a tribute to the captain's gallant defence of the Castle, Sir Ralph, under the orders of Lord Fairfax, victor of many battles, would be pleased to discuss terms of surrender. All the honours of war would be given to the brave defenders and, to ensure that the captain understood this, the phrase 'To march out with your colours and arms and free to leave the county without let or hindrance' was added. A response was respectfully required by the following noon. The sealed letter was delivered under a flag of truce by Will and two sidesmen, all well mounted and in gleaming helmets and breastplates, with all due courtesy, and salutes were exchanged. Sergeant-at-Arms Cummins and his party would take residence at the Swan Inn and await an answer.

The reply came less than two hours later by the hand of a roughly dressed and frightened looking trooper, his buff coat dirty and worn, who let slip that they had no beer left. Will, who was already enjoying himself, called for the landlord, instructed him to give the trooper all the ale he could drink pending his return, clapped the soldier on the shoulder, told him our troops were better fed and clothed and why didn't he join us when we'd taken the Castle, and rode back to Downham at speed.

Sir Ralph looked at the wax. 'No actual seal on this, Doctor, just the melted wax, so already we know that the Captain is of no real account. Let's see what the has to say to my offer.' He ripped the paper from the wax. 'Humm. Can't spell, but we'll forgive him that.' He fell silent for a few seconds. 'Yes, It's done. He asks that I come with what he calls *a sizeable party*, fire a few muskets and he will open the gates. I think we can give him that, Doctor. Of course, it's all for show, but if it saves lives as well as his face, that's good.' He turned to Will. 'Well done, Sergeant Cummins. Round up as many men as we can mount, as quick as you can. You know where the stores are. Helmets and plates if you please. All with swords and muskets.' He raised his eyebrows. 'I probably don't need to say it, but make sure they can all ride and not make us look stupid. Report back as soon as you're ready.' Will saluted and near ran from the room.

'Now, Doctor, do you choose to see the fun?'

We near galloped into the town, a real martial band, six plus Sir Ralph, the Assheton banner flying proudly at his side, and me following at the rear. Nate had pleaded to come when I called for Bay, but Will sequestered his horse for the duration, and his face fell.

The Keep and its curtain wall towered above us on its rocky knoll as we rode up the main street. There were a few curious faces as we gathered below the pathway rising to the Castle's gate. Will dismounted and walked steadily up to the slope, banged on the heavy door, and a small postern was opened for him. He was inside for several minutes before returning to Sir Ralph's side.

'I watched them loading their muskets, making sure there was no ball. Didn't want this to be a trap, us standing here like sitting ducks, sir.' Sir Ralph nodded. 'When I shout for surrender, they'll fire, we'll fire, and then they'll open up for us. Just give me the signal, sir.' Our leader gave another brief nod and Will shouted clear and loud, his voice echoing off the rock. There was a short delay before the defenders gave a ragged fusillade and, on our swifter reply, the gates were opened with effort, grating against the ground as if they had not been moved for some time, and we rode slowly up into the outer bailey. As we did so, I looked back to see Nate coming up behind on Pod's small pony, with the younger boy on behind, Nate's legs almost reaching the ground. I frowned at them. 'Did I say you could come, boys?'

'Begging your pardon, sir, but you didn't say we couldn't, just that I couldn't come on Dob, which Will lent to John Chamley.' He had me there.

'Now you're here, stay close and keep out of mischief,' I said, 'Have you been in here before?' They shook their heads before Pod said, with a touch of pride in his voice, that he had been in Lancaster Castle, which was much bigger. He then seemed to recall that visit and grew pale, before saying in a lower voice, 'But I'm glad I'm not there now.' That had been a very traumatic trip for the mite, with a trial and a hanging to witness.

In front of us stood the Steward's House, though the official himself had long abandoned it. The enemy Captain invited Sir Ralph in whilst Will was sent first to the Keep, with instructions to then search all the outbuildings and take an inventory. The defeated Royalists stood around looking glum, until Will instructed two of our men to get beer for them from the Swan. 'You'll be on your way soon, lads,' he shouted across the Bailey, 'unless any of you want to join us?' I wandered around, looked in the old chapel, now empty, unused, and close to ruin, and climbed into the Keep where the sharp wind whistled through the arrow loops. With no signs of a fire having been lit there for a long time, it was a damp and cheerless place, I thought.

By the time I returned to the Bailey, the surrendered troops were being formed up by their captain, to march out of the town, accompanied by four of our mounted men. I knew a number of them were from the town, so I guessed that, as soon as they were clear of Clitheroe, they would throw down their buff coats and simply walk back to their homes. It was little more than a farce.

Will was to be left at the Castle with two men until the expected increase to our forces arrived.'Never expected to be King of my own Castle, Doctor.' he said, with the usual grin adorning his face.'Did you ever play that game when you were a child? Were you ever a child, in fact?"

'If you weren't armed and armoured, I'd give you a smack for that, Cummins.'

'Given your advancing age, and the fact that I might have need of your services at some point, I would probably not retaliate, sir.' That made me laugh out loud.

Nate asked to stay with Will, to which I had no objection, and I returned to Downham with Sir Ralph and Pod.

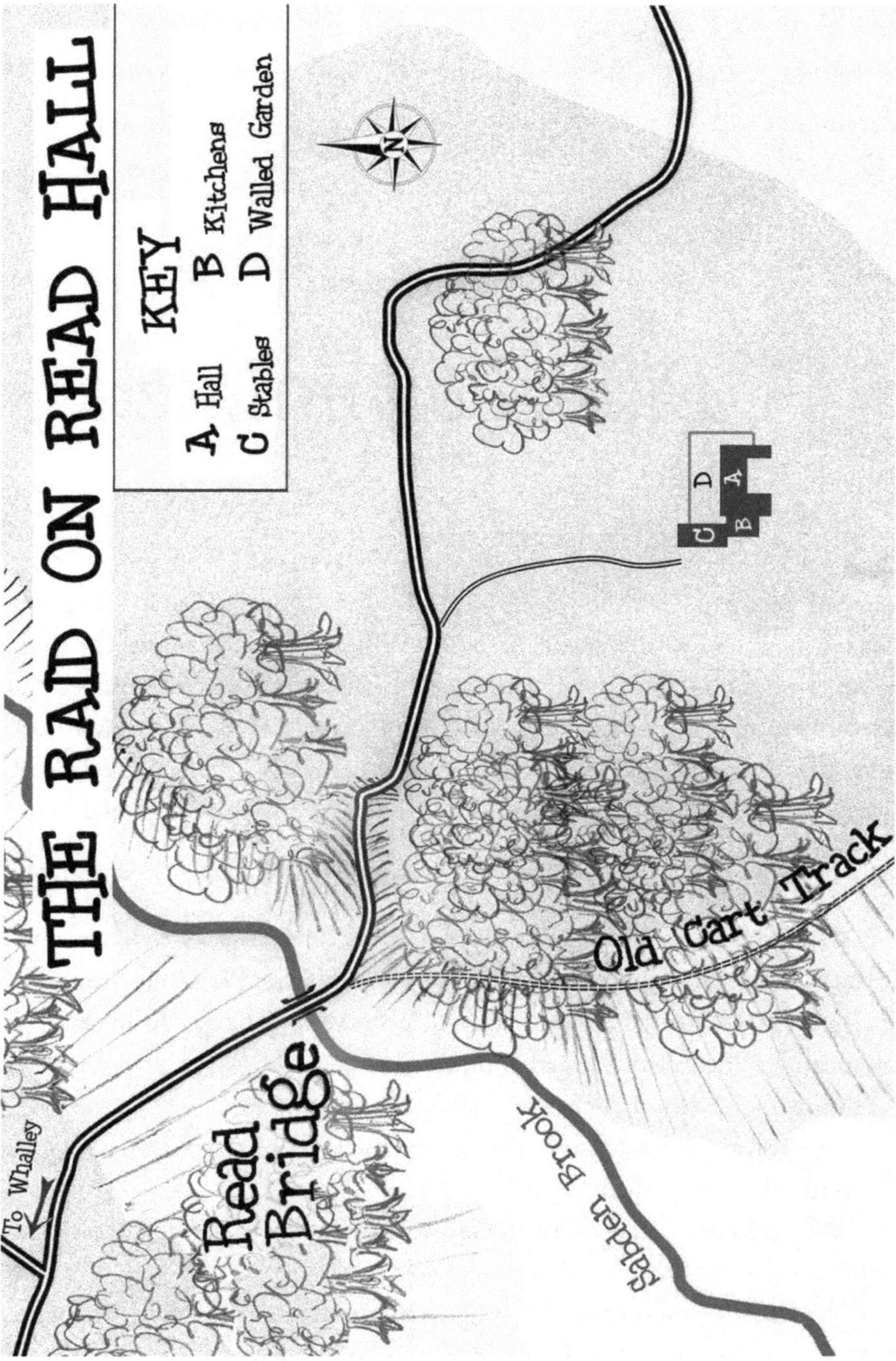
THE RAID ON READ HALL
KEY
A Hall
B Kitchens
C Stables
D Walled Garden
N
To Whalley
Read Bridge
Sabden Brook
Old Cart Track
A
B
C
D

Fifty Four

A Plan Formulated

It was the last week of November before our reinforcements arrived. Four and twenty troopers and a Sergeant Mason marched to the castle, relieving Will, who was thankful for their appearance as he was already running short of supplies. Nate proved his usefulness by bringing the news to Downham and then returning to the Castle with instructions to Mason to take command there but release a dozen of his men into the charge of Sergeant Cummins, who would bring them to us.

'My son has done well by us, I feel. I asked for at least twelve men, and he has sent twice that figure.' We were gathered in the Hall to further plan the descent on Read Hall, I merely to observe and happy to leave such organising to people of a martial mind.

'How many are we then, sir?' I asked.

'I must leave at least four here to guard the Hall, but two dozen I would say, plus myself and Will.'

'We could take a few more of Mason's men,' suggested Will, 'just for the attack.'

'We could,' responded Sir Ralph, 'but that's a large force to move without gaining attention. I should like us to be discreet. The element of complete surprise would be most useful.'

'I do have an idea, sir, if I may?' Sir Ralph nodded his assent and indicated the rough map on the table, and Will continued. 'From the Whalley road and before you descend onto the bridge, there is a part ruined barn in the woods to the right, roughly here. It can't be seen from the road and can give some shelter. I only found it accidentally when I was spying out the Hall. We march over, rest there till dawn, and then attack.'

'Not a bad plan, Will. Let's just mull it over.' said Sir Ralph. 'Tench moves at night, as we have found to our cost, but I like the idea of moving in at dawn.' He turned to Will. 'You are thinking that to march directly from here in the night would leave our men tired before the fight. If fight there is, of course. We may have no opposition.'

'With God's help, we can hope for no fight, sir, but we must plan for one.' I murmured an Amen. 'Better still if we could get food there. We'll fight better with full bellies.' The conversation descended into detail, but a thought occurred to me. I cleared my throat.

'Is Whalley not an option? It's what, two and a half miles to Read? Surely your son wouldn't be unhappy if your men camped at the Abbey for a day or so? That would be safer, would it not?' They both turned and stared at me.

The old Hospitium of Whalley Abbey is a long high building that had filled one side of a cloister, if the remains of grubbed out walls close by are to be believed. The Abbey Church once stood to its North and East and must have been a sight before it was knocked down on King Henry's orders. Our building wasn't what one would call comfortable, but it did provide good shelter for our party. The Abbey's refectory and kitchens were long gone, but the housekeeper and servants of Colonel Assheton's household provided us with good fare, his house, home to past Abbots, being less than a hundred yards away. His father, Sir Ralph, was warmly welcomed and taken in by his Daughter-in-Law.

We had arrived in the afternoon, our men marching in a rather ragged manner for the eight or so miles from Downham, joined part way by a further six of Mason's men. A few villagers watched us as we approached the Abbey, and one called out to ask was the Colonel coming home, which we declined to answer, though hats were raised at the sight of his father. After much pleading by Nate I had allowed him to come with us as my assistant, in case there was bloodshed, and he was first of use in the unsaddling and stabling of our horses, now housed at one end of the Hospitium. I vowed to his mother that I would ensure that he kept a good distance from Read Hall when we attacked.

It occurred to me that, given the scale of this building, the old Abbey must have welcomed many visitors and, as I knew that Lord Derby's force had camped here before being routed earlier in the year, we were likely not its first martial occupants. Whether this place had been a site of pilgrimage I didn't know, but as a site of Roman worship and a sign of the great wealth of that church, I'm glad it has gone. I have seen a number of grand churches and even cathedrals, such as York and Westminster but, whilst their sight does overwhelm the senses, I cannot but decry them as idolatrous places.

At Sir Ralph's request, Will had picked three men who could be trusted to understand and follow instructions. Robb, usually the gate-keeper at Downham, was one of them. The first thing he did as we grouped together was ask me to look at his troublesome feet, something he'd been pestering me about for months and which I'd always managed to avoid. Now I felt obliged to consider them. The removal of his toe-rags revealed the problem, which I'd long suspected. Each foot had a large bunion.

'I know this is not possible when you are, like now, asked to march,' I said, 'but I can do little for such feet other than to say rest them as much as possible. Whenever you stop, take off your boots and let the air to your feet, pad the swellings with cloth when you do put on your boots. A paste of rabbit's fat and comfrey well rubbed in may offer some relief, though you'll have to wait until we reach home for that.' Though I doubted that such an ointment would give true relief, it was the best I could suggest. Robb seemed happy, having had the care of a physician, by God.

Our Commander joined the four of them as they pored over Will's rough map, a lanthorn lighting the scene. I listened in on the periphery as they planned the attack.

A picket of four men would stay on the road above Read Bridge and a further six were to detour though fields and get to the trees on the far side of the Hall. All armed with muskets and swords, they were to prevent any flight from the place to the North or East. The remainder were to take the cart track to the West of the property and secrete themselves in the woods. Six of these were to continue on to the South edge of the wood to cover the Southern aspect of the Hall, leaving fourteen plus Will and Sir Ralph to cross from the wood to the Hall.

'That looks good, Will.' said Sir Ralph, 'But are there dogs to raise an alarm? What about horses in the stables?'

'We just don't know, sir. It's a chance we'll have to take. We don't even know if there will be any resistance, or how many may oppose us.' Will paused. 'I believe that you should stay within the trees, Sir Ralph, until we can be sure of our position. I will lead the attack.'

I thought Sir Ralph might take exception at this, but he seemed to understand Will's logic and, after thinking it over for a moment, nodded his head. It was agreed that Nate and I would stay close to the cart track with the horses, only exposing ourselves when the house had been cleared. That being settled, we tried to get some sleep. It was doubtful that we'd see sunrise, as the days had been cloudy, but there would be light enough by seven, by which time the action should have begun. We needed an hour to march the near two miles, plus time to arrange ourselves, so we were to be wakened by four, eat and move off. In the event, sleep didn't come, nerves keeping me awake, though around me many were snoring.

As we rose in the dark, Will came over and handed me a blue riband to tie round my arm. We would all wear the Assheton colours to avoid any misunderstandings. He also gave me a pistol, 'With Sir Ralph's compliments' and an instruction to check my flint. It felt heavy in my hand. I hoped I wouldn't need it.

Fifty Five

The Girl, Rachel

Bay seemed a little wary as I mounted. She is little used to being ridden in the dark, but she walked out of the village and up the steep hill on the Padiham Road willingly enough, Nate's horse at our side, he being wound up tight in his cloak and drooping as though still asleep. I was cold and fusty and still troubled by thoughts of the last time we'd passed this way to battle. All were quiet as we trudged along, just the sound of footfall, an occasional clink of a sword or horse's harness. A fat badger crossed before us, disappearing quickly into the undergrowth. He would be soon going to ground for winter.

Clattering across the bridge, we stopped close to the site of my wounding seven months back. With hurried whispers the pickets were dispatched, and we turned onto the old cart track that would take us close to the Hall. As we entered the woods the dark and damp seemed to close in around us. Twigs cracked underfoot, there were the vague rustlings of small animals around us, and an owl took off suddenly above us, causing Bay to snort and toss her head. The track was rough indeed, deeply rutted but overgrown, and one of our men fell heavily, cursed, and a sharp whispered 'Quiet!' came from behind me.

Now Sir Ralph, Will and our other riders dismounted and came stumbling to us, handing their horses' reins to Nate. Off they disappeared into the trees, leaving us alone. Nate tied the horses loosely to a birch tree and we sheltered between them, taking some of their warmth, though the cold was already rising through my boots. We could see nothing of the Hall, though if our map was correct it was only some two hundred yards away.

How much time had passed I didn't know, possibly only twenty minutes but it felt like a lifetime. A cockerel crowed though it was still not full light, and I determined to see what was happening. Whispering for Nate to stay with the horses, I scrambled through the trees, getting a sharp bramble in my face for my trouble. I almost fell onto our men, crouched and near invisible as they were, looking out over a close-cropped and open pasture to the loom of the Hall. No-one spoke.

In minutes the buildings became more defined, and it was clear that dawn was near. The cockerel spoke again, answered by another, and now I could see Will and Sir Ralph standing just before me. Our commander clapped my friend on the shoulder, raised a hand, clicked his fingers, and all but two of our soldiers moved out into the field, crouching, and sloping off towards the stables, the house as yet showing no sign of life.

I crept to Sir Ralph's side. He gave me a quick glance and a nod of his head and resumed his scrutiny of Will's progress. They were half-way when a dog barked once. Will made a motion with his hand and all dropped flat to the ground, but nothing further disturbed the silence, and within a few seconds they were up and running for the stables. A quick movement and they were inside. Still no sound reached us. If there were horses within, they made little noise. I presumed that, from the barn, they could see and gain access into the walled garden that ran behind the Hall proper, but no attack had been planned for that quarter, and shortly our men re-appeared, creeping towards the kitchen block. Someone was up and about within as smoke now curled from a chimney before being blown away, a bitter wind beginning to rise like the tension in my breast.

And now Will and his fellows could be seen clearly, he with pistol in hand and others holding their swords in readiness, as they ducked beneath a shuttered window to reach the adjacent door. Two men continued past, to peer round a corner to the front of the edifice, before signalling all clear to Will, standing right by the door.

Then things happened with speed, for the door opened, a small fellow came out and, in the instant he noticed Will, was flattened by a mighty blow which sent him slumping to the ground. Whether he had made a sound, I couldn't tell, but our men were quickly in the building. I found I was sweating despite the cold.

Muffled and confused sounds now reached me, and the unseen dog set up a continued barking, though from the sound of it he was out in the walled garden. Two soldiers came back out, one to wave across at us, the other to drag the still comatose fellow into the corner betwixt the stables and kitchens and to stand over him as Sir Ralph and his two supporters walked quickly across. I so wished to be there in the action that, despite my orders, I thought I had reason enough to treat the wounded man and ran across to where he lay.

It was Seddon, looking pale and unkempt beneath the blood flowing from a mighty gash to his head. I open his jacket, tore at his shirt, and ripped off a piece to bind his wound. Turning to his captor, I said, 'If you can find something to tie him with, you can just leave him here, the turncoat, and join your friends inside.' and went to peek inside the house.

Here, in the very kitchen, where a fire was already burning well, all seemed calm, all sound of action being further through the building. I heard a sniffling, and beyond an upset pail of water tucked aside a dresser in a corner of the room, found a girl, a mere child, shaking, frightened and with tears on her cheeks, brown hair matted and uncombed, thin almost to emaciation and with dark circles under her eyes. 'Who are you?' I demanded, roughly, but she was in no state to answer. I looked round, spied a flagon of beer, passed it to her and told her to drink. I could smell that the beer was stale, but it was of no consequence.

As soon as she was calm, I took her arm, took her from the wet, and seated her on a stool, crouching down beside her. 'What's your name, child, how old, and what do you do here?'

'Rachel, sir, aged eight years I think, and just a maid.' She looked at me in fear. 'Am I to be hanged?'

'Why would you think that?

'Because of the man below. I believe him to be bad and was told if I spoke of him I would die.'

'And have you done anything evil to warrant a hanging, Rachel?'

'On my life I have not, sir. I am only here for I am frightened to leave on pain of death. I never wished to stay here, for I am beaten when I won't do for him.' She began to cry again.

I was puzzled and asked, as gently as I could, 'And who is the man below, Rachel? Do you mean the Devil?' She shook her head. 'Is it a man called Tench?'

'No not him, though he comes and goes, frightening me more than the Mistress.'

'When did you last see Tench, my dear?'

'Three or four days since, I think.'

'So, he isn't here now?' She shook her head. 'Who else is in the house? Do you know the man Adam?'

'Adam and his wife have only been here a short while, but he is the only one who is kind to me. His wife is in the attic and never comes down, though I've heard her crying at night.'

'Then Adam and wife, you, your mistress who is…?'

'Says we must call her Lady. See, she burned me when I forgot to say it.' The girl pulled up a dirty sleeve to reveal a wide and deep welt across her upper arm, a branding, the skin clearly dead and flaking, a horrible wound to give such a mite.

'Have you no mother near, Child?' She shook her head. 'Have you no-one to keep you?' She started to cry once again, deep sobs shaking her. It was pitiful and I was much moved.

Now came a pistol shot and further sounds of battle from within the house, which stopped my questioning. I picked Rachel up, telling her she was now safe, and ran with her from the building. Plunging into the trees and now out of breath, I put her down to compose myself before traversing the woods in search of Nate. I saw the horses first and then he appeared from round a tree with sword in hand. 'Is it done, sir, have we won the day?'

'To be true, I little know, Nate. A fight still rages within the house, but I have rescued this young maiden,' I smiled down at her, 'who needs your protection. Say hello to Rachel. Rachel, this is Nate, as brave a fellow as I know.' As quickly as I could, I returned to the Hall.

Adam, bound as he was, was now awake. He looked completely forlorn and beaten. I lifted his head and tried to get him to answer my questions, but he would not reply. At first I thought his brain might be away, but his eyes looked clear enough, though he tried to avoid looking at me, so I believed he was simply refusing to speak. I smacked him across the face. 'Where is Tench? Where is Tench? Who is in the house? How many?' I shouted, but he wouldn't answer.

Within the house, I found signs of the fight. In the first apartment, which contained little but chairs and a table, they were all upset. The next apartment showed a heavy tapestry, which had been ripped from the wall and trampled by many boots, which led me into the Great Hall. A figure came out onto the Minstrel's gallery at the far end, levelling a musket at me and my heart skipped a beat, but it was one of our men, who quickly raised his gun and raised an apologetic hand. I called to him, 'How goes it?'

'Slowly I think, sir. There's a bloody witch and three others who have barricaded themselves in a room just beyond. Sergeant Cummins has taken some few men around and hopes to gain the attics, to shoot down from above.'

As he said this came a muffled scream from somewhere, and I wondered whether Seddon's wife had been discovered. Suddenly, beyond the far doorway, I saw a flash of white, the merest glimpse of a pale face, that disappeared in the blink of an eye. Clicking my fingers to the guard above and pointing, I cried 'This way. Get men down here.' And without thought, ran after the vision, pulling my pistol from my belt as I did so.

I looked around the dark panelled corridor. At the far end I could just make out the first steps and newel post of a stairway coming from above. On my right hand were two doors and on the left three more, and between each were more tapestries, whose details I could not make out. I felt sure that the woman that I glimpsed had moved to my left, so gingerly tried the first door. It was locked. I tried to peer through the keyhole but could see nothing. The other two doors led into bare apartments. My friend from above now clattered down the stairs and ran to me. 'We must break through this door.' I cried, and he threw himself against it, but it remained immovable. Two more troopers arrived to assist, trying to batter it down together, but despite their combined weight it was to no avail.

Will strode down the corridor, holding the arm of a weeping woman, followed by more of his men escorting a further prisoner at the point of a sword. 'Look who I've found, Doctor' he said angrily, 'Seddon's woman, the bitch. See what she's done to my hand.' He had a nasty cut across his knuckles. 'You'll fucking regret that.' He glared at her then turned to me. 'What are you about, Doctor?'

'I think our prize went this way.' I responded, 'Through this door.'

Literally throwing the woman to another trooper with an instruction to hold her tight, Will told us to stand back, drew his pistol and fired at the door lock. The report near deafened me and as I ducked, the ball ricocheted past my ear. The wood had splintered and, although the lock still held, the door was burst through at the cost of a couple of bruised shoulders. The room was empty, and I felt stupid.

Fifty Six

'Did You Fire Your Pistol?'

'I know what I saw, Will. She disappeared on this side of the corridor.' He had regained some of his humour at my discomfort and said, 'I believe you, Doctor, though most wouldn't. It's a bloody warren, this place. We've already discovered two Priest-holes.' Sending others off to find Sir Ralph and to tell the outer pickets to converge on the Hall whilst maintaining a watch for escapees, we set to in the hope of finding a concealed exit from the room, banging on the carved and decorated panelling, and stamping on the floor to discover the hollow sound that would reveal an exit. It was to no avail. All seemed solid.

Sir Ralph arrived looking somewhat downcast and annoyed. 'No Lady, no Tench. So far we've got one prisoner plus Seddon and his wife, who I know not what to do with, plus one of their men dead. We've gone to so much trouble for near to no return.' He turned to Will. 'I want this place taken apart, with care, mind, and put back as near as can be.' And to me, 'If you believe someone is still concealed within these walls, then find them.' He stalked out. It was the nearest to anger I'd ever seen him.

'Will,' I said, 'Would you mind sending someone over for Nate? He has a young child in his care, a maid from here who might help us.'

'I'll try anything. I agree the Harpy must still be in the house.' He thought for a second and then said 'I haven't seen any cellars. Have we checked for cellars?' he went out to direct his men.

I went back to the kitchen to see Nate carrying Rachel from the wood. 'Don't be afraid, little one,' I said with as sweet a smile as I could manage, 'but when you had to visit the man below, how did you get down? Do you know a secret way beyond the Hall?' She nodded.

'You won't have to go down there again, but can you show me the door?' Again, she nodded and, taking my hand, we walked once again through the building.

There was more noise from below us as we passed through the Great Hall. In the corridor, Rachel pointed to the panelling, and I once again thumped on it but, as before, it gave no echo of space behind. It was so frustrating. But keeping my voice as level as possible I asked the child if she knew how it opened, and she pointed vaguely at the oak carvings some six feet off the ground. I quickly reached up, trying to push, lift or turn each one, my heart in my mouth, until I heard a click and a whole section of the wall seemed to depress by no more than a couple of inches.

'Nate,' said I, keeping my voice light, 'It's time you took Rachel from here. Get Dob and take her down to Whalley, till we are finished here. Go to Robb's picket at the top of the cart track, tell him to send someone with you. One of our Downham men, mind.' I patted Rachel's head. 'Keep with Nate and I'll come on later. Don't worry, you're safe now, child.' Nate opened his mouth and I guessed he would ask to stay, but I simply said 'Go, now.' and off they went.

I returned to my task, pushing heavily on the oak. Though it was heavily constructed it swung open easily and quietly, and from inside came an awful reek. I was contemplating this and the darkness within, daring myself to enter, when two of our troopers walked down the staircase, and I recognised Rich Sykes of Downham's Home Farm, and I grabbed him. 'Richard, can you find a glim? I want to find what's down here, and you can help me.'

'Surely, Doctor. Is there treasure below?'

'I don't know but be quick. And make sure your pistols are primed.'

'Ain't got no pistols, sir. It's swords or nowt. But I'll get a light.'

With Richard and lanthorn before, the edge of my cloak held to my nose against the increasing stench and my heart beating loud enough for all to hear, we crept our way down a narrow stone stair, a deep, echoing banging coming from below, as if the house was to fall about our heads. I was dreading what we would find before us, as one might imagine, and gripped my pistol tightly, my mouth dry. The stair turned before us, and we made the bottom. Then all was confusion. A crash of bricks, a choking cloud of dust and, in the same second, the flash of a gun, which lit a dim figure not ten feet from us. Its boom deafened me, and darkness reigned as the shot smashed the lanthorn. I pointed and snapped my pistol as the figure seemed to disappear, but it failed to fire, as a dusty Will and several of his men literally fell through the wall at our side.

Near blind and ears ringing from the gunshot, tears streaming down my face and coughing near to burst from the dust, all my senses were astray. I think somebody tried to yell in my ear, but the sound just echoed around my head and didn't resolve itself into anything like words. My arm was grabbed, I felt myself being dragged across a pile of rubble, falling heavily and badly twisting an ankle as I did so, the pain forcing its way into my brain. Bodies pushed past me and, as the dust began to settle and the gloom lessened, I saw Will. I spoke but couldn't hear my own words, never mind what Will was mouthing to me. Now he grabbed me and pulled me back across the rubble, barking my shins, then up, up on a sloping path, where we burst out into the light and fell in a heap onto a bed of dead leaves.

Coughing enough to make me retch, I rolled on my side, trying to blink my eyes free of dust. Lying there for a few minutes I worked my way round my body, moving my fingers toes, arms shoulders, to check where else I may have been damaged besides my legs and ankle. I found myself whole, which seemed a miracle, though my lungs still felt full of dust and stone. I managed to sit up as my hearing started to return, and there was Will, coloured grey from head to foot, talking to me. "What?' I asked.

'I said, did you fire your pistol?' He was holding it out to me by the barrel. I nodded. 'Did you check the flint like I said?' he continued.

I tried to say 'Yes, of course' but descended into another coughing fit.

'You didn't tighten the flint when you put it back. It had dropped out.' I looked at the hammer and saw the void, and with, I believe, a touch of contempt, he said, shaking his head, 'For a person of high intelligence and knowledge beyond the common, the simplest things escape you, Doctor. How you survive I don't know. I really don't know.' He passed me his hand and pulled me to my feet, where I nearly fell again from the pain in my ankle.

'What happened?' I croaked.

'You came down your stair, I came through the wall. One of the two people down there got out the way we've just come. I'm sure it was the woman, but don't worry, I can't see she'll have got far, for the House and buildings are locked down. I doubt a mouse could move without us knowing.' I began to laugh, I couldn't stop, and Will looked at me as if I'd gone mad but, would you believe it, just as he'd said that a mouse had emerged from our escape route, ran along the edge of the wall, and disappeared from sight.

'When you've composed yourself, you'd better come back below. There's a friend of yours down there, and he's not looking too well.'

Fifty Seven

'Beyond Recognition…'

WE STOOD OUTSIDE AS THE WOMAN WAS BROUGHT FROM THE barn, I still stunned by what had happened, Sir Ralph looking grim, and Will looking triumphant if anything, I would say. He had brushed himself down and, though his breastplate was dented in more than one place, it still shone, and not even the tear in his right boot took anything away from his commanding look. If his Cat had seen him as Sergeant-at-Arms Cummins, I'm sure she would have been impressed, though I preferred him as plain Will.

The first search of the cellars, whilst I was struggling to find my mystery door, had revealed nothing except, within a mountain of chests, timber, and other detritus such as tends to accumulate in such places, a full barrel of wine. The men being what they were, this was breached and several of them were now looking very sorry for themselves and vomiting copiously against the wall of the barn. After first chastising them as he went below, Will noticed that the vaulted cellars, consisting of a long passage with chambers off, ended suddenly at a bricked-up doorway. This he had broken through just as I arrived at the foot of the stairs, and thus the noise and cloud of blinding dust. I am just thankful that I didn't descend on my own to face the she-devil that now stood before us.

She had got no further than the hay-loft of the stables, but was still full of fight when cornered, pushing one man off the ladder and running another through the arm with a pitchfork before being overpowered, I was told.

There was nothing but contempt and anger in her gaze as she spat at us, as gaunt, common-looking, and with as poor a complexion as when I first saw her in Aspinall's Hall. I didn't believe she was a lady then, and I was even surer of it now.

Her shift was torn, revealing more of her than most would have wished, and she was covered in a dark cloak. There was no sign of the yellow dress that I had last seen her in, and which first led me to know her falsehood. Sir Ralph motioned that she was to be taken from our sight. 'But tie her well to a horse, and if she tries to bolt, shoot her,' he called as she was hauled away. 'She'll hang, of course,' he said, almost to himself.

I hesitate to state the scene that met my eye as I returned to the cellar. It is a sight that haunts me still. Chained to the wall was something that had lately been a man of small stature, his once expensive clothes filthy and torn, beard and long hair untended and dirty. To say I recognised him would be untrue, for he was beyond recognition, but I knew who it was, indeed had guessed some time before. I had last seen him seven months before, screaming and running his sword into me, another vision that wakes me in a sweat on troubled nights, but I thought back to one of the first times I'd seen him, finely dressed in grey doublet and breeches, mimicking King Charles in style and manner, as he descended the fine staircase at his opulent home. Even then there had been an evil feeling around him. Theft and murder were his legacies.

His left arm was missing, that was clear, and possibly part of his shoulder too, probably as the result of the musket shot that saved my life at Read Bridge. I wondered who had performed the necessary surgery. If that wasn't striking enough, the sight of still wet blood soaking the front of his tunic lent the scene a truly diabolical edge. I lifted his head up. There was still a little warmth in his body, even if the slice across his throat had drained most of his life-blood. I let the head fall back and shivered. Whilst I would normally revel in the examination of such body to improve my chirurgical knowledge, I had seen enough of Sir Christopher Kendall to last me several lifetimes.

I gulped in fresh air as I sat in the walled garden of Read Hall. It was cold but sheltered from the bite of the wind, at least. I could hear Will directing measures to close up and protect the buildings. Without the Nowells being in residence or a new housekeeper and retinue being appointed I wondered, idly, what would happen to it.

Sir Ralph came and sat with me.'I never did see such a sight. How long has he been there, Doctor?'

'A few months at least, sir.' I felt numb and could drum up no emotion as I spoke. 'Possibly he sought refuge here after the battle at the bridge when he was wounded. Perhaps that ogress, that dragon took him in, even tried to nurse him at first, who can say. Someone amputated his arm, at least. You don't think she really did marry him, do you?' He shrugged his shoulders.'I doubt it myself, sir. I think Tench must have some part to play in the story. She, whatever her name really is, only came into the picture when Tench's attempts to get into your cellars failed.'

'Yes, Doctor, but something still doesn't add up. If Tench is part of this, why was he not part of her attempted theft on All Saints Day, why is he not here, and why did she cut Kendall's throat before we could speak to him.'

'To be honest, I'm almost beyond caring, Sir Ralph. We can speculate, but might never know. I presume you'll try to question her but, as no-one would even try to save her from the gallows, I doubt you'll get answers from her.' He shook his head slowly.

'I might get something from our prisoners.' he said, 'And Seddon, I want some answers from him. He's worked for me for years, why would he betray me?'

'Gold, I would think, for what else could induce such a thing? Perhaps losing his son twisted his mind a little. Or could Tench have had some hold over him? The thing is, I don't see him as completely bad, as he seemed to have been shocked when your man was shot at the robbery. He turned and tried to help, did he not?'

'But I can't let him stay in Downham. I must turn him out at the very least, if not prosecute him.' he sighed heavily.'it's a mess, a true mess.'

As we rose, a further thought struck me. 'What will happen to Kendall's valuables stored at your home? What about Waddow Hall?'

'That's the one good thing to come from this, Doctor.' He near smiled. 'Those goods, that gold and silver, can now be confiscated and used to finance our fight against the King. I doubt anyone can say otherwise. Waddow lies across the river and is in the Riding of Yorkshire, so I'm unsure of my powers of seizure there, but we'll see.' He clapped me on the shoulder. 'Let's for home. How's your ankle?' But I first had patients to see.

Thankfully, my professional expertise was confined to looking at Will's knuckles, easily bound, and the arm wound of our soldier from the hayloft, which was quite serious, as the fork had run through both the bicep and tricep muscles. It would be painful for some time, and I would need to watch for infection, but it should mend, and the arm retain its use. Thankfully, the fork had missed the bone.

Fifty Eight

Some Sweet Lullaby

I HAD ONE FURTHER CALL TO MAKE BEFORE RETURNING TO Downham. Riding up to the massive gatehouse of Whalley Abbey, I shouted for the keeper to open up. As the great oak doors creaked apart, I pulled Bay to a mounting block, cautiously climbed down with my painful ankle, passed her reins to a waiting boy who stared and watched me climb, with difficulty, the steps to the Old Abbot's house, now the residence of the younger Assheton.

'If you're wanting your boy and girl, they're across behind the stables.' He said with a smug and unattractive smile after seeing me struggle. I roundly cursed him beneath my breath as my ankle throbbed. 'Go and get them, then.' I said, angrily. As I remounted, Bay turned round to look at me, and I'm sure she was saying what I was thinking, that the boy either liked to see people struggle or was part imbecile. Perhaps I'm wrong, as she is a sweet-tempered horse.

Nate appeared in the distance, waved, and shouted that he'd get Dob and would be with me directly, and shortly he rode out, Rachel sitting comfortably in front of him.

I thought that Slater might curse me for bringing another mouth into our home but, whilst she was rather taken aback for a moment, proved to be as contrary as ever by taking Rachel on her knee, cuddling her, and singing some sweet lullaby as she pulled a comb through the mite's thick hair.'And isn't it so matted, child? Deary me, it's ever so, but if I pulls too hard, you can smack my hand, little one.'

Pod too was taken with the new arrival."But she is very pale and thin, sir.' he whispered to me.'Then we must feed her and treat her well and she will improve.' I replied. Put down in Slater's bed, the poor mite quickly fell asleep and, with Pod and Cas sat at my feet, I revealed my adventure, in part at least.

'...and brave Nate spirited our little maiden away to safety.' I came to the end of my tale with the boys eyes and mouths opened wide in astonishment, and not a word did they say. Nate had stood, arms folded and leaning on the wall, looking serious and nodding, as though he'd been at my side every step of the way, and now blushed with pleasure. His mother, after the usual wringing of hands and the occasional cry of 'Oh, My lord' and 'Heaven save us' whilst rocking back and forth in her chair in agitation, beamed at him with pride.

Later, after Nate had poulticed my ankle with comfrey and I was sitting warm and relaxed by the fire, Slater quizzed me about the girl.'If she has no-one to claim here, what will become of her?' I shrugged and, after a few moments she said, quietly, as if to herself"I've never had a girl to look after. There's lots I could teach her...'

I smiled contentedly.

Two days had passed, and all had been invited to feast and drink in the large barn in the grounds of Downham Hall. Slater had worked all day with Sir Ralph's cook to prepare pies of various sorts, though pride of place went to a full ox, roasted over a pit outside, the fat causing flames to dance wildly as dusk fell. A fiddler played tunes, though few set to dance, and the most popular thing, with the men at least, was the seeming endless supply of strong ale.

Though it had not yet been established where they might live, Will had brought Cat, to meet Sir Ralph and his Lady and, if their smiles were to be believed, all went well. Later, just as things began to flag, old Robb stood and sang a song which he dedicated to the young lovers:

Be merry my friends and list awhile
Unto a merry jest,
It may from you produce a smile
When you hear it first expressed,
Of a young man lately married,
Which was a boon good fellow,
This song in his head he always carried
When drink had made him mellow:
I cannot go home, nor will I go home,
It's long of the Oil of Barley.
I'll tarry all night for my delight,
And go home in the morning early.

It didn't seem the most appropriate song to sing, but all, including Cat, laughed, and joined in the chorus.

Postscript

The snow came early, and not a little. Hard frosts set in on the last day of November, and by the third of December all was blanketed in white, with just the black skeletons of the trees revealing distances across the landscape. Nature herself seemed silenced by the weight of snow, and our movements created narrow tracks across the bright expanse between cottage, stable and Hall. Though the boys larked in it as boys do in their careless ways, coming in wet and near frozen, with bright red faces and hands, and noses running free, most of my days were spent huddled round the fire, with Slater complaining that I was in her way. All the signs of a long winter had been there, a profusion of berries on holly and elder, fat squirrels and fatter badgers and the like. Richard Towneley was pleased as it confirmed his prediction.

Starved of news, worried how Colonel Assheton and our men were coping out in the field, and wondering if they would ever make it home, we were surprised and gladdened when a starved and frozen courier arrived, carrying a number of messages for Sir Ralph and even myself. His revival took some time, there were touches of frostbite on nose, hands, and feet, and he was laid up in a heated room for several days. His horse was not so lucky. Having been pressed hard, she died two days later, despite the good care of Pod and Cas, constantly rubbing her down and trying to get her to eat a mash of bran and beer.

The messages were both good and bad. Good, in that we learned that the Colonel and his men were bedded down in the Town of Liverpool, having averted a landing from a Royal fleet anchored in the Mersey river. He would return to Whalley as and when there was an improvement in the weather.

Good too was news that the Scots had signed a covenant with our Parliament to oppose the King's forces and had promised to field an army on our behalf in the coming year, which will give good relief.

The saddest news was in a letter to me that I had never expected, it being from William Lilly, no less. I had sent letters to him over time, with questions related to his science but, to date, had never received a reply and thought he had forgotten me. Now he wrote to tell me and, I suppose, many others, of the illness of John Pym, and that his examination and divination of the stars told him that Pym could not live. Pym, that icon of our struggle; Pym, who more than anyone had opposed the absolute power of the King; Pym, one of the famous Five Members, who escaped from Charles' invasion of Parliament. What a loss, what a blow this will be to our cause. I believe him to be the greatest and truest Member of Parliament we have ever had.

I don't doubt that Lilly's forecast is true, for I know his powers, but I would wish for better news, and also to hear his predictions for the future, even though I feel there will be little to the good. So much of what is happening around us seems to indicate the End of Days, with the world in uproar, turned on its head, father fighting son, brother fighting brother, and no end in sight. Though I see these things and tremble, I pray for our deliverance and a better world.

We are close to the death of the year, which brings on these melancholy thoughts I believe. It is a year whose passing I won't regret. I have been wounded, nearly drowned, dispossessed, had more adventure than I would ever wish, and yet I am still here. One key adversary is gone, and a mystery solved, in part at least, and, though the devilish Tench is still at large, I am back in health and with my friends and family close about me. I have said in the past that my books, my very library is my family, and it is certainly true that I wouldn't part with them, but I have come to realise that my real family, my true family, my growing family, is Joan Slater, Nate, Pod, and perhaps even Cas, should his improvement continue. There is also the likelihood that little Rachel will soon be counted amongst them. Outside of them, I seem to have unwittingly adopted the family currently residing at my property in Clitheroe, where I hope soon to return. The School also is beginning to prosper again under the hand of Usher Brierley. Finally, to my good friend and sometime saviour Will and his erstwhile bride, I must lift my glass and wish them health and happiness, if not wealth.

This under my hand in Downham, the twentieth of December in the year of Our Lord MDCXLIII.

Johannes Hyphastes *sive* Webster

Author's Comments and Historical Notes

Historical Background to the Civil War within Lancashire

In the English Civil Wars there were a number of regional conflicts that formed the whole. Lancashire saw one of those regional conflicts. In some ways, the fighting in the county could be seen as a separate theatre of war and a microcosm of the wider conflict. The towns mainly supported Parliament whilst the landowners, gentry and aristocracy mostly supported King Charles. The exception was the town of Preston, whose population seemed to sway towards the King, although, after changing hands on a couple of occasions, it finally recognised Parliament.

It was a time of great social and economic tension between the towns and landowners, and this was exacerbated by the religious divides: Puritan and non-conformist sects versus Anglicans versus the Roman Catholic families that still existed in the surrounding countryside, for Lancashire had long been a religious "hothouse". Various sects arose here, including the 'Grindletonians', precursors of the Quakers, whose ideas spread across the whole of the North and Midlands.

It is also interesting to remember that, as far as the 17th Century goes,

Lancashire was considered a rather isolated, remote and possibly even backward part of the country, as the great historian of Lancashire's Civil War, Ernest Broxap, readily identified. With the purge that followed the Gunpowder Plot of 1605, Catholics sought refuge in the County because of its perceived isolation and, especially after 1612 and the Pendle Witch trials, it also had the taint of lawlessness and "Devilish works".

Additionally, the geography of the county split it on an east/west axis, the hilly eastern side rising into the Pennines whilst the west fell into the flat coastal plains. The main east/west route across the county was the Ribble Valley and, though after the period covered by this novel, both Royalist and Parliamentarian armies would cross to and from Yorkshire through this area.

In the year of 1644, the issue of "Parliament or the King" was decided within the county and effectively without external interference.

Characters

Dr Webster was a real person and a good number of the personal details included in this book are true. He was an ex-Anglican priest and was Master of Clitheroe Royal Grammar School. He is credited with finding financial anomalies in the school's accounts and recovering monies, a fact I use as the main plot line in the first novel. He also served as a surgeon to Sir Richard Shuttleworth's Parliamentary forces in the English Civil War, though he was not present (as far as I am aware) at the Battle of Read Bridge (or Battle of Whalley as it is sometimes called) or any of the actions detailed in this or my first Webster novel. All the books mentioned in the text are known to have been in Webster's Library which, at the time, was one of the most extensive private libraries in the country. An auction catalogue of his library still exists. He learned some chemistry from Hungarian Dr Hunyades in London. And he was cantankerous and litigious!

His study was demolished in the mid 1900's I believe, and his house, substantially altered, is now a solicitor's office.

Of Webster's household his housekeeper, the widow Slater, did exist but Nate, Pod & others are all figments of my imagination.

School Usher Amos Brierley and his sister are fictitious, though the school did have an Usher, or under-master. Most of the detail of the Grammar School given here is accurate.

Sir Christopher Kendall as I've written him is fictitious. However, there was a Grammar School governor called Christopher Kendall. Waddow Hall exists but has no connection with anyone called Kendall.

Roger Nowell of Read Hall was real and was a school governor at this time, as was Aspinall of Standen Hall, but I fear I've traduced them in the book. There is nothing to suggest that they were anything like the characters I've made them. I apologise to any extant descendants they may have.

There were three Ralph Asshetons at this time: the elder Sir Ralph of Downham Hall, who was a governor of the Grammar School at Clitheroe; his nephew, Sir Ralph of Whalley Abbey, who was MP for Clitheroe and fought on Parliament's side; and a Sir Ralph of Middleton, Manchester, Colonel in the Parliamentary cause and who was also an MP. To avoid confusion, I have ignored the Manchester Assheton and fudged the Downham Hall and Whalley Abbey Asshetons somewhat. The Assheton family is still resident at Downham Hall and, as I write, the current Ralph Assheton is the 2nd Baron Clitheroe.

Sir Richard Shuttleworth of Gawthorpe Hall was also a real person. Governor of Clitheroe Grammar School, MP, and a colonel in the Parliamentary forces.

For historical context, for troop movements and actions in Lancashire. and one that gives a suitable overview of these times, my main source document was "The Great Civil War in Lancashire 1642-1651" by Ernest Broxap, published in 1910.

England did not adopt the Gregorian Calendar until 1752, so in Webster's day the New Year did not occur until 25th March. For the purposes of this novel and clarity I have ignored that and used the Gregorian throughout.

The following notes relate to various chapters and episodes in the book which may be of interest. I have made use of historical records wherever possible and weaved the story around them.

Notes to Chapters

Chapter 1. 'The Stars They Do Shine...'

Webster may not have known his exact birth date. His baptism is on record, but it was usual for that to happen between two and four weeks after birth.

William Lilly (1602-1681) was an astrologer in much demand during and after the English Civil War, and there are hints (but no more than that) that Webster knew him.

Chapters 6 – 12

A Royalist picket was routed at Emmott Lane Head, Colne, and details relating to the Battle of Adwalton Moor and the defence of Heptonstall are substantially correct, though I've adjusted the dates to fit my narrative.

Chapter 13.

Richard Towneley (1629 -1707) was a most interesting and important person, though not a resident of Towneley Hall during the war. His family was Royalist, Catholic, and in Lincolnshire at the time. He did indeed keep important weather records from an early age and became a mathematician, natural philosopher (or scientist, as we would now say) and astronomer. By the 1670's he was in residence at the family home in Burnley, and in correspondence with the Astronomer Royal, John Flamsteed, who asked Towneley to help him prove that the Earth rotated at a constant speed. Towneley designed a novel clock for this purpose. Towneley Hall has one of his astronomical clocks with a 24-hour face on display,

Chapter 15

Richard Hakluyt (1553-1616) was the chief promoter of English colonization of North America, collecting details of navigation and voyages in support of this. The Hakluyt Society still exists, publishing accounts of voyages and travels.

Chapter 16

In writing about Webster beating someone up, this is not just my imagination, as he might well have been a bit of a bruiser. A few years later than the period covered by this novel he was taken to court after assaulting a town official in Clitheroe.

Chapter 17

Though the character of Mistress Whittle is fictional, the shadow of the Pendle Witches still loomed large in the area and, to a degree, still does. I've referenced it in places throughout this novel because Webster was, in a way, involved in its aftermath, causing him to write *The Displaying of Supposed Witchcraft* in 1677.

Chapters 33-37

Details of Hornby and the siege of the Castle are, I believe, substantially correct. The church tower still shows chips in its stonework from musket balls. The Parliamentary troops did climb into the Great Hall of the Castle through a window, acting on information from a deserter (who was not, in reality, a Spanish ex-sailor!)

The Castle is a private residence and completely altered since 1643.

Chapter 38

Details of Lancaster and its trade are, I believe, accurate. Tobacco and Salt were two of the most important commodities brought into the port, and *Sleechers* did indeed produce salt from Morecambe Bay.

Chapter 39

The Chapter House is an intriguing structure, and all that remains of Cockersands Abbey. The housing there of the Spaniards is my invention.

There were possibly two hundred Spaniards marooned in the Fylde after their ship was destroyed in the River Wyre in 1643. Some must have survived, and I wonder whether a trace of their DNA remains in the area.

Chapter 41

Details of the 'Kirkham Monster' are taken verbatim from a Tract, illustrated with a woodcut and published in London in 1645. It demonstrates the amount of "Fake News' that abounded at this time.

Chapter 43

The Battle of Farington Moss is my fiction (*unless you know different!*). I wanted to give Webster some more medical work, and also an indication of the tactics of the time. The Royalist Lord Molyneux and his troops had been thrown out of Liverpool by Colonel Shuttleworth, as I state, and were somewhere around Ormskirk at this time.

Chapter 4–49

The customs surrounding All Hallows were culled from various sources, as is the moving of the traditional bonfire to the fifth of November.

Chapter 50

Jonas Moore (1617-1679) was a Mathematician and Astronomer who became Surveyor of the King's Ordnance (which would eventually devolve into the Ordnance Survey) and was knighted by King Charles II. His early history was as I state, including the supposed 'bewitching to death' of his elder brother by Demdike.

Chapter 52.

When Webster's book, *The Displaying of Supposed Witchcraft* was published in 1677. Jonas Moore, then Vice-President of the Royal Society, gave his imprimatur to allow it to be printed.

Chapter 53

Clitheroe Castle was held by a small group of Royalists, who were then ousted in mid to late 1643, but I can find no details of how this was managed. Sir Ralph Assheton's diplomacy is, therefore, my invention.

Chapter 54

The old Hospitium of Whalley Abbey still exists. The ruins of the whole Abbey are worth a visit.

Chapter 55

Read Hall, altered beyond recognition since 1644, is now a private residence. It was the home of the Nowell family, one of which was intimately connected to the story of the Pendle Witches and their prosecution.

Postscript

John Pym (1584-1643) played a major role in creating what would become the modern Parliamentary system. His attempted arrest by Charles I in Parliament in January 1642 was one of the sparks that led to the first of the English Civil wars.

In late 1643, William Lilly examined John Pym's star chart and his urine and deduced that Pym would die just eight days later. Pym duly obliged, exactly as predicted.

John Webster Biography

John Webster (1610–1682), also known as **Johannes Hyphastes**, was an English clergyman, physician and chemist with interests in astrology, the occult, and was a sceptic about witchcraft. He was very argumentative and controversial in his views.

Born: Thornton on the Hill, Coxwold, North Yorkshire (not, as I incorrectly stated in *A Sea of Contumely*, in Thornton in Craven).

Claimed education at Cambridge University. There is no proof of this but his acceptance as a clergyman and the fact that his literary works show a high level of education would support that claim. He studied under the Hungarian alchemist Johannes Hunyades (János Bánfi-Hunyadi), who is known to have worked at Gresham College in London.

Became curate at Kildwick in 1634. He followed Grindletonian Roger Brearley in this post, and had accepted most of the Grindletonian views, such as salvation coming from following the spirit of Christ, rather than the conventions and form of worship of the Church of England. Though nonconformist he did not consider himself a Puritan and is generally classified as antinomian. During 1st English Civil War, he left a position as Master of the Grammar School at Clitheroe and became surgeon and army chaplain in the Parliamentarian forces under Colonel Richard Shuttleworth. In 1648 he became vicar at Mitton, Whalley, though still held nonconformist views (he moved closer to the views espoused by the later Quakers).

He preached on October 12, 1653, when minister at All Hallows, Lombard Street, in a dispute with two London ministers. Serious disorder resulted after he argued aggressively against the established clergy.

Back in Clitheroe in the late 1650s. In 1658 he was arrested and had papers seized. He gave up the ministry and practiced as a physician. He died at Clitheroe.

He owned one of one of the largest libraries in the North of England, some volumes of which are now at Chetham's Library in Manchester.

Clitheroe's Parish Church of St Mary Magdalen, next to what was his house, has an unusual plaque to his memory. It's in the form of a six-pointed star surrounded by astrological symbols with the sun in the centre. Underneath is an inscription in Latin that reads:

"Those who understand this figure will know me to have understood it too. Here lies a man unknown and sunken in a sea of contumely, yet bore it well and cherished much of times gone by, that he might learn the secrets of wise men and come to know what fire and water do. John Hyphantes or Webster, in Spinosa, his Country House among the hills in a woodland Yorkshire Parish where the cuckoo sings. Born Feb 3 1610, and parted from this life at 72, June 18 1682, and thus on his deathbed bade farewell to this world. Golden peace to the living and eternal rest to the dead. With fire and water he will at last be restored to grace."

Webster's writings

The Saints Guide (April 1653) rejected the worldly wisdom taught in schools as of no spiritual value. He made the case against any kind of university-educated clergy. Some consider this pamphlet, dated April 1653, was probably a response to the dissolution of the Rump Parliament.

Academiarum Examen of 1654 made detailed proposals for the reform of the university curriculum; it was dedicated to General John Lambert, a highly placed officer of the New Model Army. Webster wanted to combine ideas from the experimental philosophy of the time with those of astrology and alchemy.

He edited William Erbery's works and wrote his biography in 1658, as *The Testimony of William Erbery*.

Metallographia (1671) was a work about the history and chemistry of metals. It attributed to minerals the property of growth. He had a corpuscle theory of matter and drew on the work of Robert Boyle, the father of modern chemistry in England. It became the textbook on metals for almost a hundred years. Isaac Newton used this book in his own alchemical work.

The Displaying of Supposed Witchcraft (1677) was a critical and sceptical review of evidence for witchcraft. Webster went as far as suggesting that the Bible had been mistranslated to support the belief in witches. Jonas Moore, then Vice-President of the Royal Society, gave his imprimatur to allow it to be printed. It was also translated and published in Germany.

Medical Practise in the Seventeenth Century

Medicine, as practised in Webster's day, was based on the idea that there were four main liquids (the Humours) in the body, each connected to the four earthly elements of earth, air, fire and water. They were:

Blood, the sanguine humour, related to air and spring, and thus hot and wet.

Yellow bile, or choler, related to fire and summer, so hot and dry.

Black bile, or melancholy, related to earth and autumn, so cold and dry.

Phlegm, related to water and winter, so cold and wet.

Personality and one's health were determined by the ratio of each of these humours in the body. It would be assumed, for instance, that an angry person had too much yellow bile in their body, or a melancholic person had too much black bile.

It was a physician's job to balance these four humours in a patient, as the way to ensure, or return someone to, health. The main ways to achieve this were through bloodletting (exsanguination), emetics to induce vomiting, cupping to draw malign humours through the skin, the use of leeches or herbal remedies and diet.

If a person was thought to be suffering from phlegm, the cold and wet humour, for instance, they would be treated with an opposite - something to reinforce the warm and dry such as spicy food or herbs that were classified as hot, such as hyssop.

The humours theory stemmed from Hippocrates of around 460BCE. Treatments for balancing the humours by the application of opposites came from Galen (circa 200CE). These ideas began to fall out of favour in Webster's time – for instance he was aware of William Harvey who proved, in the 1620's that the body had a single circulatory system, and thus disproving the humoral theory that blood was produced part in the heart and part in the liver. Humorism was definitively disproved in the 19th century by the advent of germ theory.

Acknowledgements

THANKS TO MY PARTNER JILL FOR HER SUPPORT AND encouragement in this and all my other projects; Isobel Norton and John Coventry for initial readthroughs; Bill Honeywell and Jill Crocker for proofreading; and the staff of Matador Publishing for their assistance.

Thanks too to Lord Thomas Grey's Regiment of Foote (English Civil War re-enactment group) for the front cover image, and Ruth Lochrie Photography for the back cover image.

All maps, illustrations and cover design are my own work.

This book is printed on paper from sustainable sources managed under the Forest Stewardship Council (FSC) scheme.

It has been printed in the UK to reduce transportation miles and their impact upon the environment.

For every new title that Troubador publishes, we plant a tree to offset CO_2, partnering with the More Trees scheme.

MORE TREES
LET'S PLANT A BILLION TREES

For more about how Troubador offsets its environmental impact, see www.troubador.co.uk/sustainability-and-community